THE SAVAGE BEARD OF SHE DWARF

D0063162

AN ONI PRESS PUBLIC...

THE SAVA

SHE

Written & Illustrated

By

KYLE LATINO

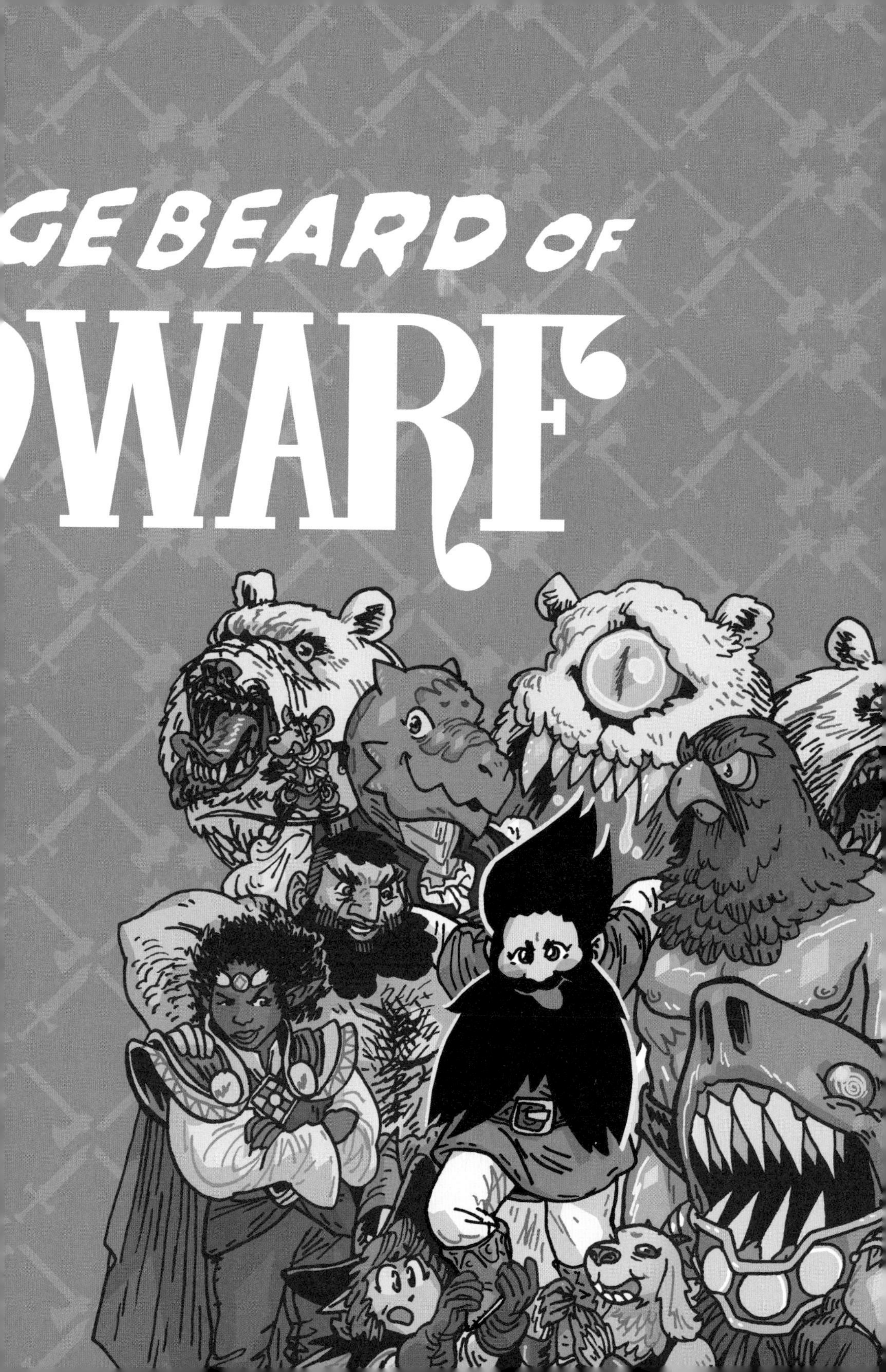
GE BEARD OF
WARF

PUBLISHED BY ONI-LION FORGE PUBLISHING GROUP, LLC
Written and illustrated by Kyle Latino
Designed by Sonja Synak
Lettered by AndWorld Design
Color Assistance by Angus Hannigan and Ginger Dee

For Elise.

For all who wander.

James Lucas Jones
president & publisher

Sarah Gaydos
editor in chief

Charlie Chu
e.v.p. of creative & business development

Brad Rooks
director of operations

Amber O'Neill
special projects manager

Harris Fish
events manager

Margot Wood
director of marketing & sales

Jeremy Atkins
director of brand communications

Devin Funches
sales & marketing manager

Katie Sainz
marketing manager

Tara Lehmann
marketing & publicity associate

Troy Look
director of design & production

Kate Z. Stone
senior graphic designer

Sonja Synak
graphic designer

Hilary Thompson
graphic designer

Sarah Rockwell
junior graphic designer

Angie Knowles
digital prepress lead

Vincent Kukua
digital prepress technician

Shawna Gore
senior editor

Robin Herrera
senior editor

Amanda Meadows
senior editor

Jasmine Amiri
editor

Grace Bornhoft
editor

Zack Soto
editor

Steve Ellis
director of games

Ben Eisner
game developer

Michelle Nguyen
executive assistant

Jung Lee
logistics coordinator

Joe Nozemack
publisher emeritus

onipress.com | lionforge.com
facebook.com/onipress | facebook.com/lionforge
twitter.com/onipress | twitter.com/lionforge
instagram.com/onipress | instagram.com/lionforge

First Edition: May 2020

ISBN 978-1-62010-738-6
eISBN 978-1-62010-741-6

1 3 5 7 9 10 8 6 4 2

CHAPTER

I

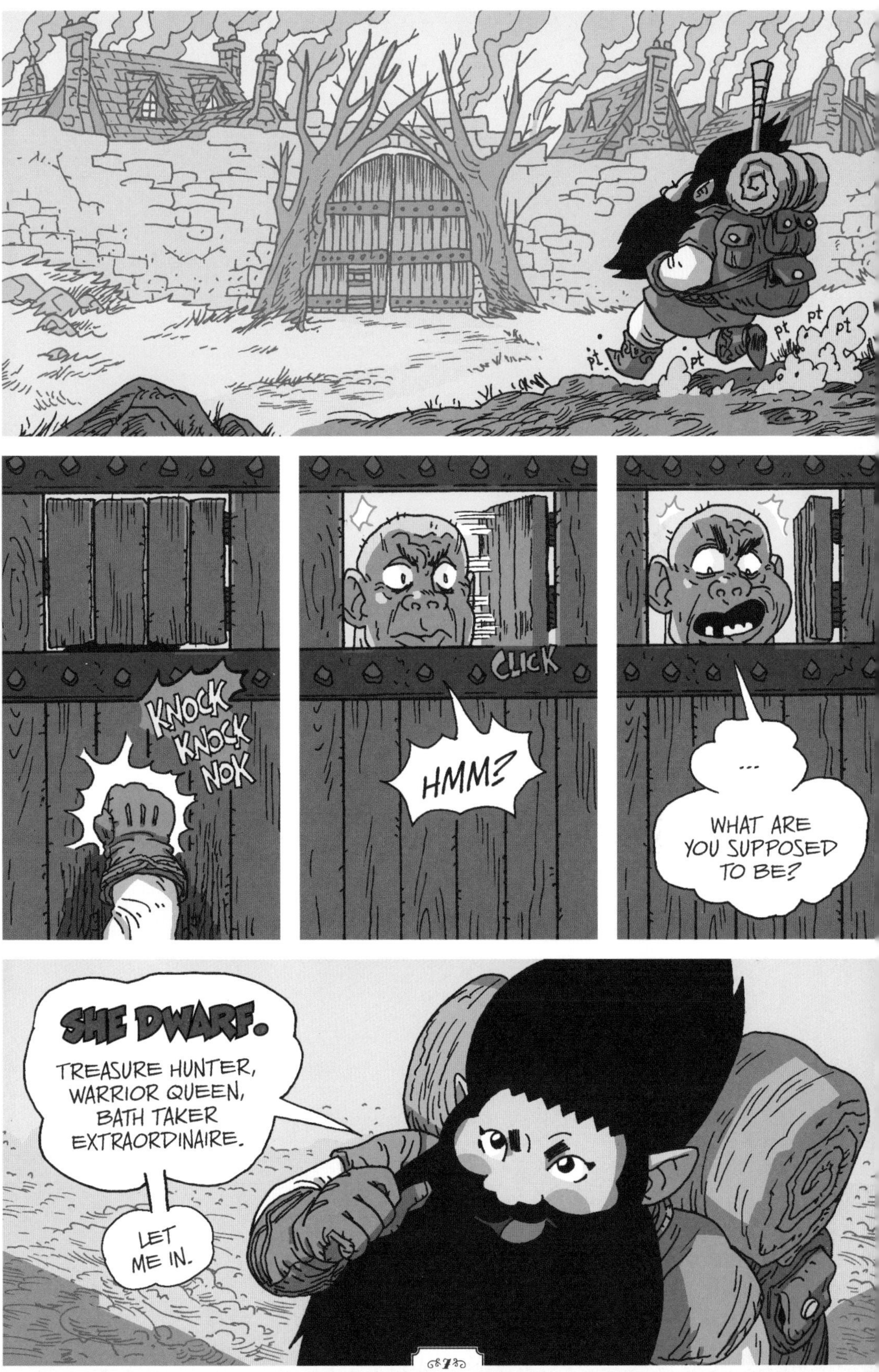
pt pt pt pt pt pt
KNOCK KNOCK NOK
CLICK
HMM?
...
WHAT ARE YOU SUPPOSED TO BE?
SHE DWARF.
TREASURE HUNTER, WARRIOR QUEEN, BATH TAKER EXTRAORDINAIRE.
LET ME IN.

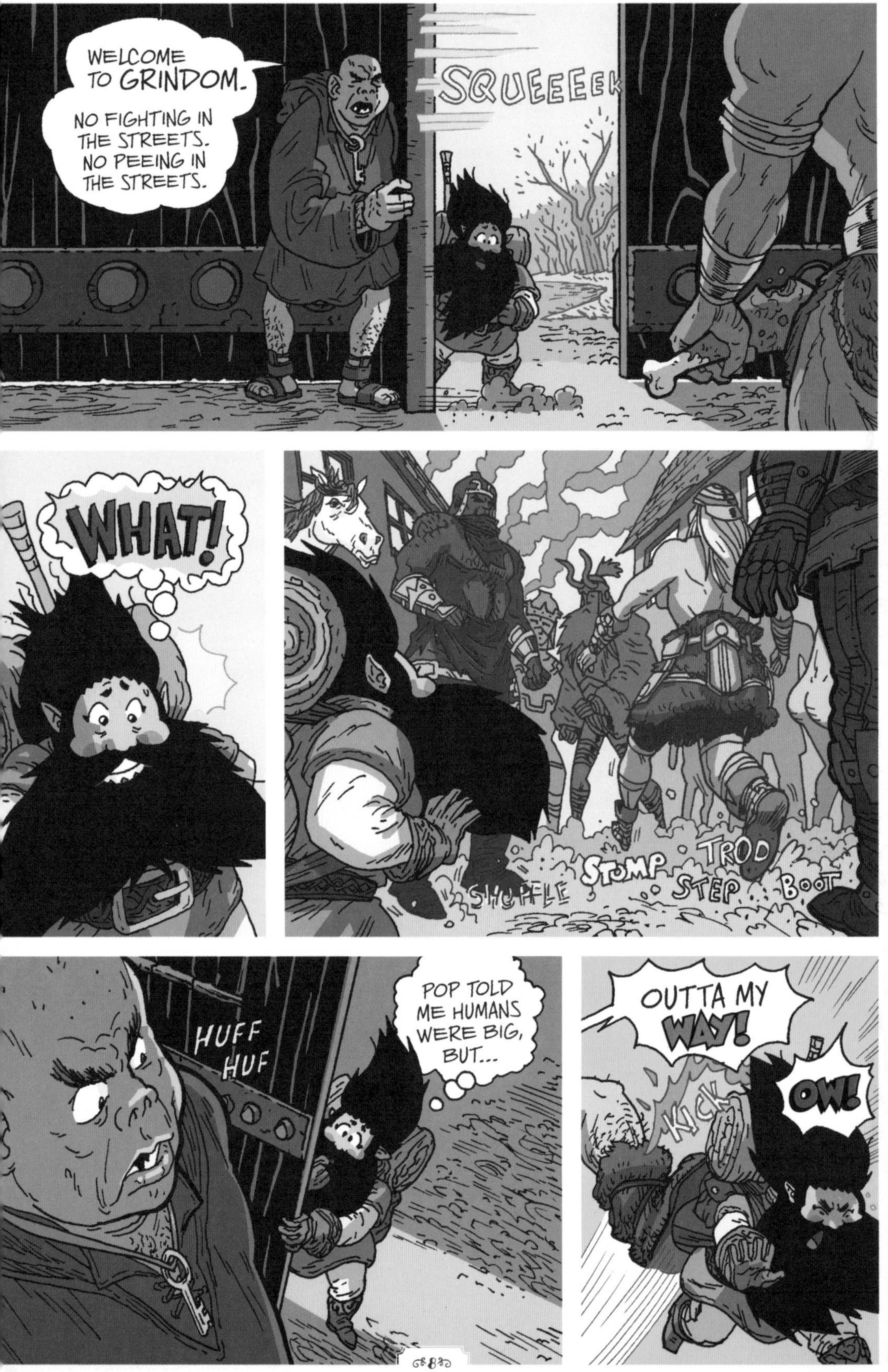

WELCOME TO GRINDOM.
NO FIGHTING IN THE STREETS. NO PEEING IN THE STREETS.
SQUEEEEEK
WHAT!
STOMP
TROD
SHUFFLE
STEP
BOOT
HUFF HUF
POP TOLD ME HUMANS WERE BIG, BUT...
OUTTA MY WAY!
KICK
OW!

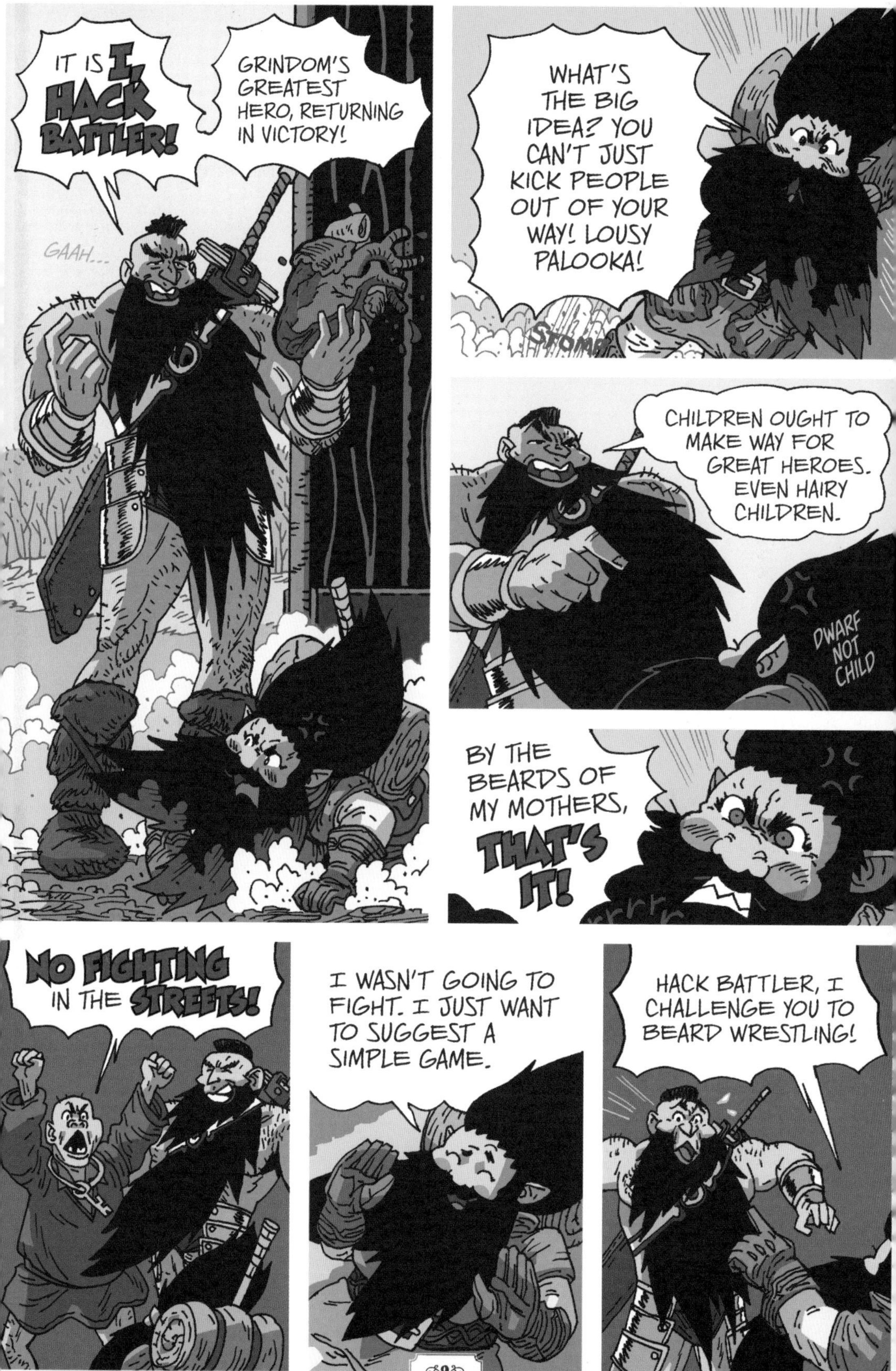
IT IS I, HACK BATTLER!
GRINDOM'S GREATEST HERO, RETURNING IN VICTORY!
GAAH...
WHAT'S THE BIG IDEA? YOU CAN'T JUST KICK PEOPLE OUT OF YOUR WAY! LOUSY PALOOKA!
STOMP
CHILDREN OUGHT TO MAKE WAY FOR GREAT HEROES. EVEN HAIRY CHILDREN.
DWARF NOT CHILD
BY THE BEARDS OF MY MOTHERS, THAT'S IT!
NO FIGHTING IN THE STREETS!
I WASN'T GOING TO FIGHT. I JUST WANT TO SUGGEST A SIMPLE GAME.
HACK BATTLER, I CHALLENGE YOU TO BEARD WRESTLING!

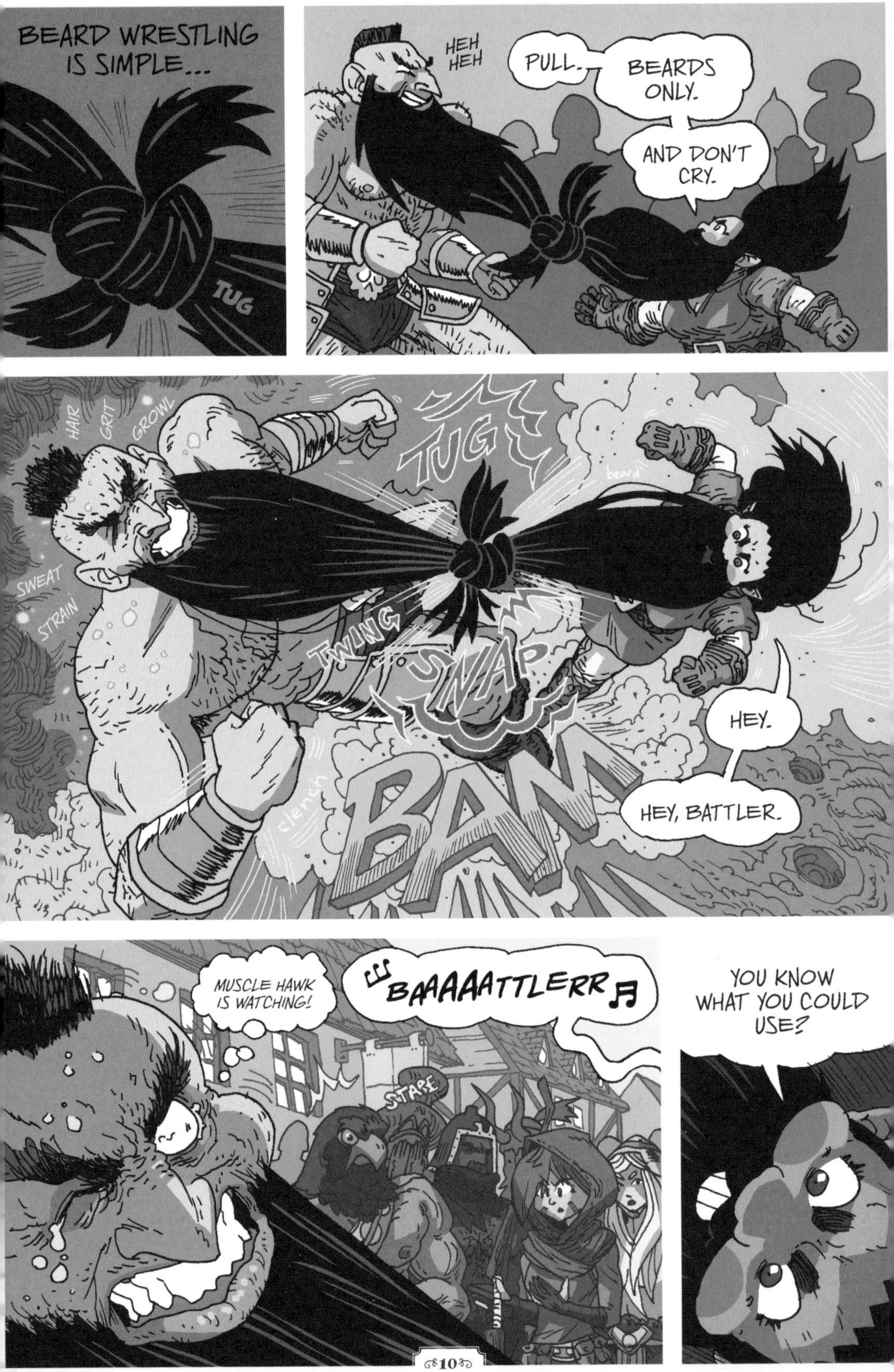
BEARD WRESTLING IS SIMPLE...
TUG
HEH HEH
PULL.
BEARDS ONLY.
AND DON'T CRY.
HAIR
GRIT
GROWL
TUG
beard
SWEAT
STRAIN
TWING
SNAP
clench
BAM
HEY.
HEY, BATTLER.
MUSCLE HAWK IS WATCHING!
BAAAAATTLERR
STARE
YOU KNOW WHAT YOU COULD USE?

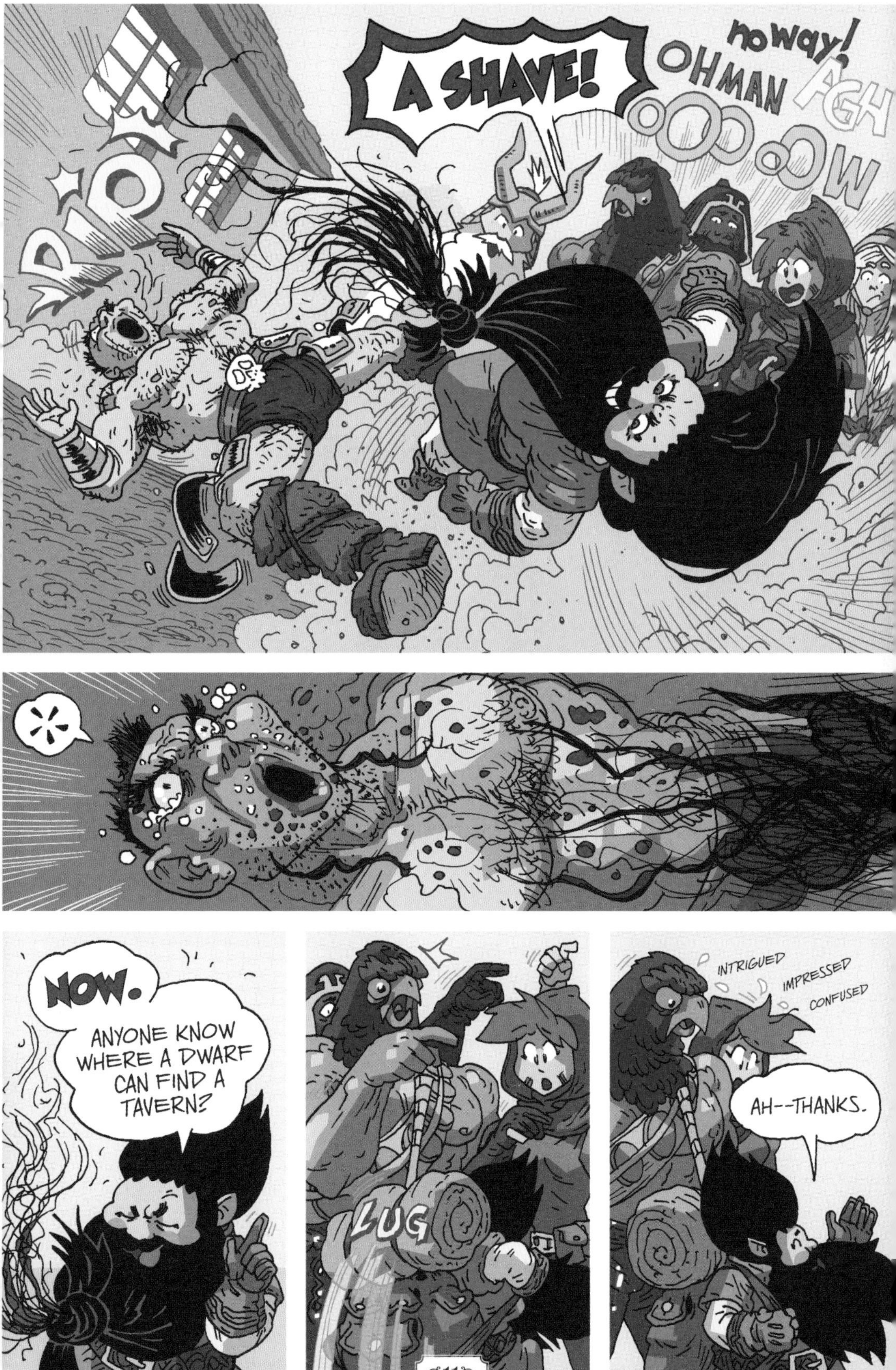
RIP
A SHAVE!
noway!
OHMAN
AGH
OOO..OOW
NOW.
ANYONE KNOW WHERE A DWARF CAN FIND A TAVERN?
LUG
INTRIGUED
IMPRESSED
CONFUSED
AH--THANKS.

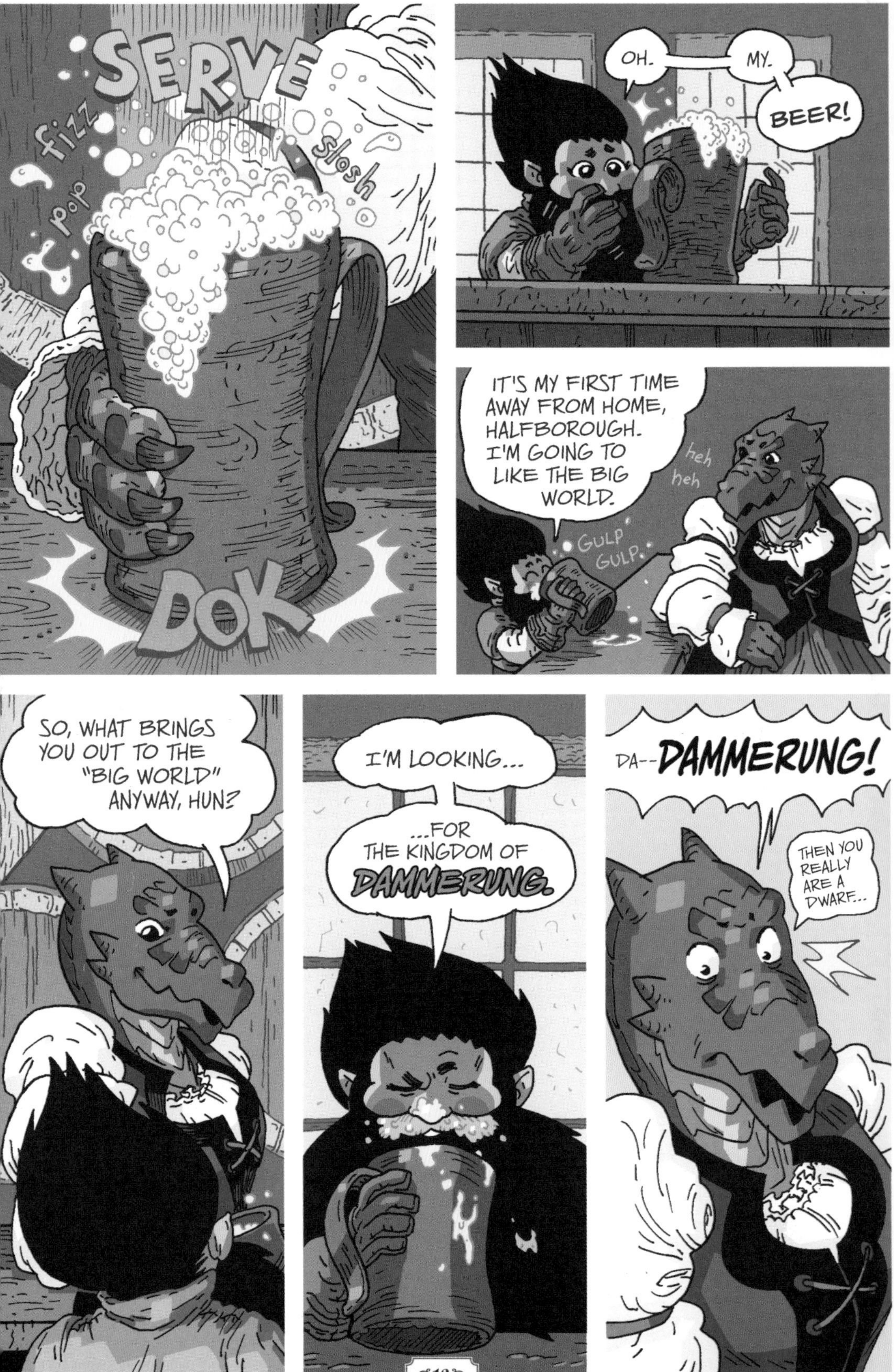
SERVE
fizz
pop
slosh
DOK
OH.
MY.
BEER!
IT'S MY FIRST TIME AWAY FROM HOME, HALFBOROUGH. I'M GOING TO LIKE THE BIG WORLD.
heh heh
GULP GULP
SO, WHAT BRINGS YOU OUT TO THE "BIG WORLD" ANYWAY, HUN?
I'M LOOKING...
...FOR THE KINGDOM OF DAMMERUNG.
DA--DAMMERUNG!
THEN YOU REALLY ARE A DWARF...

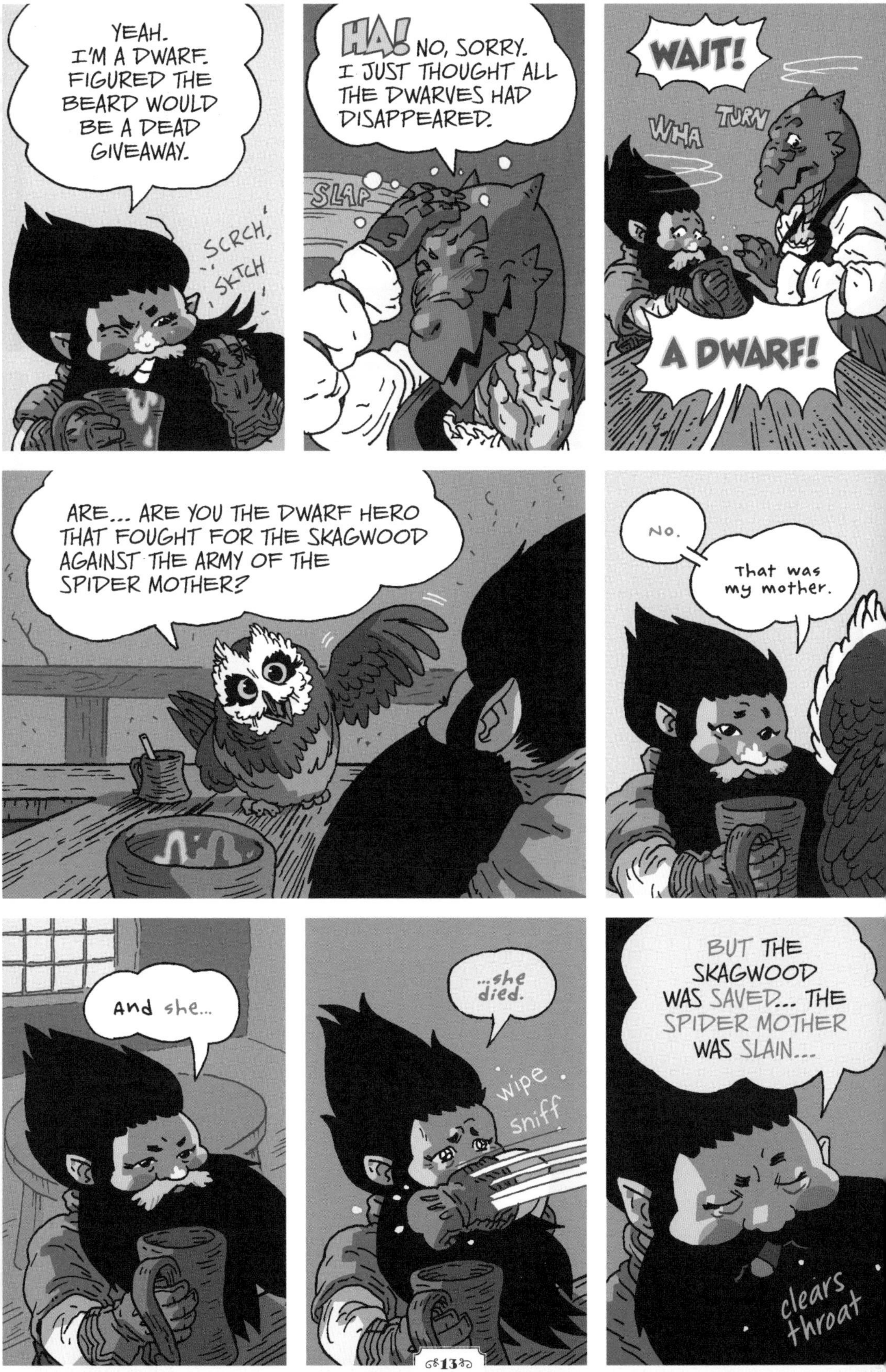
YEAH. I'M A DWARF. FIGURED THE BEARD WOULD BE A DEAD GIVEAWAY.
SCRCH, SKTCH
HA! NO, SORRY. I JUST THOUGHT ALL THE DWARVES HAD DISAPPEARED.
SLAP
WAIT!
WHA
TURN
A DWARF!
ARE... ARE YOU THE DWARF HERO THAT FOUGHT FOR THE SKAGWOOD AGAINST THE ARMY OF THE SPIDER MOTHER?
NO.
That was my mother.
And she...
...she died.
wipe
sniff
BUT THE SKAGWOOD WAS SAVED... THE SPIDER MOTHER WAS SLAIN...
clears throat

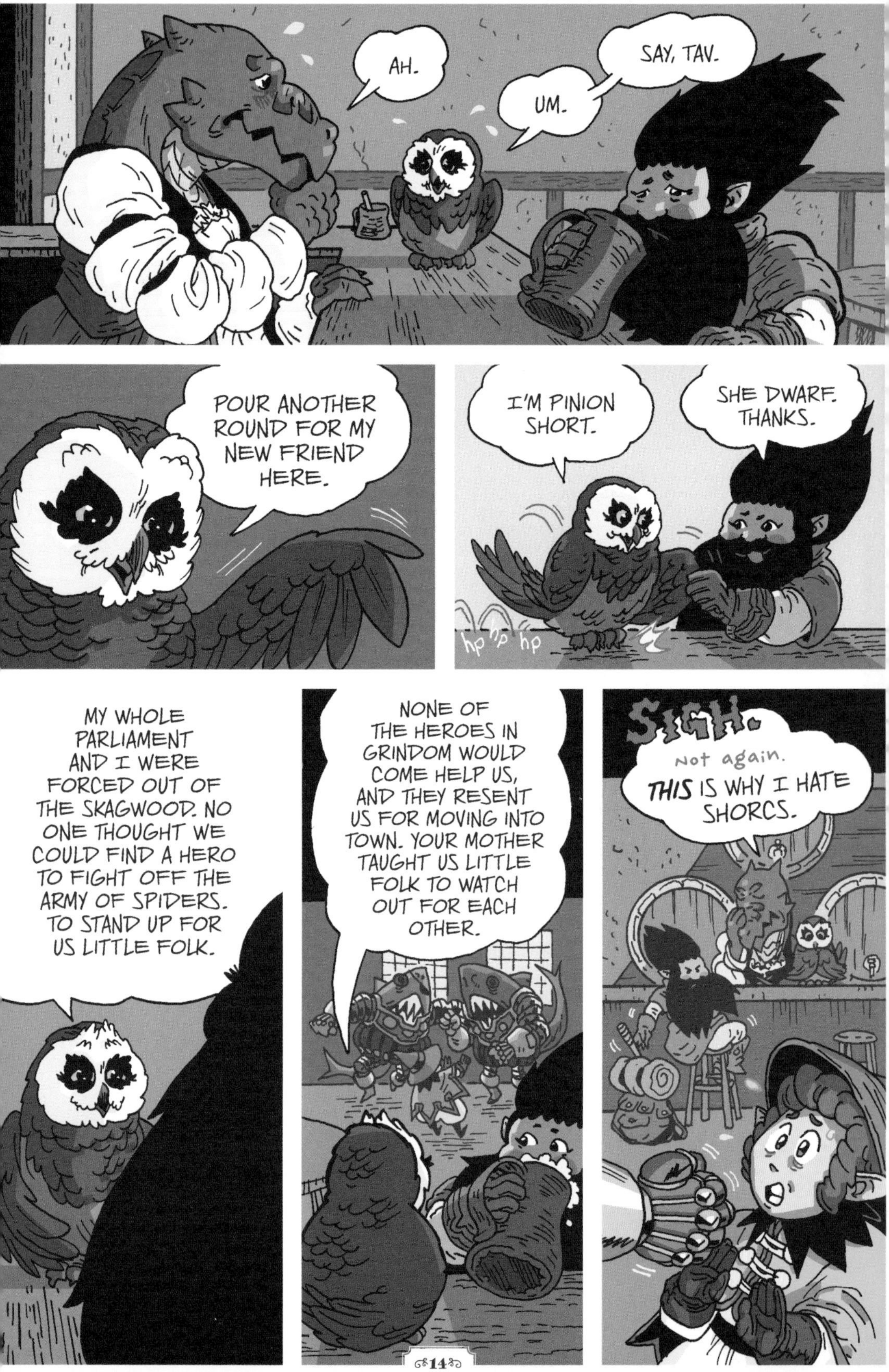
AH.
UM.
SAY, TAV.
POUR ANOTHER ROUND FOR MY NEW FRIEND HERE.
I'M PINION SHORT.
SHE DWARF. THANKS.
hp hp hp
MY WHOLE PARLIAMENT AND I WERE FORCED OUT OF THE SKAGWOOD. NO ONE THOUGHT WE COULD FIND A HERO TO FIGHT OFF THE ARMY OF SPIDERS. TO STAND UP FOR US LITTLE FOLK.
NONE OF THE HEROES IN GRINDOM WOULD COME HELP US, AND THEY RESENT US FOR MOVING INTO TOWN. YOUR MOTHER TAUGHT US LITTLE FOLK TO WATCH OUT FOR EACH OTHER.
SIGH.
not again.
THIS IS WHY I HATE SHORCS.

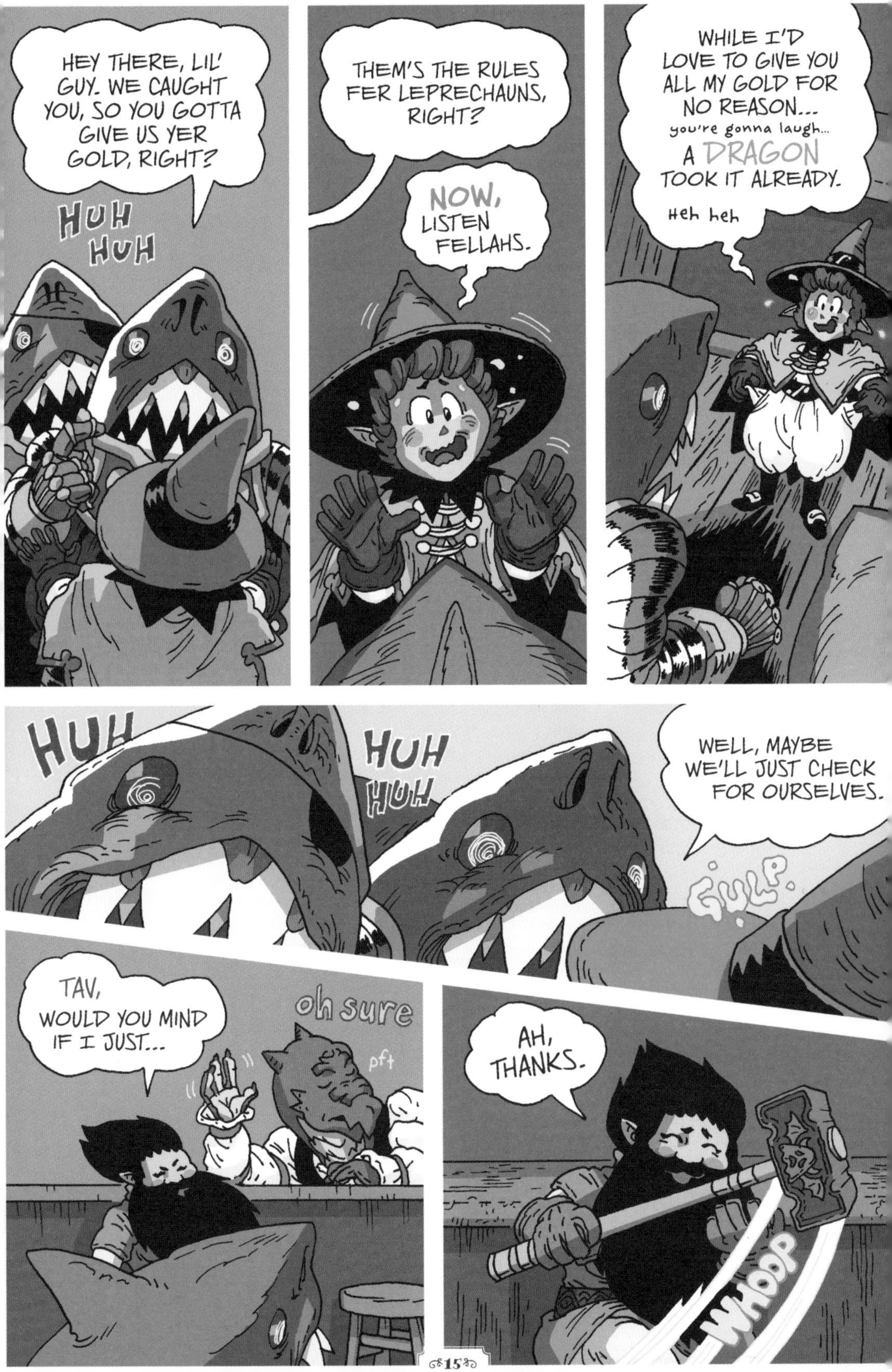
HEY THERE, LIL' GUY. WE CAUGHT YOU, SO YOU GOTTA GIVE US YER GOLD, RIGHT?
HUH HUH
THEM'S THE RULES FER LEPRECHAUNS, RIGHT?
NOW, LISTEN FELLAHS.
WHILE I'D LOVE TO GIVE YOU ALL MY GOLD FOR NO REASON...
you're gonna laugh...
A DRAGON TOOK IT ALREADY.
Heh heh
HUH
HUH HUH
WELL, MAYBE WE'LL JUST CHECK FOR OURSELVES.
GULP
TAV, WOULD YOU MIND IF I JUST...
oh sure
pft
AH, THANKS.
WHOOP

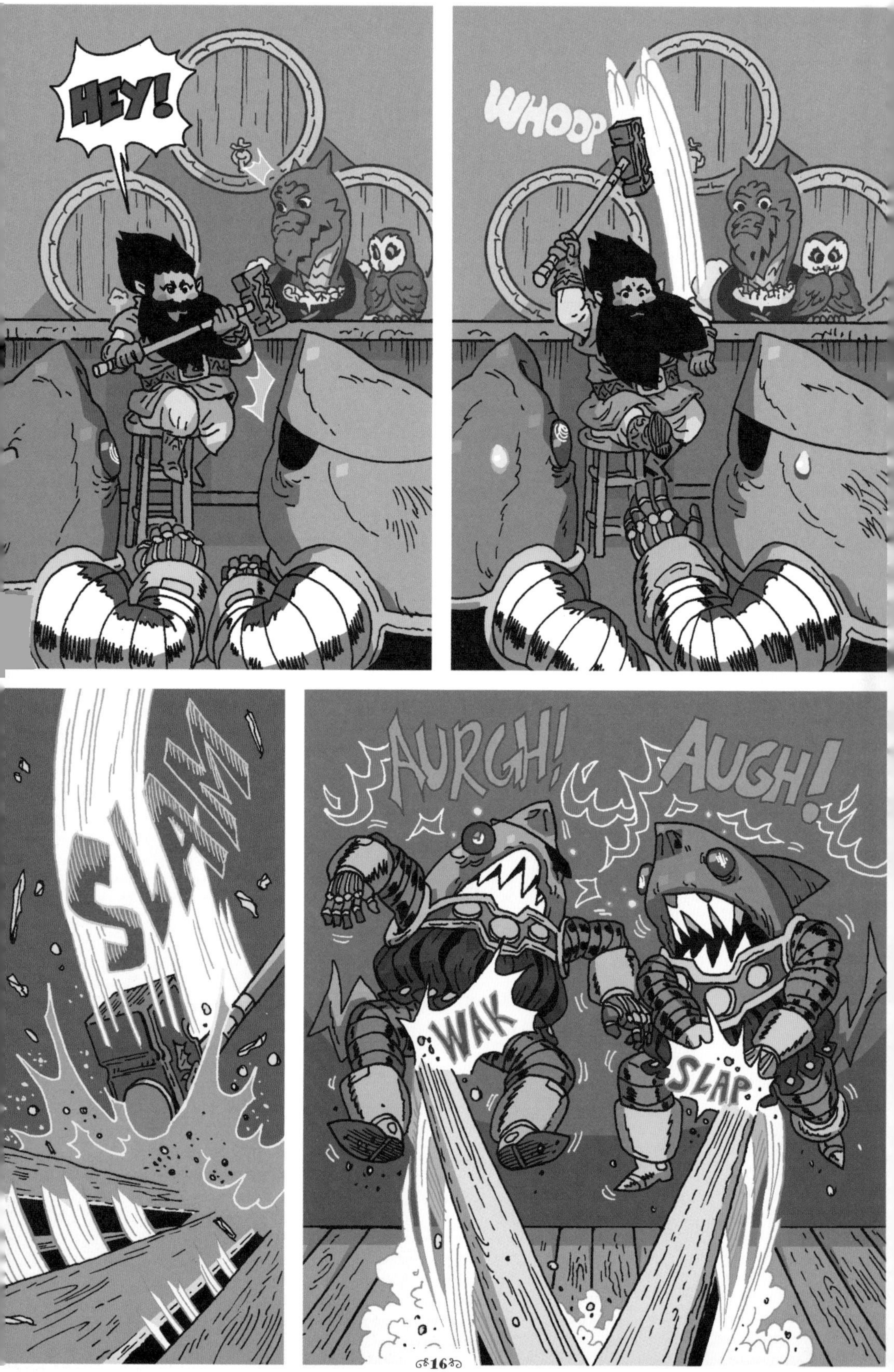
HEY!
WHOOP
SLAM
AURGH!
AUGH!
WAK
SLAP

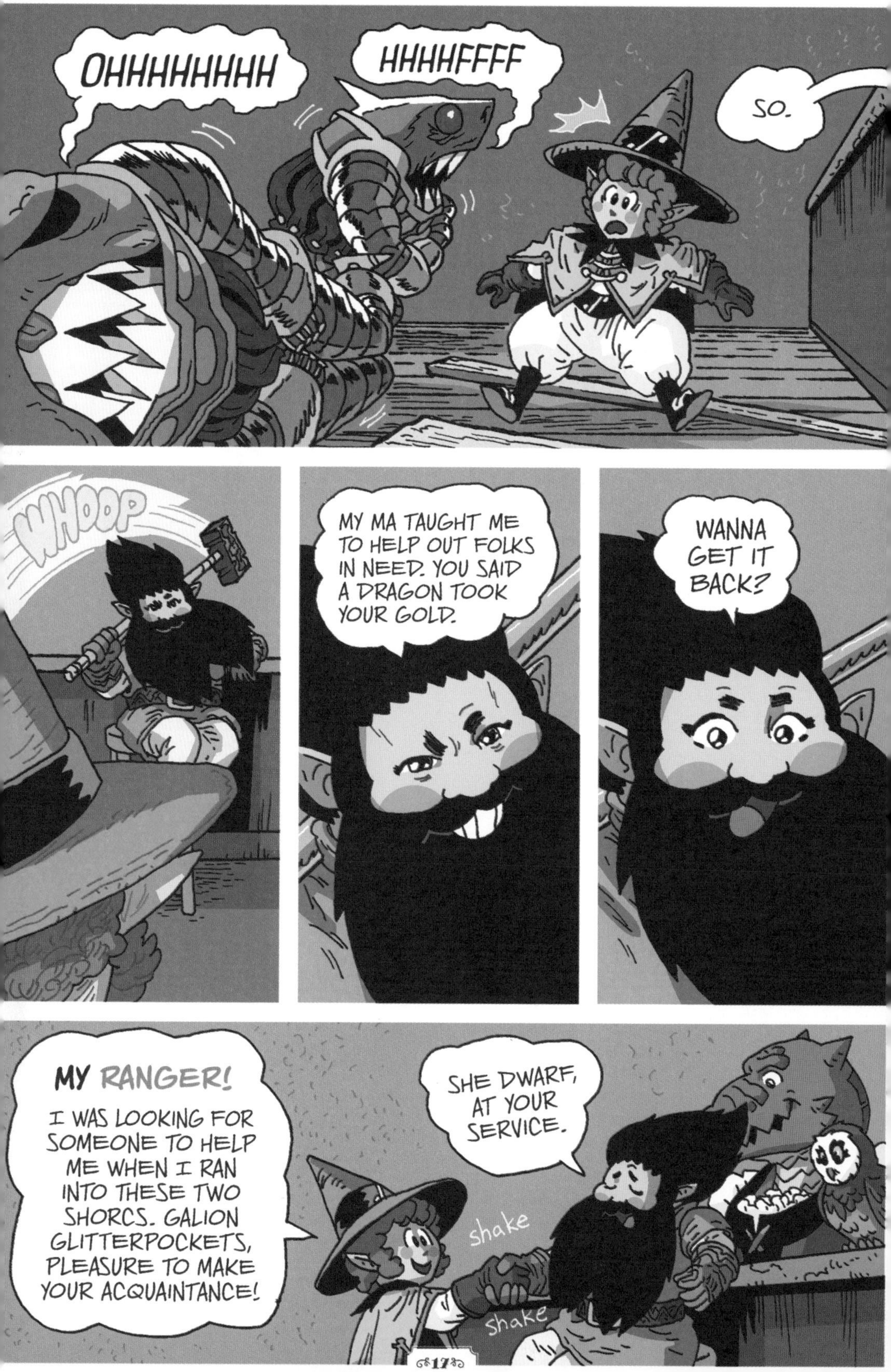
OHHHHHHHH
HHHHFFFF
SO.
WHOOP
MY MA TAUGHT ME TO HELP OUT FOLKS IN NEED. YOU SAID A DRAGON TOOK YOUR GOLD.
WANNA GET IT BACK?
MY RANGER!
I WAS LOOKING FOR SOMEONE TO HELP ME WHEN I RAN INTO THESE TWO SHORCS. GALION GLITTERPOCKETS, PLEASURE TO MAKE YOUR ACQUAINTANCE!
SHE DWARF, AT YOUR SERVICE.
shake
shake

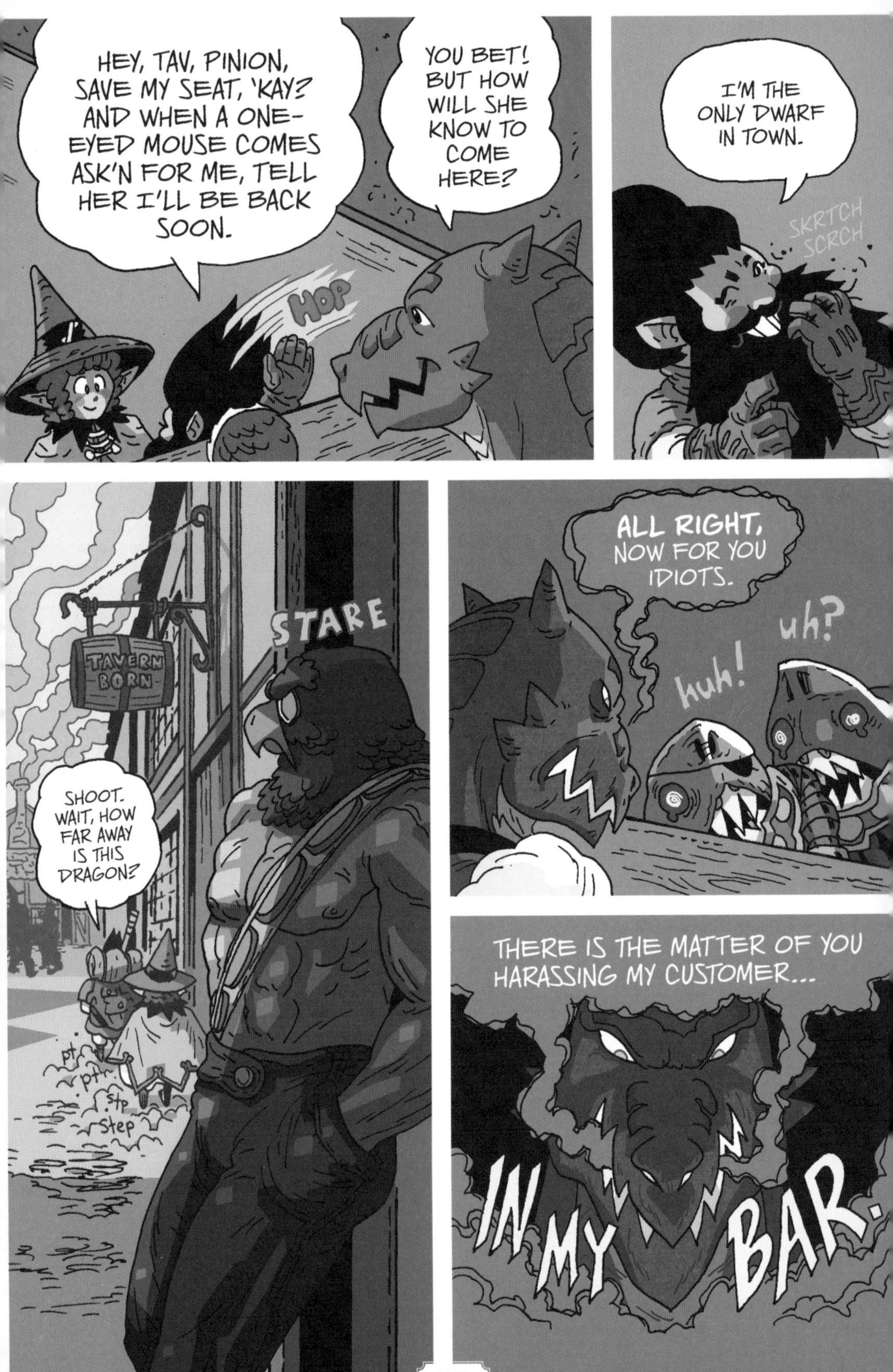
HEY, TAV, PINION, SAVE MY SEAT, 'KAY? AND WHEN A ONE-EYED MOUSE COMES ASK'N FOR ME, TELL HER I'LL BE BACK SOON.
YOU BET! BUT HOW WILL SHE KNOW TO COME HERE?
HOP
I'M THE ONLY DWARF IN TOWN.
SKRTCH SCRCH
TAVERN BORN
STARE
SHOOT. WAIT, HOW FAR AWAY IS THIS DRAGON?
pt pt stp step
ALL RIGHT, NOW FOR YOU IDIOTS.
huh!
uh?
THERE IS THE MATTER OF YOU HARASSING MY CUSTOMER...
IN MY BAR.

CHAPTER
II

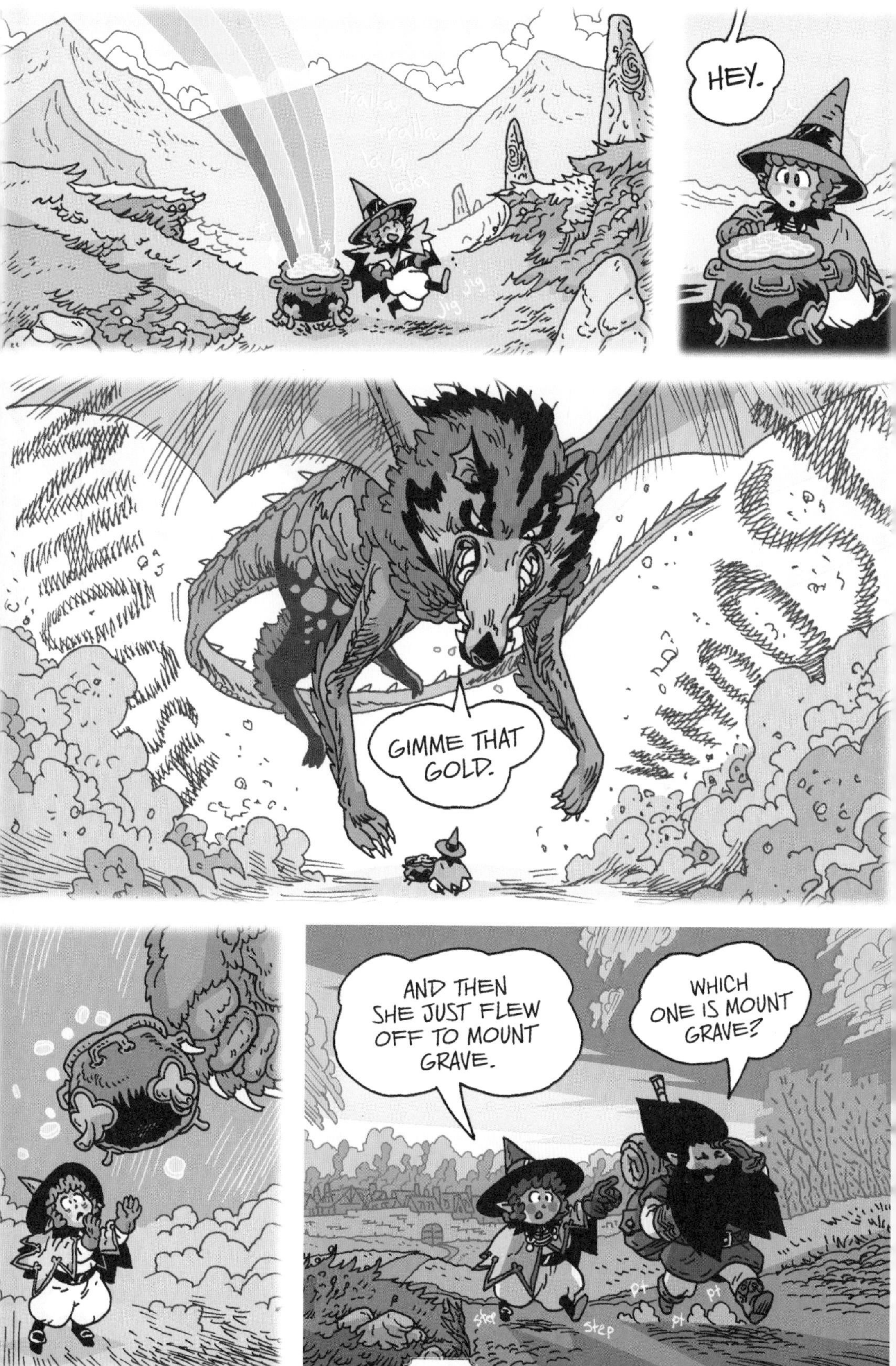
tralla
tralla
la la
lala
jig
jig
jig
HEY.
GIMME THAT GOLD.
AND THEN SHE JUST FLEW OFF TO MOUNT GRAVE.
WHICH ONE IS MOUNT GRAVE?
step
step
pt
pt
pt

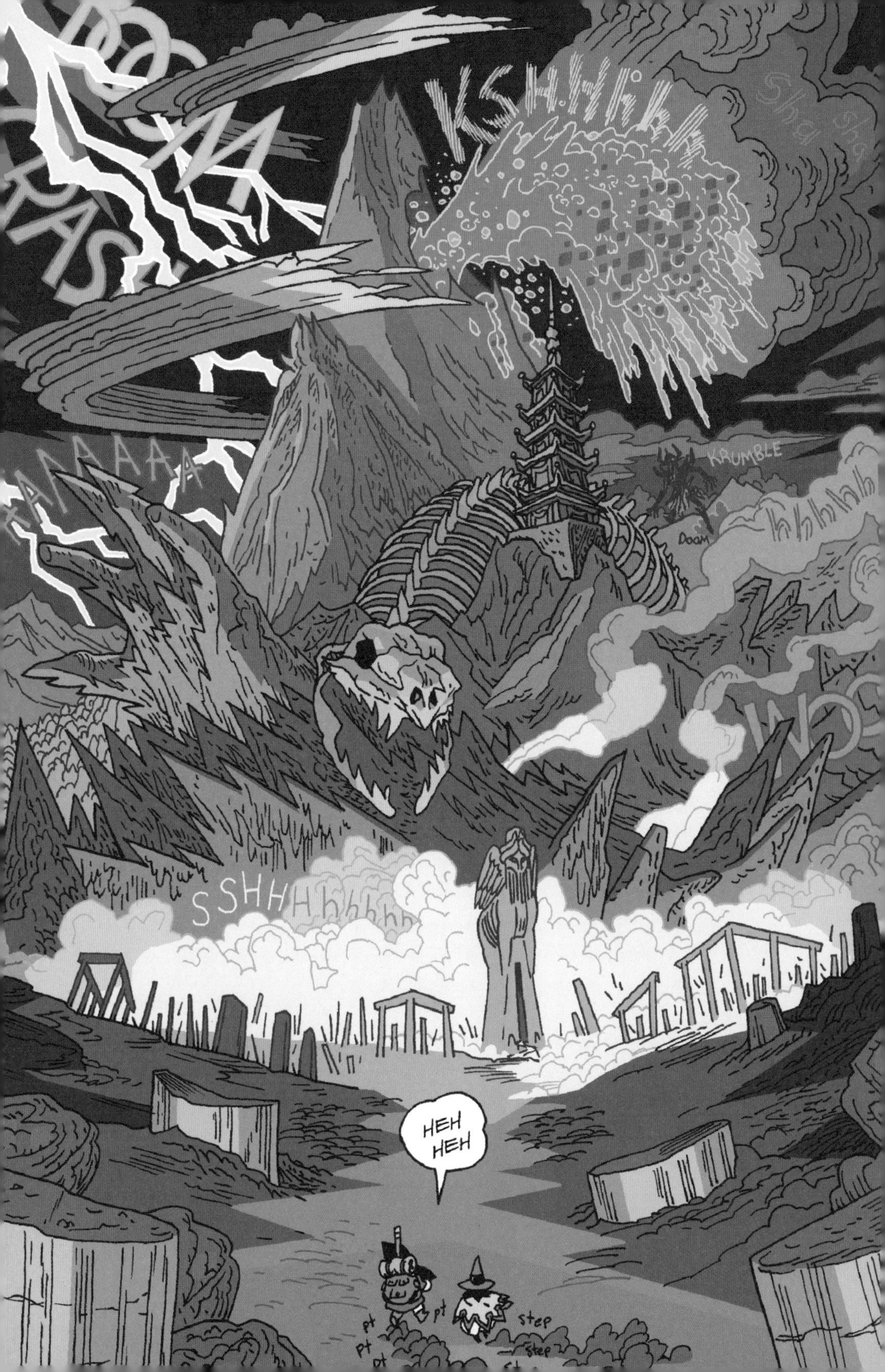
KSHHHHH
sha sha
AAAAAAA
KRUMBLE
hhhhhh
DOOM
SSHHHhhhhh
HEH HEH
pt pt
pt pt
step
step

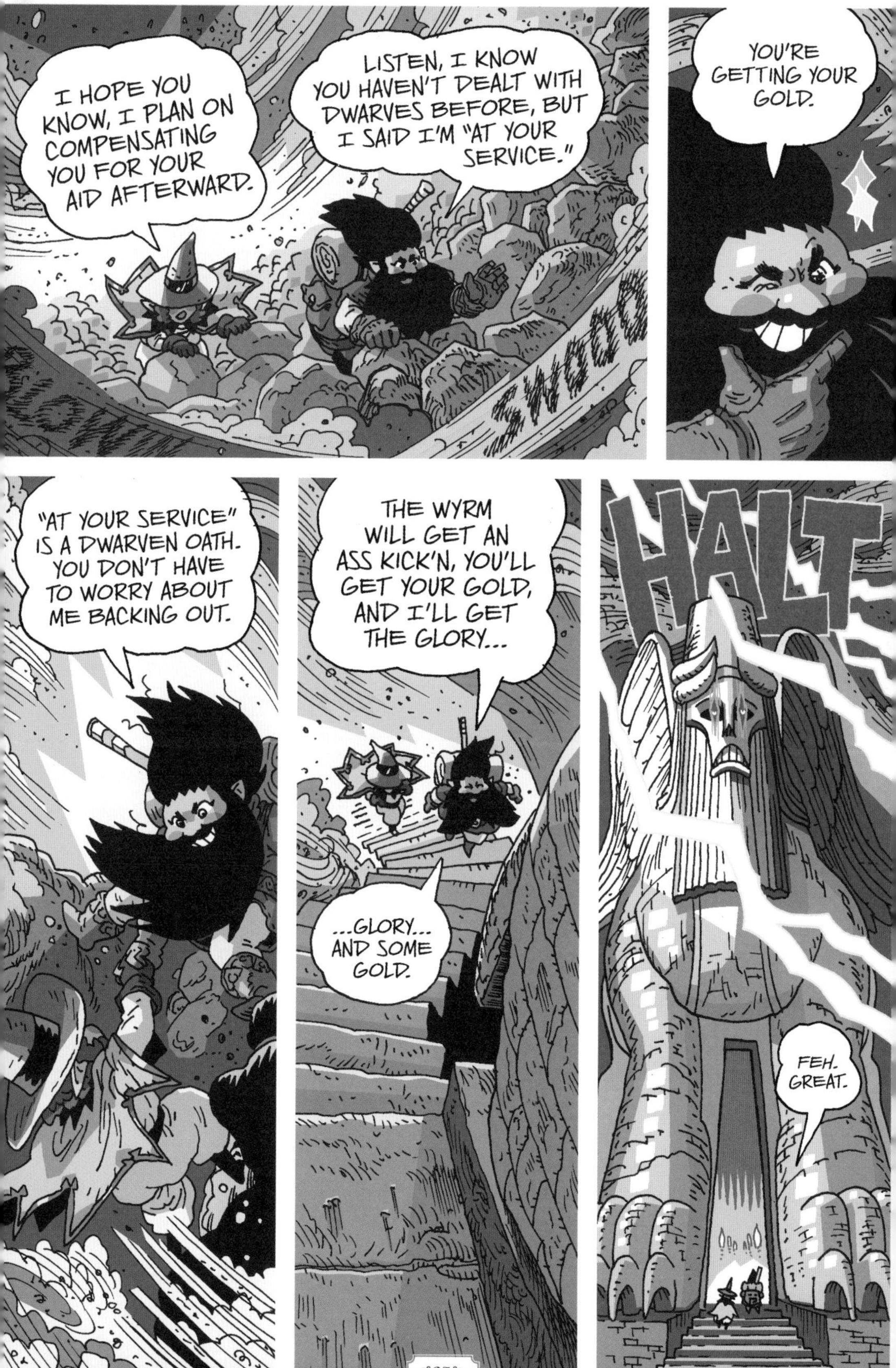

I HOPE YOU KNOW, I PLAN ON COMPENSATING YOU FOR YOUR AID AFTERWARD.
LISTEN, I KNOW YOU HAVEN'T DEALT WITH DWARVES BEFORE, BUT I SAID I'M "AT YOUR SERVICE."
YOU'RE GETTING YOUR GOLD.
"AT YOUR SERVICE" IS A DWARVEN OATH. YOU DON'T HAVE TO WORRY ABOUT ME BACKING OUT.
THE WYRM WILL GET AN ASS KICK'N, YOU'LL GET YOUR GOLD, AND I'LL GET THE GLORY...
...GLORY... AND SOME GOLD.
HALT
FEH. GREAT.

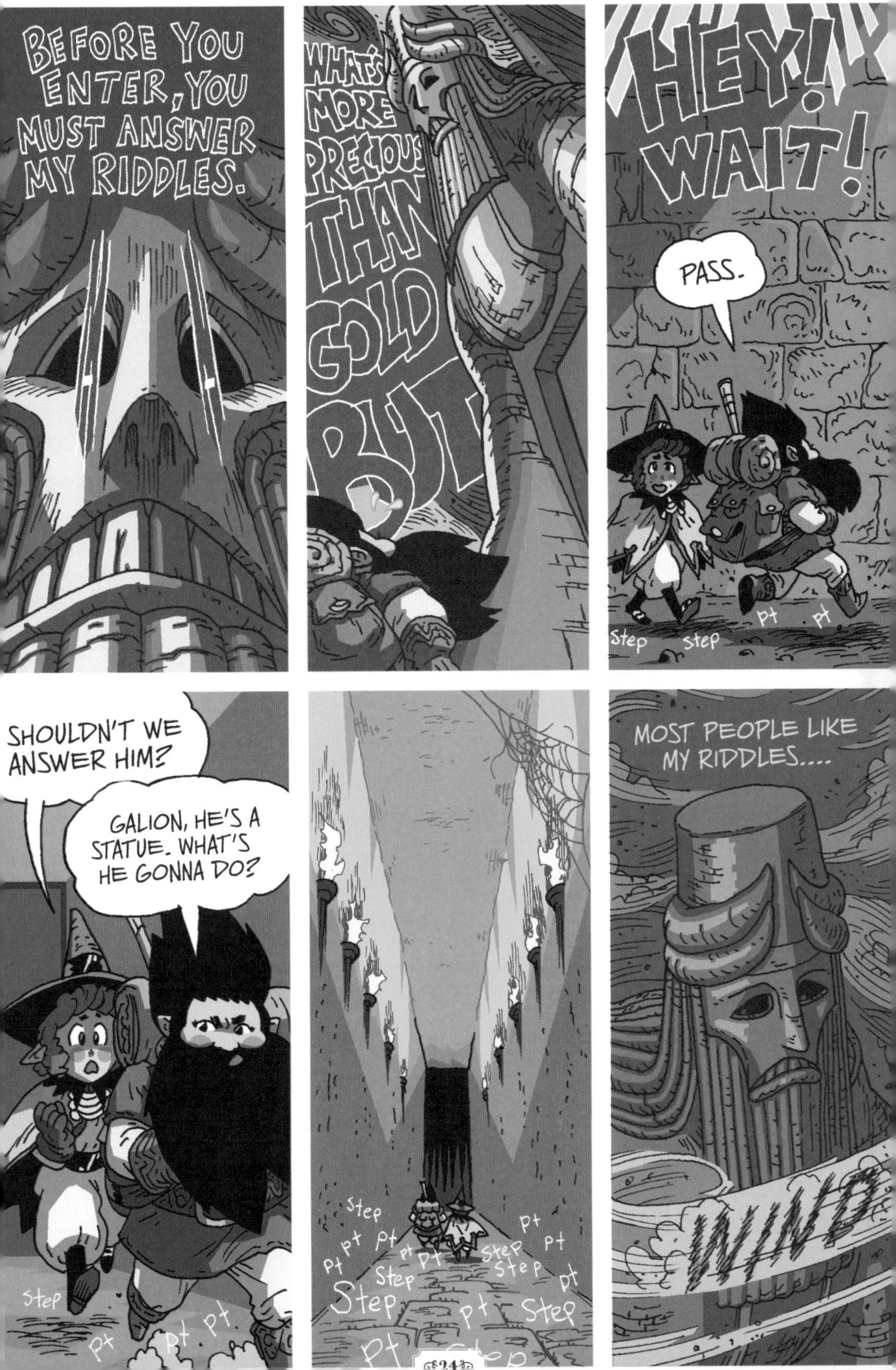
BEFORE YOU ENTER, YOU MUST ANSWER MY RIDDLES.
WHAT'S MORE PRECIOUS THAN GOLD BUT
HEY! WAIT!
PASS.
Step step pt pt
SHOULDN'T WE ANSWER HIM?
GALION, HE'S A STATUE. WHAT'S HE GONNA DO?
Step pt pt pt
Step pt pt pt pt pt Step Step Step pt Step pt Step pt pt
MOST PEOPLE LIKE MY RIDDLES....
WIND

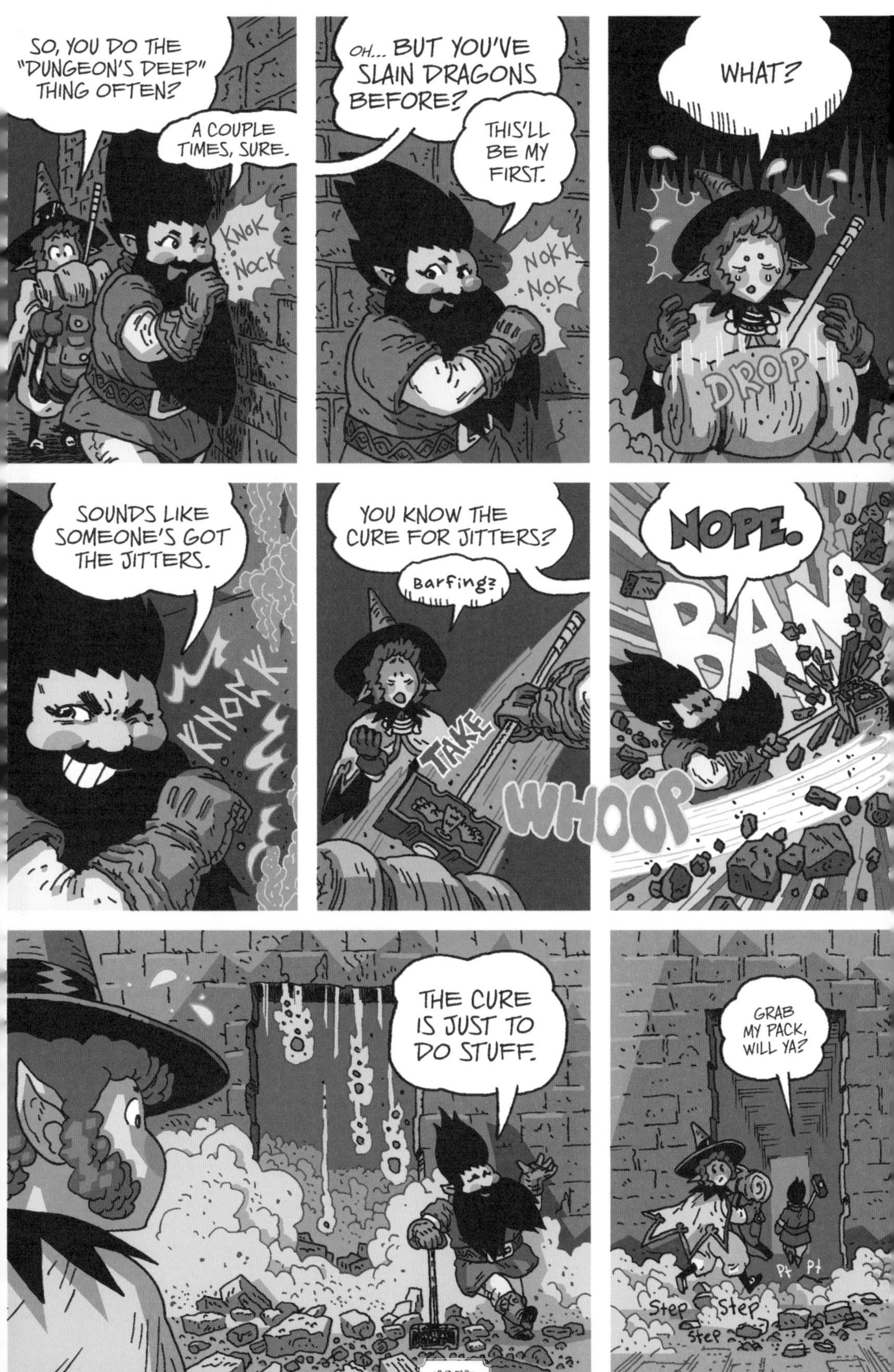
SO, YOU DO THE "DUNGEON'S DEEP" THING OFTEN?
A COUPLE TIMES, SURE.
KNOK NOCK
OH... BUT YOU'VE SLAIN DRAGONS BEFORE?
THIS'LL BE MY FIRST.
NOKK NOK
WHAT?
DROP
SOUNDS LIKE SOMEONE'S GOT THE JITTERS.
KNOCK
YOU KNOW THE CURE FOR JITTERS?
Barfing?
TAKE
NOPE.
BAM
WHOOP
THE CURE IS JUST TO DO STUFF.
GRAB MY PACK, WILL YA?
Pt Pt
Step Step Step

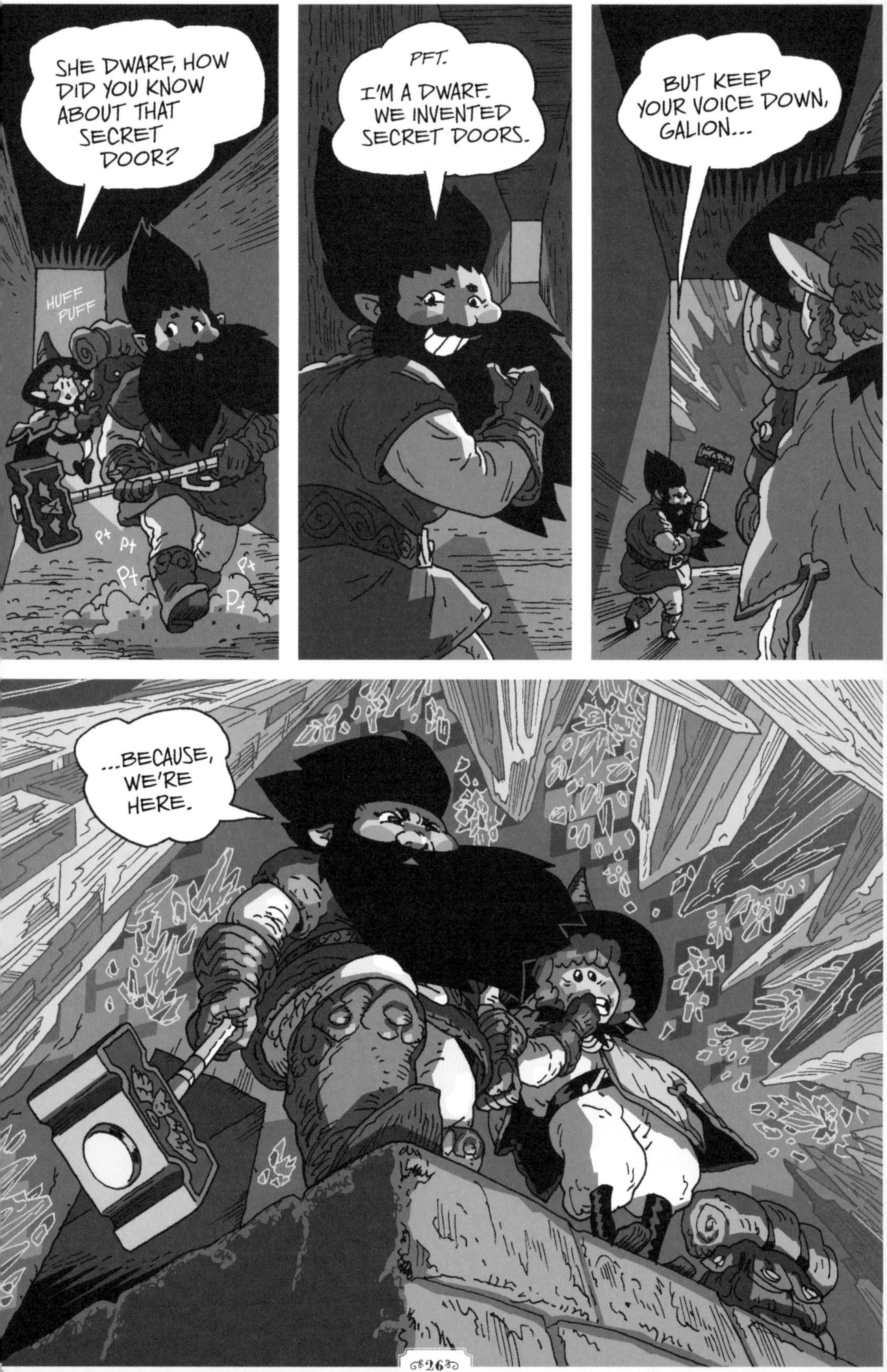
SHE DWARF, HOW DID YOU KNOW ABOUT THAT SECRET DOOR?
HUFF PUFF
Pt Pt Pt Pt Pt
PFT.
I'M A DWARF. WE INVENTED SECRET DOORS.
BUT KEEP YOUR VOICE DOWN, GALION...
...BECAUSE, WE'RE HERE.

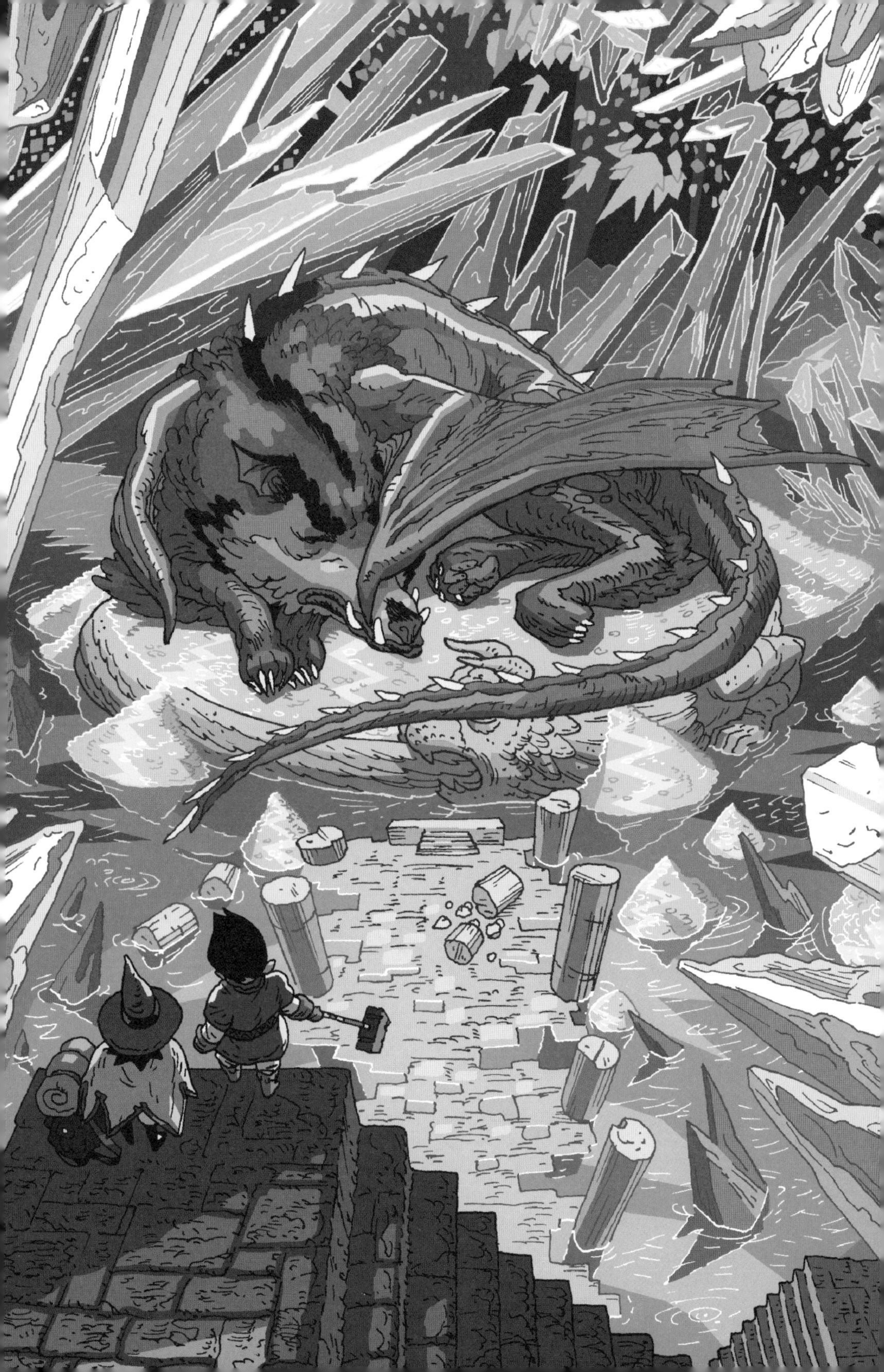

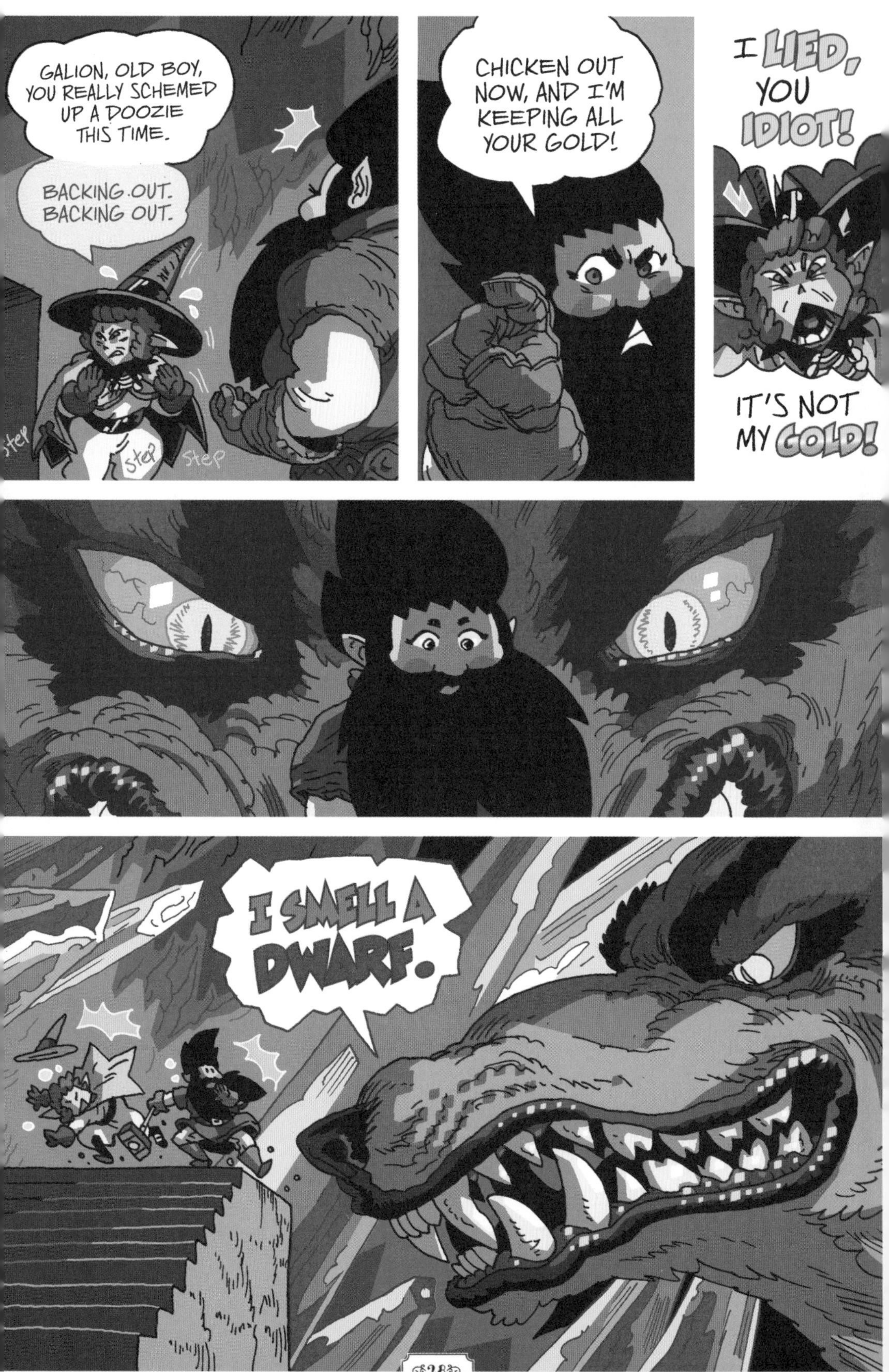
GALION, OLD BOY, YOU REALLY SCHEMED UP A DOOZIE THIS TIME.
BACKING OUT. BACKING OUT.
step
step
step
CHICKEN OUT NOW, AND I'M KEEPING ALL YOUR GOLD!
I LIED, YOU IDIOT!
IT'S NOT MY GOLD!
I SMELL A DWARF.

UH. LISTEN, MA'AM, I WAS LED HERE ON FALSE PRETENSES. SO, I'LL JUST GET OUT OF YOUR HAIR NOW.

SCOOT SHUFFLE

CRASH

THE DOOR!

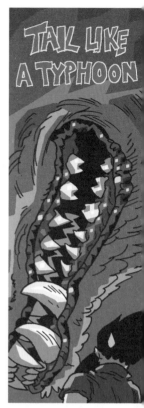

TAIL LIKE A TYPHOON

BACK LIKE A SEA,

AND YOU'VE GOT THE NERVE TO COME DOWN TO ME?

WE DON'T HAVE TO DO THIS!

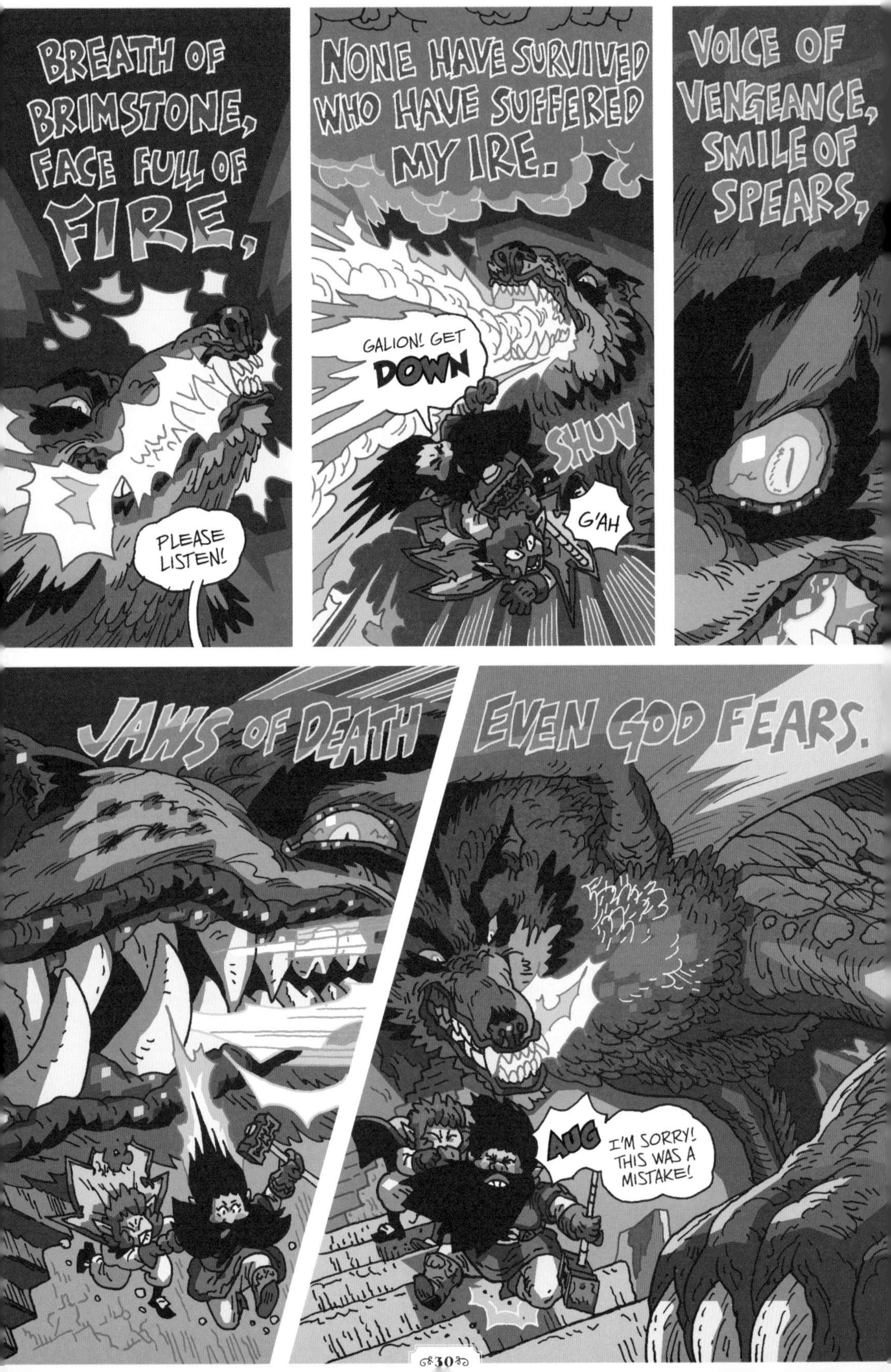
BREATH OF BRIMSTONE, FACE FULL OF FIRE,
PLEASE LISTEN!
NONE HAVE SURVIVED WHO HAVE SUFFERED MY IRE.
GALION! GET DOWN
SHUV
G'AH
VOICE OF VENGEANCE, SMILE OF SPEARS,
JAWS OF DEATH
EVEN GOD FEARS.
AUG
I'M SORRY! THIS WAS A MISTAKE!

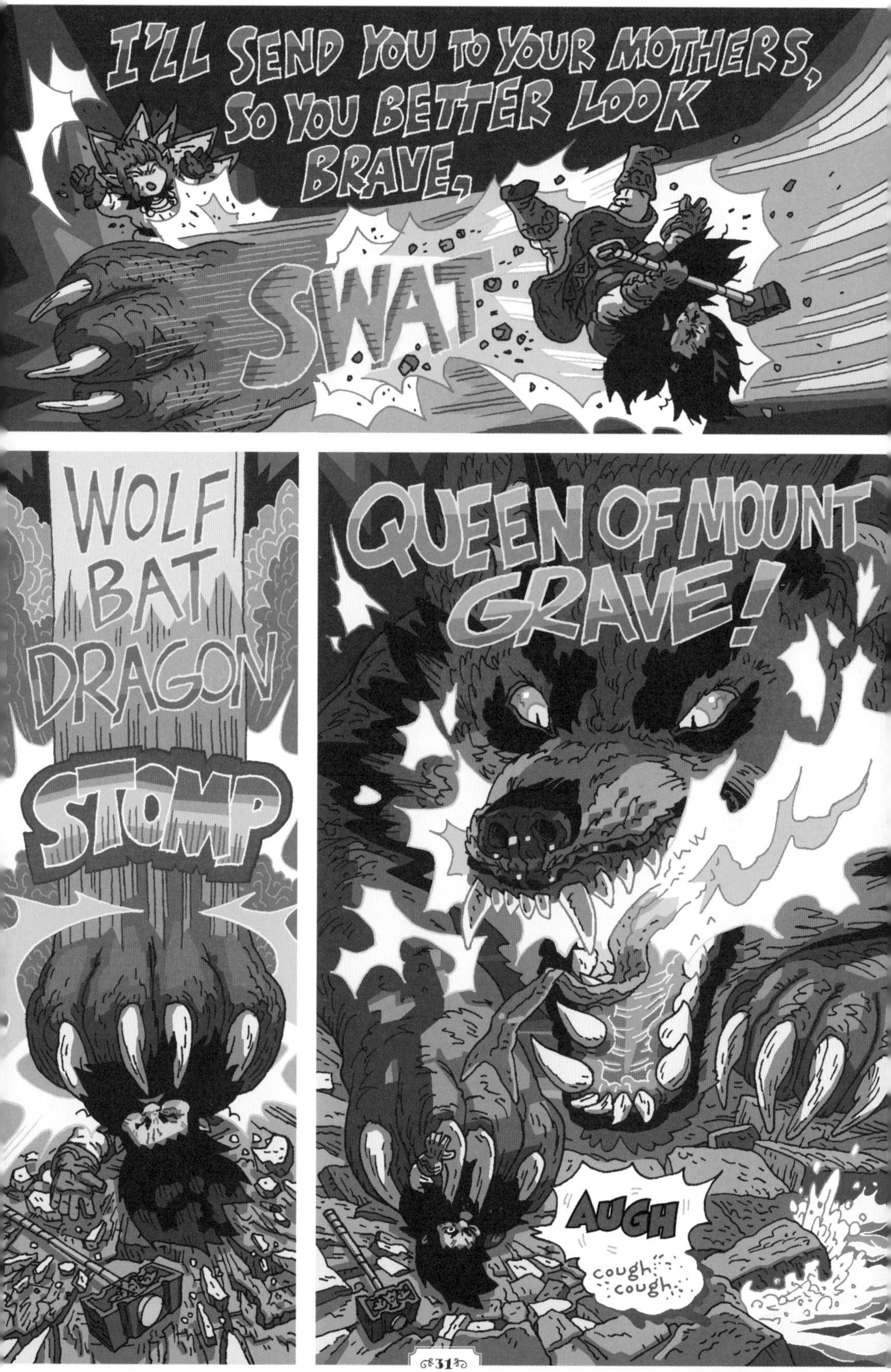
I'LL SEND YOU TO YOUR MOTHERS, SO YOU BETTER LOOK BRAVE,
SWAT
WOLF BAT DRAGON
STOMP
QUEEN OF MOUNT GRAVE!
AUGH
cough cough

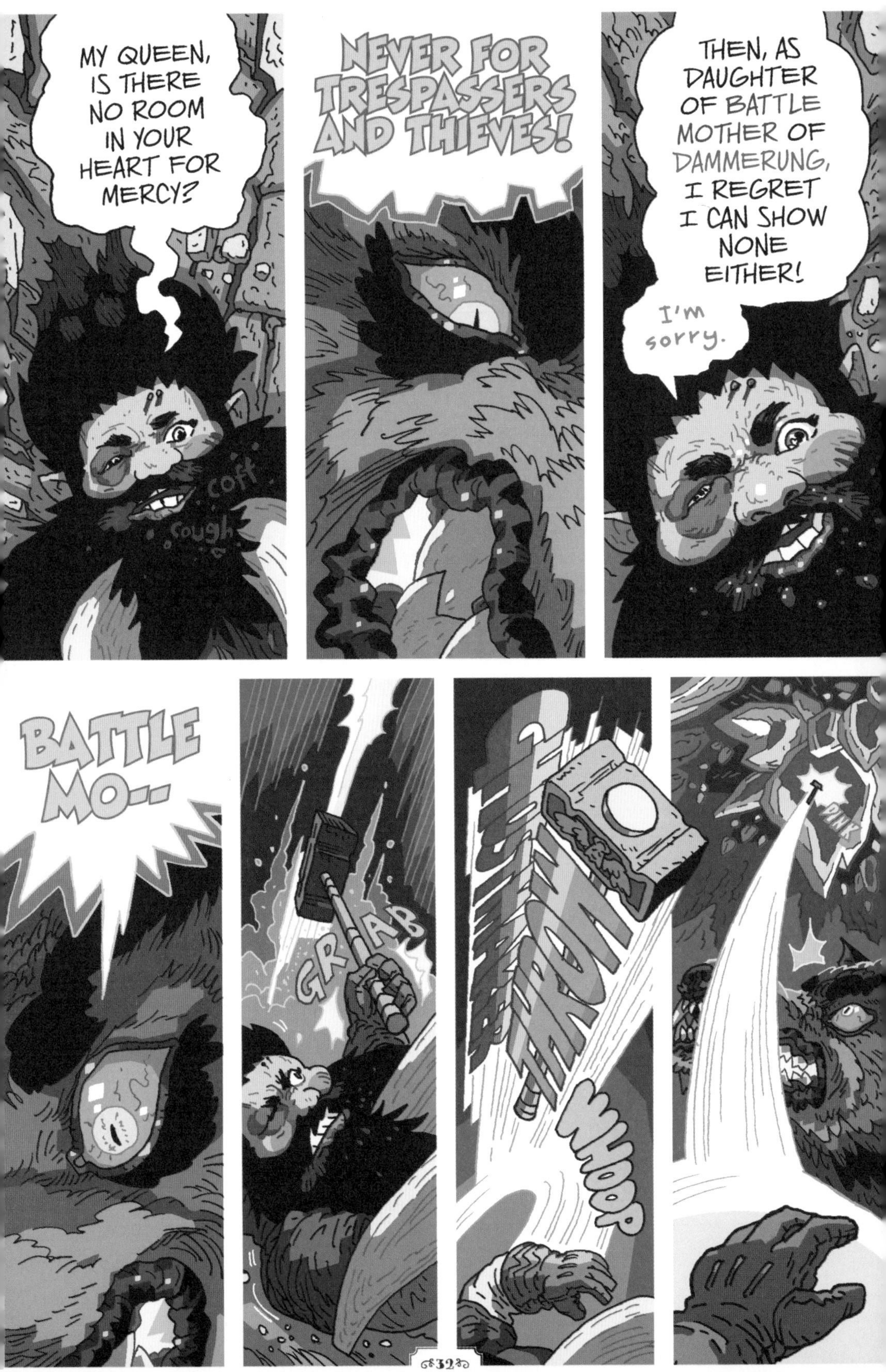

MY QUEEN, IS THERE NO ROOM IN YOUR HEART FOR MERCY?
coff
cough
NEVER FOR TRESPASSERS AND THIEVES!
THEN, AS DAUGHTER OF BATTLE MOTHER OF DAMMERUNG, I REGRET I CAN SHOW NONE EITHER!
I'm sorry.
BATTLE MO--
GRAB
THROW
WHOOP
PINK

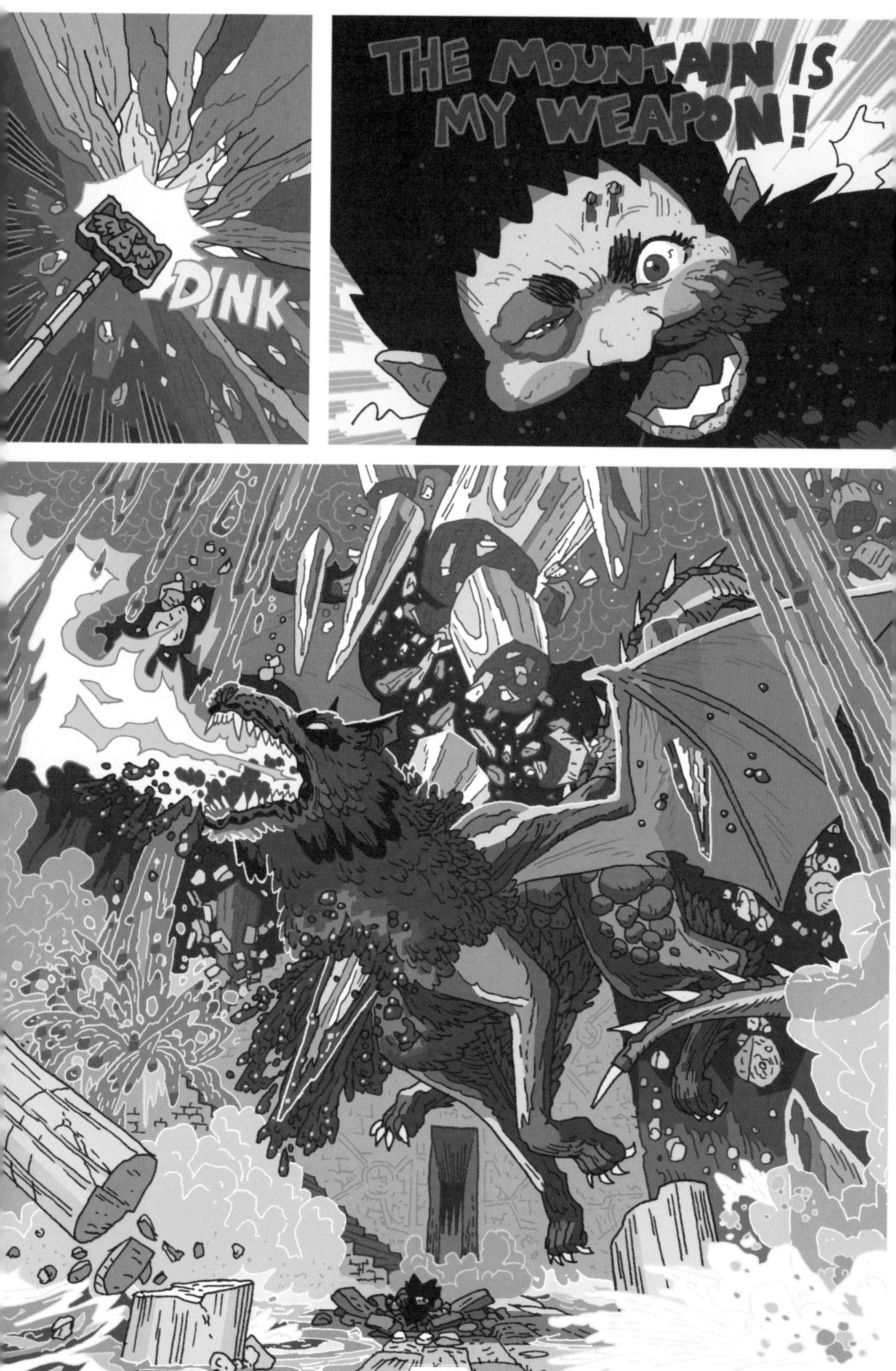
DINK
THE MOUNTAIN IS MY WEAPON!

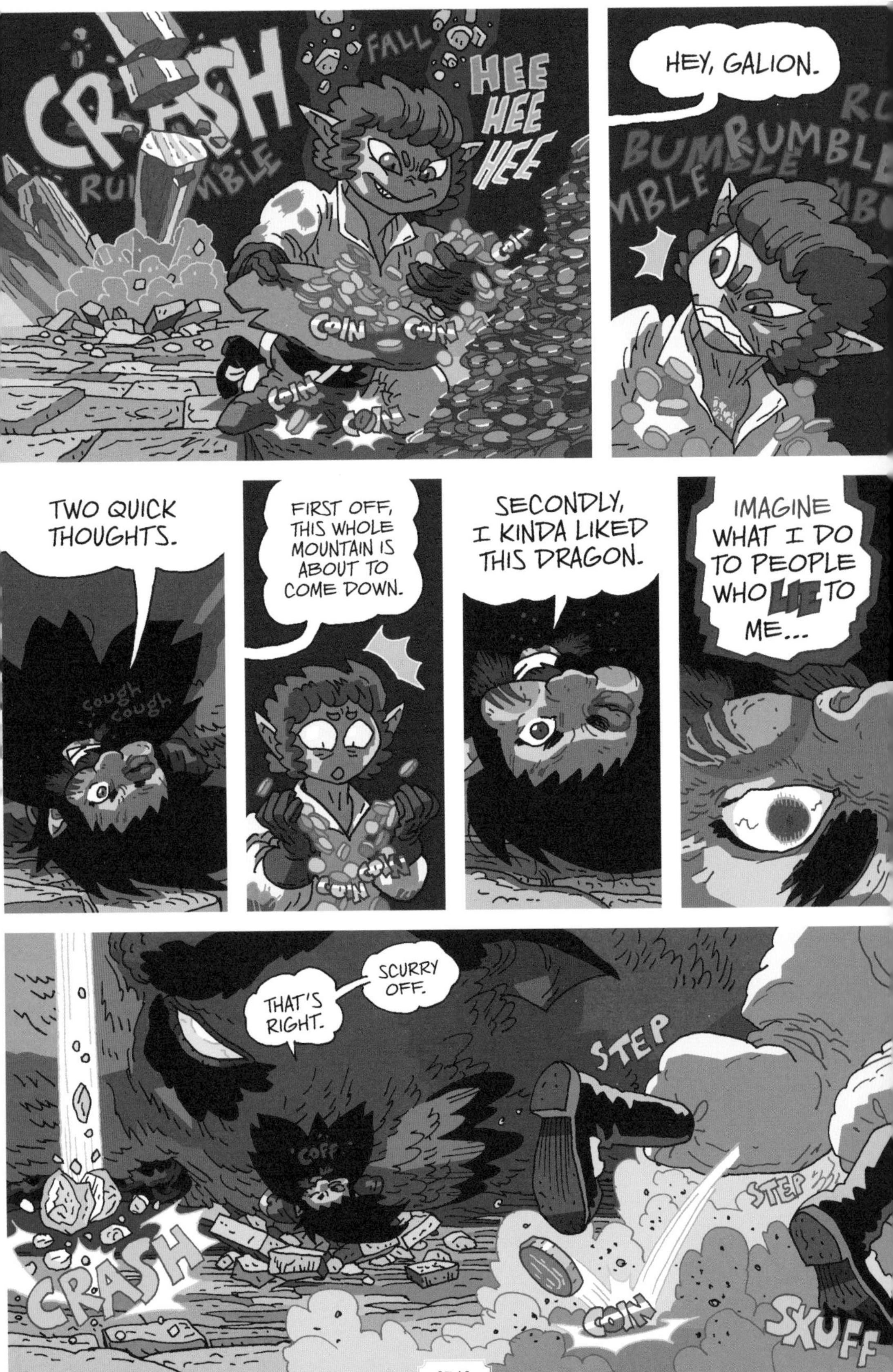
CRASH
RUMBLE
FALL
HEE HEE HEE
COIN COIN
COIN
COIN
HEY, GALION.
BUMRUMBLE
MBLE
TWO QUICK THOUGHTS.
cough cough
FIRST OFF, THIS WHOLE MOUNTAIN IS ABOUT TO COME DOWN.
COIN COIN
SECONDLY, I KINDA LIKED THIS DRAGON.
IMAGINE WHAT I DO TO PEOPLE WHO LIE TO ME...
THAT'S RIGHT.
SCURRY OFF.
STEP
COFF
STEP
CRASH
COIN
SKUFF

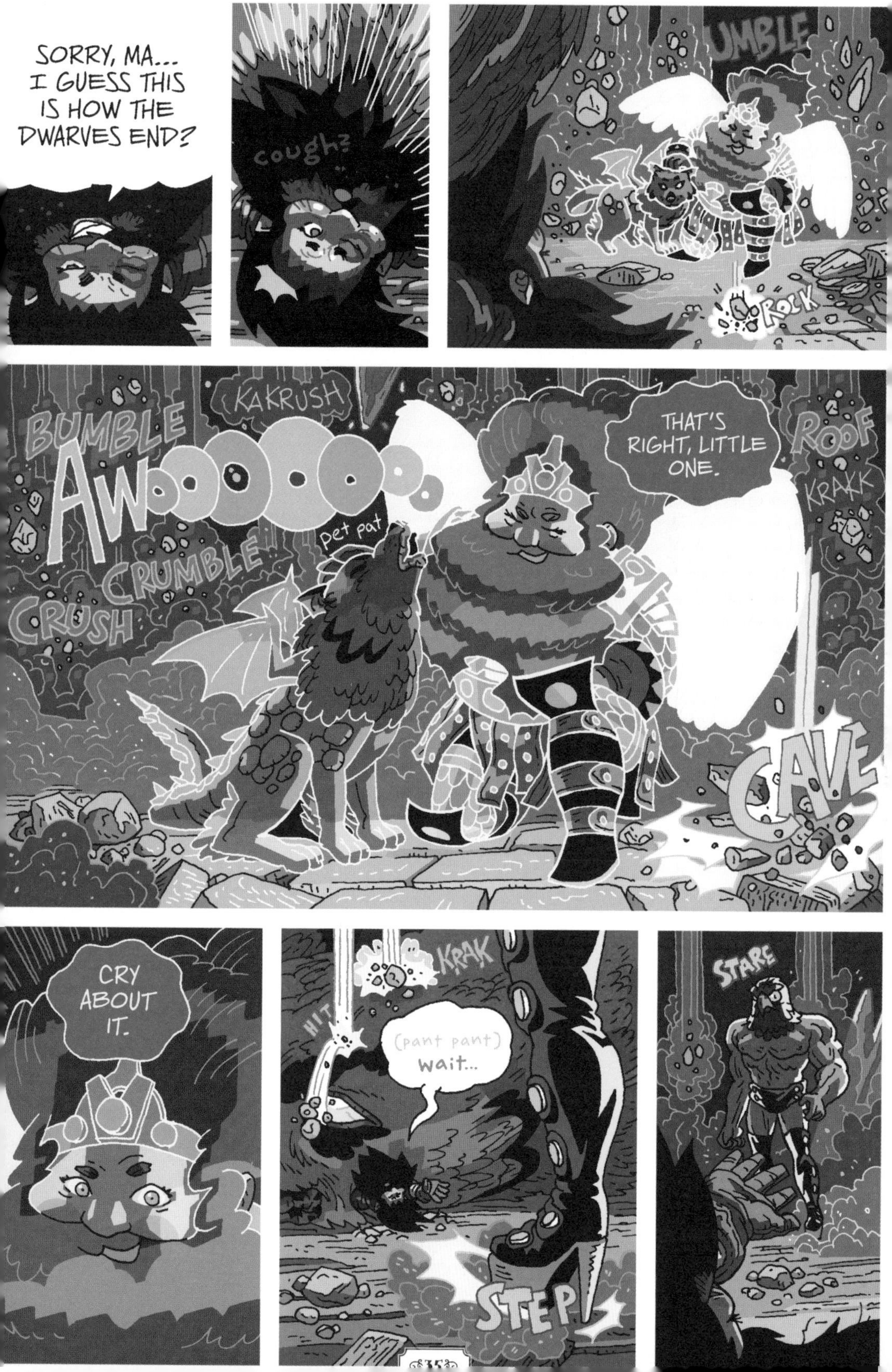
SORRY, MA...
I GUESS THIS IS HOW THE DWARVES END?
cough?
UMBLE
ROCK
KAKRUSH
BUMBLE
AWOOOOOOO
pet pat
CRUMBLE
CRUSH
THAT'S RIGHT, LITTLE ONE.
ROOF
KRAKK
CAVE
CRY ABOUT IT.
KRAK
HIT
(pant pant)
wait...
STEP
STARE

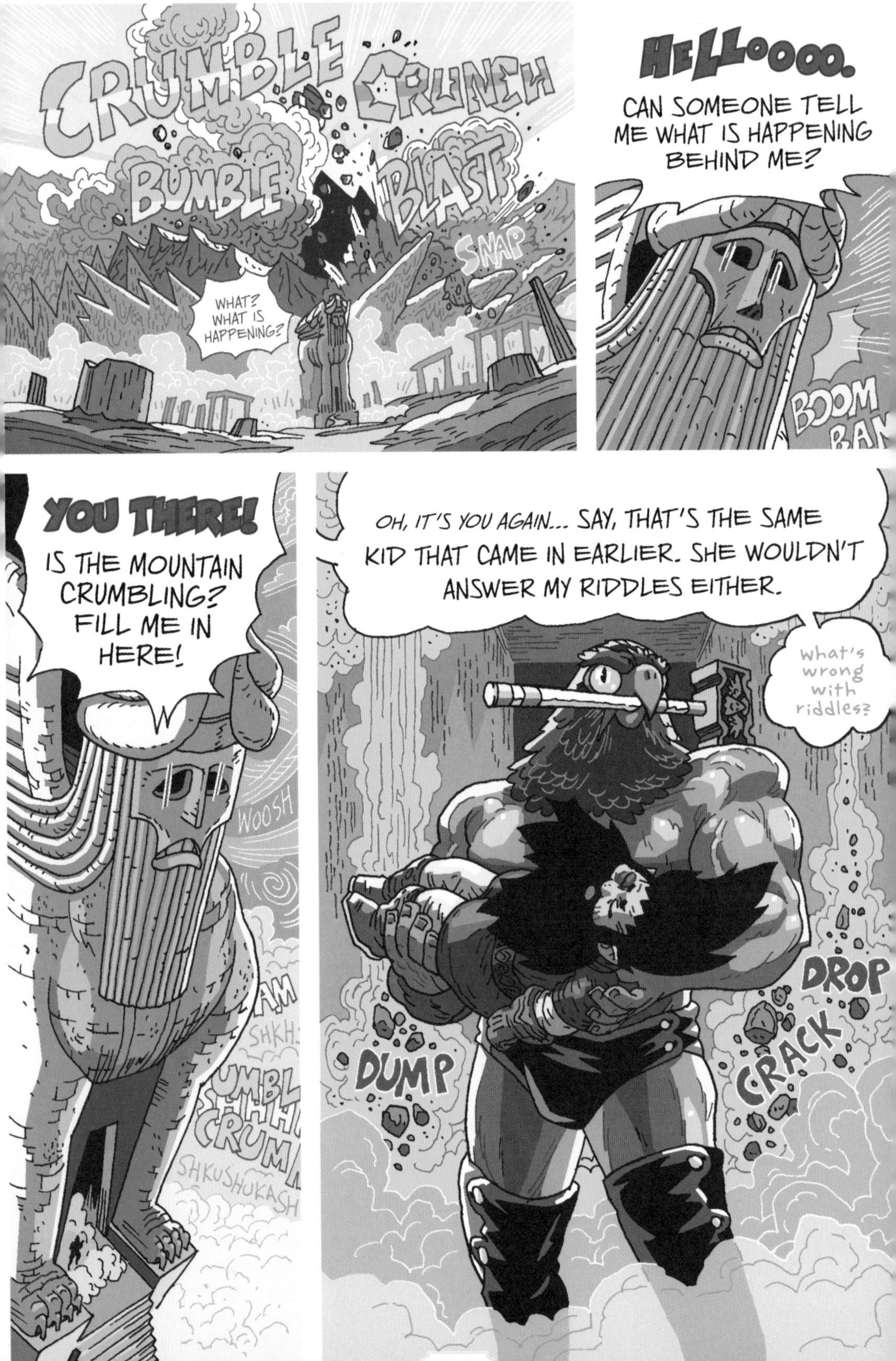
CRUMBLE CRUNCH
BUMBLE BLAST
SNAP
WHAT? WHAT IS HAPPENING?
HELLOOOO.
CAN SOMEONE TELL ME WHAT IS HAPPENING BEHIND ME?
BOOM
YOU THERE!
IS THE MOUNTAIN CRUMBLING? FILL ME IN HERE!
WOOSH
SHKUSHUKASH
OH, IT'S YOU AGAIN... SAY, THAT'S THE SAME KID THAT CAME IN EARLIER. SHE WOULDN'T ANSWER MY RIDDLES EITHER.
what's wrong with riddles?
DROP
CRACK
DUMP

CHAPTER III

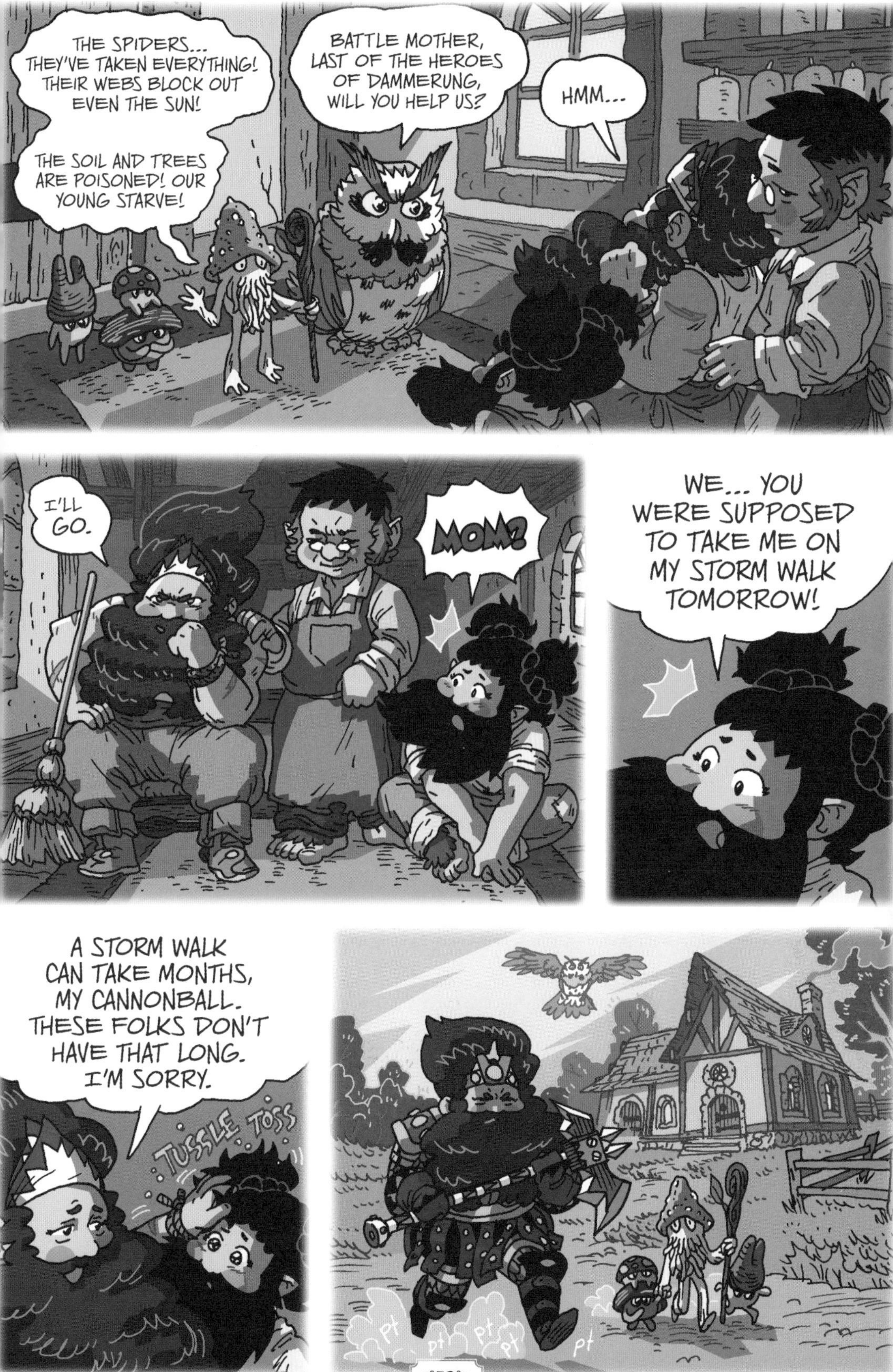
THE SPIDERS... THEY'VE TAKEN EVERYTHING! THEIR WEBS BLOCK OUT EVEN THE SUN!
THE SOIL AND TREES ARE POISONED! OUR YOUNG STARVE!
BATTLE MOTHER, LAST OF THE HEROES OF DAMMERUNG, WILL YOU HELP US?
HMM...
I'LL GO.
MOM?
WE... YOU WERE SUPPOSED TO TAKE ME ON MY STORM WALK TOMORROW!
A STORM WALK CAN TAKE MONTHS, MY CANNONBALL. THESE FOLKS DON'T HAVE THAT LONG. I'M SORRY.
TUSSLE TOSS
pt pt pt pt pt

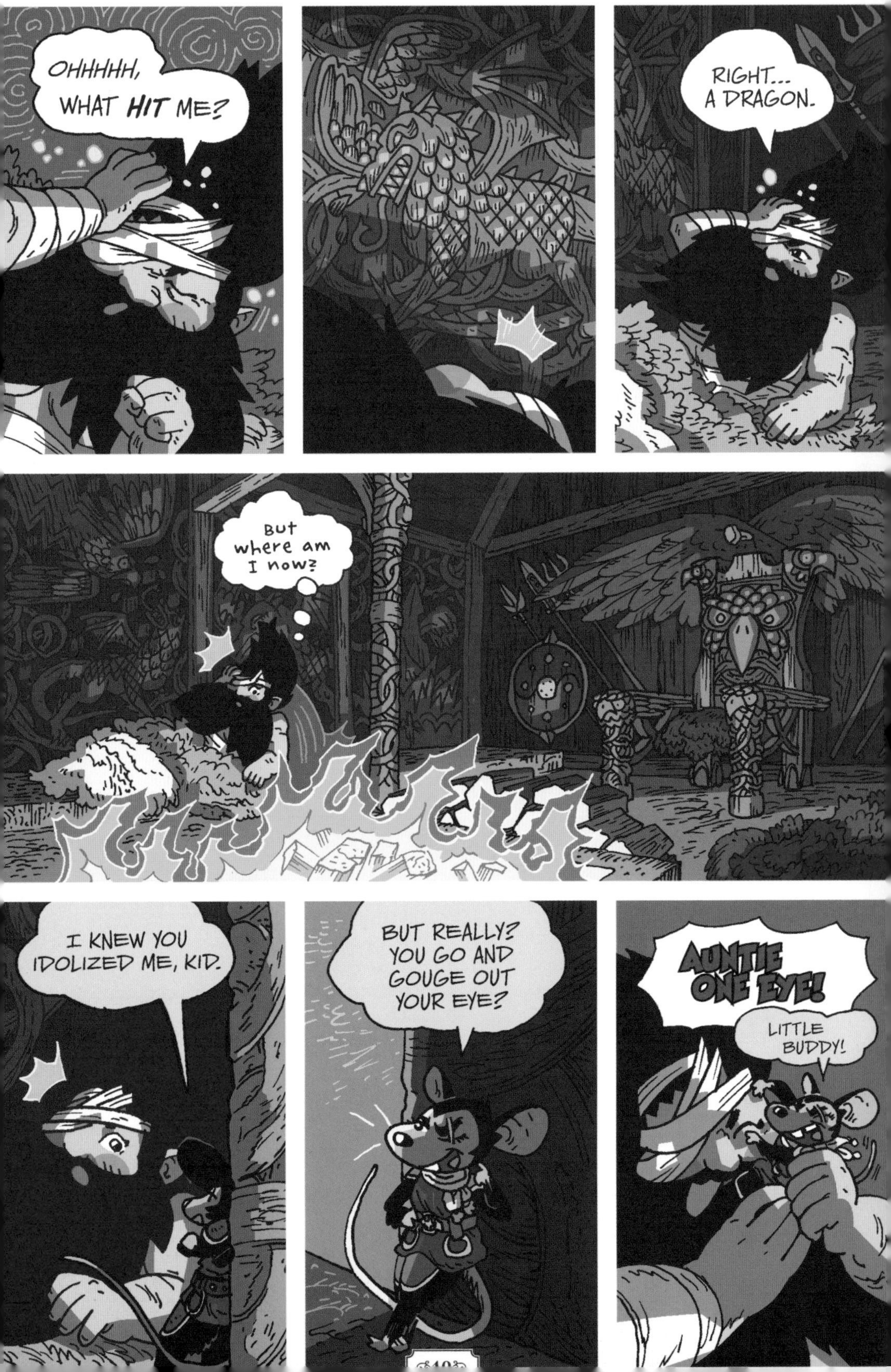
OHHHHH, WHAT HIT ME?
RIGHT... A DRAGON.
But where am I now?
I KNEW YOU IDOLIZED ME, KID.
BUT REALLY? YOU GO AND GOUGE OUT YOUR EYE?
AUNTIE ONE EYE!
LITTLE BUDDY!

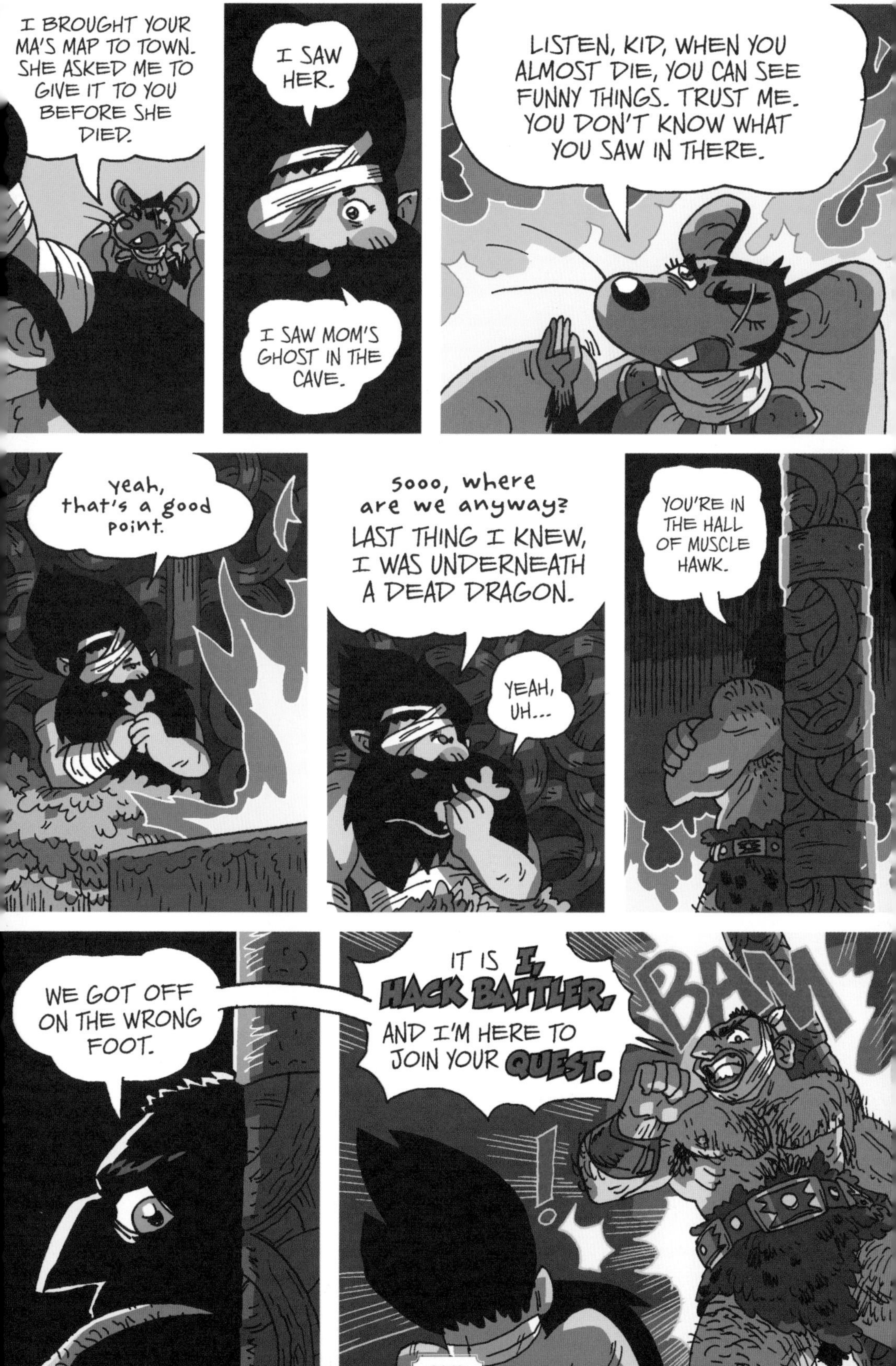
I BROUGHT YOUR MA'S MAP TO TOWN. SHE ASKED ME TO GIVE IT TO YOU BEFORE SHE DIED.
I SAW HER.
I SAW MOM'S GHOST IN THE CAVE.
LISTEN, KID, WHEN YOU ALMOST DIE, YOU CAN SEE FUNNY THINGS. TRUST ME. YOU DON'T KNOW WHAT YOU SAW IN THERE.
yeah, that's a good point.
sooo, where are we anyway?
LAST THING I KNEW, I WAS UNDERNEATH A DEAD DRAGON.
YEAH, UH...
YOU'RE IN THE HALL OF MUSCLE HAWK.
WE GOT OFF ON THE WRONG FOOT.
IT IS I, HACK BATTLER.
AND I'M HERE TO JOIN YOUR QUEST.
BAM
!

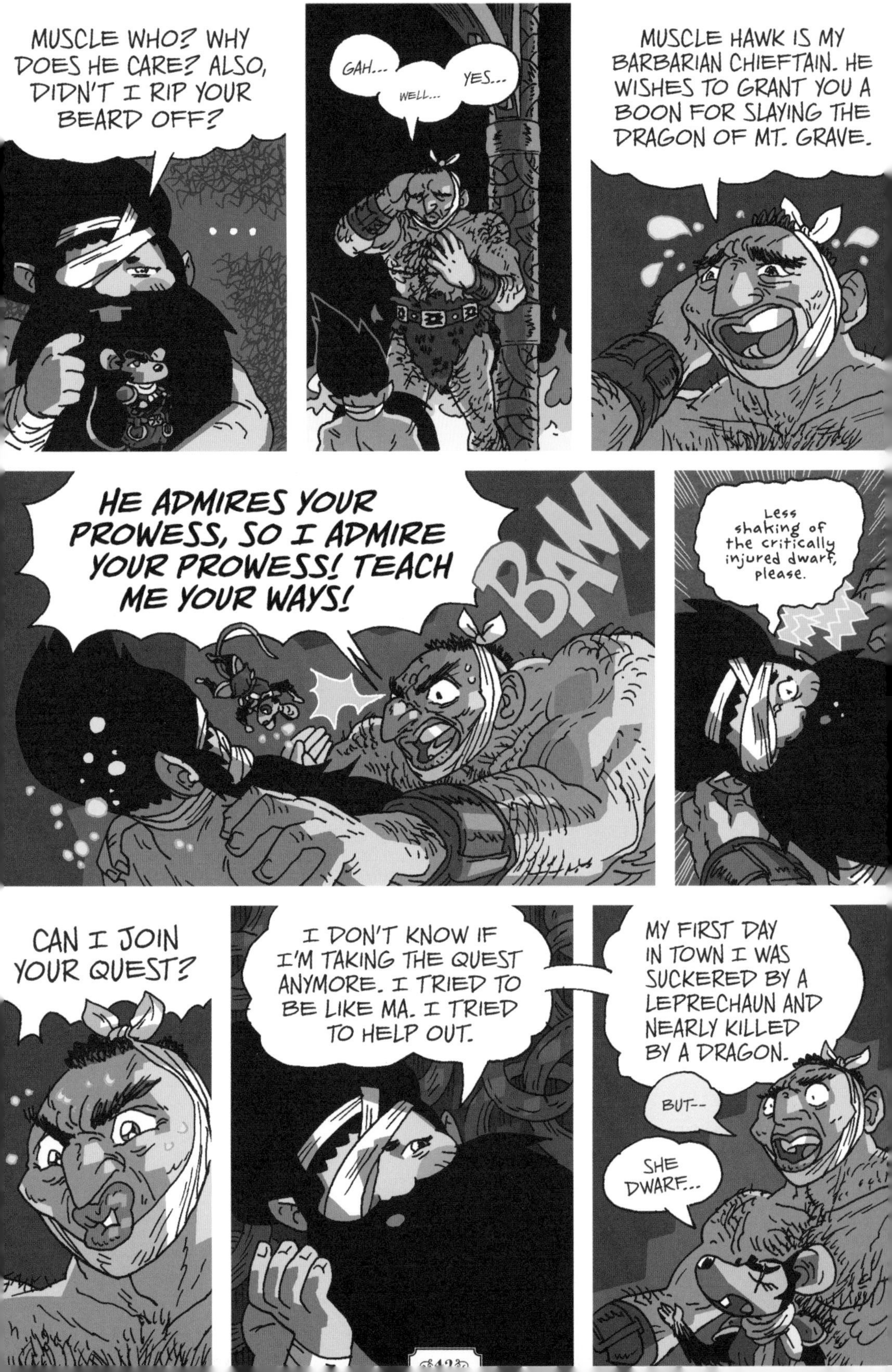
MUSCLE WHO? WHY DOES HE CARE? ALSO, DIDN'T I RIP YOUR BEARD OFF?
...
GAH...
WELL...
YES...
MUSCLE HAWK IS MY BARBARIAN CHIEFTAIN. HE WISHES TO GRANT YOU A BOON FOR SLAYING THE DRAGON OF MT. GRAVE.
HE ADMIRES YOUR PROWESS, SO I ADMIRE YOUR PROWESS! TEACH ME YOUR WAYS!
BAM
Less shaking of the critically injured dwarf, please.
CAN I JOIN YOUR QUEST?
I DON'T KNOW IF I'M TAKING THE QUEST ANYMORE. I TRIED TO BE LIKE MA. I TRIED TO HELP OUT.
MY FIRST DAY IN TOWN I WAS SUCKERED BY A LEPRECHAUN AND NEARLY KILLED BY A DRAGON.
BUT--
SHE DWARF...

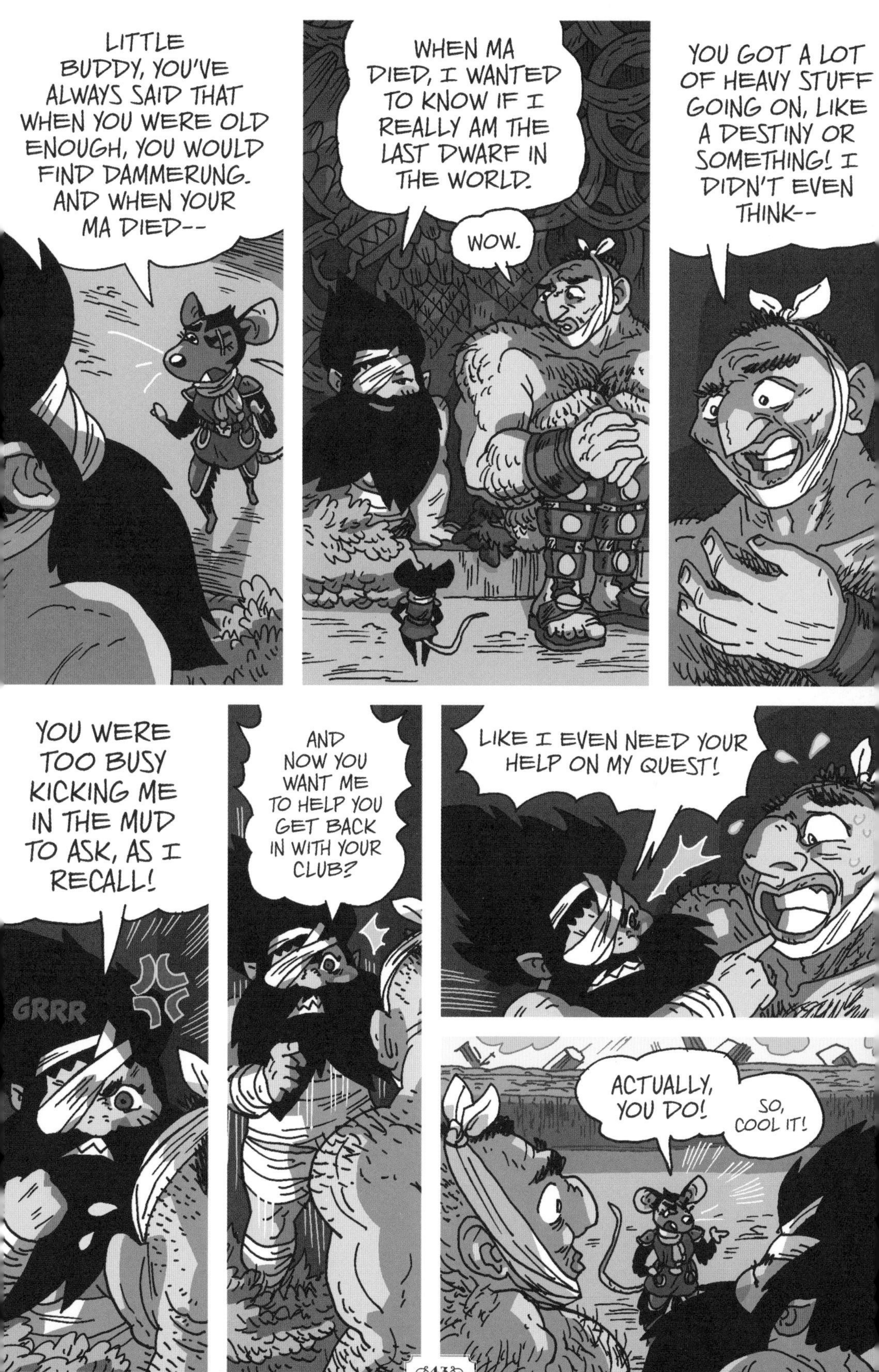
LITTLE BUDDY, YOU'VE ALWAYS SAID THAT WHEN YOU WERE OLD ENOUGH, YOU WOULD FIND DAMMERUNG. AND WHEN YOUR MA DIED--
WHEN MA DIED, I WANTED TO KNOW IF I REALLY AM THE LAST DWARF IN THE WORLD.
WOW.
YOU GOT A LOT OF HEAVY STUFF GOING ON, LIKE A DESTINY OR SOMETHING! I DIDN'T EVEN THINK--
YOU WERE TOO BUSY KICKING ME IN THE MUD TO ASK, AS I RECALL!
GRRR
AND NOW YOU WANT ME TO HELP YOU GET BACK IN WITH YOUR CLUB?
LIKE I EVEN NEED YOUR HELP ON MY QUEST!
ACTUALLY, YOU DO!
SO, COOL IT!

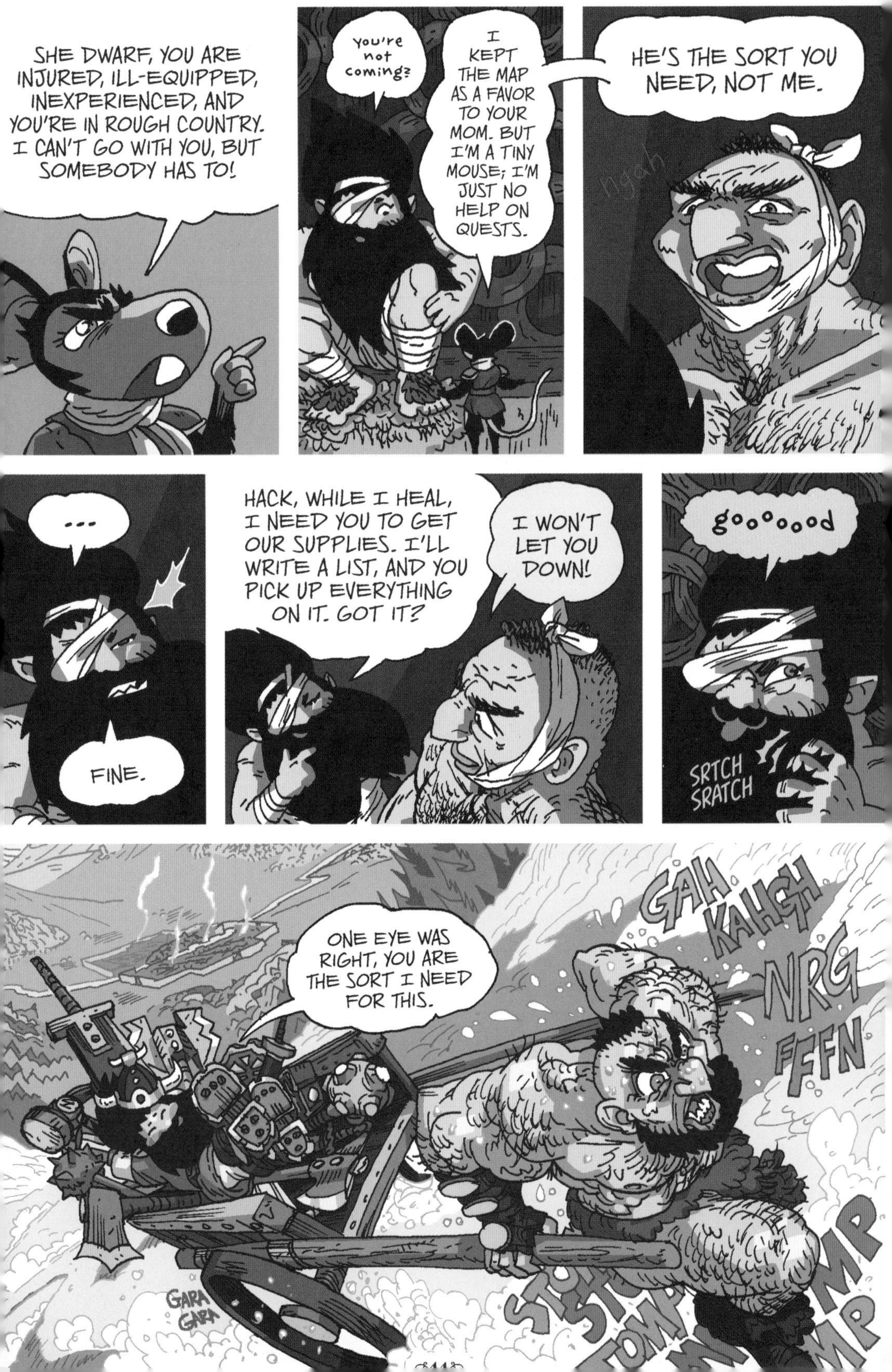
SHE DWARF, YOU ARE INJURED, ILL-EQUIPPED, INEXPERIENCED, AND YOU'RE IN ROUGH COUNTRY. I CAN'T GO WITH YOU, BUT SOMEBODY HAS TO!
You're not coming?
I KEPT THE MAP AS A FAVOR TO YOUR MOM. BUT I'M A TINY MOUSE; I'M JUST NO HELP ON QUESTS.
HE'S THE SORT YOU NEED, NOT ME.
ngah
...
FINE.
HACK, WHILE I HEAL, I NEED YOU TO GET OUR SUPPLIES. I'LL WRITE A LIST, AND YOU PICK UP EVERYTHING ON IT. GOT IT?
I WON'T LET YOU DOWN!
gooooood
SRTCH SRATCH
ONE EYE WAS RIGHT, YOU ARE THE SORT I NEED FOR THIS.
GAH
KAHGH
NRG
FFFN
GARA GARA

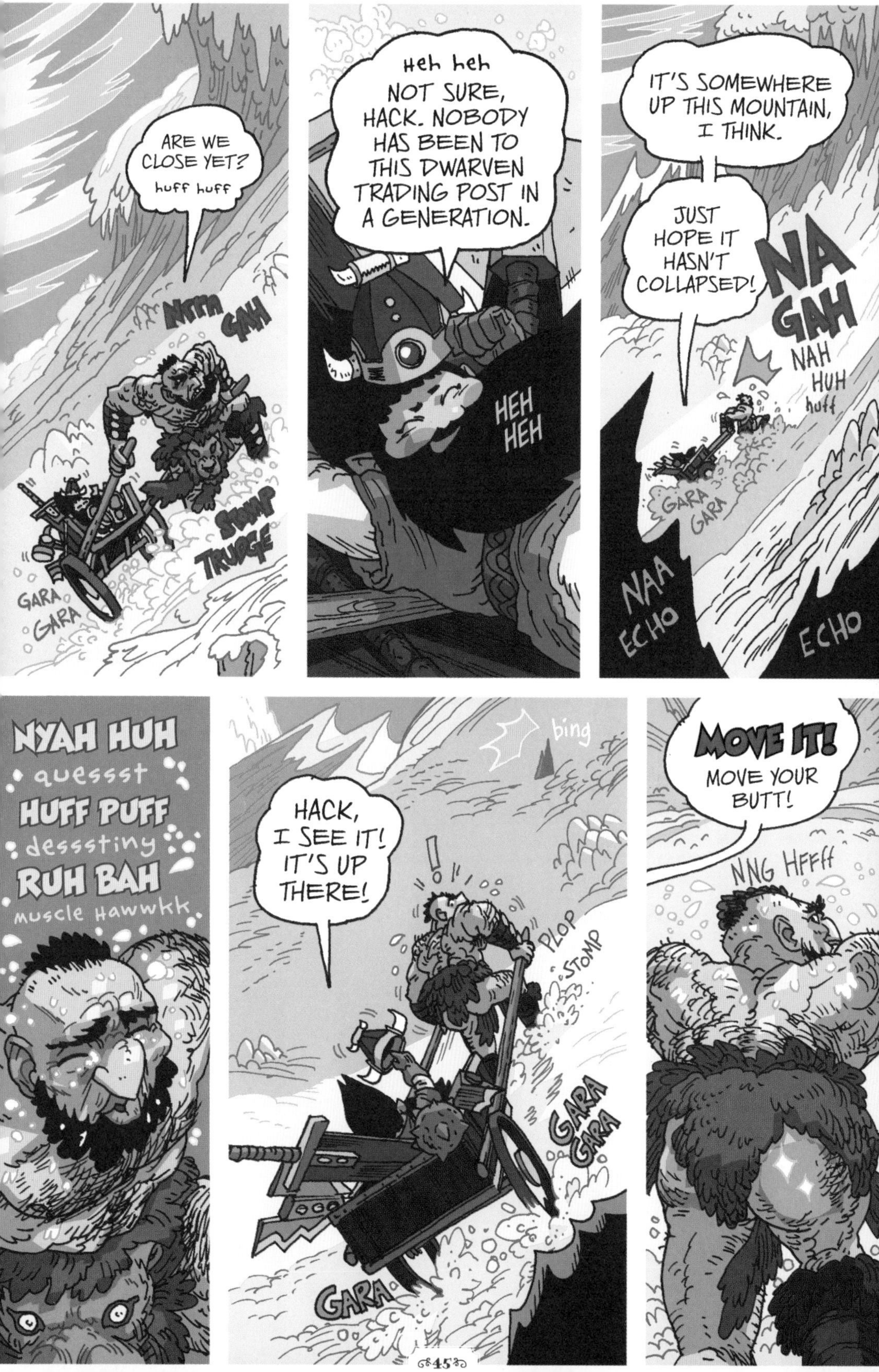
ARE WE CLOSE YET? huff huff
GAH
STOMP
TRUDGE
GARA GARA
Heh heh NOT SURE, HACK. NOBODY HAS BEEN TO THIS DWARVEN TRADING POST IN A GENERATION.
HEH HEH
IT'S SOMEWHERE UP THIS MOUNTAIN, I THINK.
JUST HOPE IT HASN'T COLLAPSED!
NA GAH
NAH HUH huff
GARA GARA
NAA ECHO
ECHO
NYAH HUH
quessst
HUFF PUFF
desssting
RUH BAH
muscle Hawwkk
bing
HACK, I SEE IT! IT'S UP THERE!
!
PLOP
STOMP
GARA GARA
GARA
MOVE IT! MOVE YOUR BUTT!
NNG HFFf

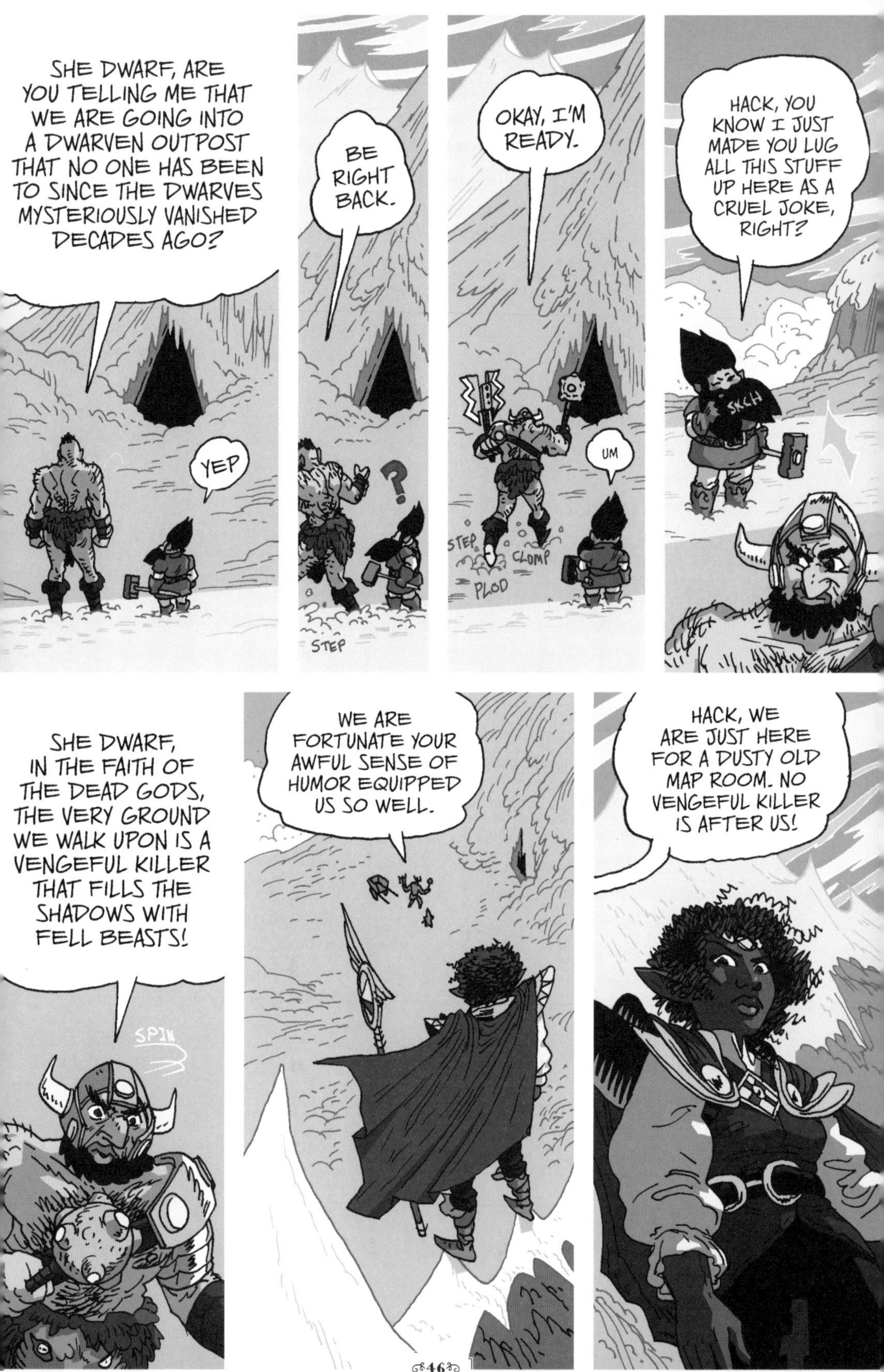
SHE DWARF, ARE YOU TELLING ME THAT WE ARE GOING INTO A DWARVEN OUTPOST THAT NO ONE HAS BEEN TO SINCE THE DWARVES MYSTERIOUSLY VANISHED DECADES AGO?
YEP
BE RIGHT BACK.
?
STEP
OKAY, I'M READY.
STEP
CLOMP
PLOD
UM
HACK, YOU KNOW I JUST MADE YOU LUG ALL THIS STUFF UP HERE AS A CRUEL JOKE, RIGHT?
SHE DWARF, IN THE FAITH OF THE DEAD GODS, THE VERY GROUND WE WALK UPON IS A VENGEFUL KILLER THAT FILLS THE SHADOWS WITH FELL BEASTS!
SPIN
WE ARE FORTUNATE YOUR AWFUL SENSE OF HUMOR EQUIPPED US SO WELL.
HACK, WE ARE JUST HERE FOR A DUSTY OLD MAP ROOM. NO VENGEFUL KILLER IS AFTER US!

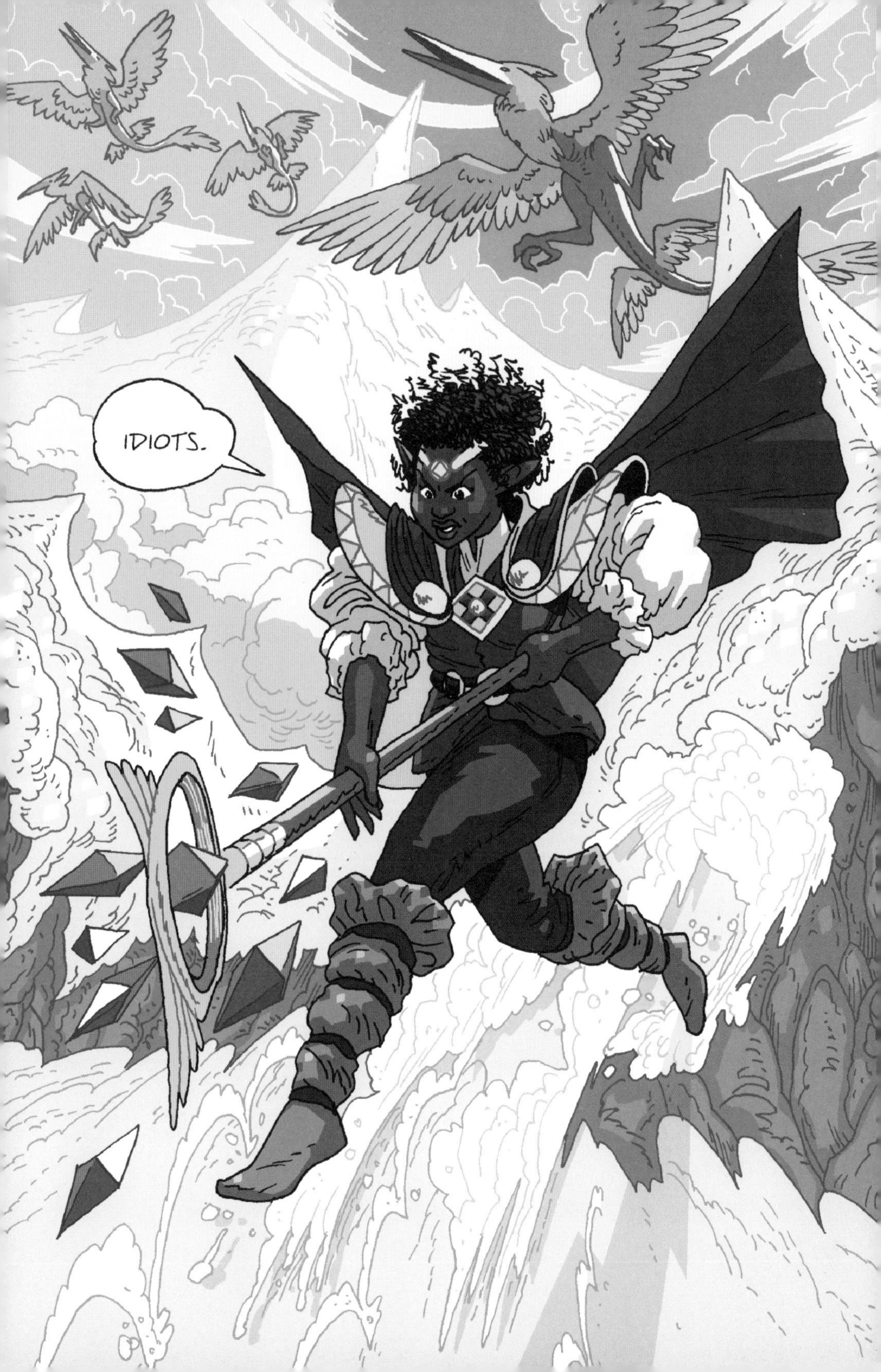
IDIOTS.

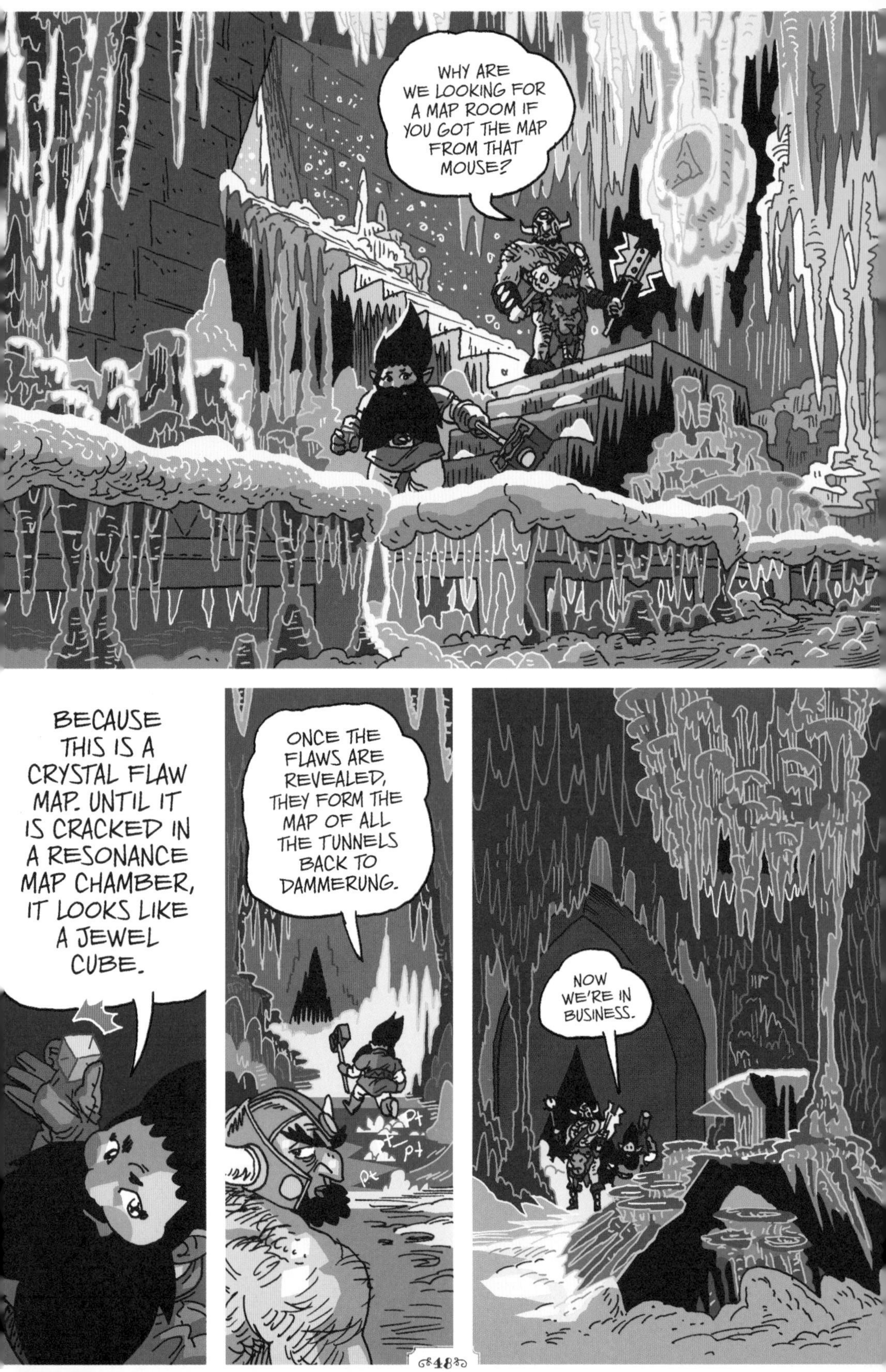
WHY ARE WE LOOKING FOR A MAP ROOM IF YOU GOT THE MAP FROM THAT MOUSE?
BECAUSE THIS IS A CRYSTAL FLAW MAP. UNTIL IT IS CRACKED IN A RESONANCE MAP CHAMBER, IT LOOKS LIKE A JEWEL CUBE.
ONCE THE FLAWS ARE REVEALED, THEY FORM THE MAP OF ALL THE TUNNELS BACK TO DAMMERUNG.
PT
PT
PT
NOW WE'RE IN BUSINESS.

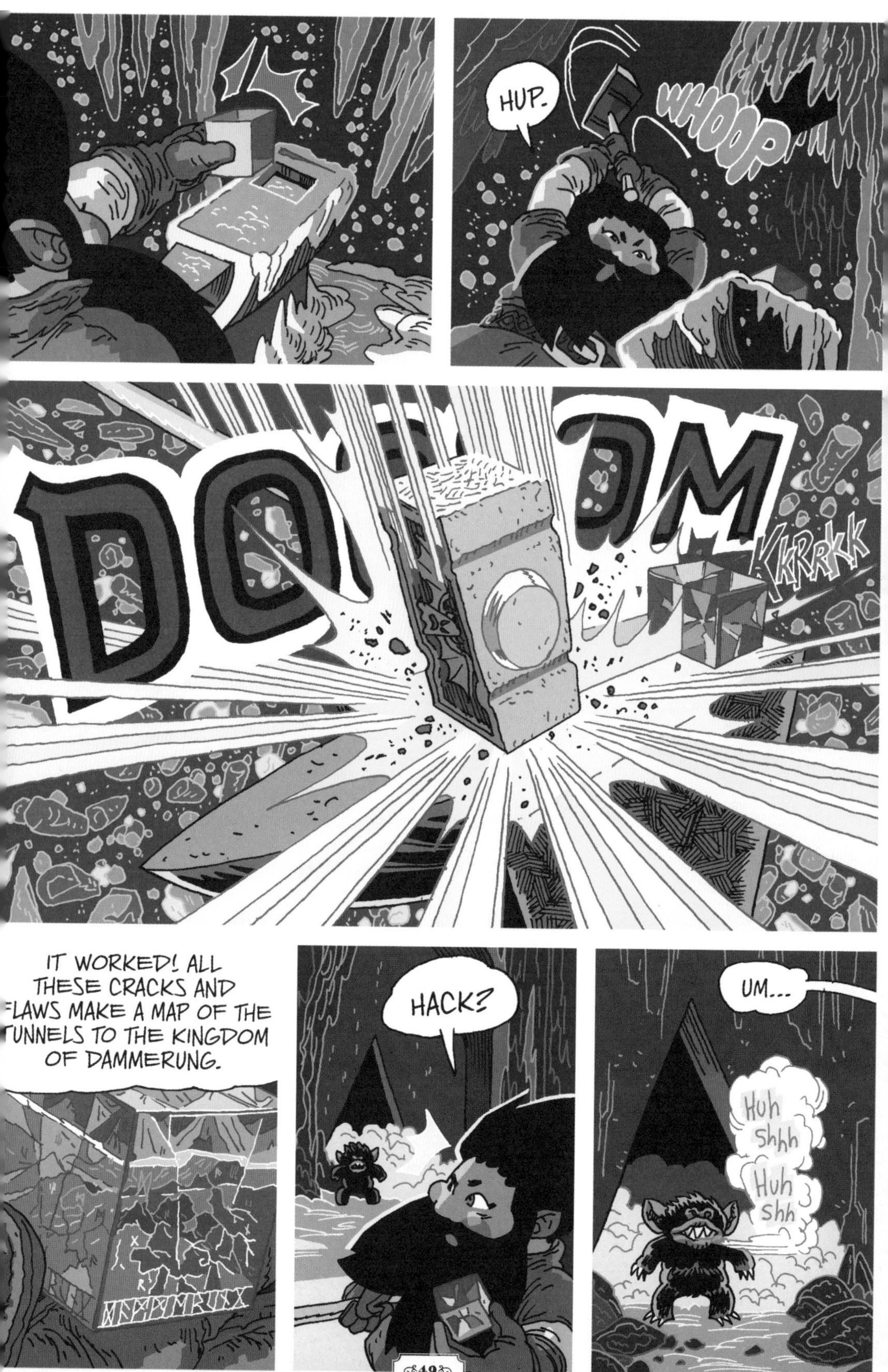
HUP.
WHOOP.
DO
OM
KKRRKK
IT WORKED! ALL THESE CRACKS AND FLAWS MAKE A MAP OF THE TUNNELS TO THE KINGDOM OF DAMMERUNG.
HACK?
UM...
Huh Shhh
Huh Shh

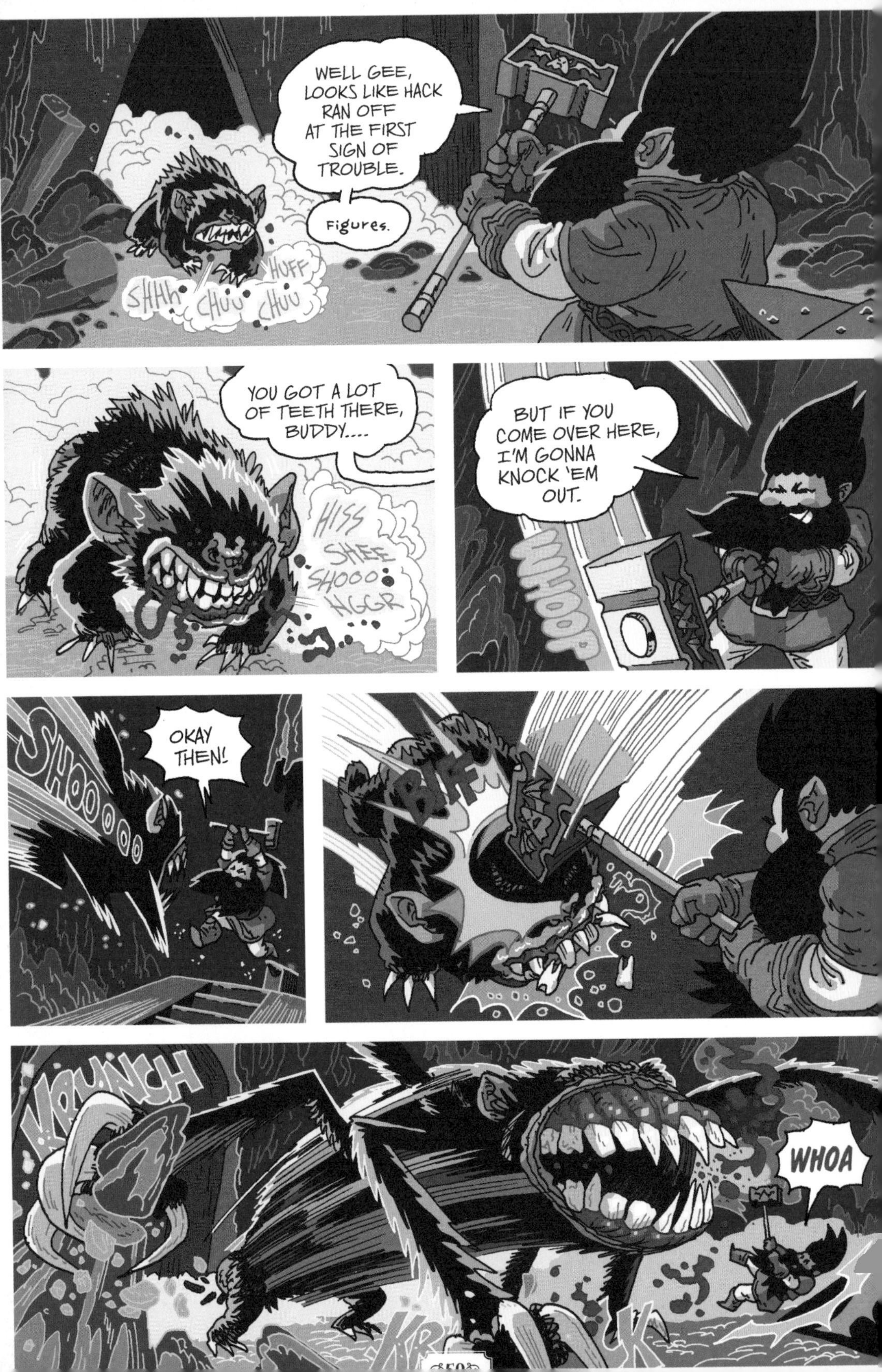
WELL GEE, LOOKS LIKE HACK RAN OFF AT THE FIRST SIGN OF TROUBLE.
Figures.
SHHH
CHUU
CHUU
HUFF
YOU GOT A LOT OF TEETH THERE, BUDDY....
HISS
SHEE
SHOOO
HGGR
BUT IF YOU COME OVER HERE, I'M GONNA KNOCK 'EM OUT.
WHOOP
SHOOOOOO
OKAY THEN!
BIFF
KRUNCH
WHOA

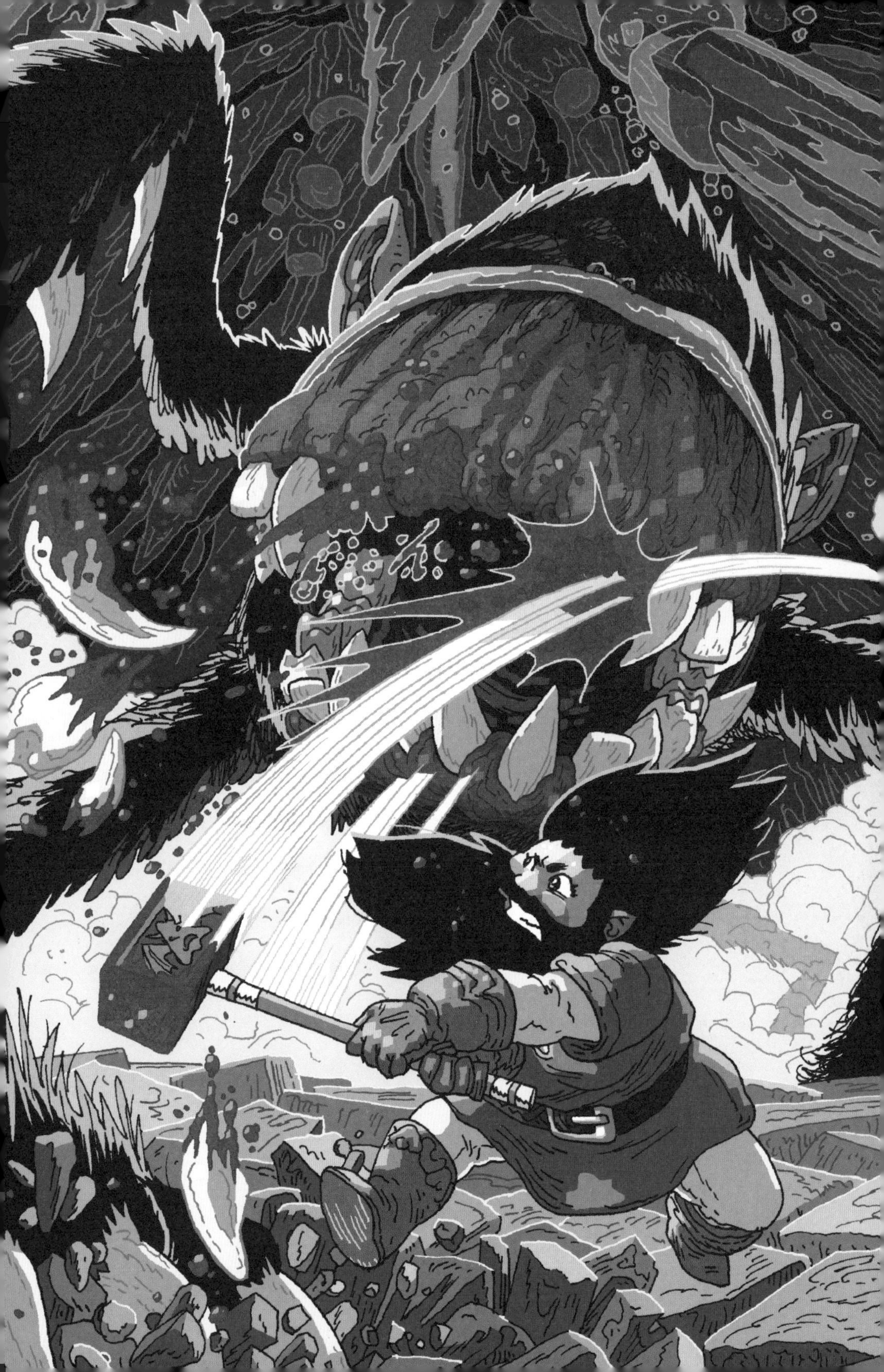

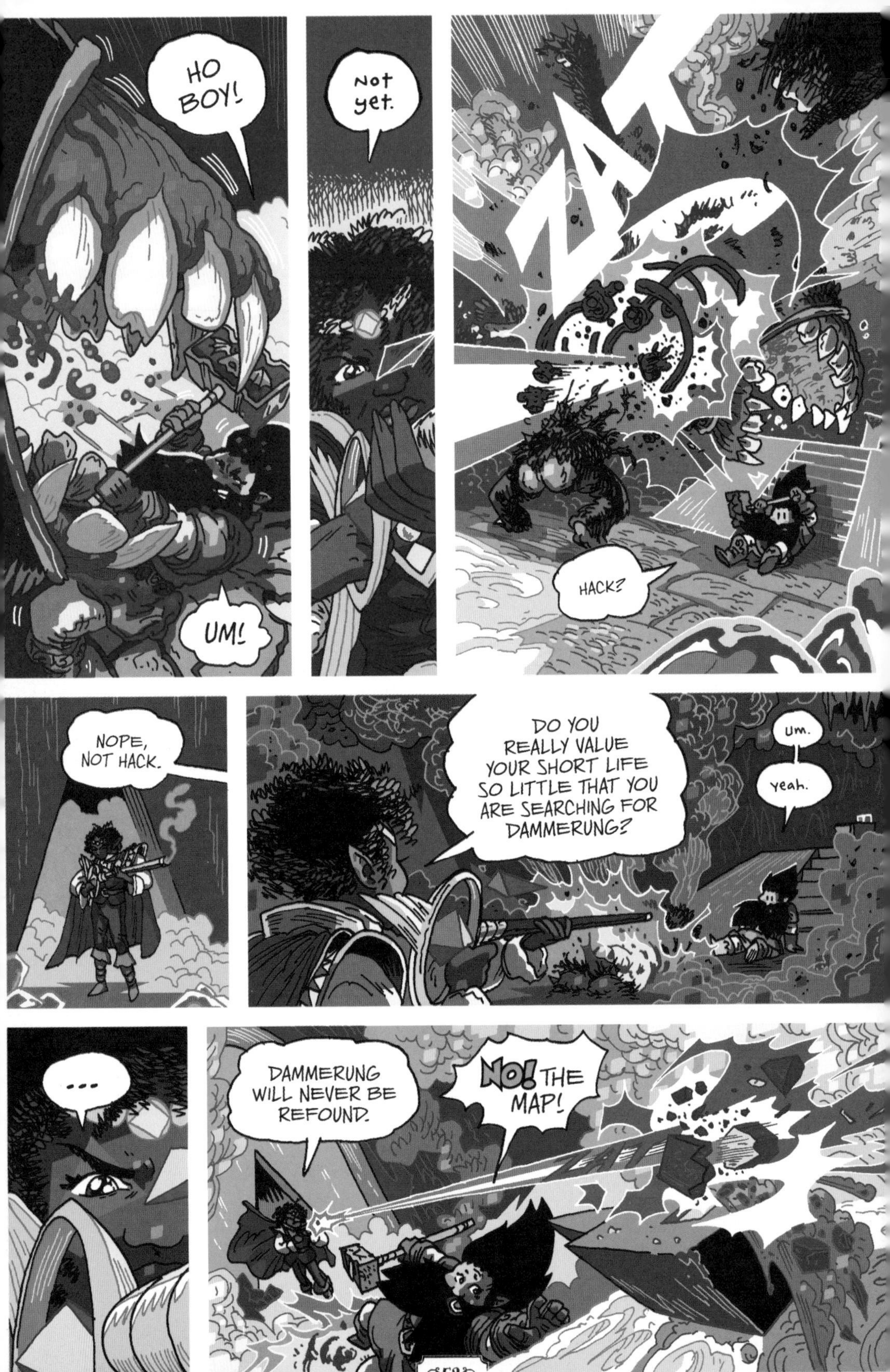
HO BOY!
UM!
Not yet.
ZAT
HACK?
NOPE, NOT HACK.
DO YOU REALLY VALUE YOUR SHORT LIFE SO LITTLE THAT YOU ARE SEARCHING FOR DAMMERUNG?
Um.
Yeah.
...
DAMMERUNG WILL NEVER BE REFOUND.
NO! THE MAP!
ZAT

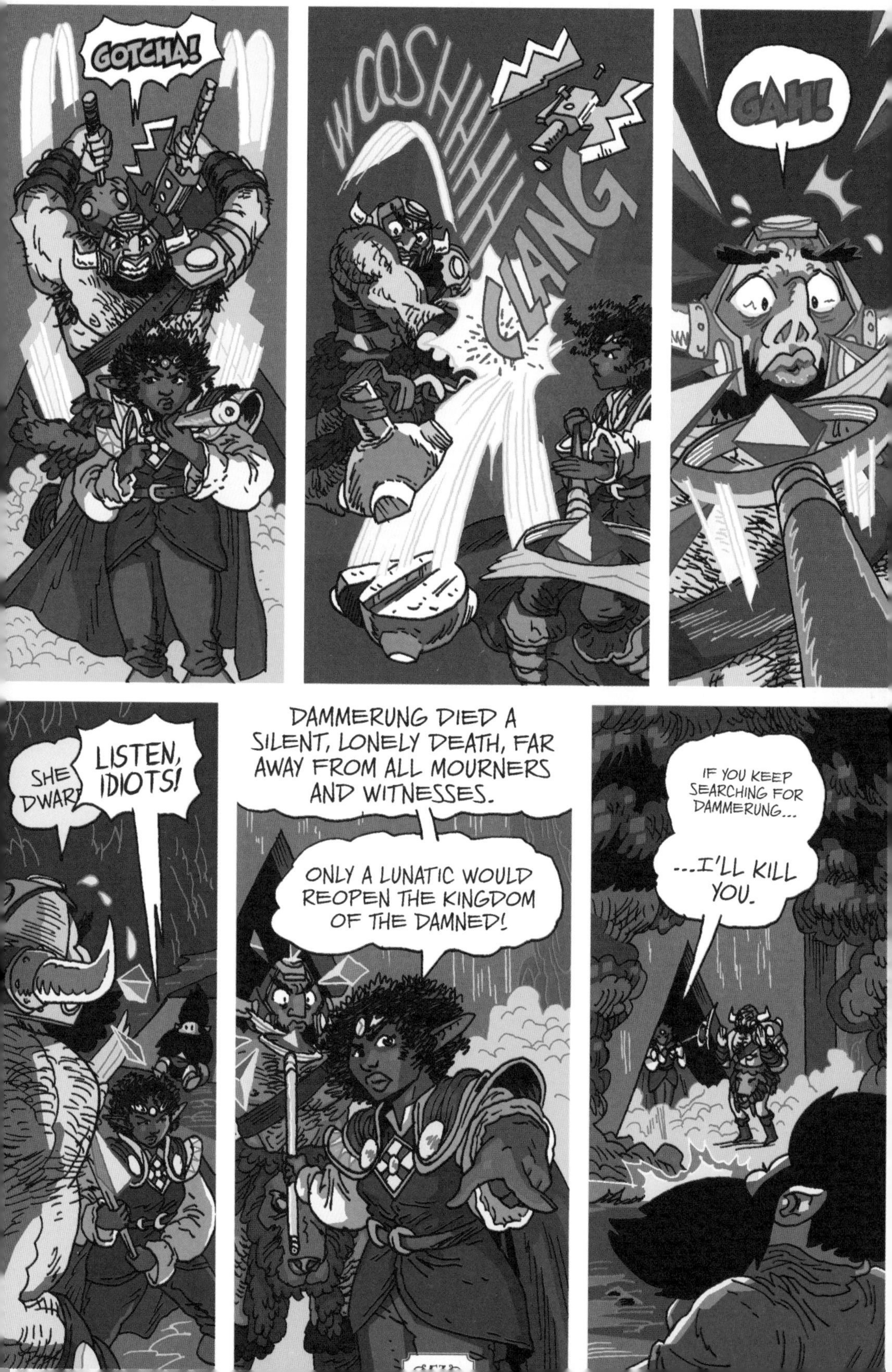
GOTCHA!
WOOSHHHH
CLANG
GAH!
SHE DWAR
LISTEN, IDIOTS!
DAMMERUNG DIED A SILENT, LONELY DEATH, FAR AWAY FROM ALL MOURNERS AND WITNESSES.
ONLY A LUNATIC WOULD REOPEN THE KINGDOM OF THE DAMNED!
IF YOU KEEP SEARCHING FOR DAMMERUNG...
...I'LL KILL YOU.

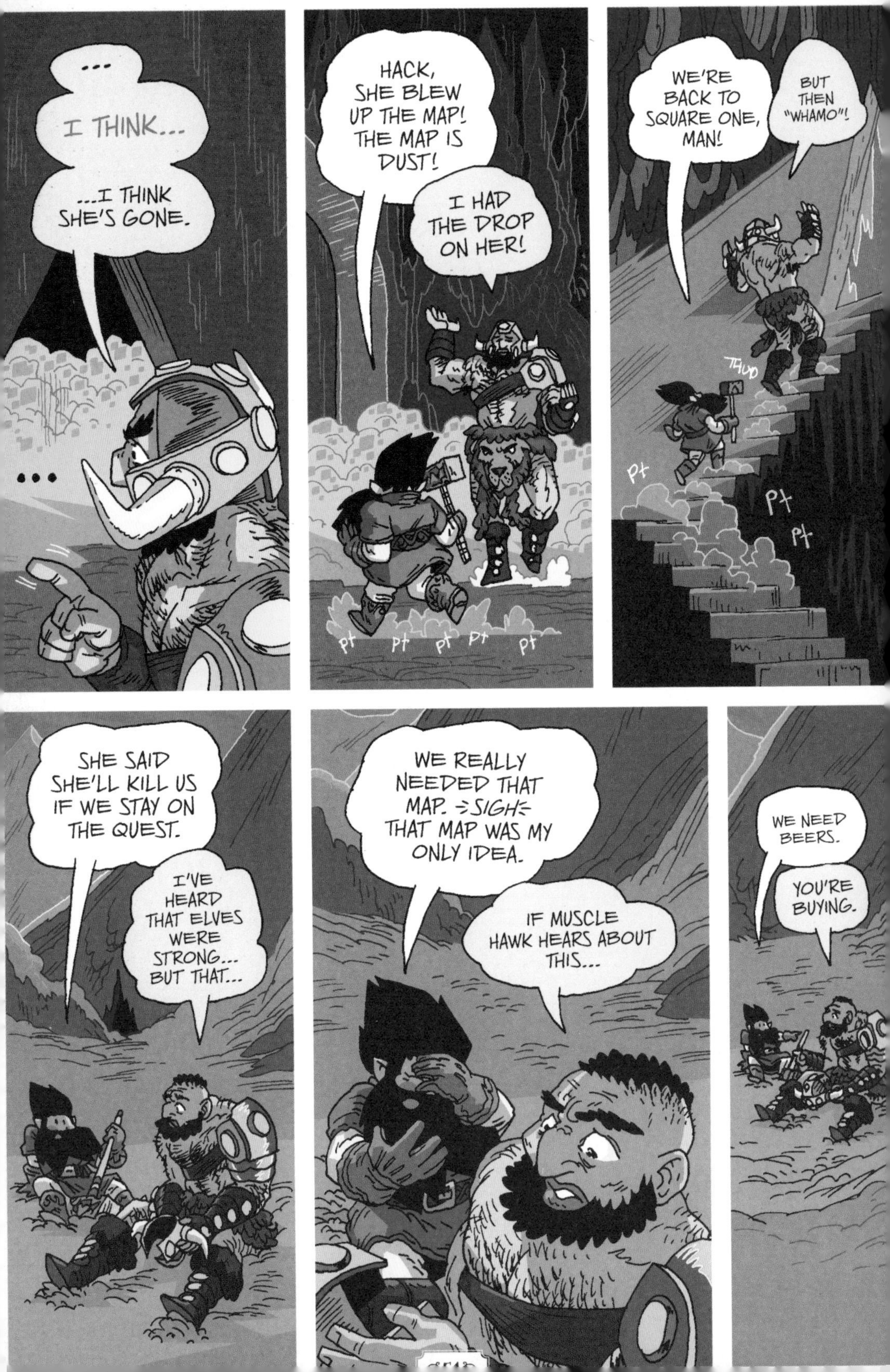
...
I THINK...
...I THINK SHE'S GONE.
...
HACK, SHE BLEW UP THE MAP! THE MAP IS DUST!
I HAD THE DROP ON HER!
pt pt pt pt pt
WE'RE BACK TO SQUARE ONE, MAN!
BUT THEN "WHAMO"!
THUD
pt pt pt
SHE SAID SHE'LL KILL US IF WE STAY ON THE QUEST.
I'VE HEARD THAT ELVES WERE STRONG... BUT THAT...
WE REALLY NEEDED THAT MAP. =SIGH= THAT MAP WAS MY ONLY IDEA.
IF MUSCLE HAWK HEARS ABOUT THIS...
WE NEED BEERS.
YOU'RE BUYING.

CHAPTER

IV

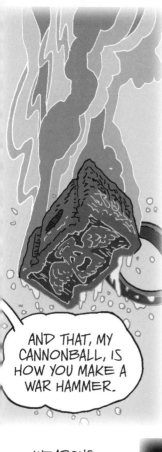

AND THAT, MY CANNONBALL, IS HOW YOU MAKE A WAR HAMMER.

WE WON'T KNOW IF THE DESIGNS SET PROPERLY UNTIL YOU POLISH THEM, THOUGH.

ARE THOSE GHOSTS? AWESOME!

"AWESOME"? HMM. LISTEN, SWEETIE.

THERE'S A GOOD GHOST AND AN EVIL ONE.

SKRT

PAT

WEAPONS DO NOT JUDGE THEIR TARGETS. WEAPONS MAKE GHOSTS OF THE GOOD **AND** THE EVIL THEY SLAY. **YOU** MUST BE JUDICIOUS IN BATTLE.

...

AND I'VE LOST HER.

DEAR?

YES, LILYPAD?

ANY THOUGHTS ON CONSEQUENCES OF BATTLE?

YES.

MEASURE TWICE, CUT ONCE, IF YOU MUST CUT AT ALL.

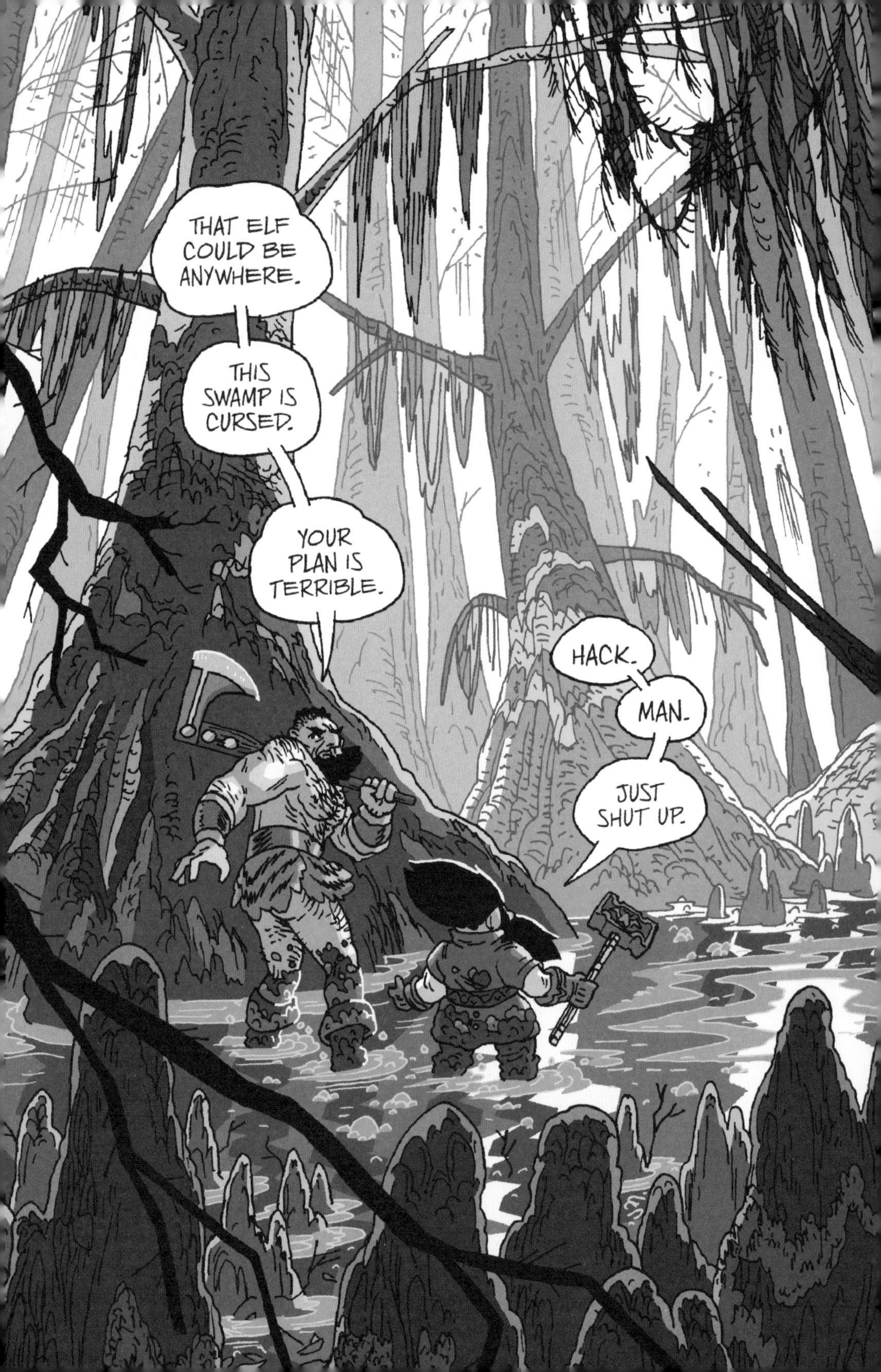
THAT ELF COULD BE ANYWHERE.
THIS SWAMP IS CURSED.
YOUR PLAN IS TERRIBLE.
HACK.
MAN.
JUST SHUT UP.

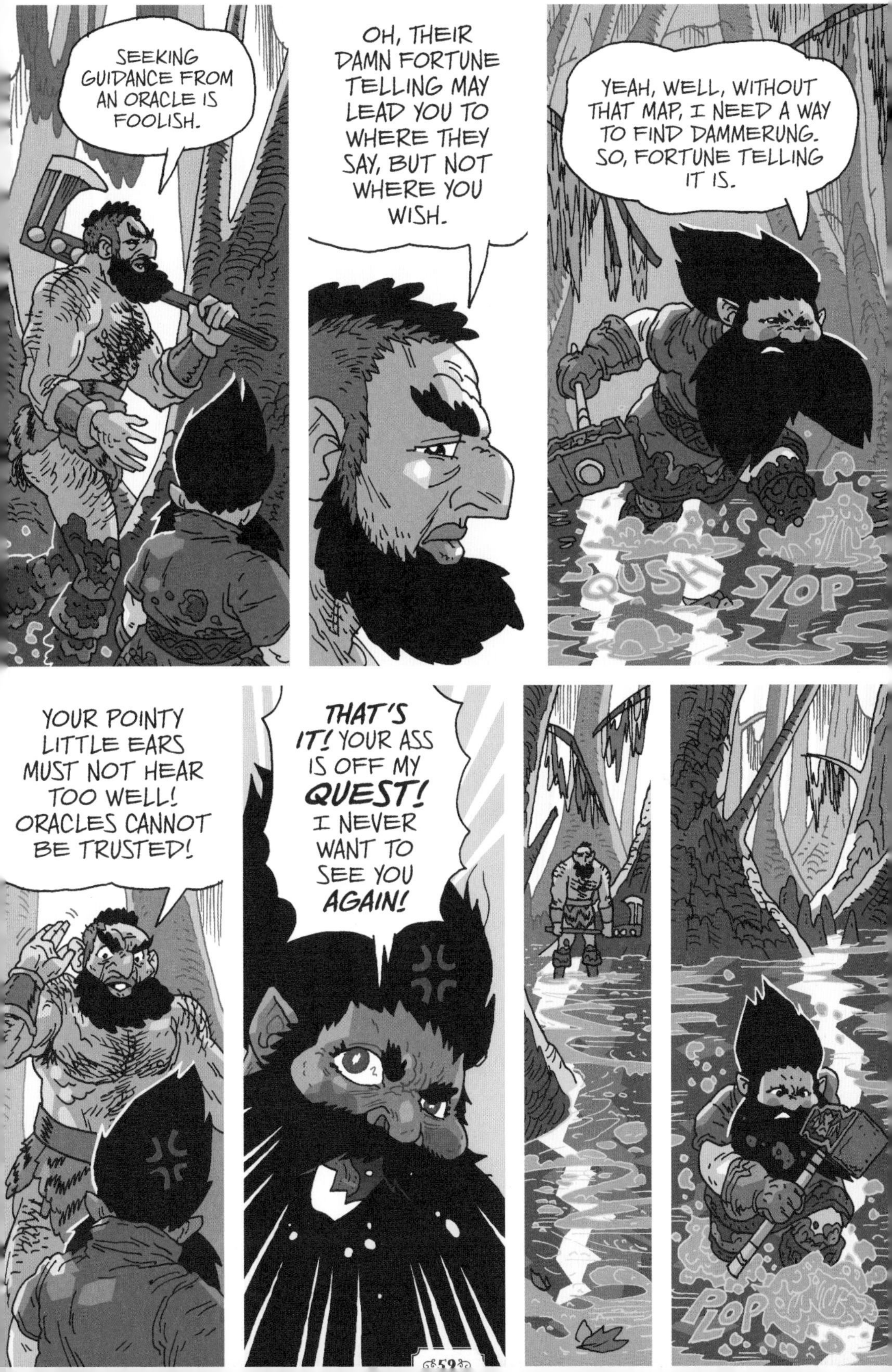
SEEKING GUIDANCE FROM AN ORACLE IS FOOLISH.
OH, THEIR DAMN FORTUNE TELLING MAY LEAD YOU TO WHERE THEY SAY, BUT NOT WHERE YOU WISH.
YEAH, WELL, WITHOUT THAT MAP, I NEED A WAY TO FIND DAMMERUNG. SO, FORTUNE TELLING IT IS.
SQUSH
SLOP
YOUR POINTY LITTLE EARS MUST NOT HEAR TOO WELL! ORACLES CANNOT BE TRUSTED!
THAT'S IT! YOUR ASS IS OFF MY QUEST! I NEVER WANT TO SEE YOU AGAIN!
PLOP

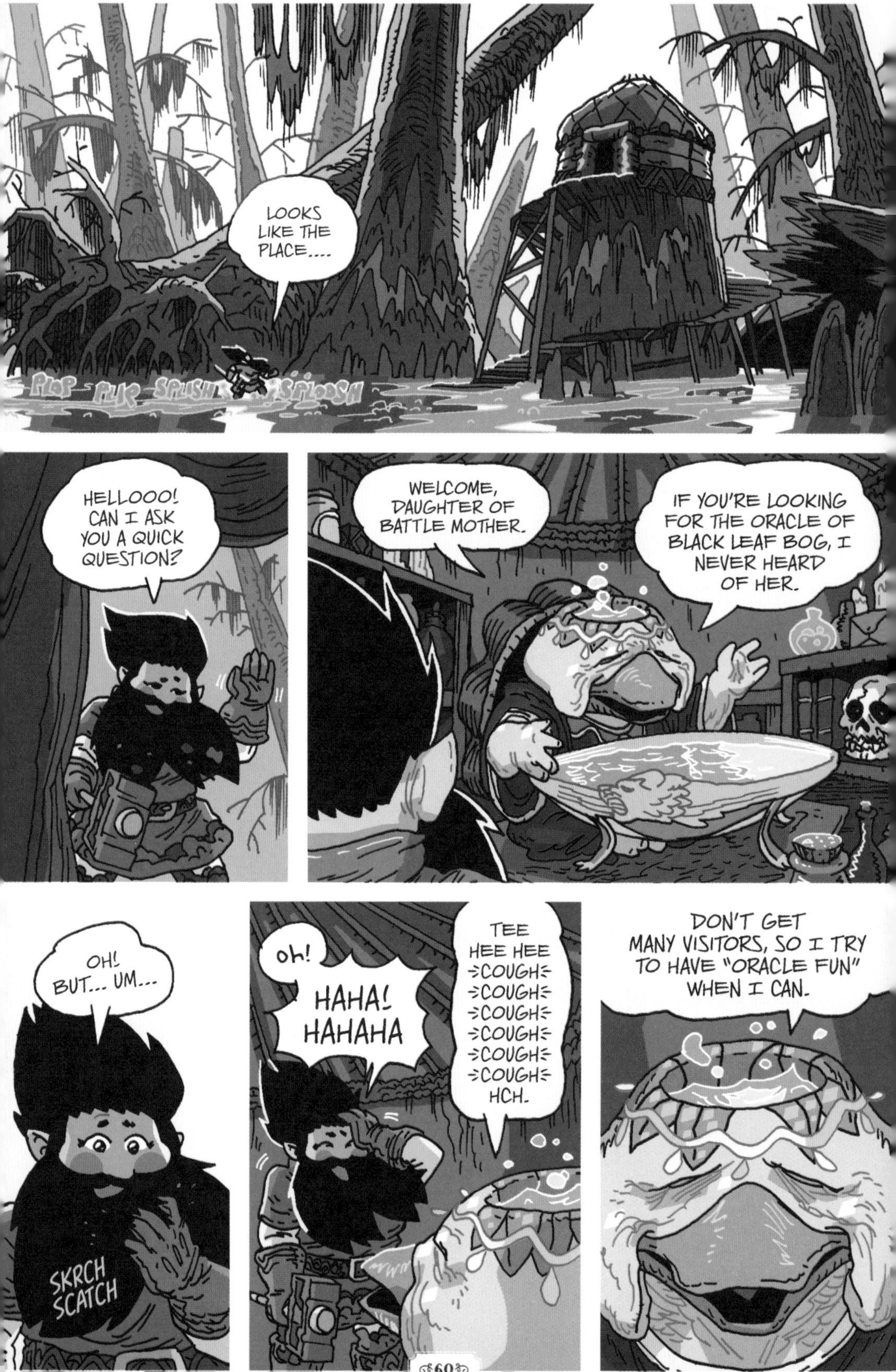
LOOKS LIKE THE PLACE....
PLOP PLIK SPLISH SPLOOSH
HELLOOO! CAN I ASK YOU A QUICK QUESTION?
WELCOME, DAUGHTER OF BATTLE MOTHER.
IF YOU'RE LOOKING FOR THE ORACLE OF BLACK LEAF BOG, I NEVER HEARD OF HER.
OH! BUT... UM...
SKRCH SCATCH
oh!
HAHA! HAHAHA
TEE HEE HEE
=COUGH=
=COUGH=
=COUGH=
=COUGH=
=COUGH=
=COUGH=
HCH.
DON'T GET MANY VISITORS, SO I TRY TO HAVE "ORACLE FUN" WHEN I CAN.

sigh
HOOKAY!

HERE'S THE RUNDOWN. I NEED TO HOLD YOUR MOST IMPORTANT POSSESSION TO DO MY SPOOKY THING.

THEN, YOU SHOUT ONE WORD, AND YOU'LL GET A PROPHECY ABOUT IT.

GOTCHA.

I'LL... I'LL GET MY HAMMER BACK, RIGHT?

YES, YES.

SPEAK THE WORD.

...

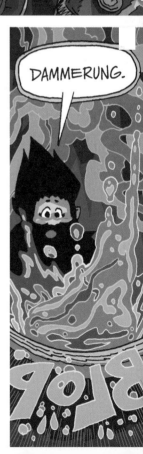

DAMMERUNG.

BLOP

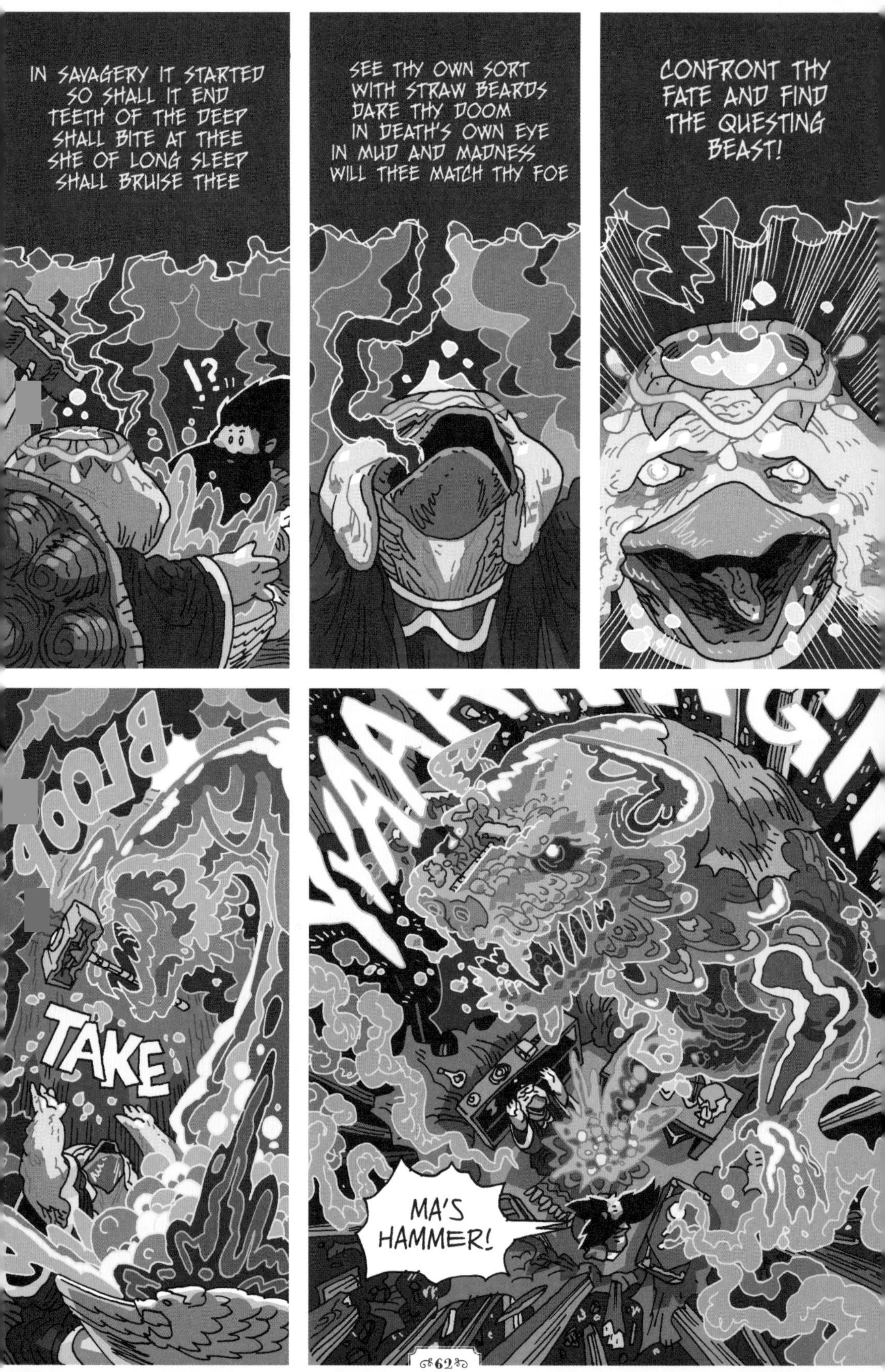
IN SAVAGERY IT STARTED
SO SHALL IT END
TEETH OF THE DEEP
SHALL BITE AT THEE
SHE OF LONG SLEEP
SHALL BRUISE THEE
!?
SEE THY OWN SORT
WITH STRAW BEARDS
DARE THY DOOM
IN DEATH'S OWN EYE
IN MUD AND MADNESS
WILL THEE MATCH THY FOE
CONFRONT THY
FATE AND FIND
THE QUESTING
BEAST!
TAKE
MA'S
HAMMER!

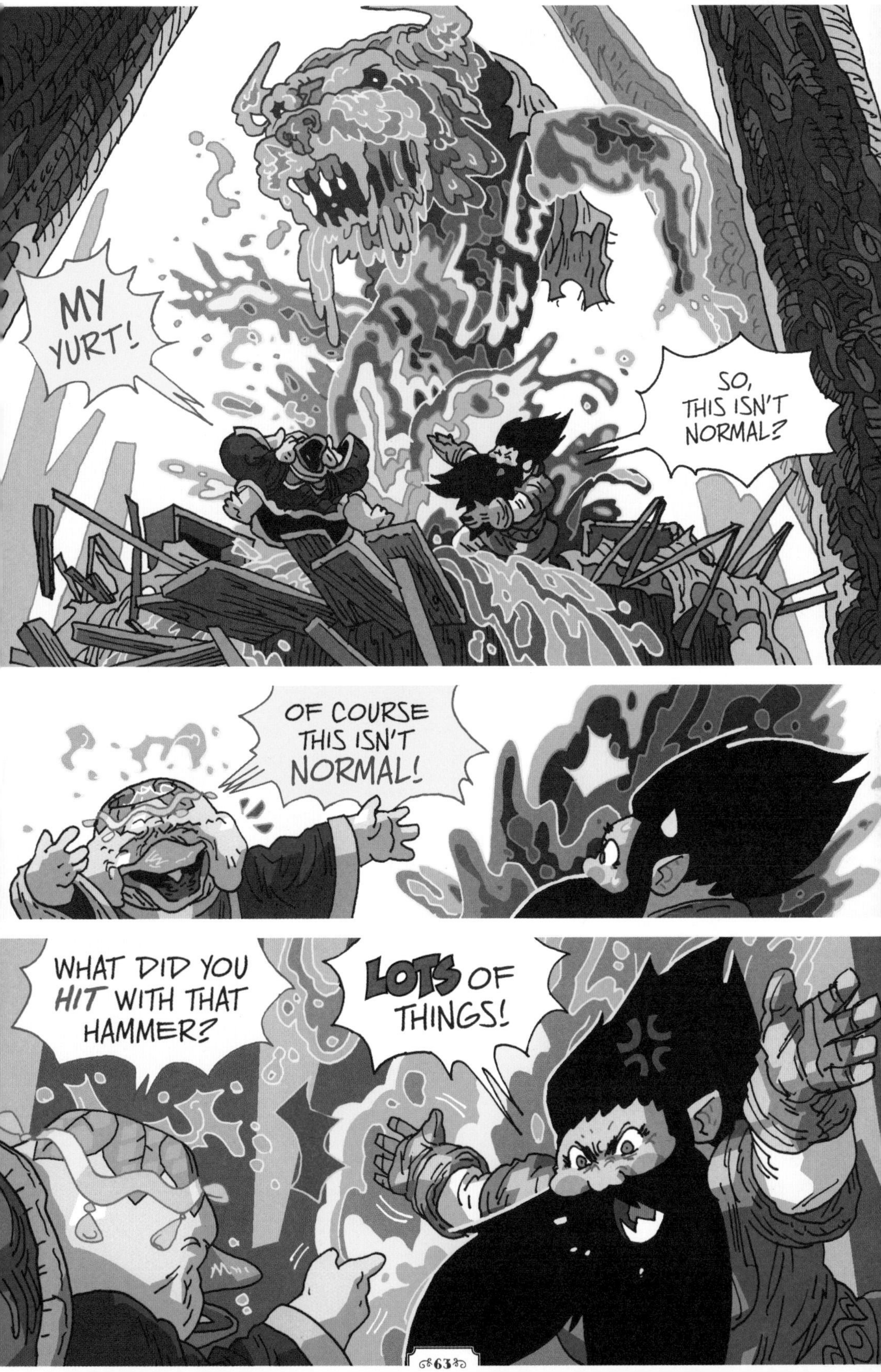
MY YURT!
SO, THIS ISN'T NORMAL?
OF COURSE THIS ISN'T NORMAL!
WHAT DID YOU *HIT* WITH THAT HAMMER?
LOTS OF THINGS!

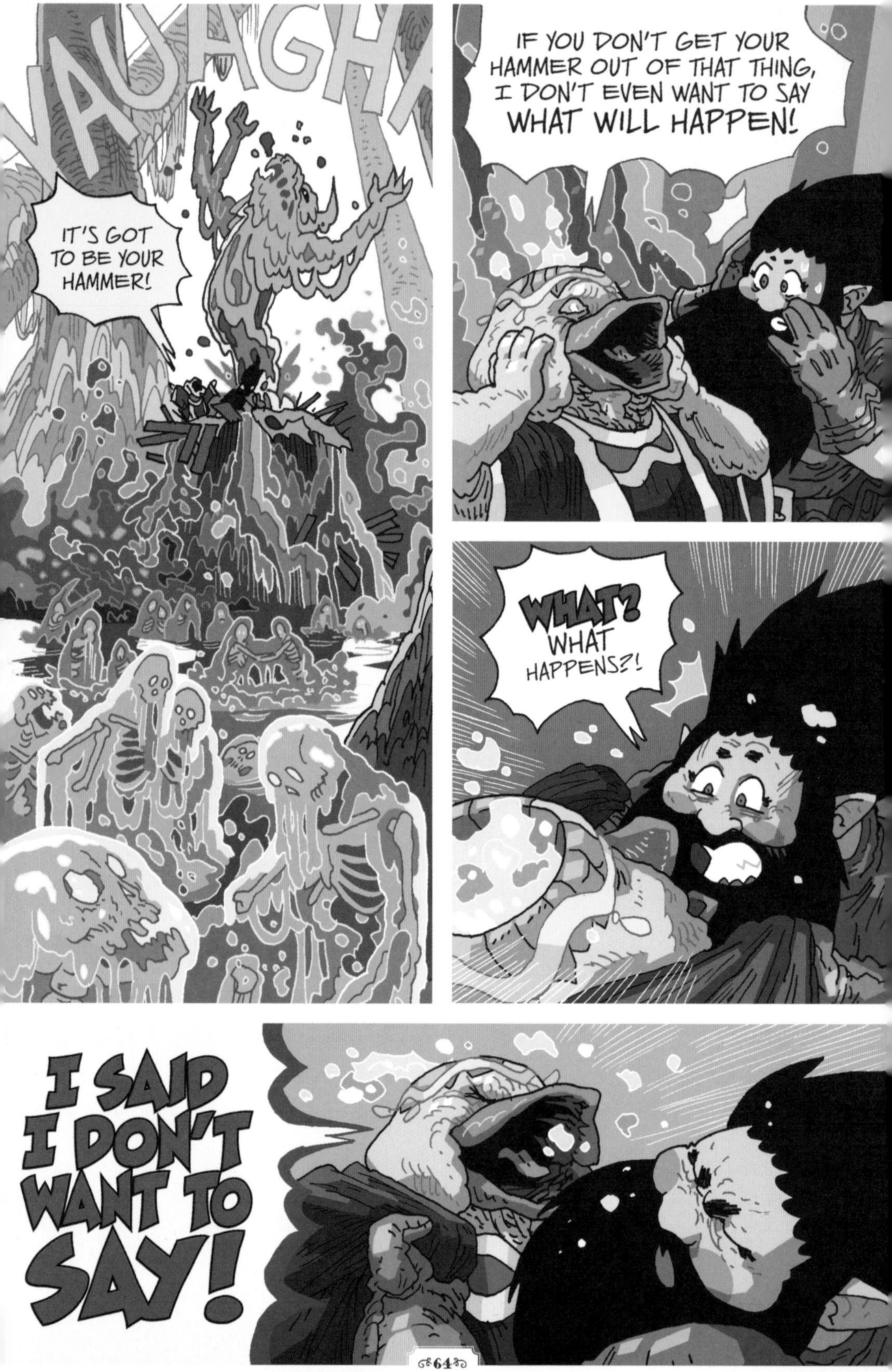
VAUAGH
IT'S GOT TO BE YOUR HAMMER!
IF YOU DON'T GET YOUR HAMMER OUT OF THAT THING, I DON'T EVEN WANT TO SAY WHAT WILL HAPPEN!
WHAT? WHAT HAPPENS?!
I SAID I DON'T WANT TO SAY!

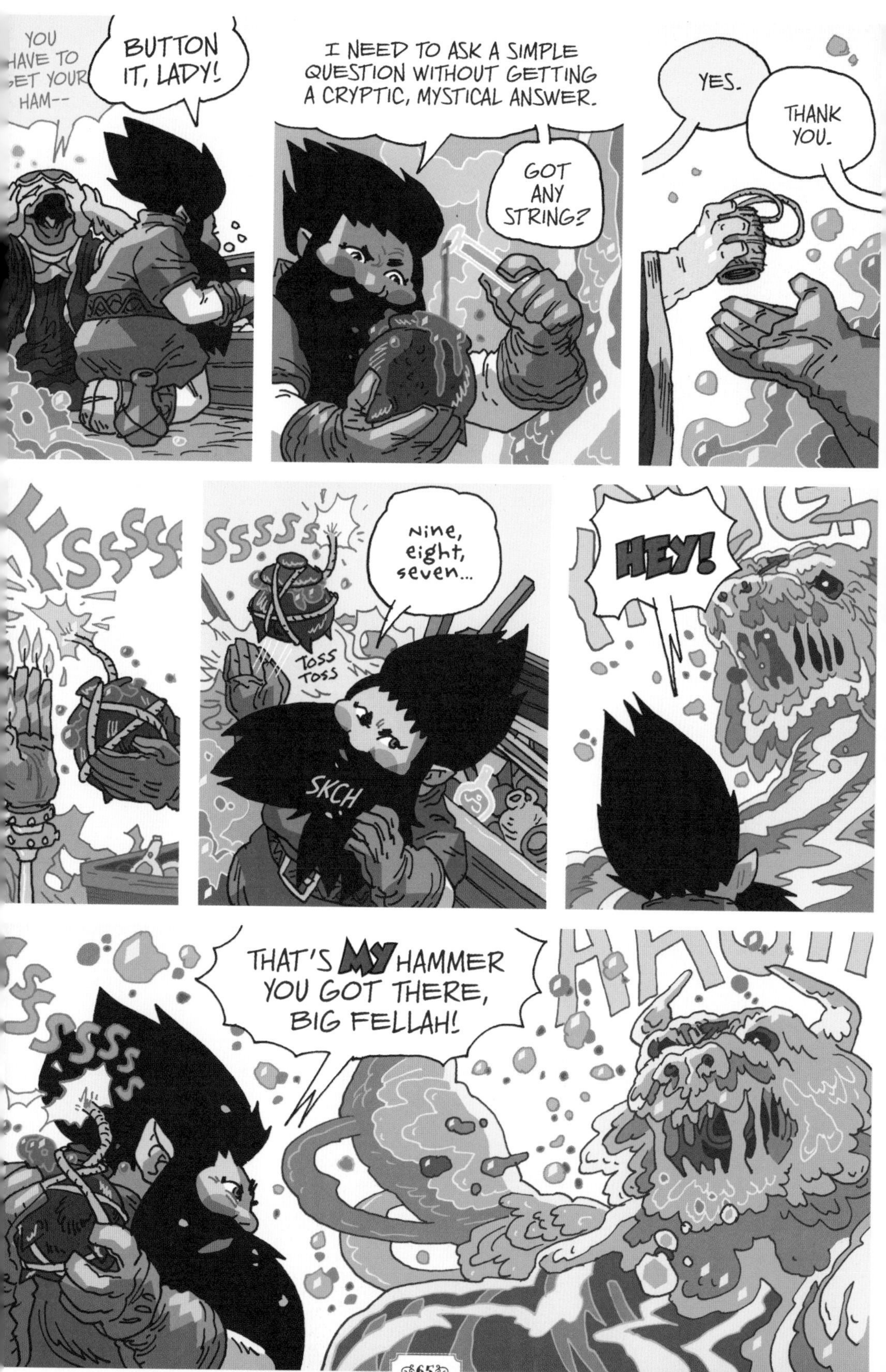
YOU HAVE TO GET YOUR HAM--
BUTTON IT, LADY!
I NEED TO ASK A SIMPLE QUESTION WITHOUT GETTING A CRYPTIC, MYSTICAL ANSWER.
GOT ANY STRING?
YES.
THANK YOU.
SSSSS
Nine, eight, seven...
TOSS TOSS
SKCH
HEY!
THAT'S MY HAMMER YOU GOT THERE, BIG FELLAH!
SSSSS

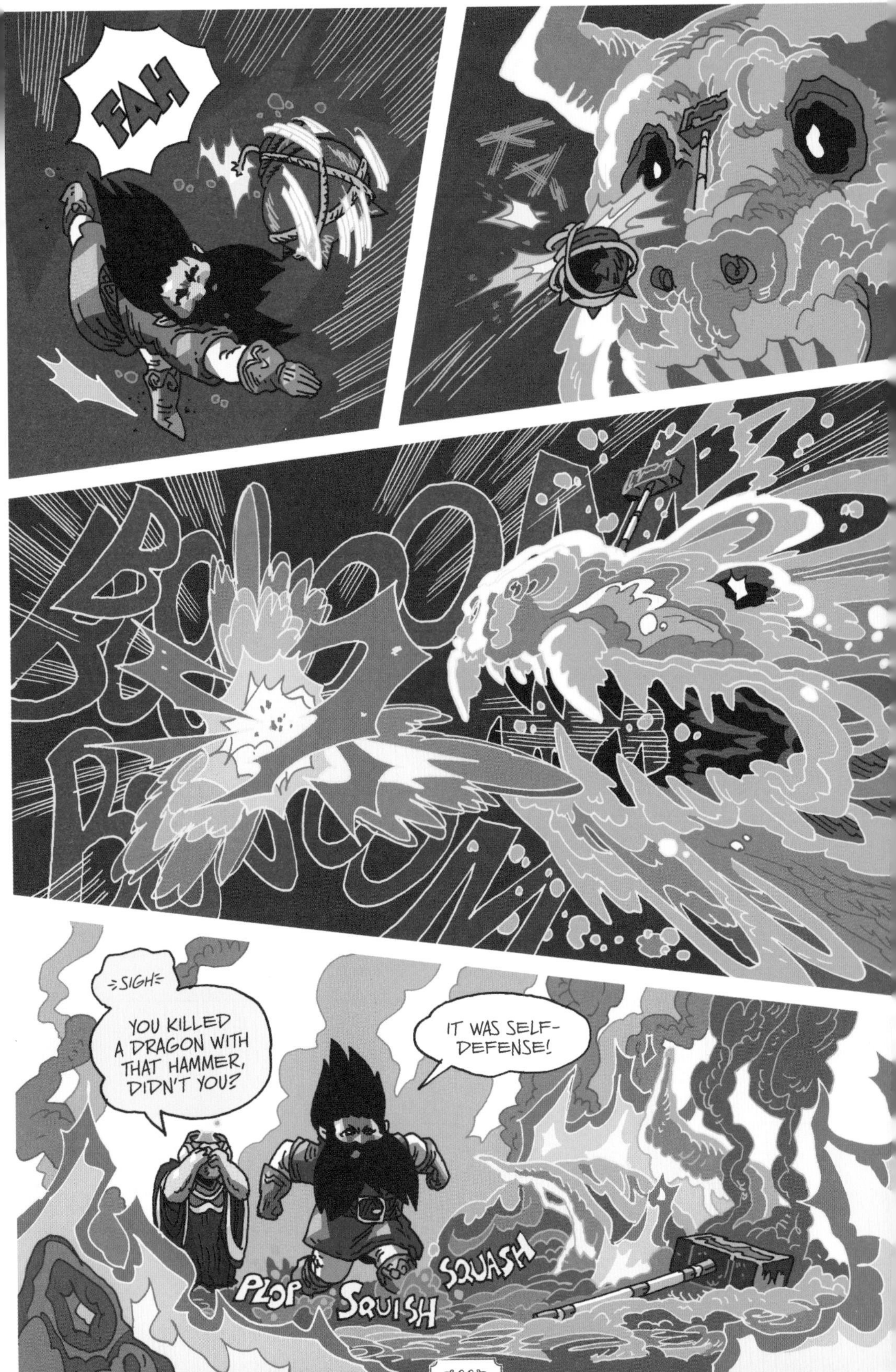
FAH
FAH
BOOOOM
≈SIGH≈
YOU KILLED A DRAGON WITH THAT HAMMER, DIDN'T YOU?
IT WAS SELF-DEFENSE!
PLOP
SQUISH
SQUASH

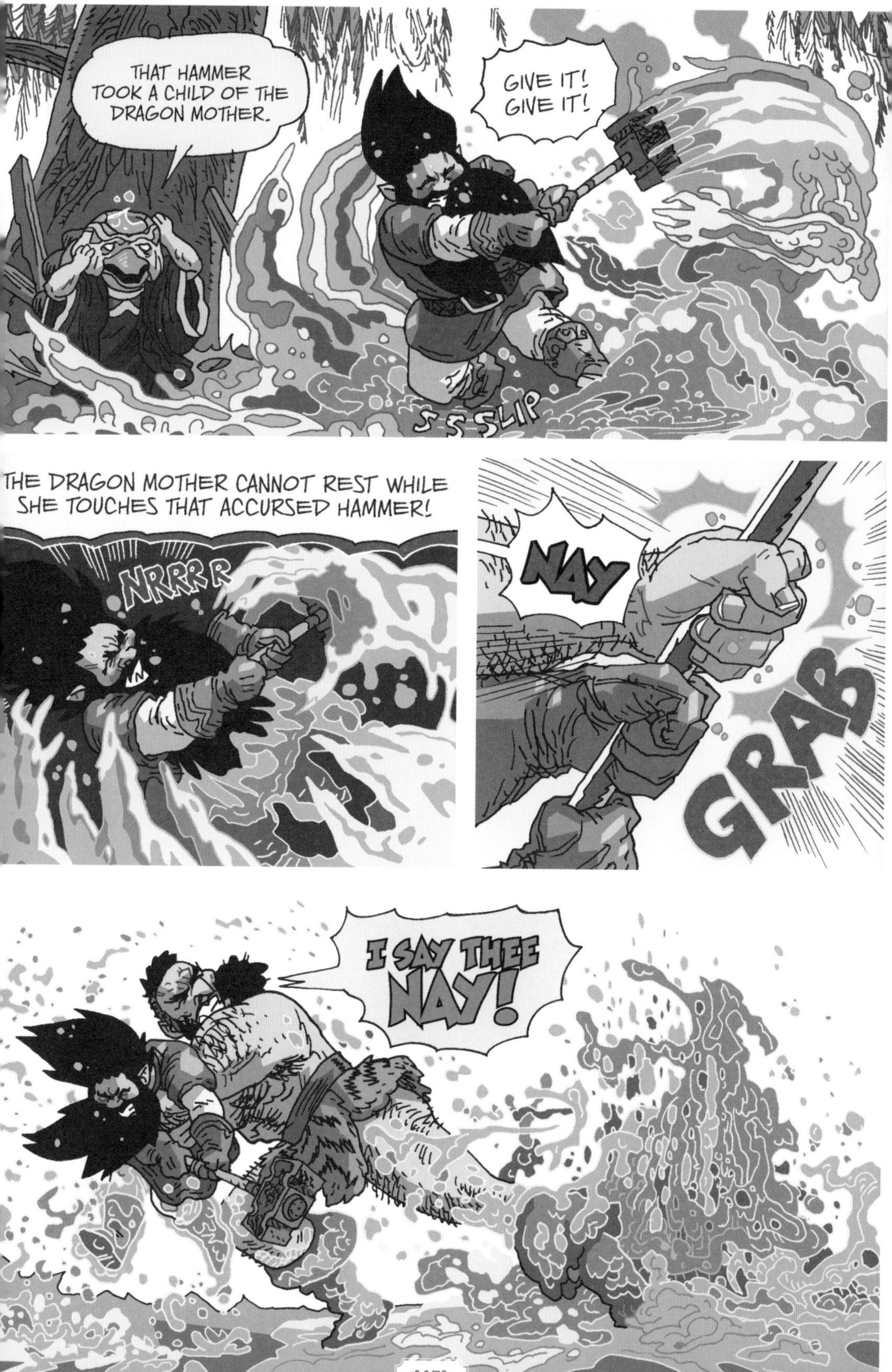
THAT HAMMER TOOK A CHILD OF THE DRAGON MOTHER.
GIVE IT! GIVE IT!
SSSLIP
THE DRAGON MOTHER CANNOT REST WHILE SHE TOUCHES THAT ACCURSED HAMMER!
NRRRR
NAY
GRAB
I SAY THEE NAY!

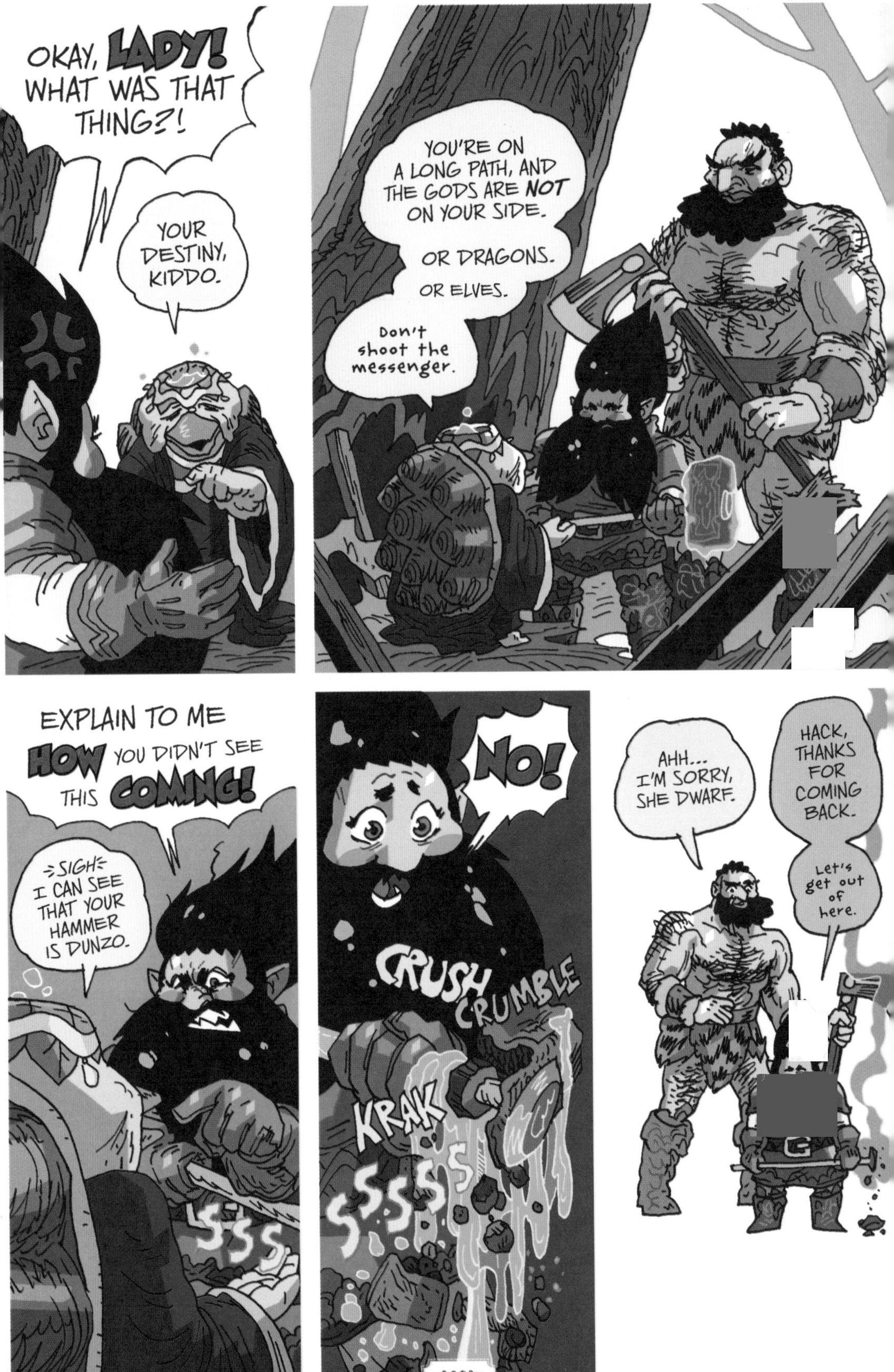
OKAY, LADY! WHAT WAS THAT THING?!
YOUR DESTINY, KIDDO.
YOU'RE ON A LONG PATH, AND THE GODS ARE NOT ON YOUR SIDE.
OR DRAGONS.
OR ELVES.
Don't shoot the messenger.
EXPLAIN TO ME HOW YOU DIDN'T SEE THIS COMING!
=SIGH= I CAN SEE THAT YOUR HAMMER IS DUNZO.
SSS
NO!
CRUSH
CRUMBLE
KRAK
SSSSS
AHH... I'M SORRY, SHE DWARF.
HACK, THANKS FOR COMING BACK.
Let's get out of here.

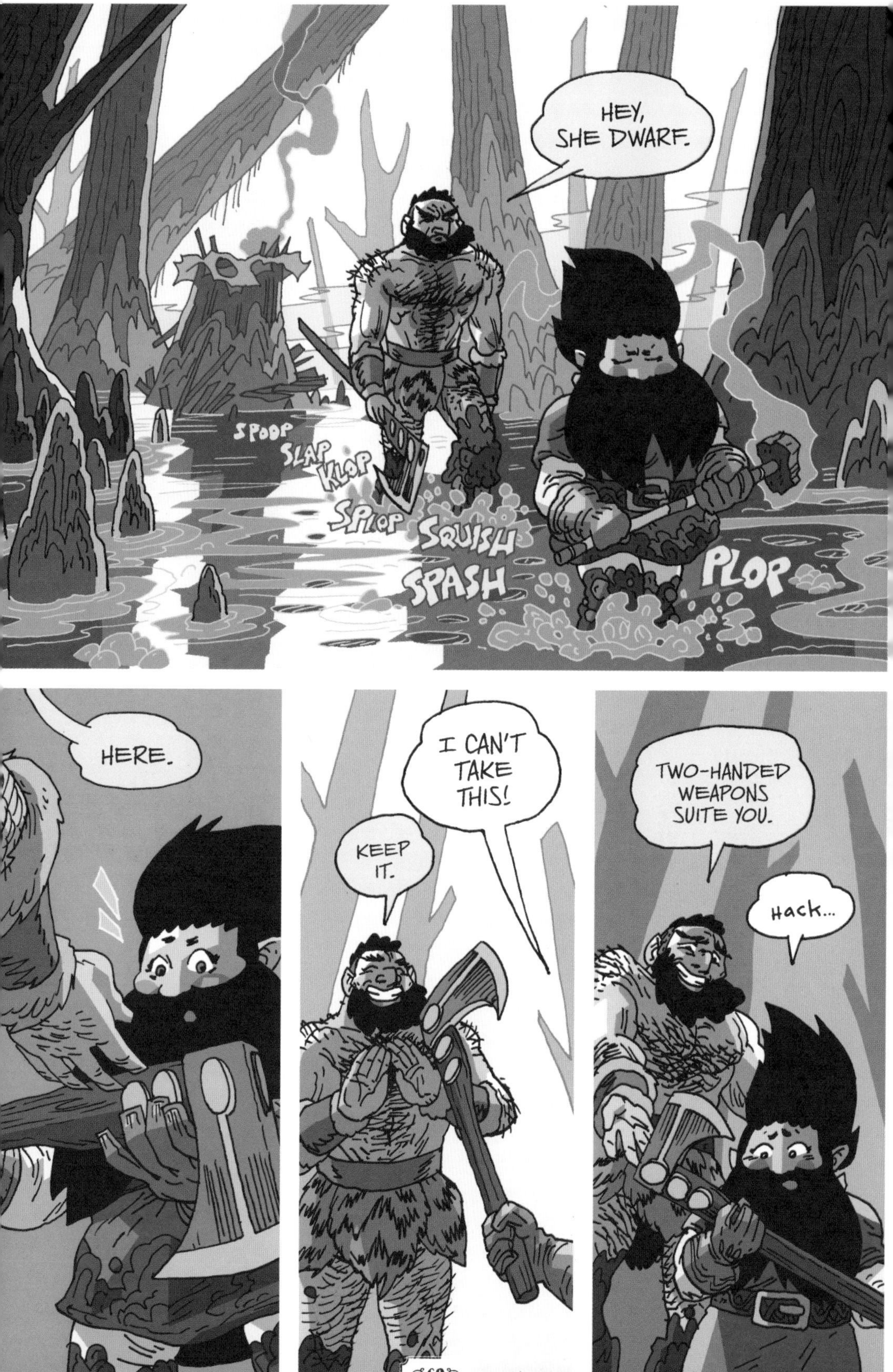
HEY, SHE DWARF.
SPOOP
SLAP
KLOP
SPLOP
SQUISH
SPASH
PLOP
HERE.
I CAN'T TAKE THIS!
KEEP IT.
TWO-HANDED WEAPONS SUITE YOU.
Hack...

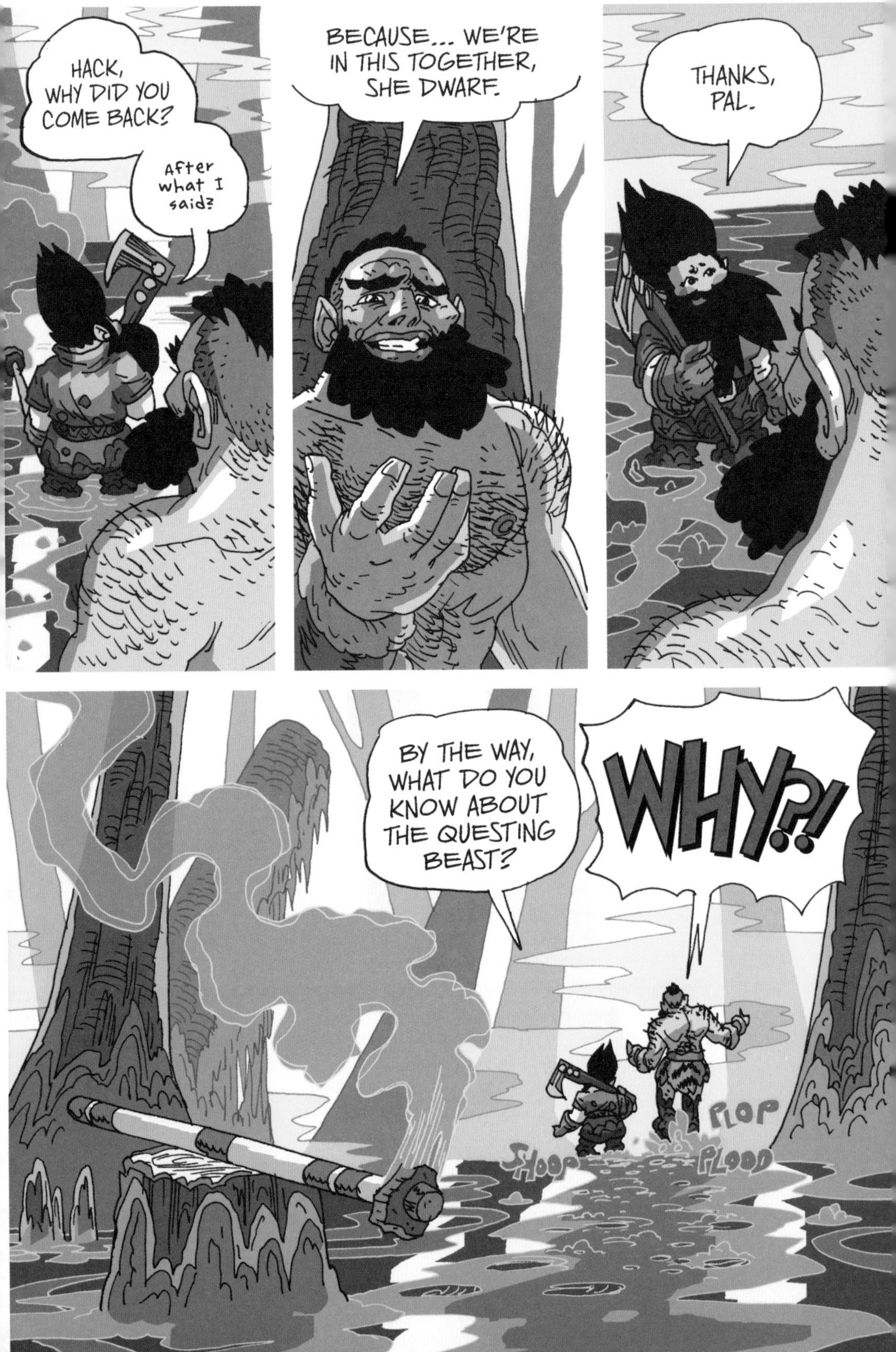
HACK, WHY DID YOU COME BACK?
After what I said?
BECAUSE... WE'RE IN THIS TOGETHER, SHE DWARF.
THANKS, PAL.
BY THE WAY, WHAT DO YOU KNOW ABOUT THE QUESTING BEAST?
WHY?!
PLOP
SHOOP
PLOOD

CHAPTER

V

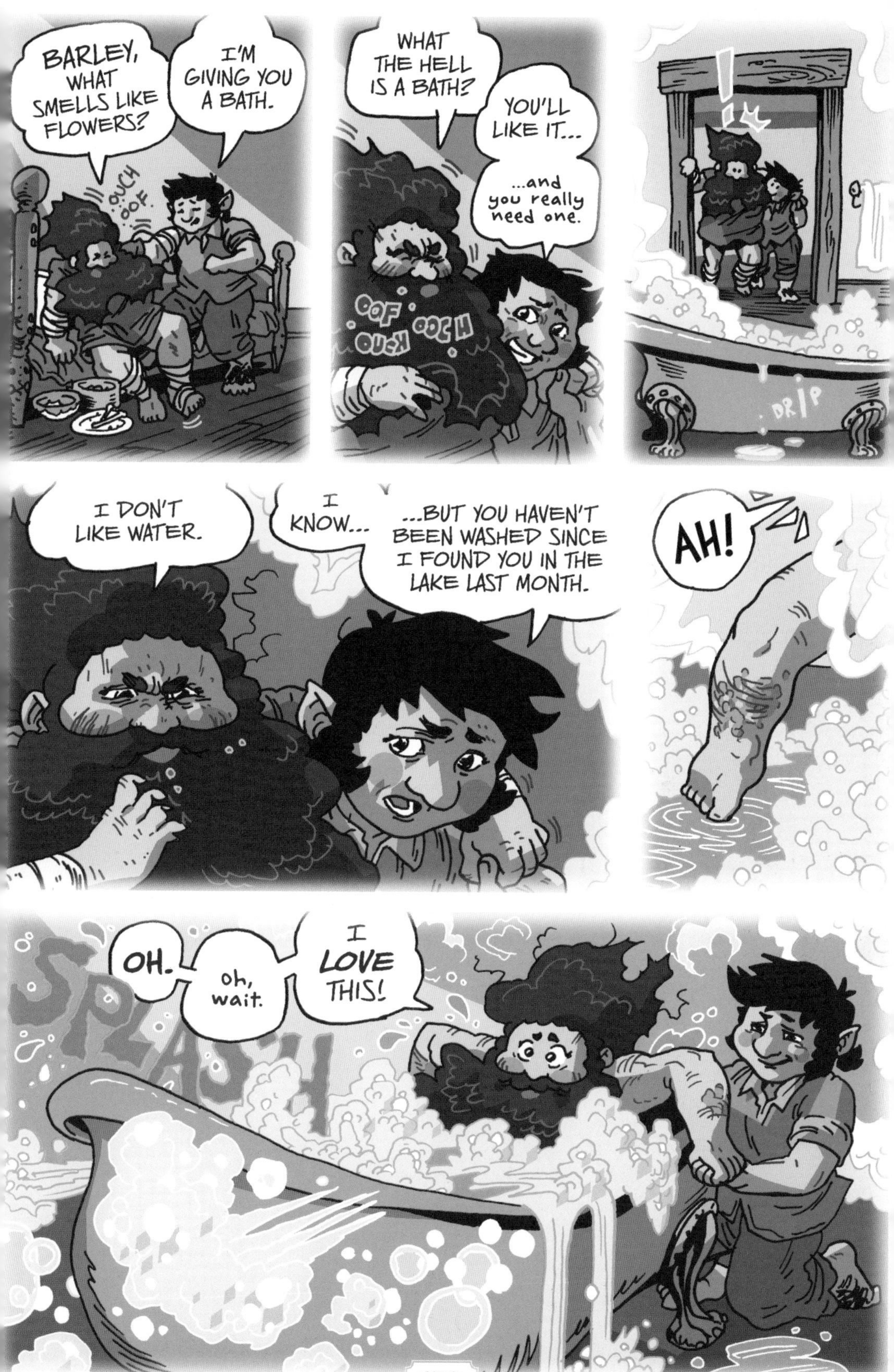
BARLEY, WHAT SMELLS LIKE FLOWERS?
I'M GIVING YOU A BATH.
OUCH
OOF
WHAT THE HELL IS A BATH?
YOU'LL LIKE IT...
...and you really need one.
OOF OUCH
OUCH OOF
!
DRIP
I DON'T LIKE WATER.
I KNOW...
...BUT YOU HAVEN'T BEEN WASHED SINCE I FOUND YOU IN THE LAKE LAST MONTH.
AH!
SPLASH
OH.
oh, wait.
I LOVE THIS!

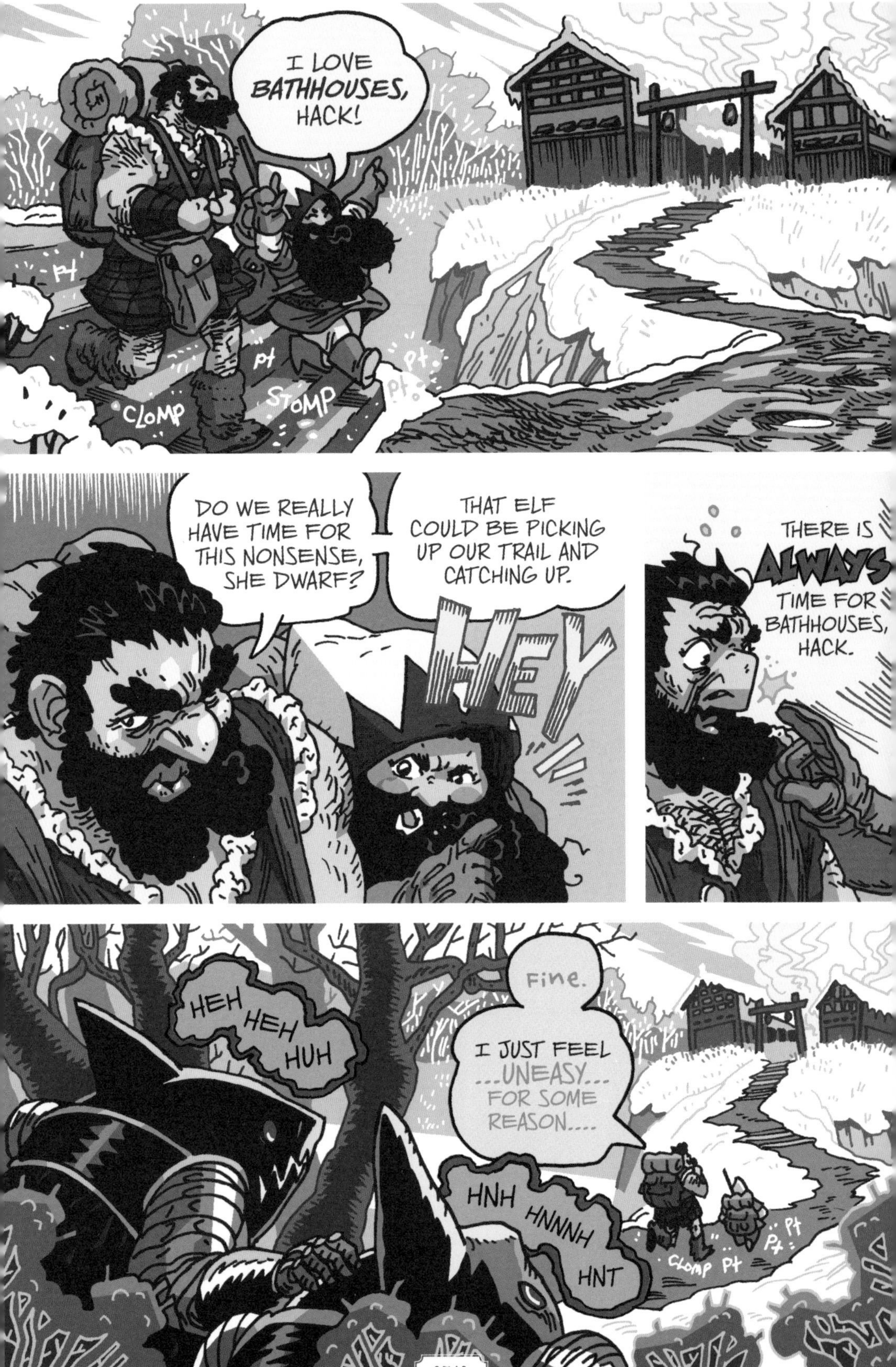
I LOVE BATHHOUSES, HACK!
Pt
pt
Pt
Pt
CLOMP
STOMP
DO WE REALLY HAVE TIME FOR THIS NONSENSE, SHE DWARF?
THAT ELF COULD BE PICKING UP OUR TRAIL AND CATCHING UP.
HEY
THERE IS ALWAYS TIME FOR BATHHOUSES, HACK.
HEH HEH HUH
Fine.
I JUST FEEL ...UNEASY... FOR SOME REASON....
HNH HNNNH HNT
CLOMP
Pt
Pt
Pt

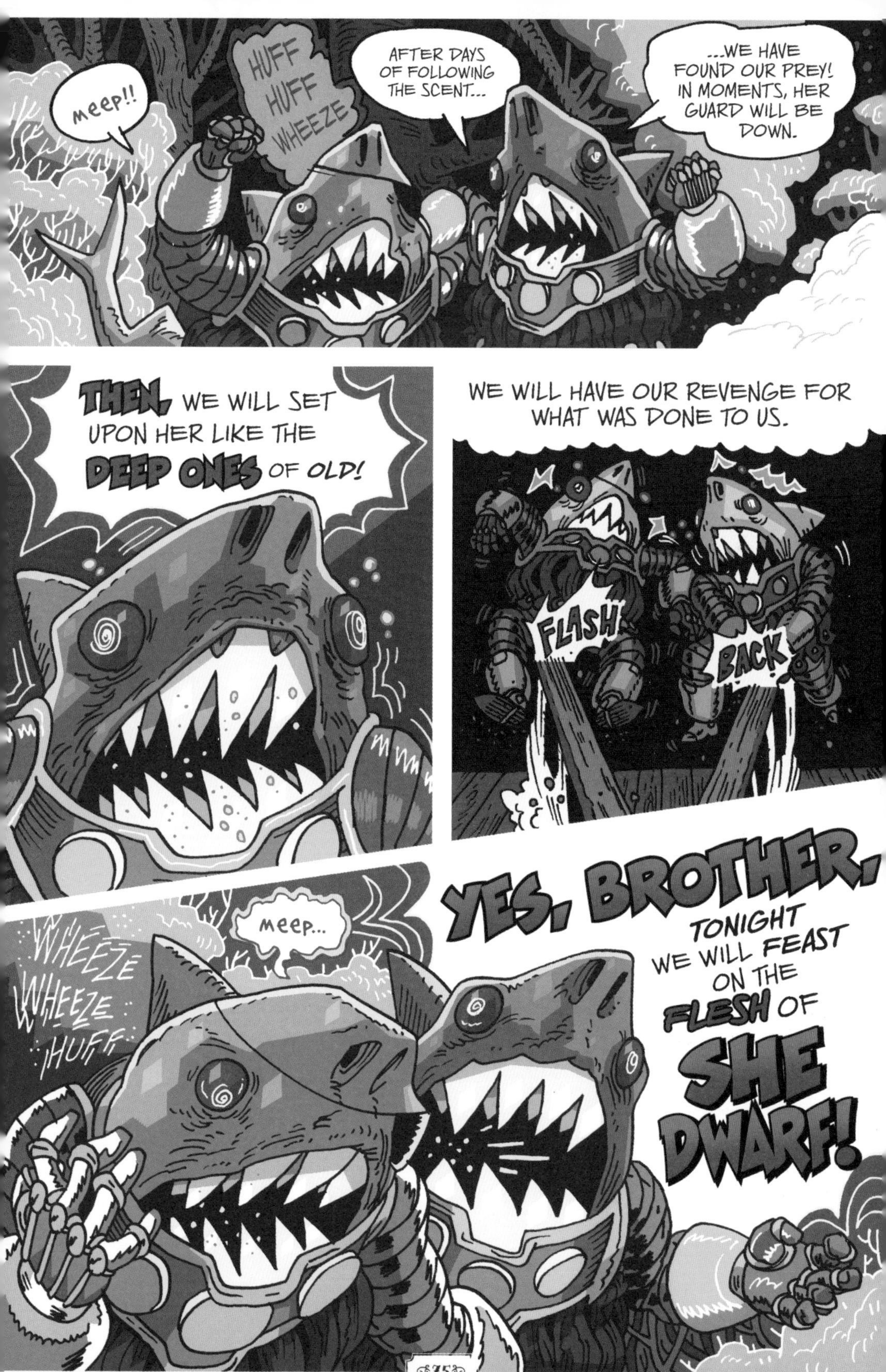
meep!!
HUFF HUFF WHEEZE
AFTER DAYS OF FOLLOWING THE SCENT...
...WE HAVE FOUND OUR PREY! IN MOMENTS, HER GUARD WILL BE DOWN.
THEN, WE WILL SET UPON HER LIKE THE DEEP ONES OF OLD!
WE WILL HAVE OUR REVENGE FOR WHAT WAS DONE TO US.
FLASH
BACK
WHEEZE
WHEEZE
HUFF
meep...
YES, BROTHER, TONIGHT WE WILL FEAST ON THE FLESH OF SHE DWARF!

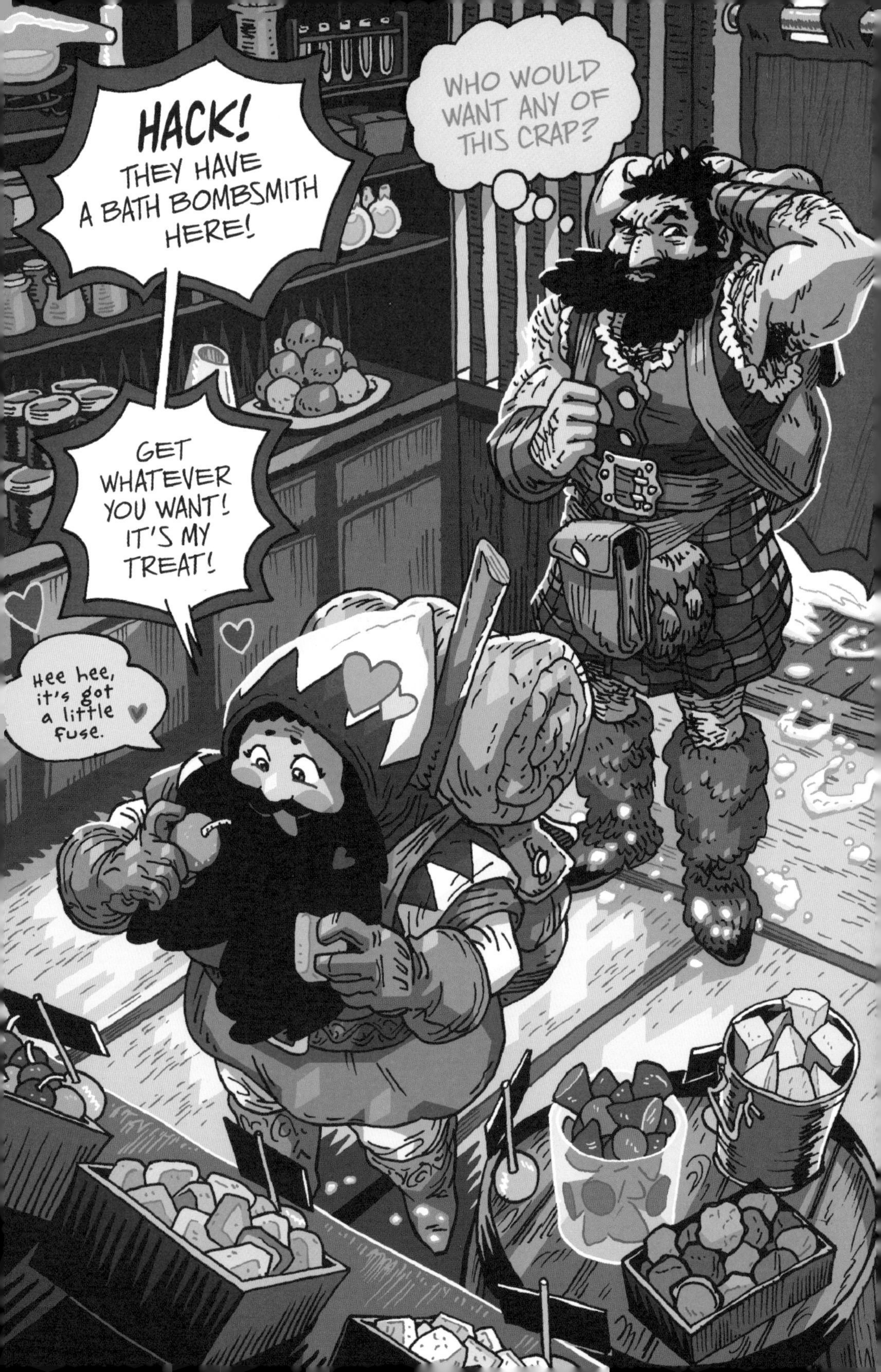
WHO WOULD WANT ANY OF THIS CRAP?
HACK! THEY HAVE A BATH BOMBSMITH HERE!
GET WHATEVER YOU WANT! IT'S MY TREAT!
Hee hee, it's got a little fuse.

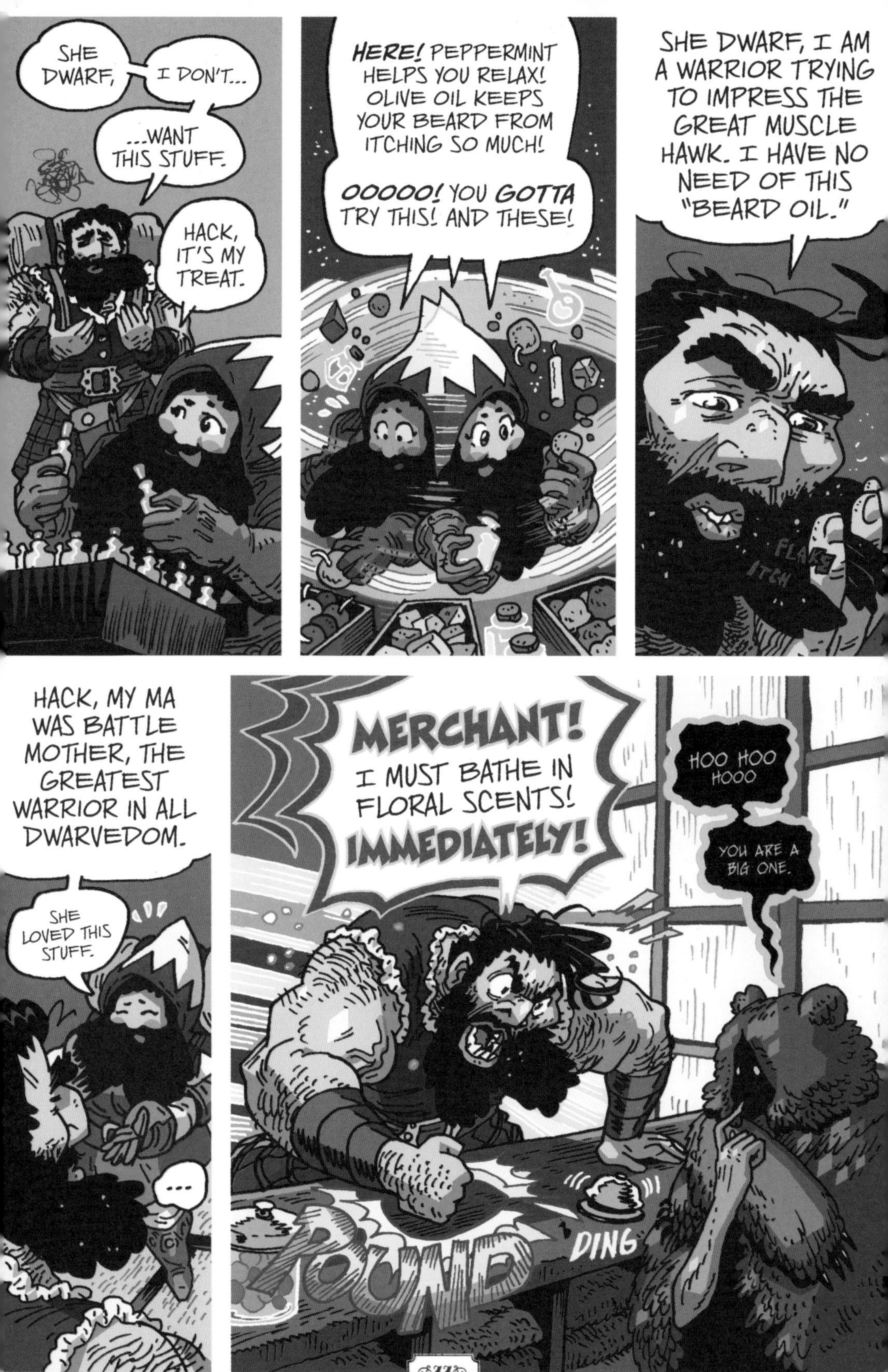
SHE DWARF,
I DON'T...
...WANT THIS STUFF.
HACK, IT'S MY TREAT.
HERE! PEPPERMINT HELPS YOU RELAX! OLIVE OIL KEEPS YOUR BEARD FROM ITCHING SO MUCH!
OOOOO! YOU GOTTA TRY THIS! AND THESE!
SHE DWARF, I AM A WARRIOR TRYING TO IMPRESS THE GREAT MUSCLE HAWK. I HAVE NO NEED OF THIS "BEARD OIL."
ITCH
HACK, MY MA WAS BATTLE MOTHER, THE GREATEST WARRIOR IN ALL DWARVEDOM.
SHE LOVED THIS STUFF.
...
MERCHANT! I MUST BATHE IN FLORAL SCENTS! IMMEDIATELY!
HOO HOO HOOO
YOU ARE A BIG ONE.
POUND
DING

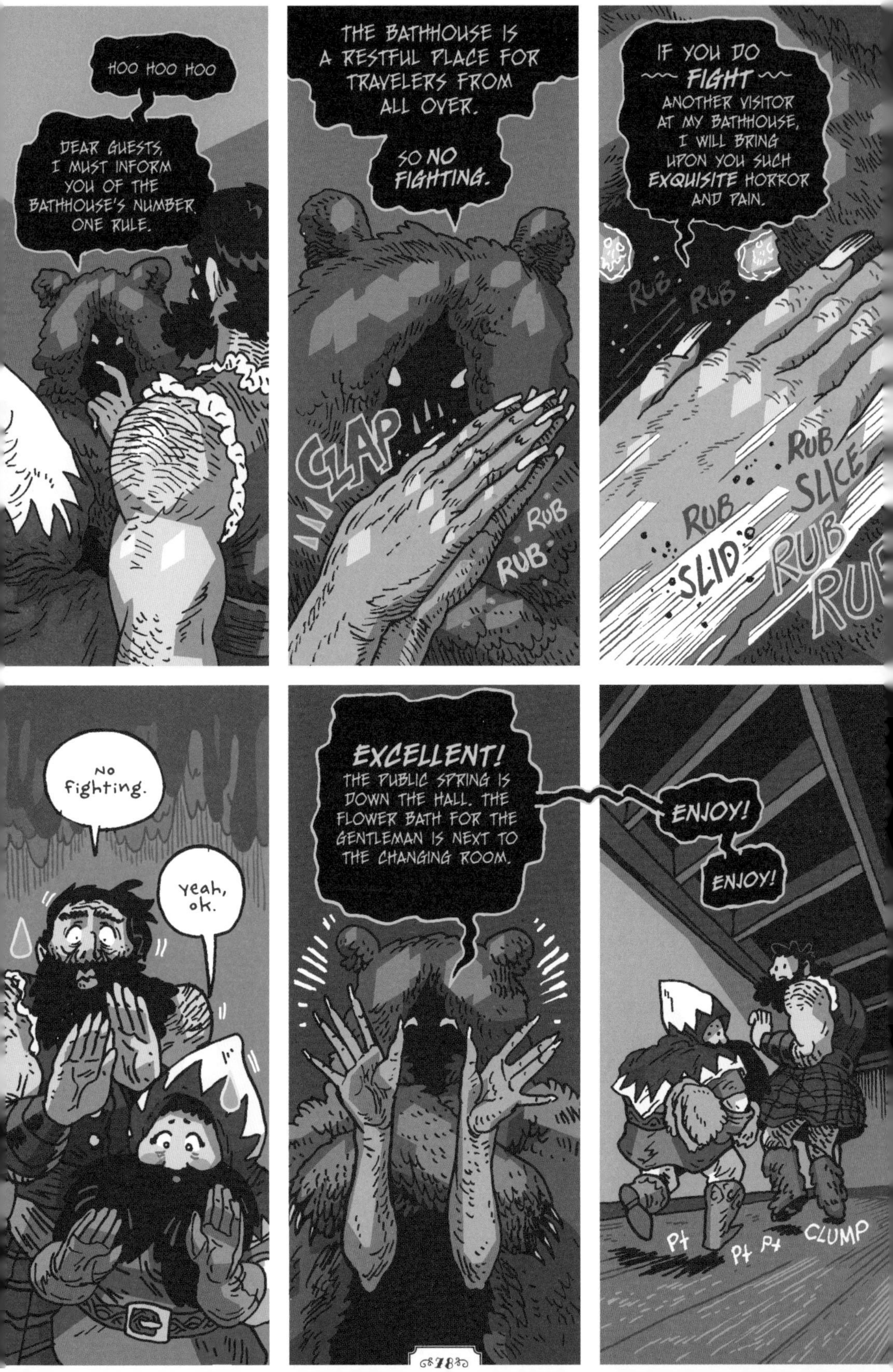

HOO HOO HOO
DEAR GUESTS, I MUST INFORM YOU OF THE BATHHOUSE'S NUMBER ONE RULE.
THE BATHHOUSE IS A RESTFUL PLACE FOR TRAVELERS FROM ALL OVER.
SO NO FIGHTING.
CLAP
RUB
RUB
IF YOU DO FIGHT ANOTHER VISITOR AT MY BATHHOUSE, I WILL BRING UPON YOU SUCH EXQUISITE HORROR AND PAIN.
RUB
RUB
RUB
SLICE
RUB
SLID
RUB
No fighting.
Yeah, ok.
EXCELLENT! THE PUBLIC SPRING IS DOWN THE HALL. THE FLOWER BATH FOR THE GENTLEMAN IS NEXT TO THE CHANGING ROOM.
ENJOY!
ENJOY!
Pt
Pt Pt
CLUMP

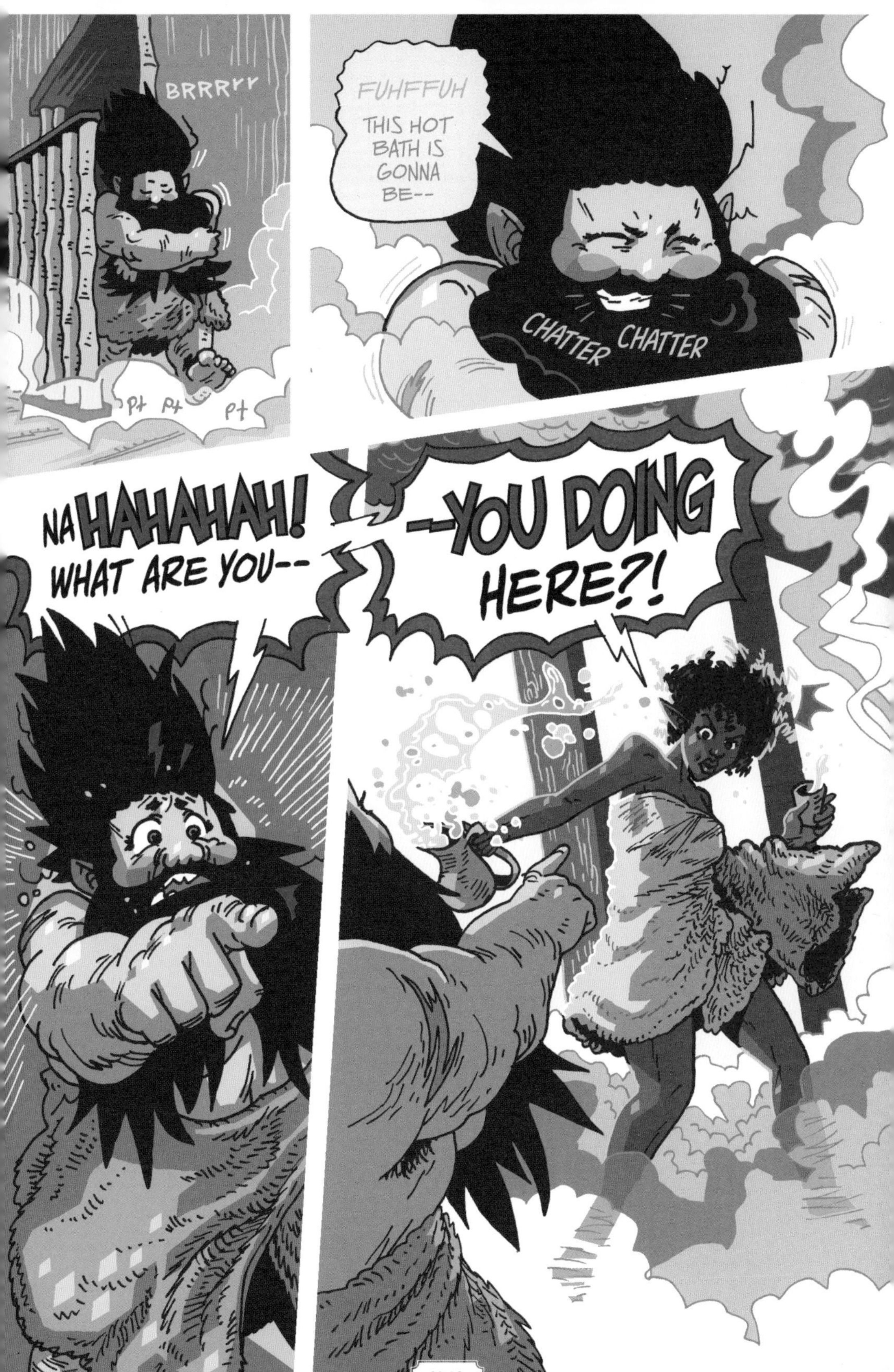
BRRRrr
Pt Pt Pt
FUHFFUH
THIS HOT BATH IS GONNA BE--
CHATTER CHATTER
NAHAHAHAH! WHAT ARE YOU--
--YOU DOING HERE?!

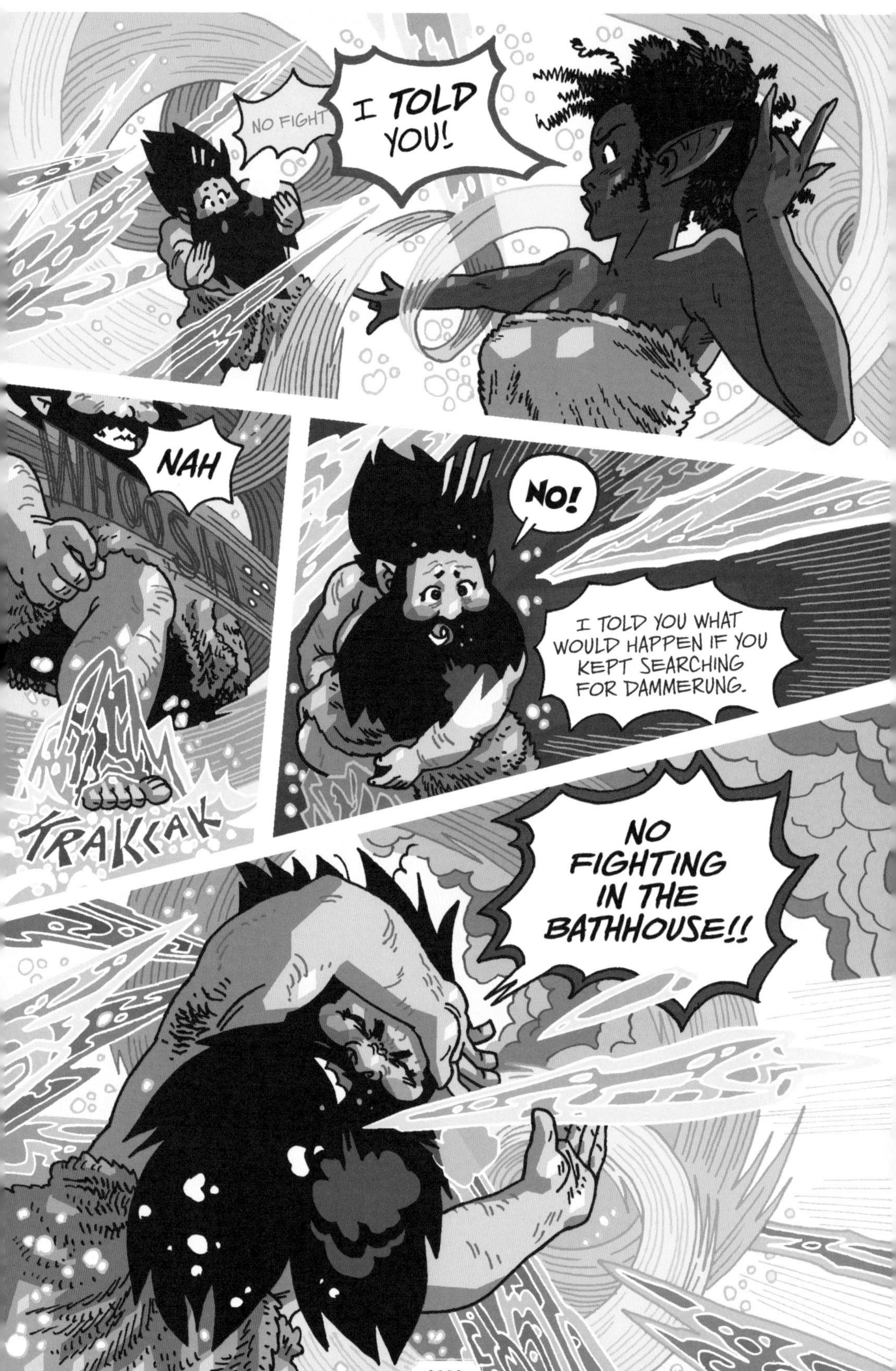
NO FIGHT
I TOLD YOU!
NAH
WHOOSH
KRAKCAK
NO!
I TOLD YOU WHAT WOULD HAPPEN IF YOU KEPT SEARCHING FOR DAMMERUNG.
NO FIGHTING IN THE BATHHOUSE!!

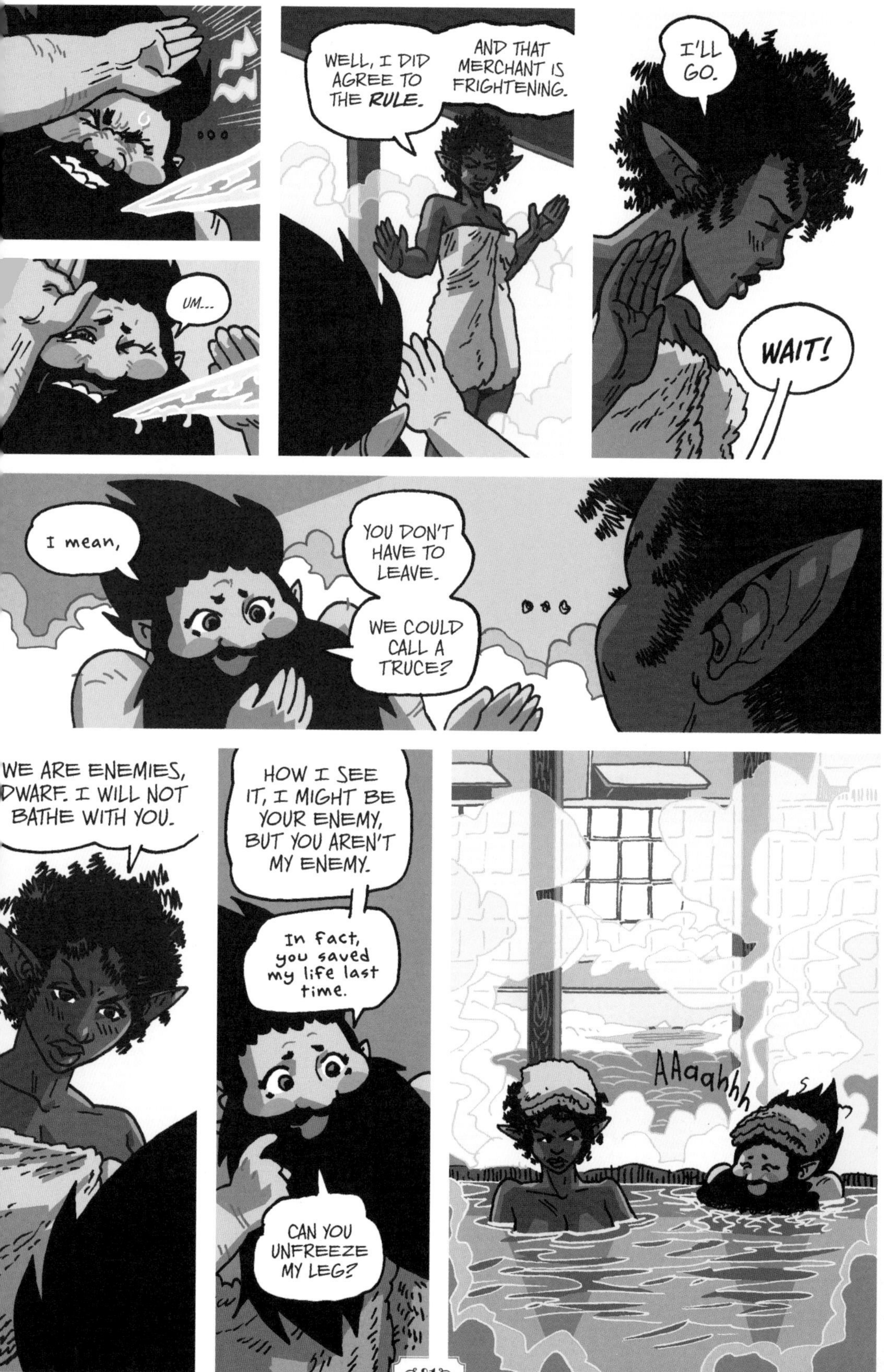
WELL, I DID AGREE TO THE RULE.
AND THAT MERCHANT IS FRIGHTENING.
I'LL GO.
UM...
WAIT!
I mean,
YOU DON'T HAVE TO LEAVE.
WE COULD CALL A TRUCE?
WE ARE ENEMIES, DWARF. I WILL NOT BATHE WITH YOU.
HOW I SEE IT, I MIGHT BE YOUR ENEMY, BUT YOU AREN'T MY ENEMY.
In fact, you saved my life last time.
CAN YOU UNFREEZE MY LEG?
AAaahhh

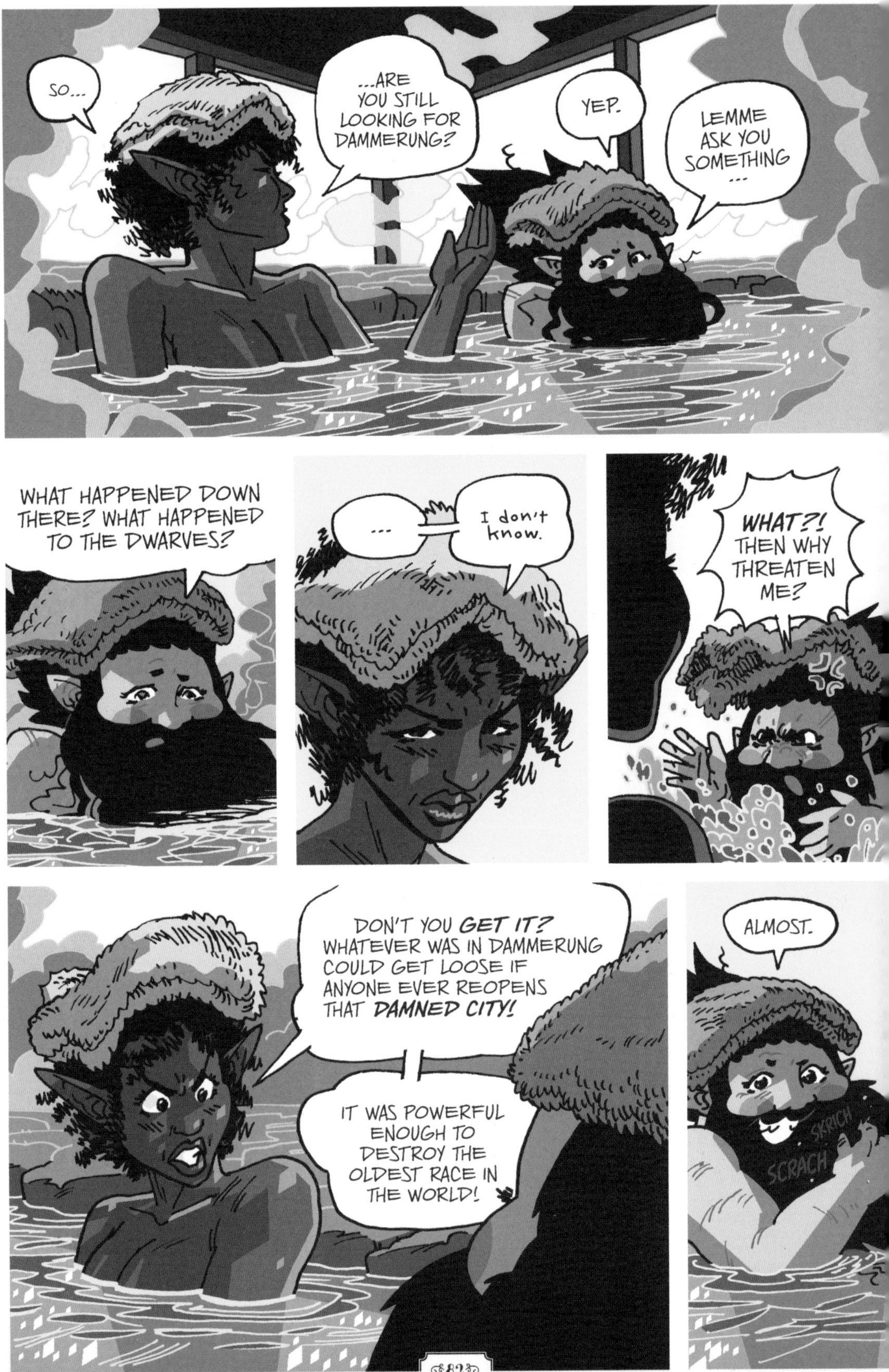

SO...
...ARE YOU STILL LOOKING FOR DAMMERUNG?
YEP.
LEMME ASK YOU SOMETHING ...
WHAT HAPPENED DOWN THERE? WHAT HAPPENED TO THE DWARVES?
...
I don't know.
WHAT?! THEN WHY THREATEN ME?
DON'T YOU **GET IT?** WHATEVER WAS IN DAMMERUNG COULD GET LOOSE IF ANYONE EVER REOPENS THAT **DAMNED CITY!**
IT WAS POWERFUL ENOUGH TO DESTROY THE OLDEST RACE IN THE WORLD!
ALMOST.
SKRICH
SCRACH

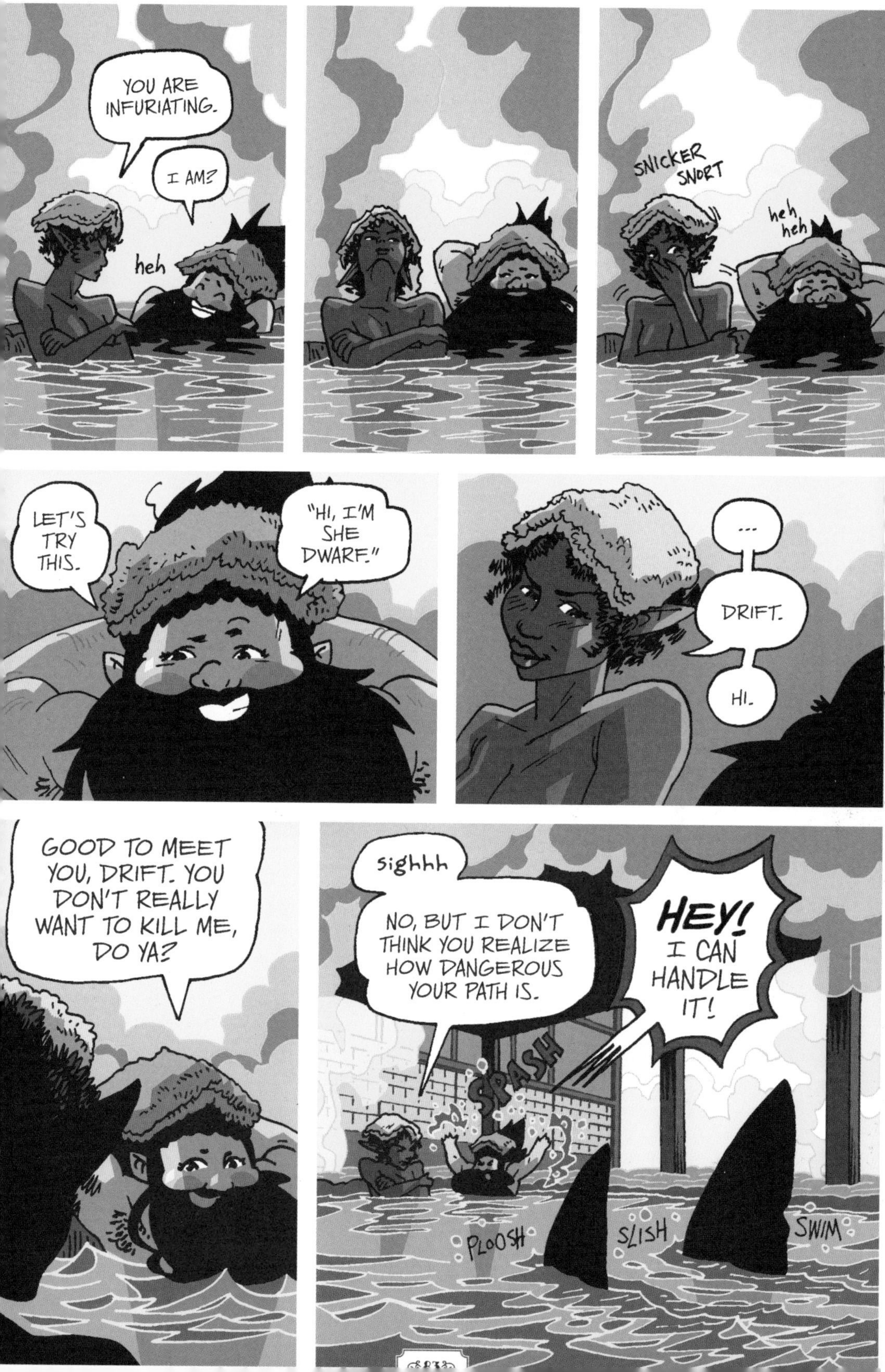
YOU ARE INFURIATING.
I AM?
heh
SNICKER
SNORT
heh heh
LET'S TRY THIS.
"HI, I'M SHE DWARF."
...
DRIFT.
HI.
GOOD TO MEET YOU, DRIFT. YOU DON'T REALLY WANT TO KILL ME, DO YA?
sighhh
NO, BUT I DON'T THINK YOU REALIZE HOW DANGEROUS YOUR PATH IS.
HEY! I CAN HANDLE IT!
SPASH
PLOOSH
SLISH
SWIM

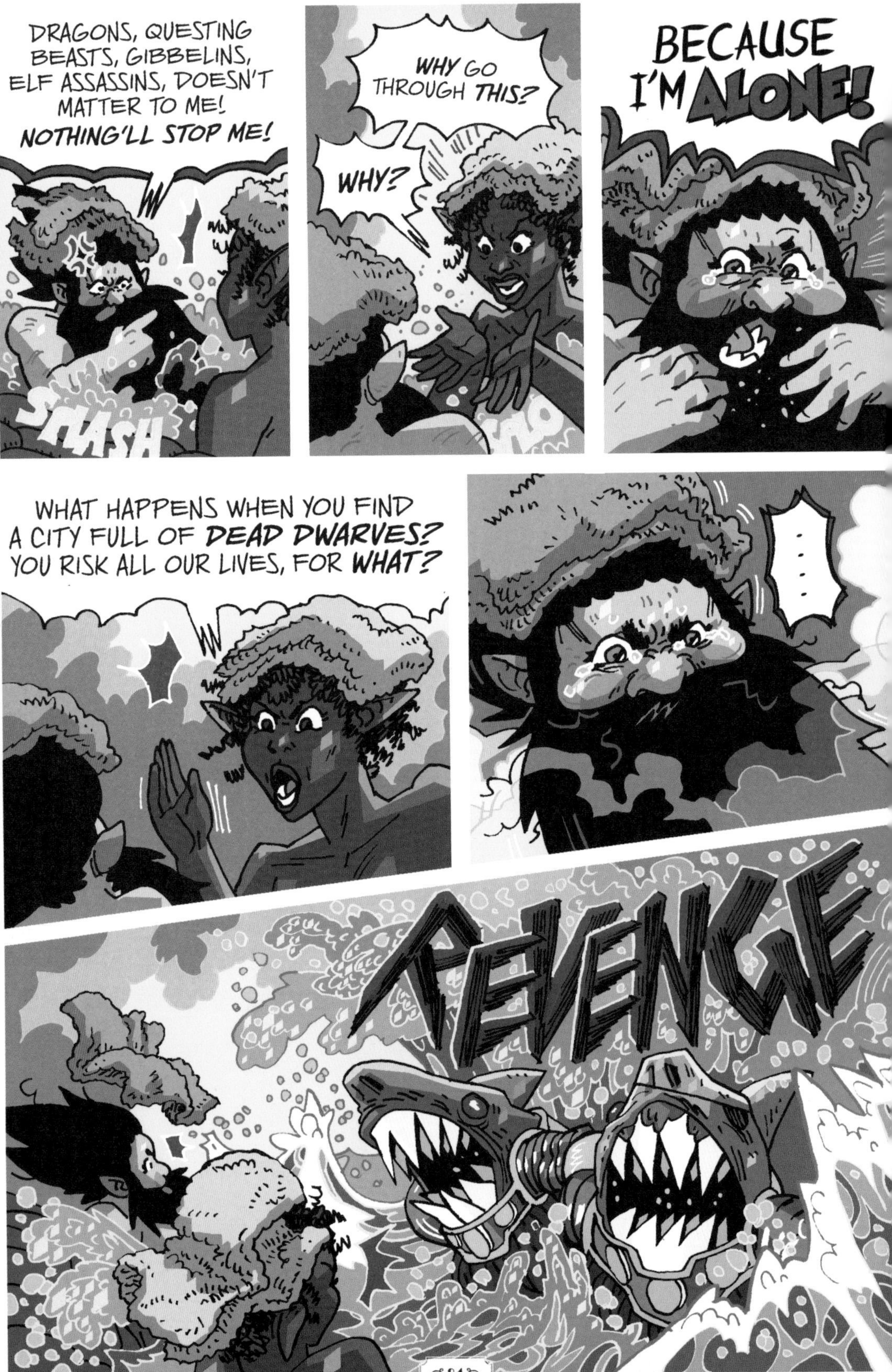
DRAGONS, QUESTING BEASTS, GIBBELINS, ELF ASSASSINS, DOESN'T MATTER TO ME! NOTHING'LL STOP ME!
SPLASH
WHY?
WHY GO THROUGH THIS?
BECAUSE I'M ALONE!
WHAT HAPPENS WHEN YOU FIND A CITY FULL OF DEAD DWARVES? YOU RISK ALL OUR LIVES, FOR WHAT?
. . . .
REVENGE

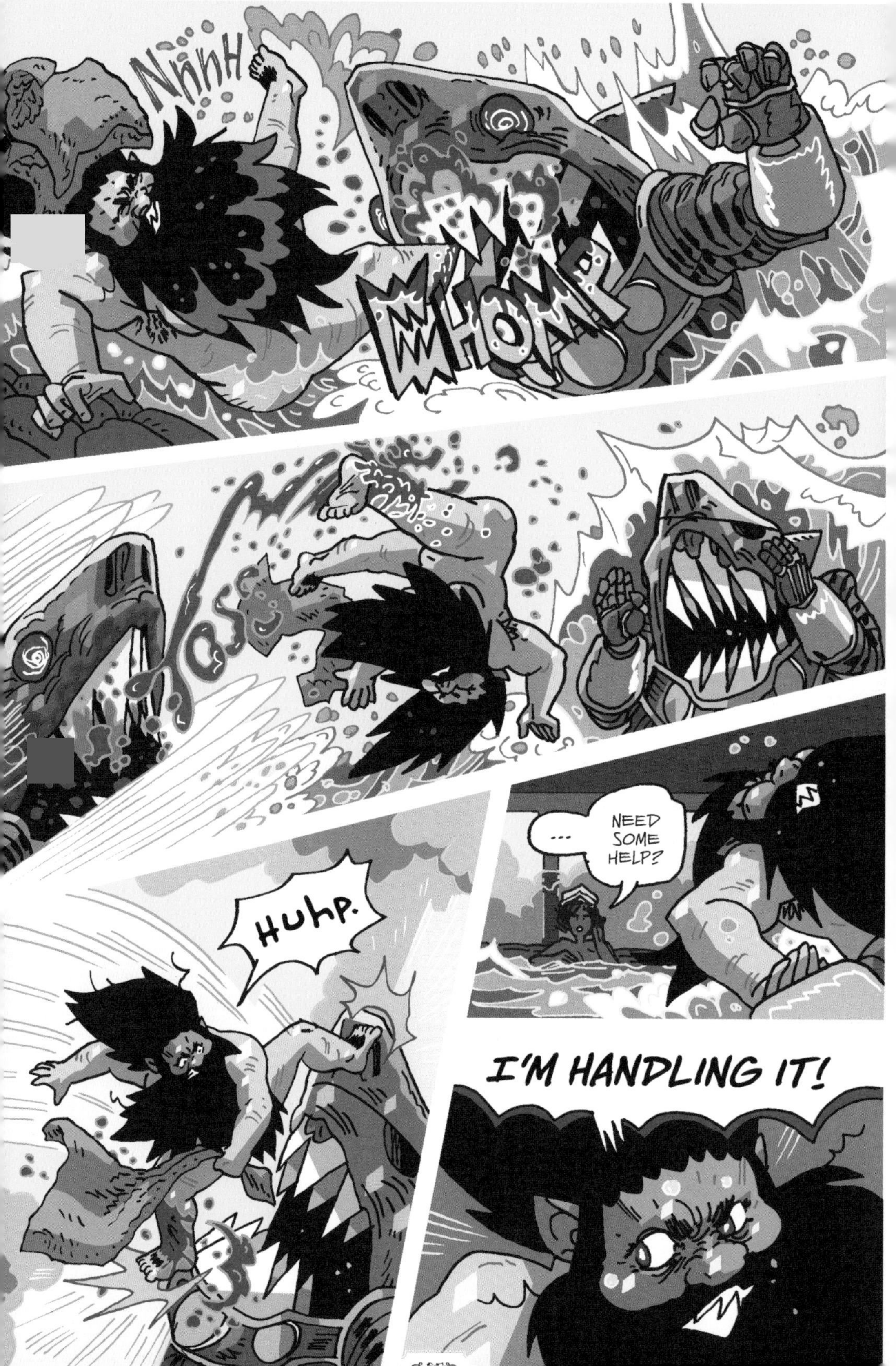
NNNH
WHOMP
HUHP.
...
NEED SOME HELP?
I'M HANDLING IT!

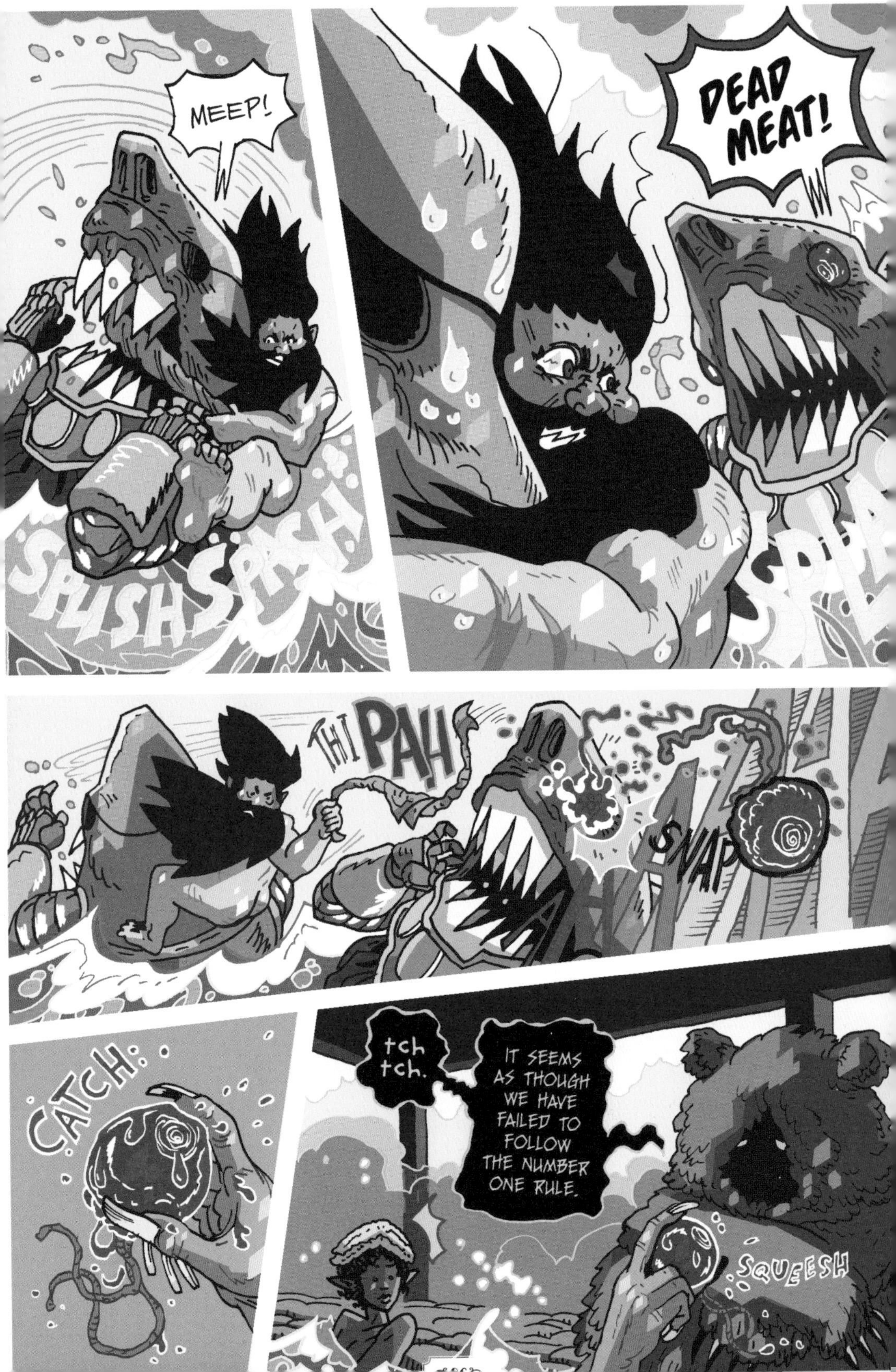
MEEP!
DEAD MEAT!
THI PAH
SNAP
CATCH.
tch tch.
IT SEEMS AS THOUGH WE HAVE FAILED TO FOLLOW THE NUMBER ONE RULE.
SQUEESH

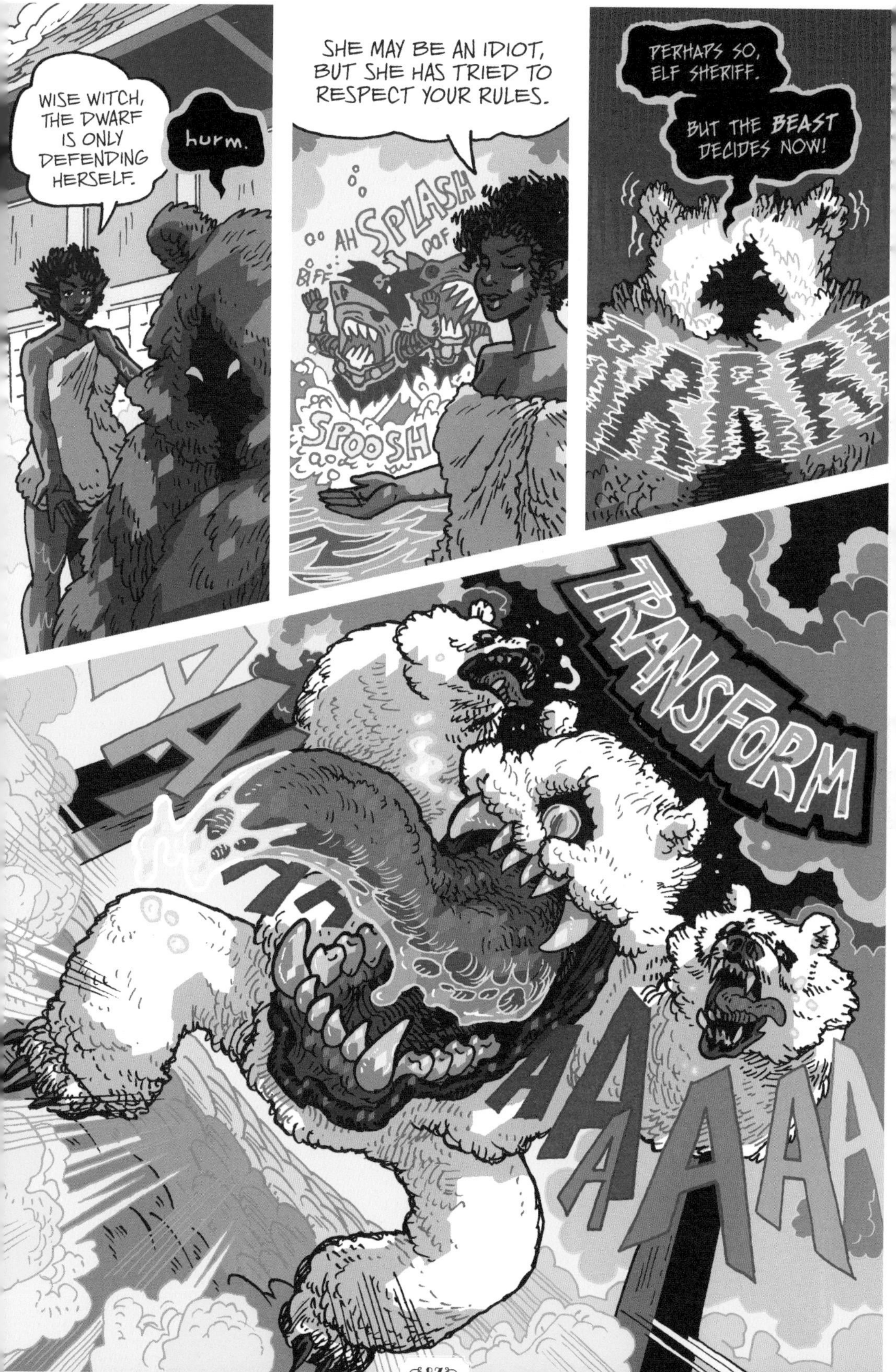

WISE WITCH, THE DWARF IS ONLY DEFENDING HERSELF.
hurm.
SHE MAY BE AN IDIOT, BUT SHE HAS TRIED TO RESPECT YOUR RULES.
AH
SPLASH
OOF
BIFF
SPOOSH
PERHAPS SO, ELF SHERIFF.
BUT THE BEAST DECIDES NOW!
RRRR
TRANSFORM
AAAAAA

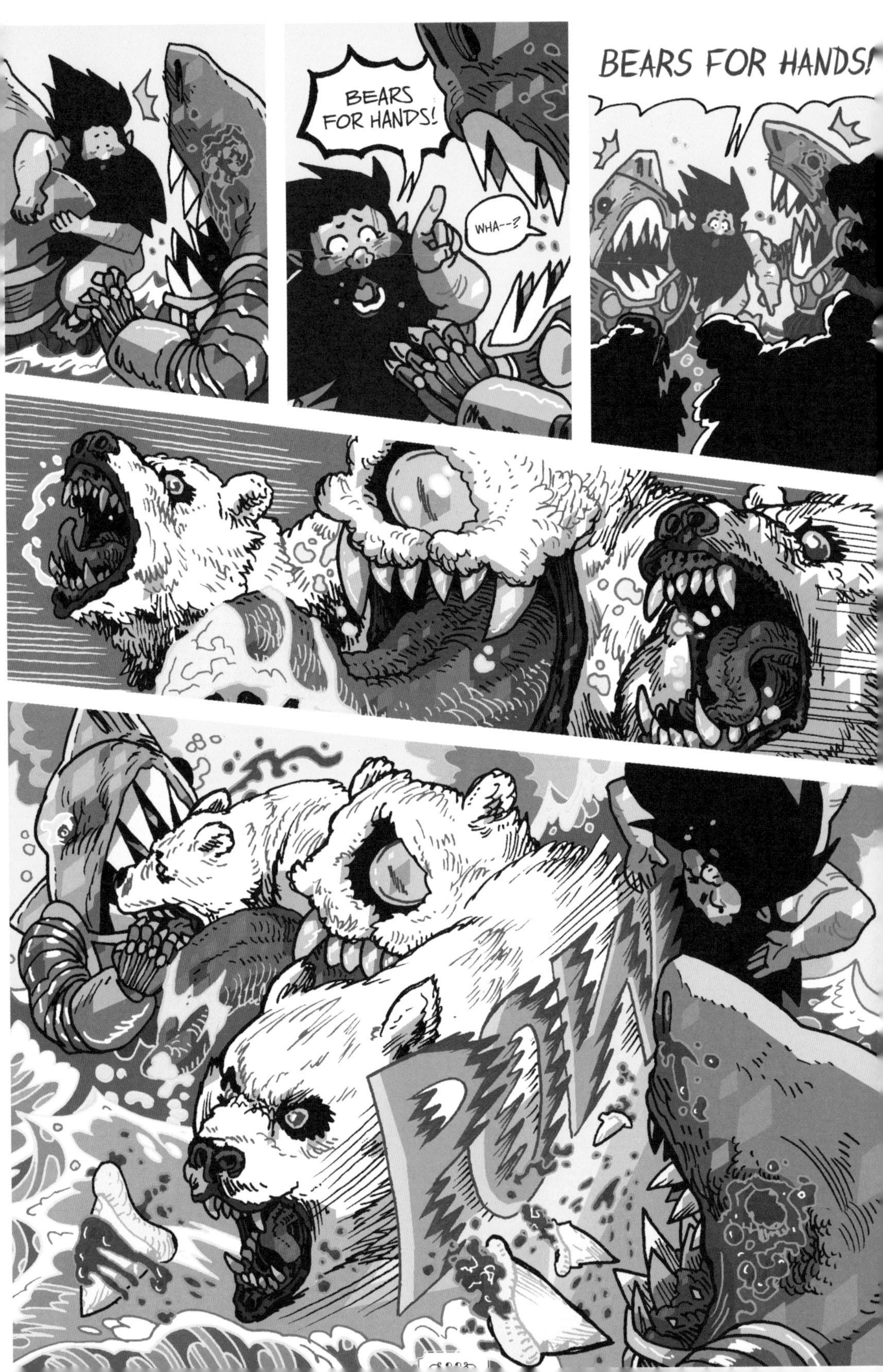
BEARS FOR HANDS!
WHA--?
BEARS FOR HANDS!

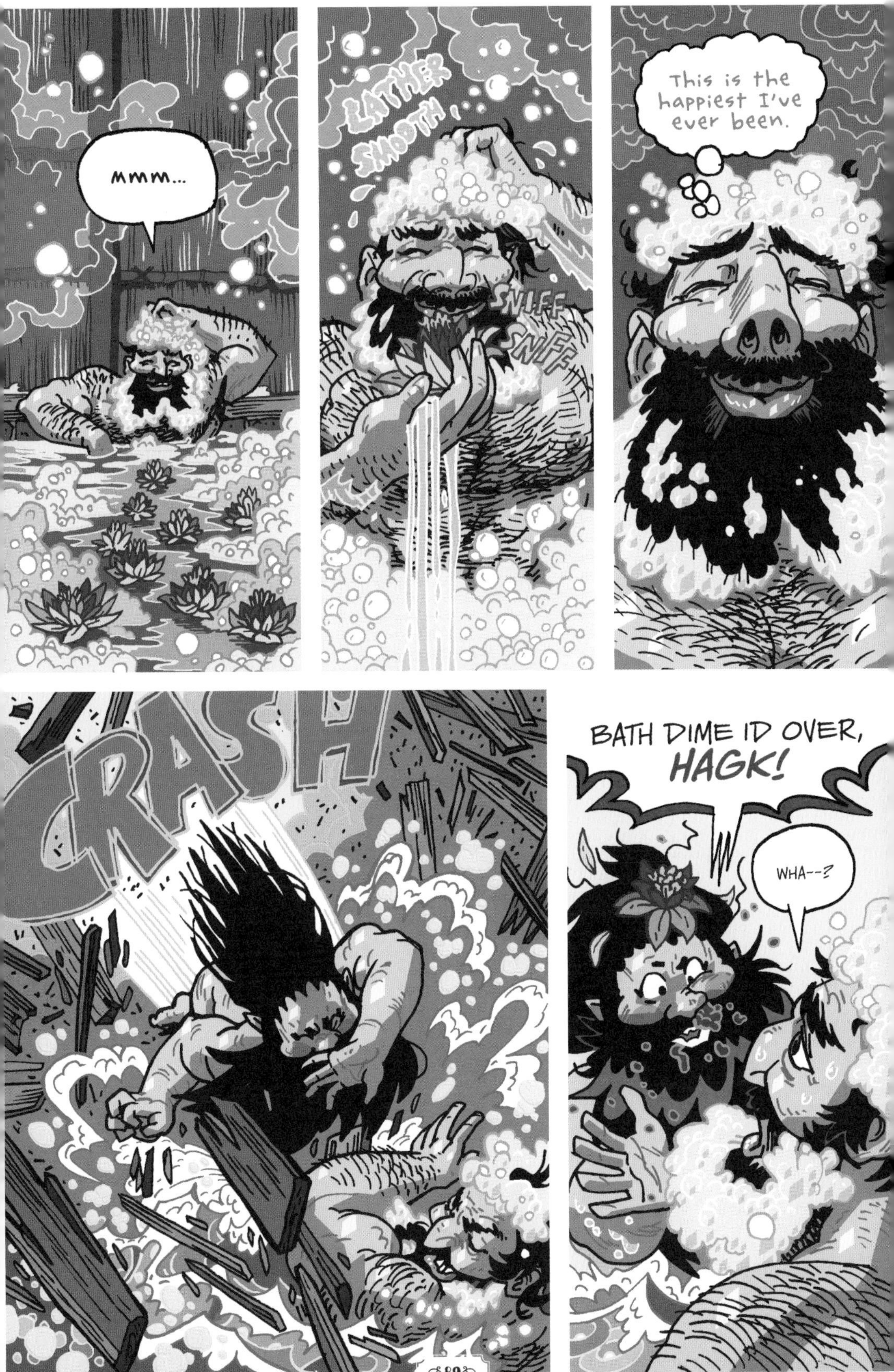
MMM...
LATHER
SMOOTH
This is the happiest I've ever been.
SNIFF
SNIFF
CRASH
BATH DIME ID OVER, HAGK!
WHA--?

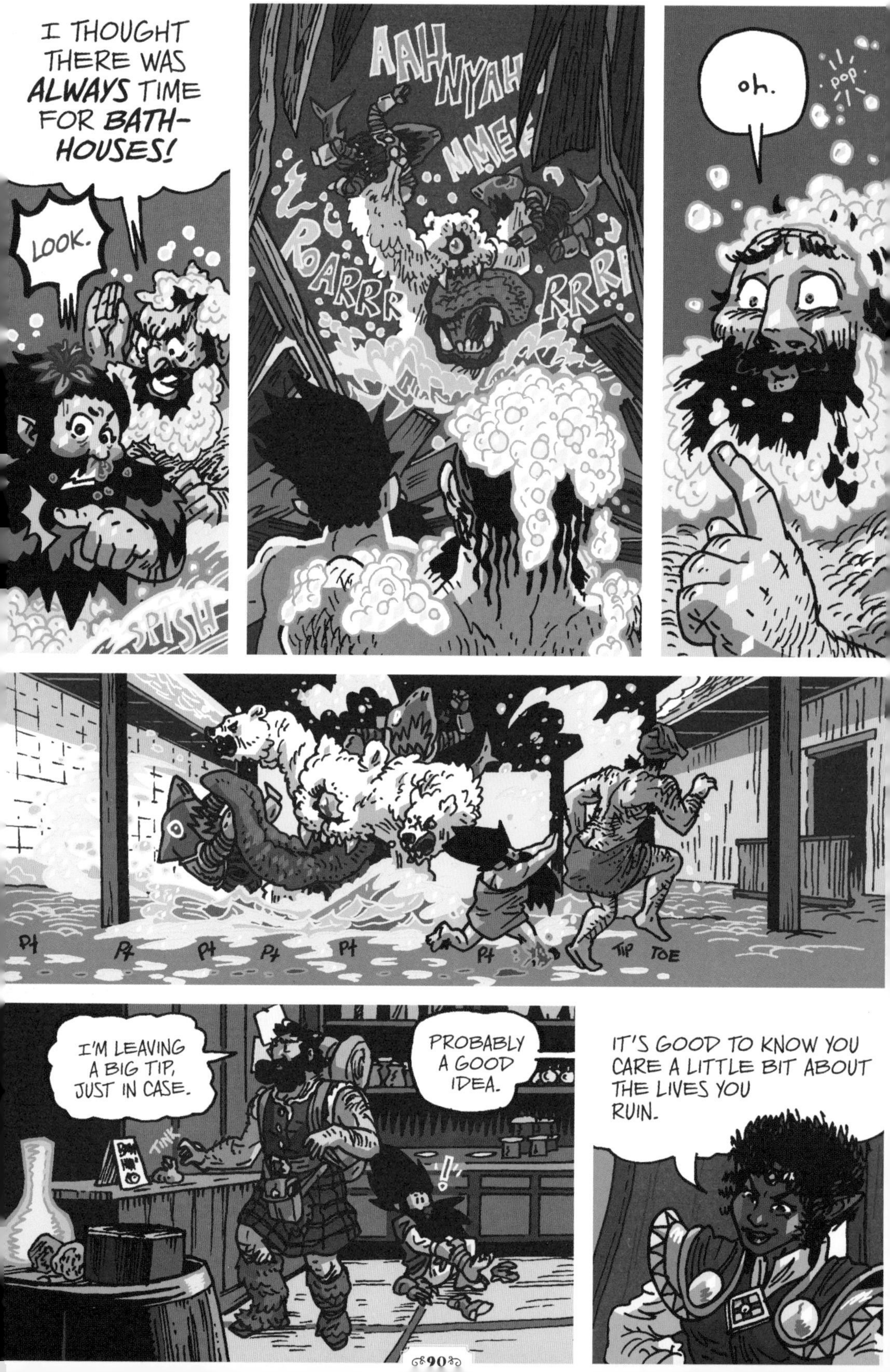
I THOUGHT THERE WAS ALWAYS TIME FOR BATH-HOUSES!
LOOK.
SPISH
AAH NYAH
MME!
ROARRRR
RRRR
oh.
pop
Pt
Pt
Pt
Pt
Pt
Pt
TIP
TOE
I'M LEAVING A BIG TIP, JUST IN CASE.
TINK
PROBABLY A GOOD IDEA.
!
IT'S GOOD TO KNOW YOU CARE A LITTLE BIT ABOUT THE LIVES YOU RUIN.

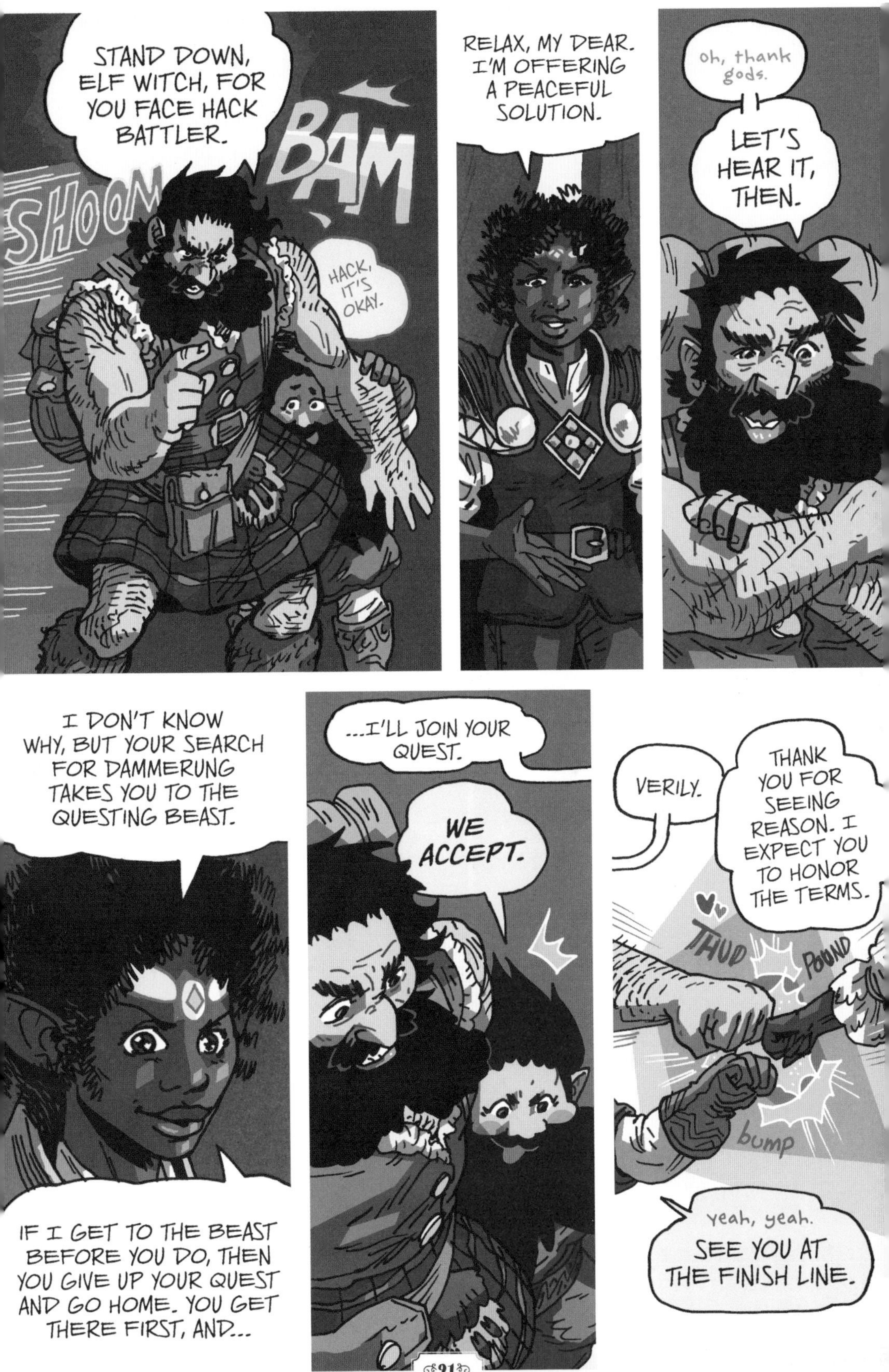
STAND DOWN, ELF WITCH, FOR YOU FACE HACK BATTLER.
SHOOM
BAM
HACK, IT'S OKAY.
RELAX, MY DEAR. I'M OFFERING A PEACEFUL SOLUTION.
oh, thank gods.
LET'S HEAR IT, THEN.
I DON'T KNOW WHY, BUT YOUR SEARCH FOR DAMMERUNG TAKES YOU TO THE QUESTING BEAST.
IF I GET TO THE BEAST BEFORE YOU DO, THEN YOU GIVE UP YOUR QUEST AND GO HOME. YOU GET THERE FIRST, AND...
...I'LL JOIN YOUR QUEST.
WE ACCEPT.
VERILY.
THANK YOU FOR SEEING REASON. I EXPECT YOU TO HONOR THE TERMS.
THUD
POUND
bump
yeah, yeah.
SEE YOU AT THE FINISH LINE.

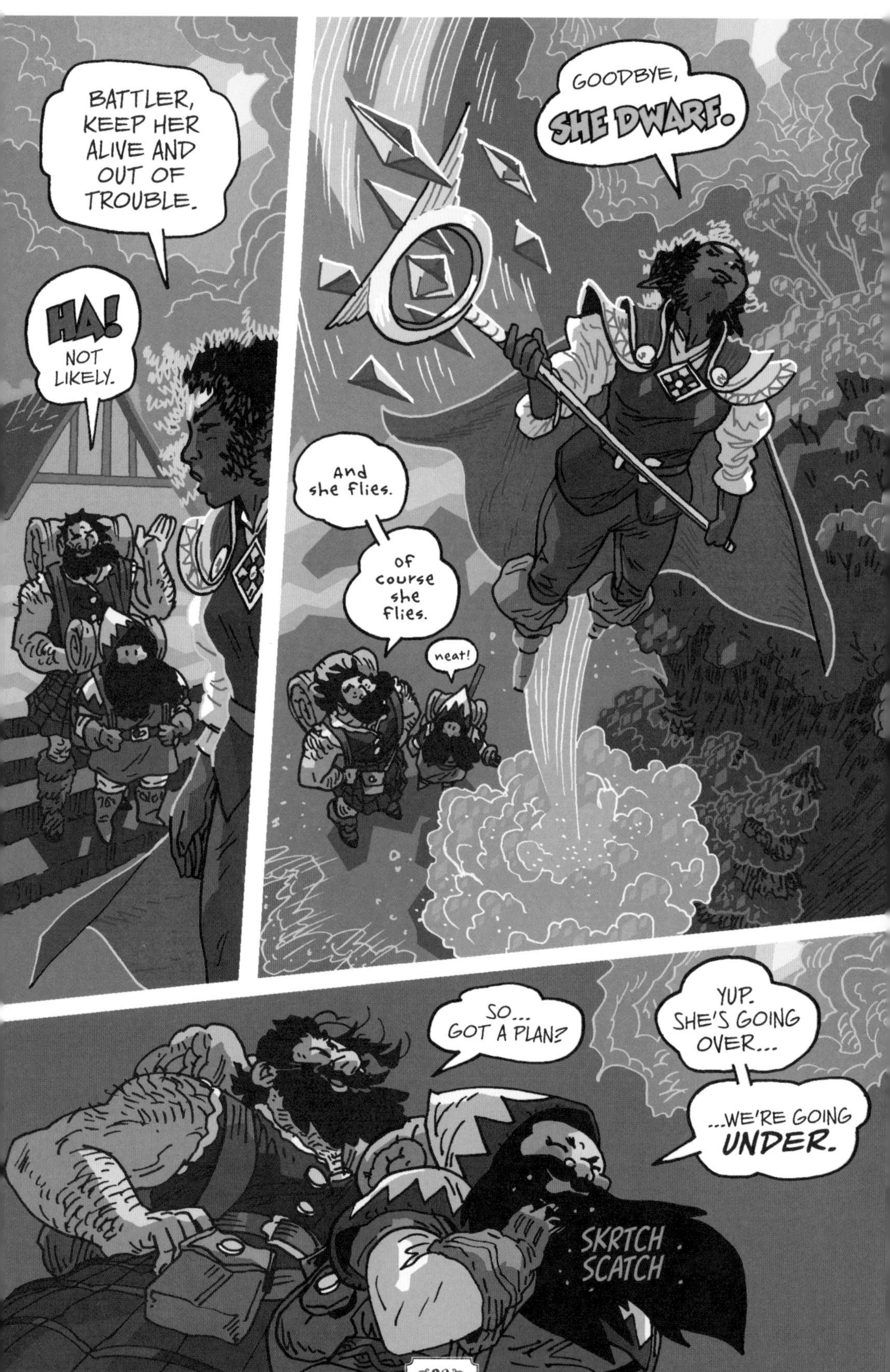

BATTLER, KEEP HER ALIVE AND OUT OF TROUBLE.
HA! NOT LIKELY.
GOODBYE, SHE DWARF.
And she flies.
of course she flies.
neat!
SO... GOT A PLAN?
YUP. SHE'S GOING OVER...
...WE'RE GOING UNDER.
SKRTCH SCATCH

CHAPTER
❦VI❧

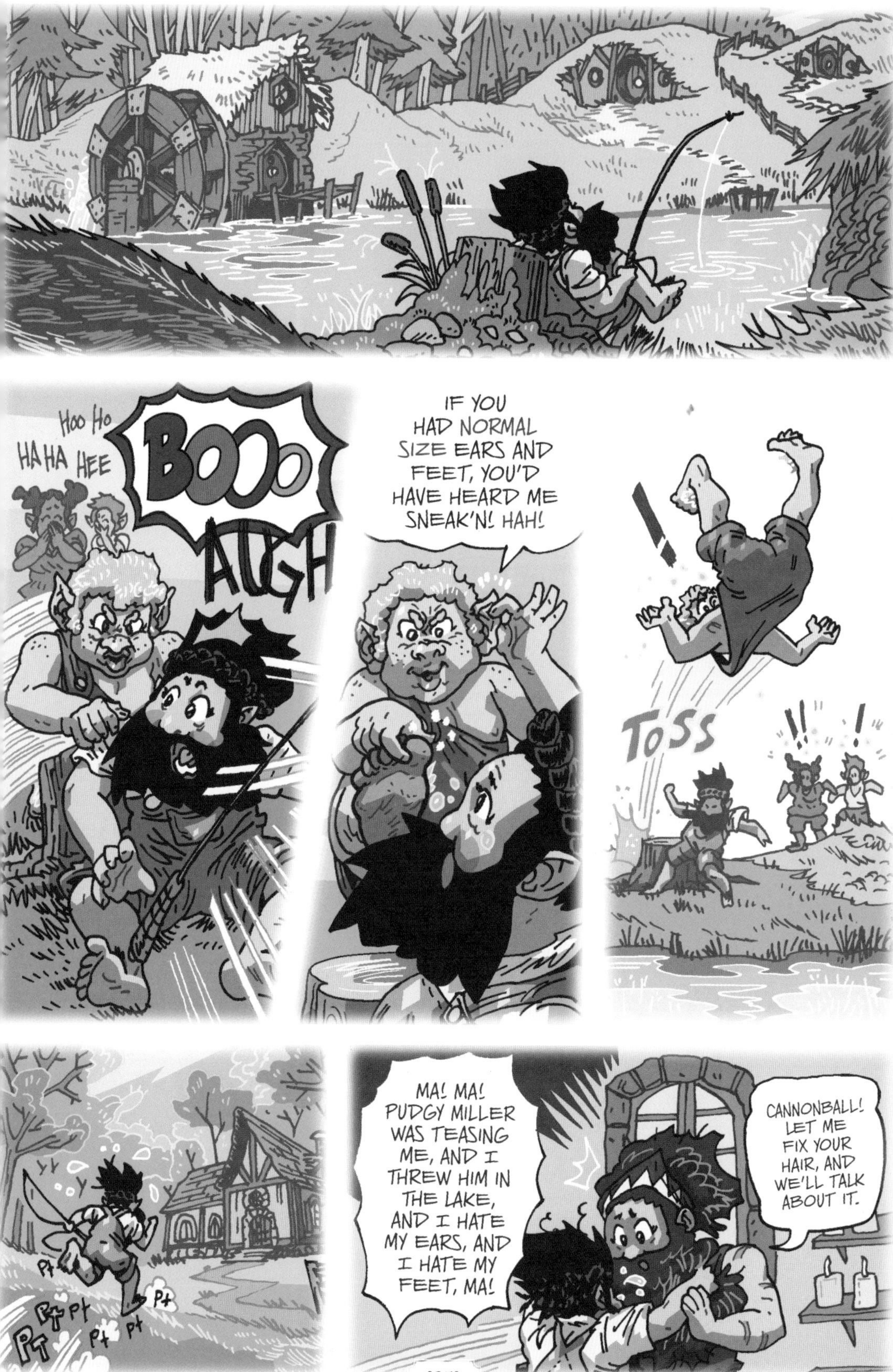

Hoo Ho
HA HA HEE
BOOOo
AUGH
IF YOU HAD NORMAL SIZE EARS AND FEET, YOU'D HAVE HEARD ME SNEAK'N! HAH!
!
TOSS
!! !
Pt Pt Pt pt Pt pt Pt
MA! MA! PUDGY MILLER WAS TEASING ME, AND I THREW HIM IN THE LAKE, AND I HATE MY EARS, AND I HATE MY FEET, MA!
CANNONBALL! LET ME FIX YOUR HAIR, AND WE'LL TALK ABOUT IT.

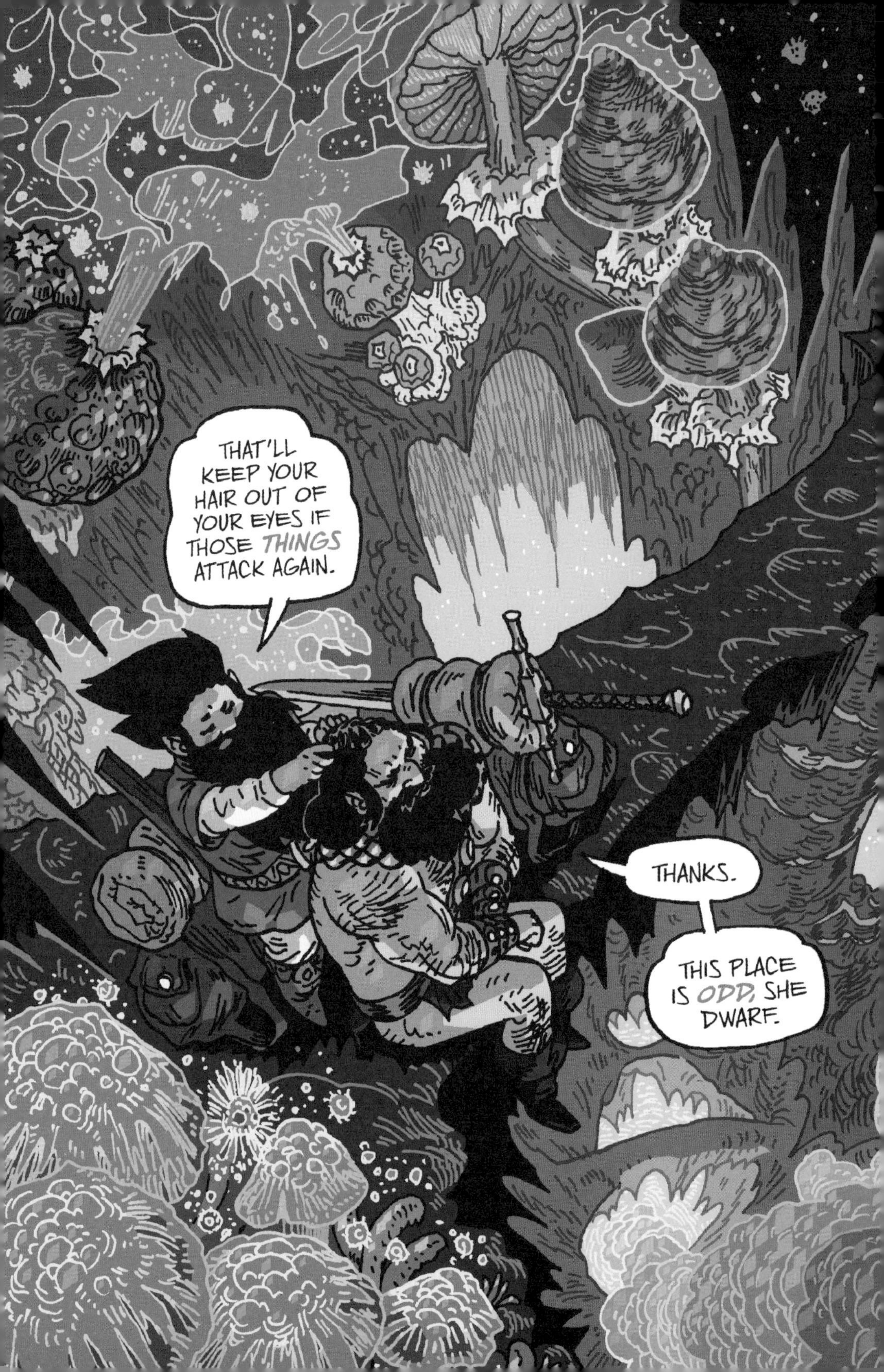
THAT'LL KEEP YOUR HAIR OUT OF YOUR EYES IF THOSE *THINGS* ATTACK AGAIN.
THANKS.
THIS PLACE IS *ODD,* SHE DWARF.

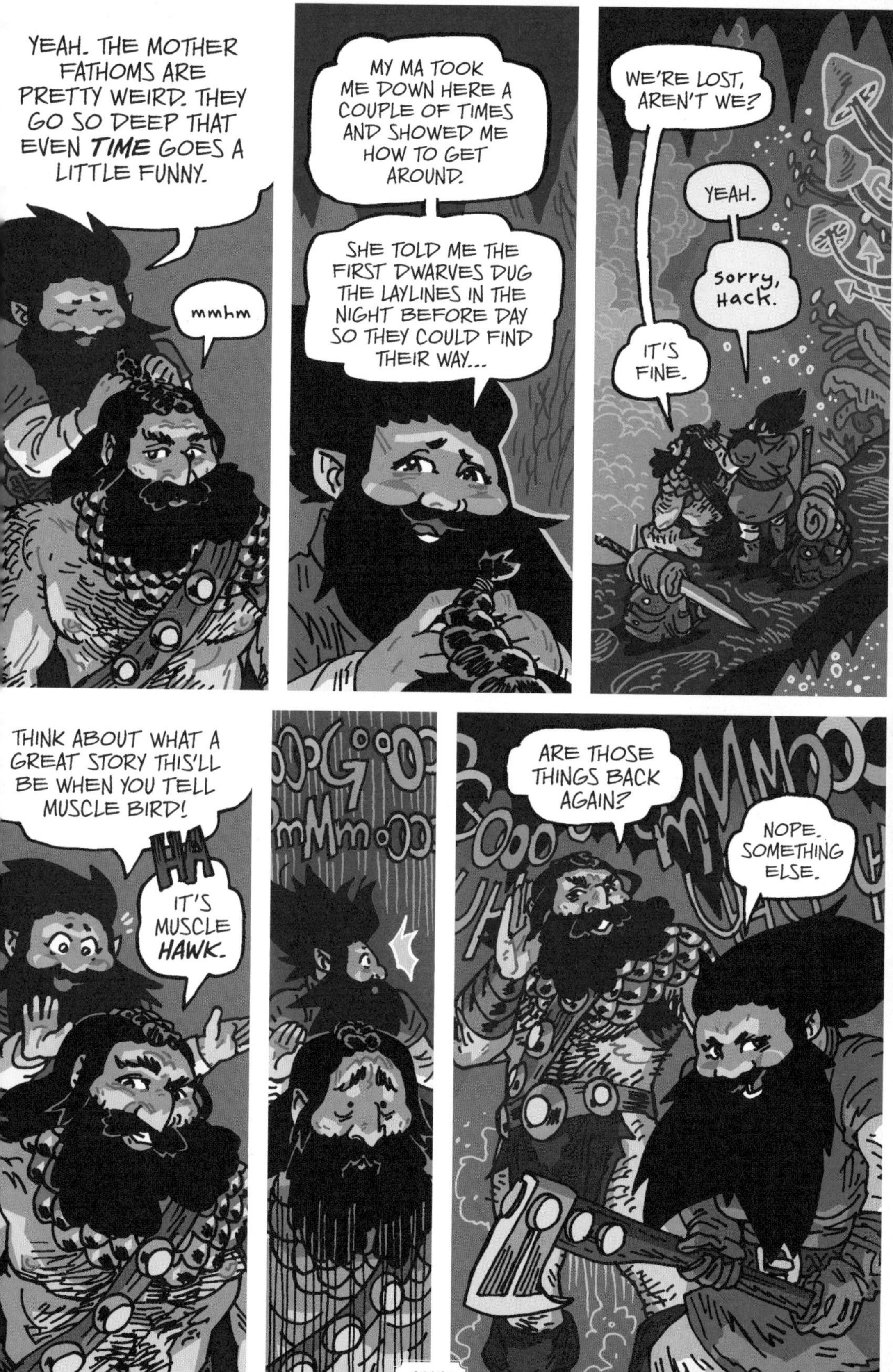

YEAH. THE MOTHER FATHOMS ARE PRETTY WEIRD. THEY GO SO DEEP THAT EVEN TIME GOES A LITTLE FUNNY.
mmhm
MY MA TOOK ME DOWN HERE A COUPLE OF TIMES AND SHOWED ME HOW TO GET AROUND.
SHE TOLD ME THE FIRST DWARVES DUG THE LAYLINES IN THE NIGHT BEFORE DAY SO THEY COULD FIND THEIR WAY...
WE'RE LOST, AREN'T WE?
YEAH.
sorry, Hack.
IT'S FINE.
THINK ABOUT WHAT A GREAT STORY THIS'LL BE WHEN YOU TELL MUSCLE BIRD!
HA
IT'S MUSCLE HAWK.
ARE THOSE THINGS BACK AGAIN?
NOPE. SOMETHING ELSE.

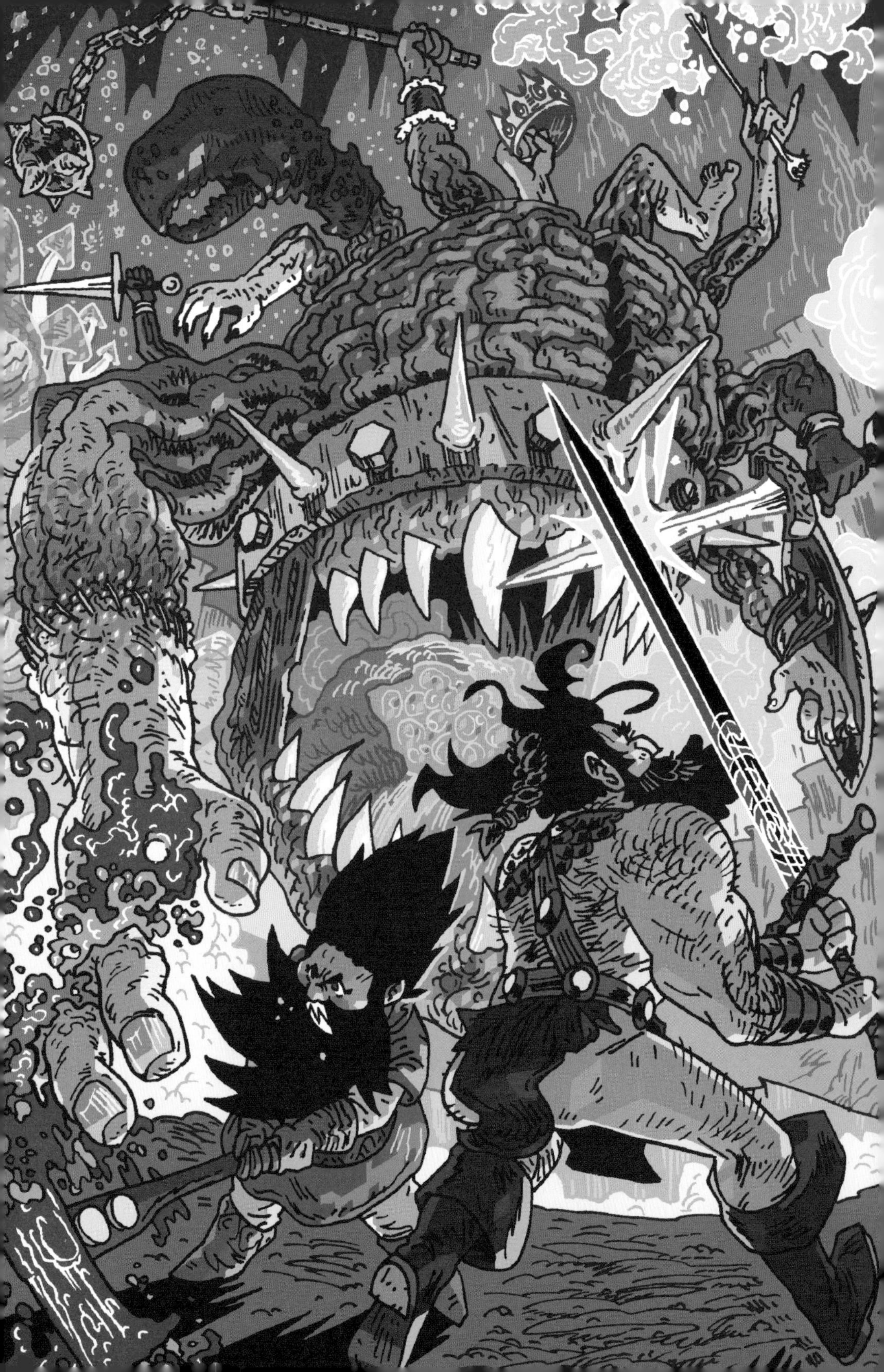

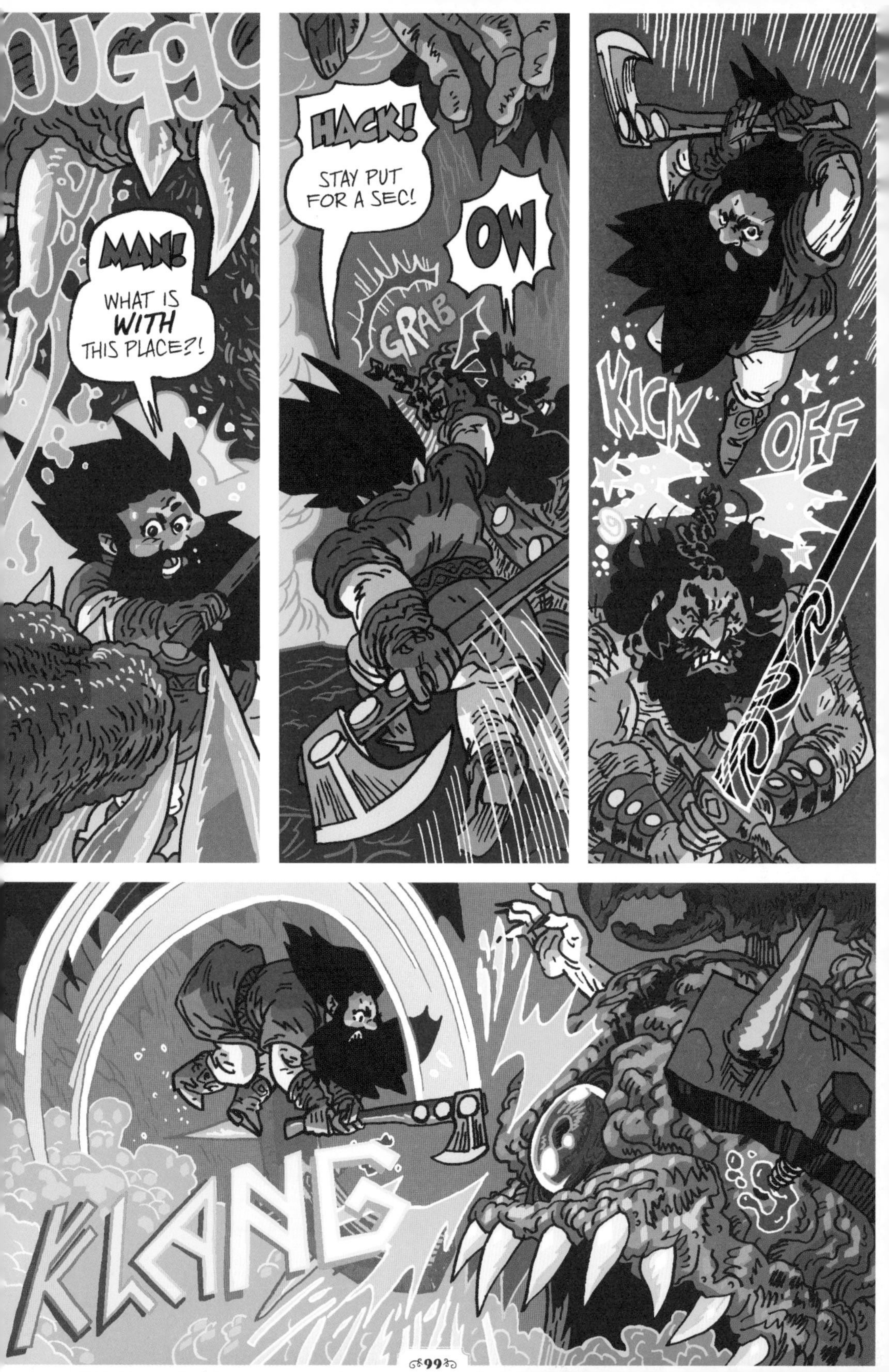
OUGGO
MAN! WHAT IS WITH THIS PLACE?!
HACK! STAY PUT FOR A SEC!
OW
GRAB
KICK OFF
KLANG

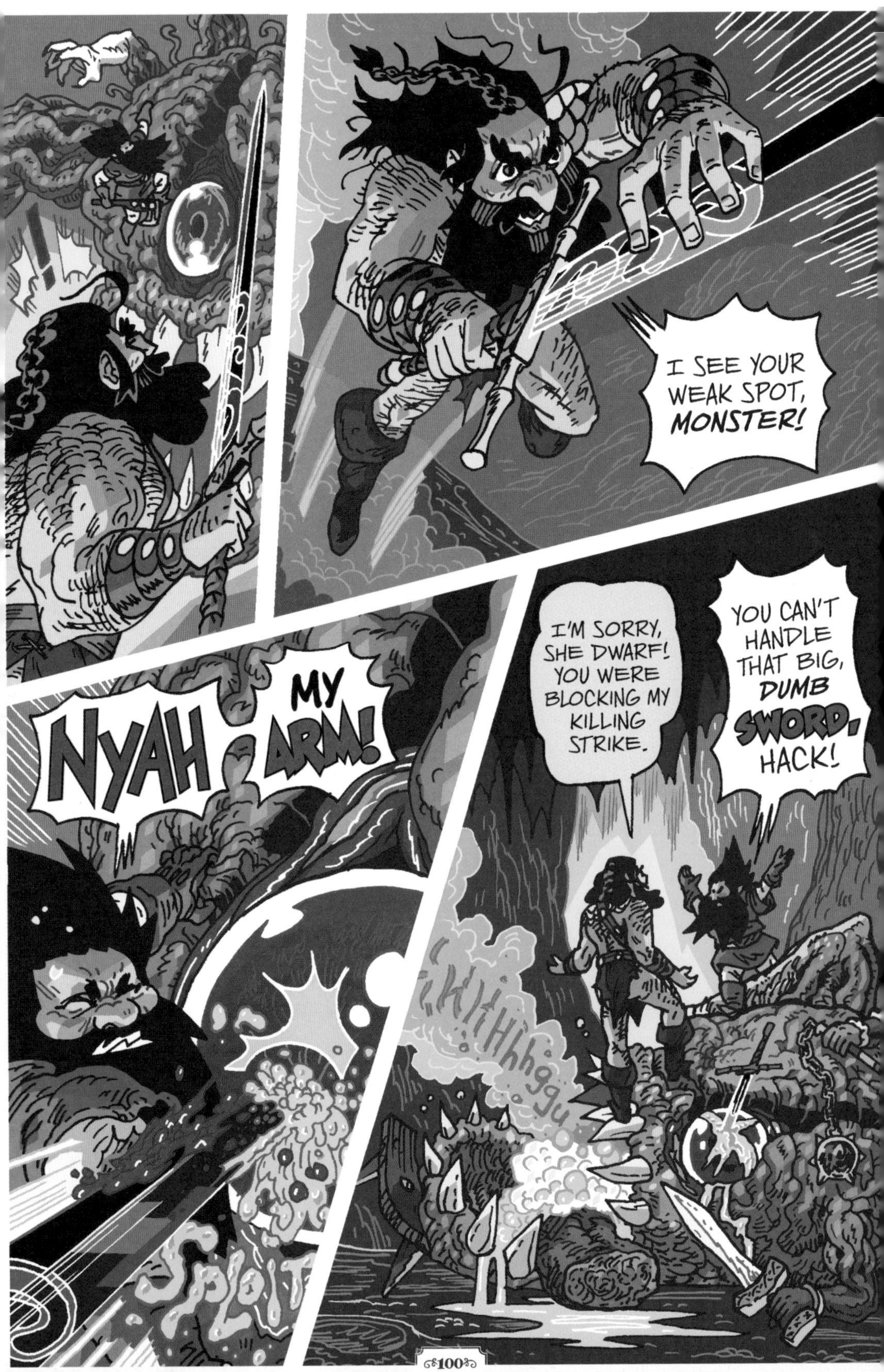
I SEE YOUR WEAK SPOT, MONSTER!
NYAH
MY ARM!
SPLOIT
I'M SORRY, SHE DWARF! YOU WERE BLOCKING MY KILLING STRIKE.
YOU CAN'T HANDLE THAT BIG, DUMB SWORD, HACK!
KKIIHhhggu

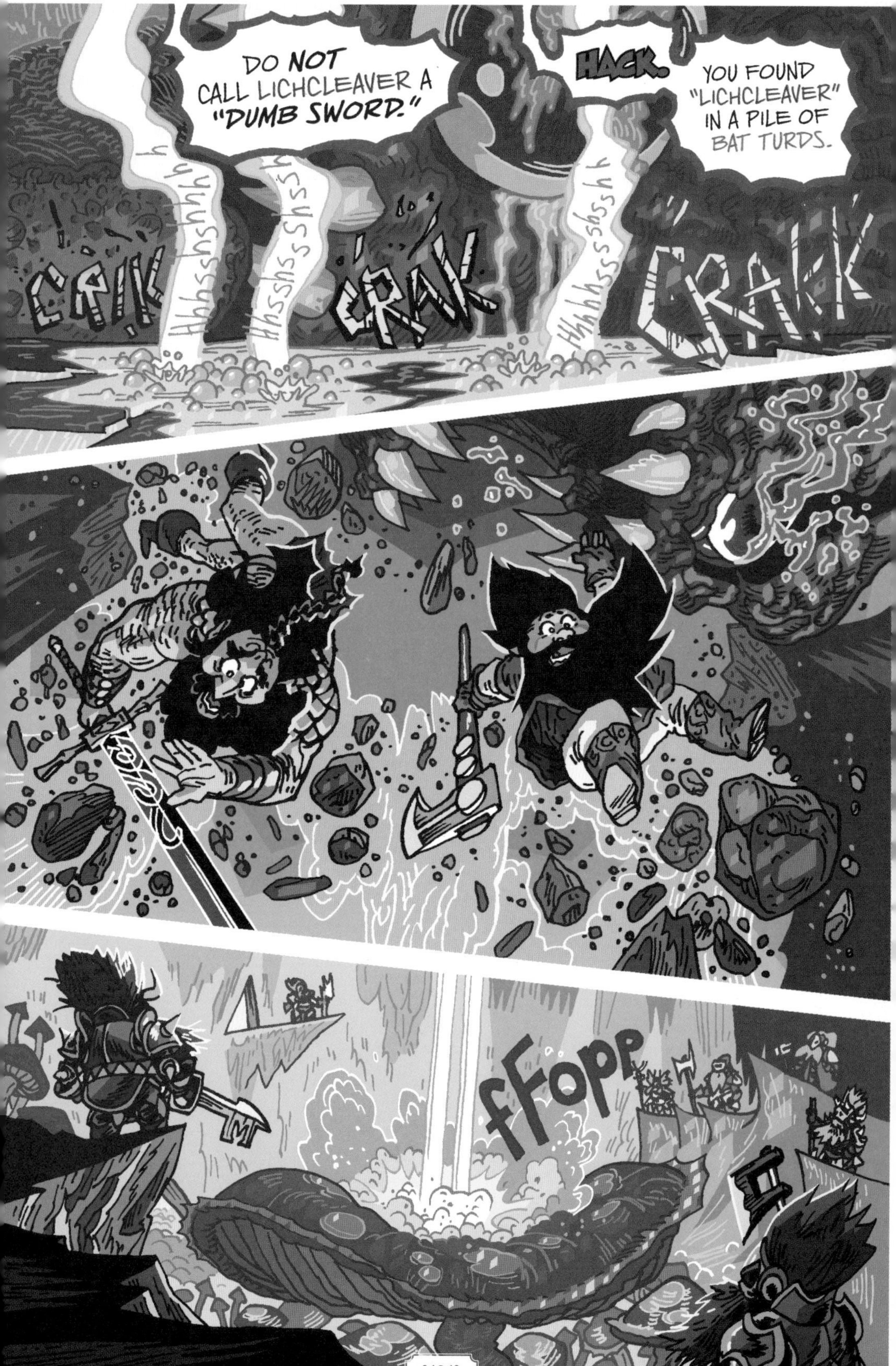
DO NOT CALL LICHCLEAVER A "DUMB SWORD."
HACK.
YOU FOUND "LICHCLEAVER" IN A PILE OF BAT TURDS.
CRIK
Hhhsshshhhh
Hhsshsssshssh
CRAK
Hhhhhssssbsshh
CRAKK
fFOPP

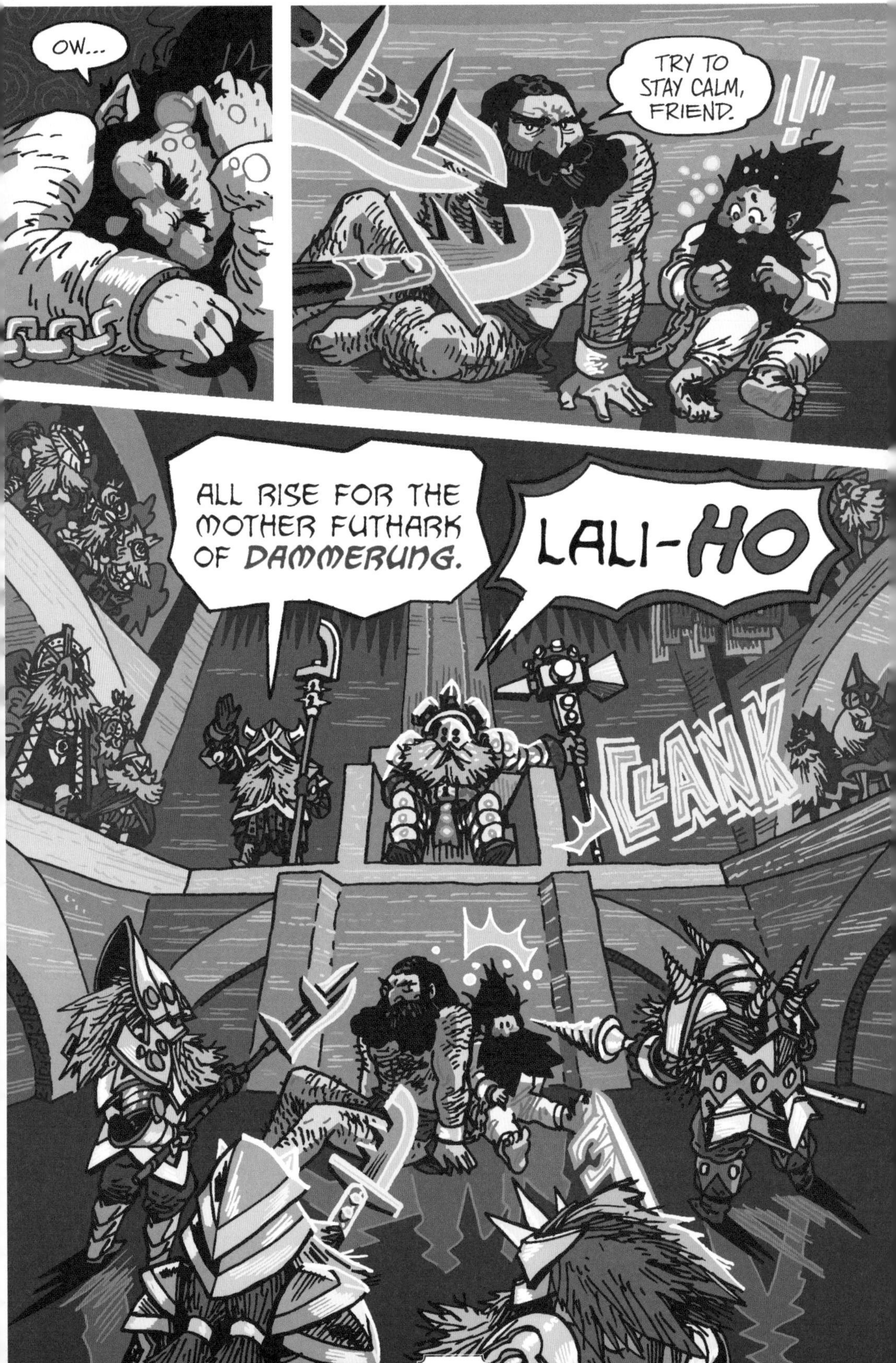
OW...
TRY TO STAY CALM, FRIEND.
!
ALL RISE FOR THE MOTHER FUTHARK OF DAMMERUNG.
LALI-HO
CLANK

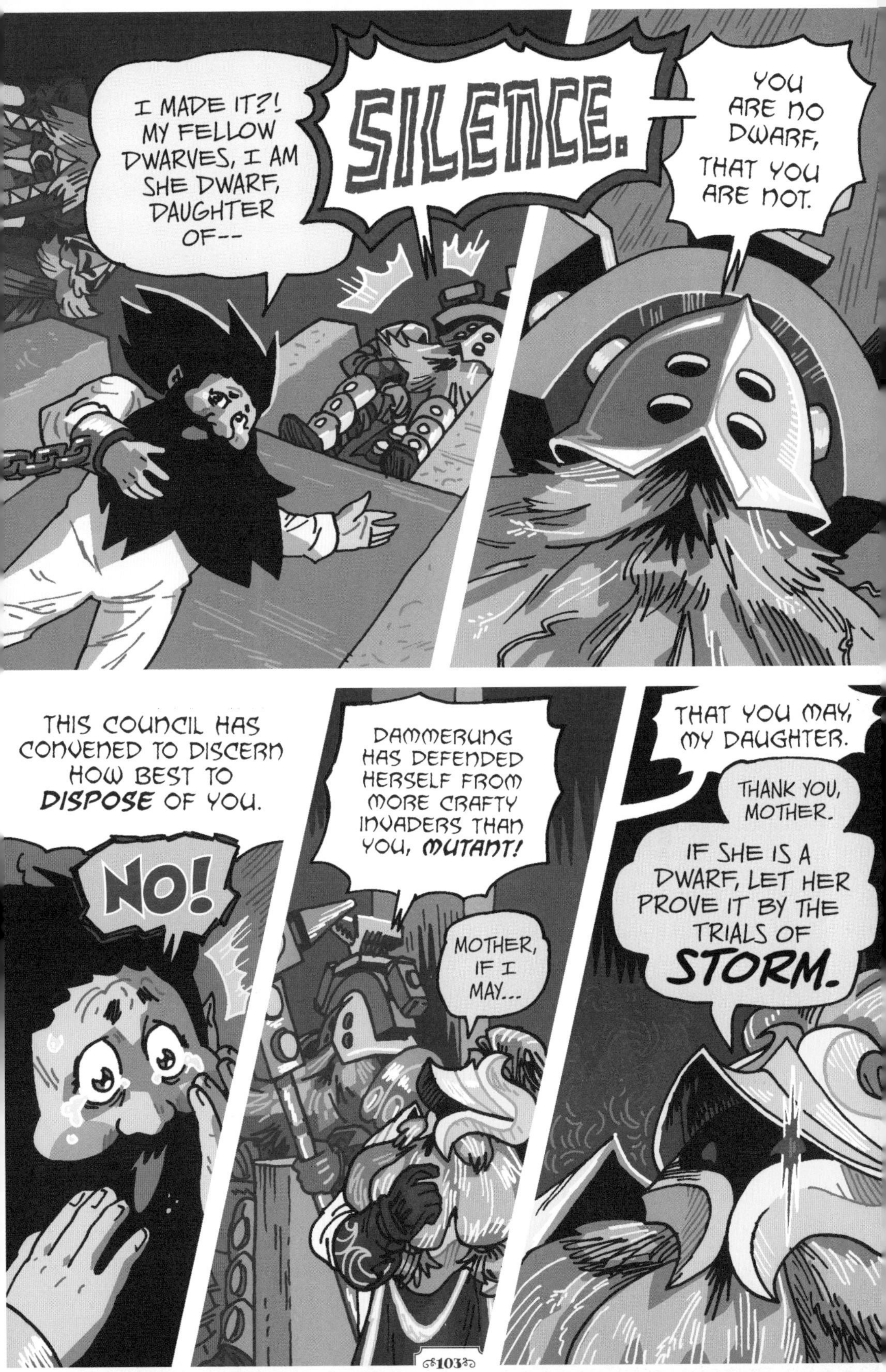
I MADE IT?! MY FELLOW DWARVES, I AM SHE DWARF, DAUGHTER OF--
SILENCE.
YOU ARE NO DWARF, THAT YOU ARE NOT.
THIS COUNCIL HAS CONVENED TO DISCERN HOW BEST TO DISPOSE OF YOU.
NO!
DAMMERUNG HAS DEFENDED HERSELF FROM MORE CRAFTY INVADERS THAN YOU, MUTANT!
MOTHER, IF I MAY...
THAT YOU MAY, MY DAUGHTER.
THANK YOU, MOTHER.
IF SHE IS A DWARF, LET HER PROVE IT BY THE TRIALS OF STORM.

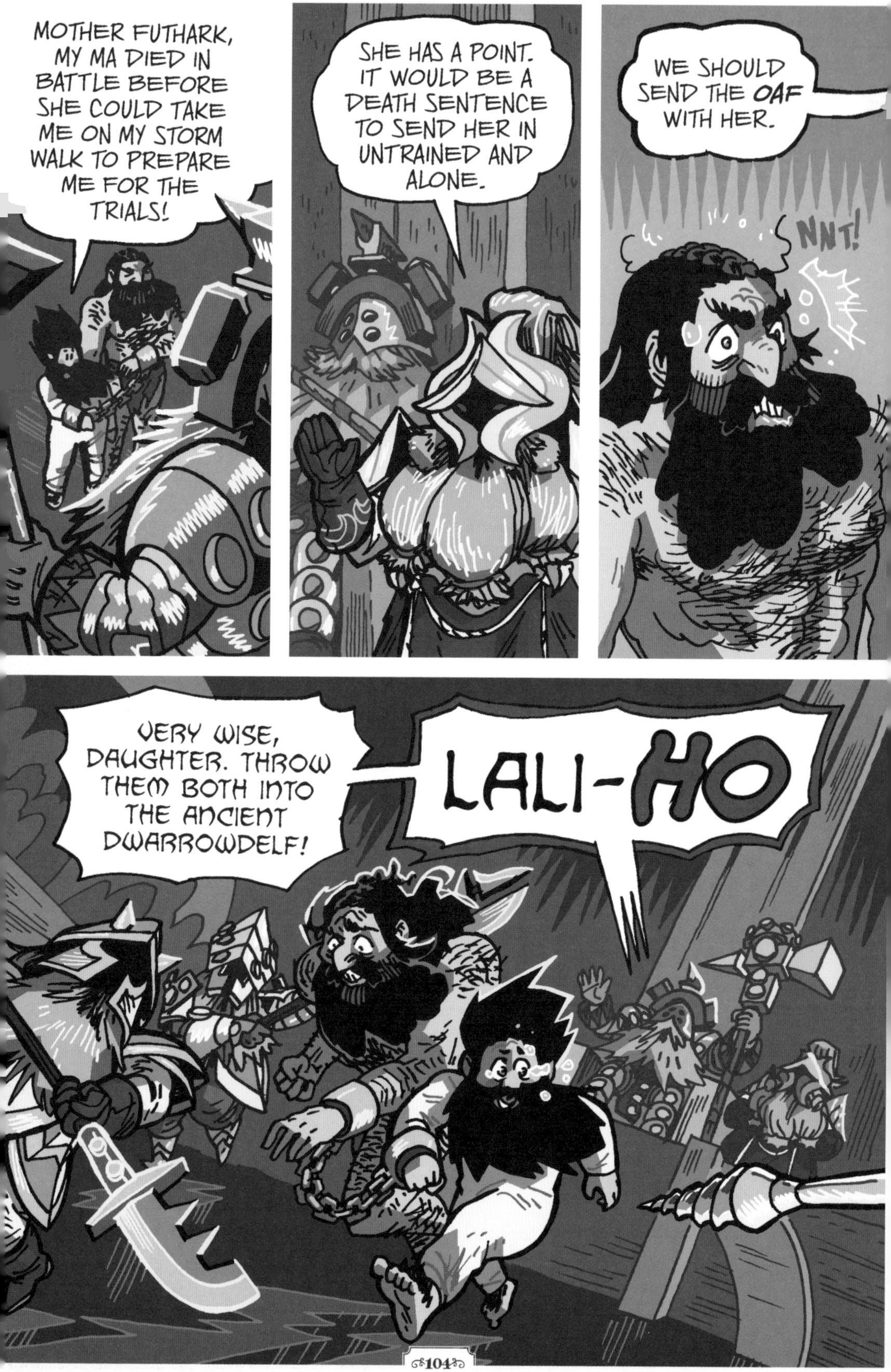
MOTHER FUTHARK, MY MA DIED IN BATTLE BEFORE SHE COULD TAKE ME ON MY STORM WALK TO PREPARE ME FOR THE TRIALS!
SHE HAS A POINT. IT WOULD BE A DEATH SENTENCE TO SEND HER IN UNTRAINED AND ALONE.
WE SHOULD SEND THE OAF WITH HER.
NNT!
VERY WISE, DAUGHTER. THROW THEM BOTH INTO THE ANCIENT DWARROWDELF!
LALI-HO

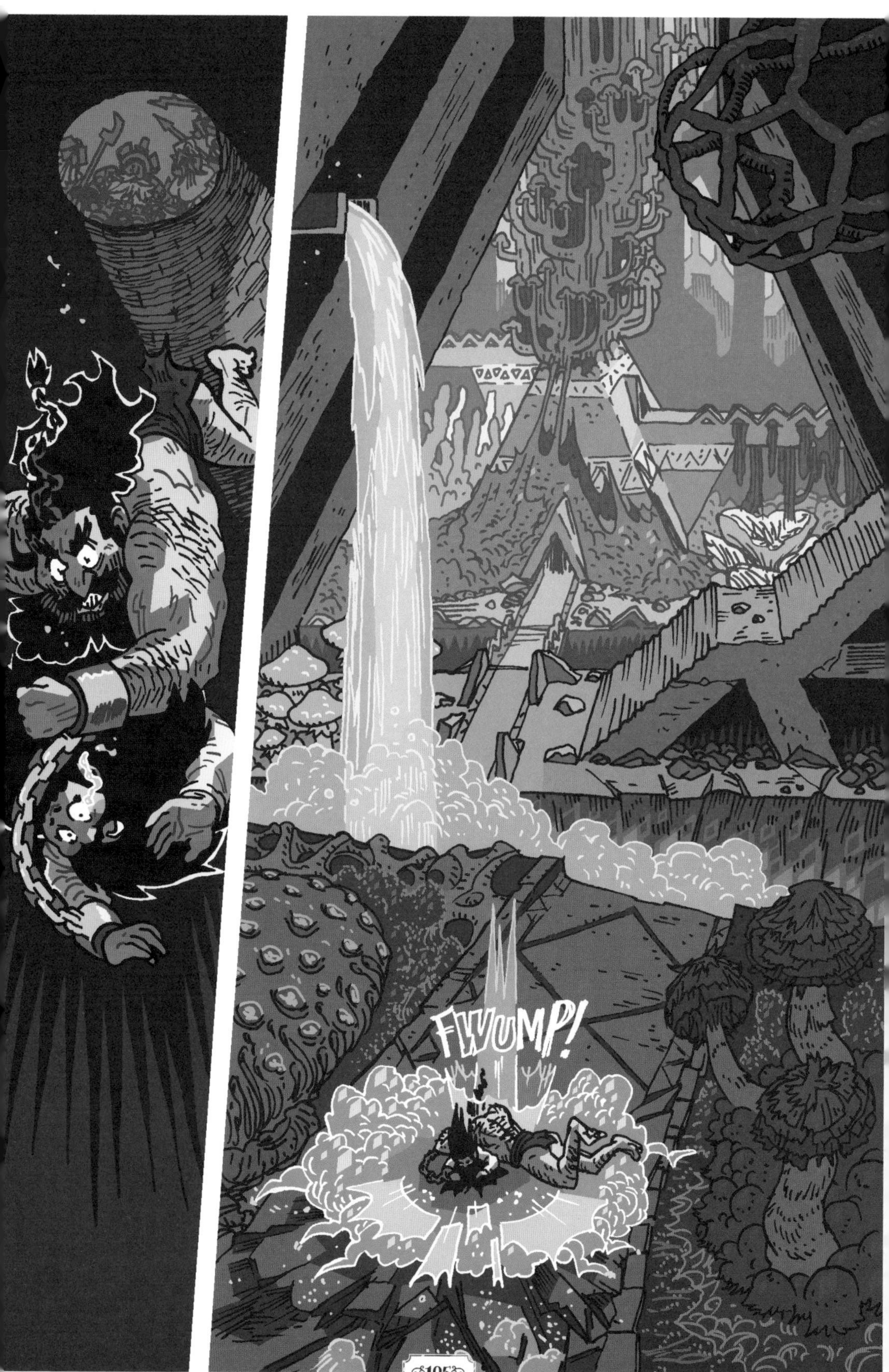
FWUMP!

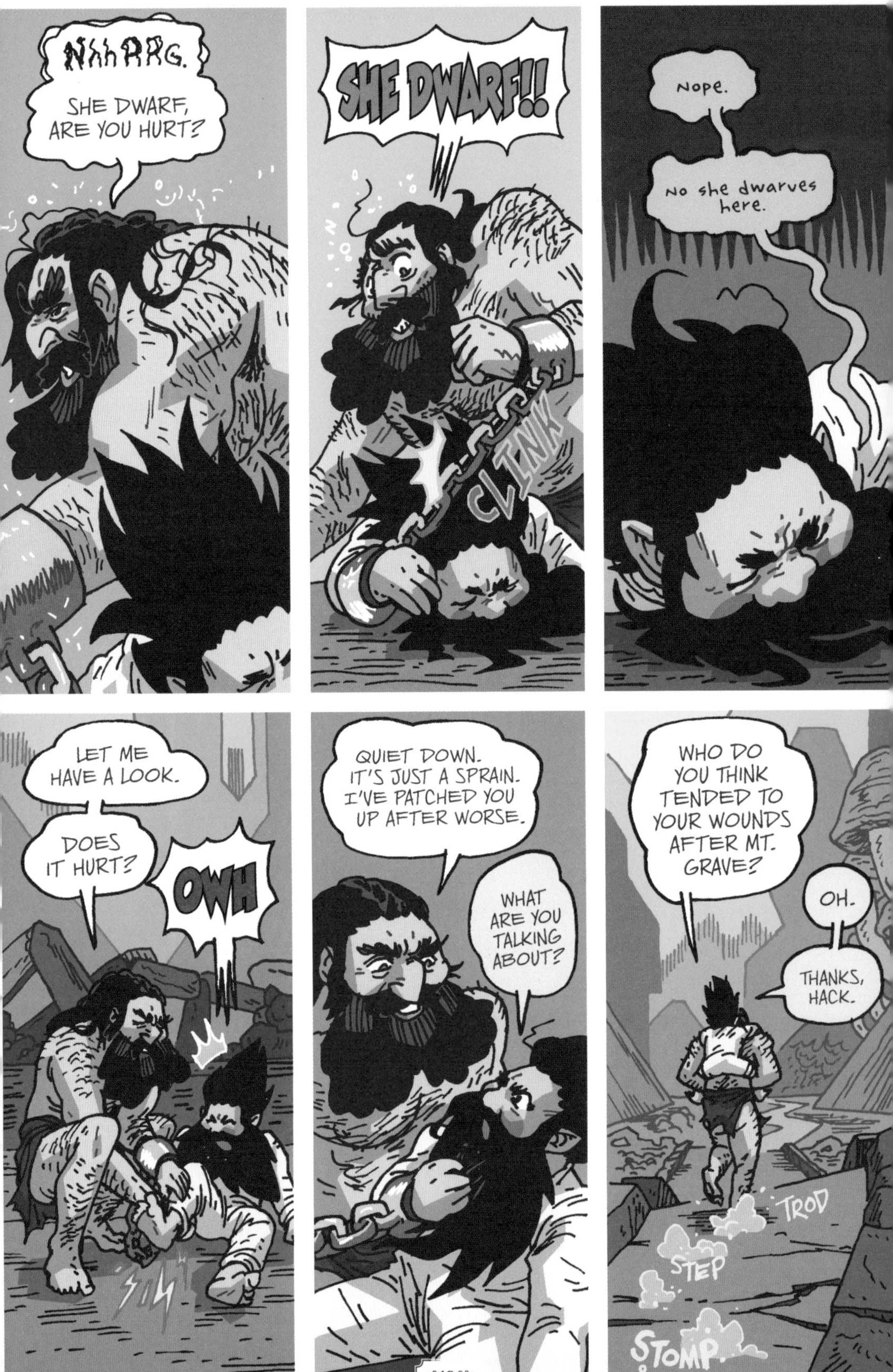
NAHARRG.
SHE DWARF, ARE YOU HURT?
SHE DWARF!!
CLINK
Nope.
No she dwarves here.
LET ME HAVE A LOOK.
DOES IT HURT?
OWH
QUIET DOWN. IT'S JUST A SPRAIN. I'VE PATCHED YOU UP AFTER WORSE.
WHAT ARE YOU TALKING ABOUT?
WHO DO YOU THINK TENDED TO YOUR WOUNDS AFTER MT. GRAVE?
OH.
THANKS, HACK.
TROD
STEP
STOMP

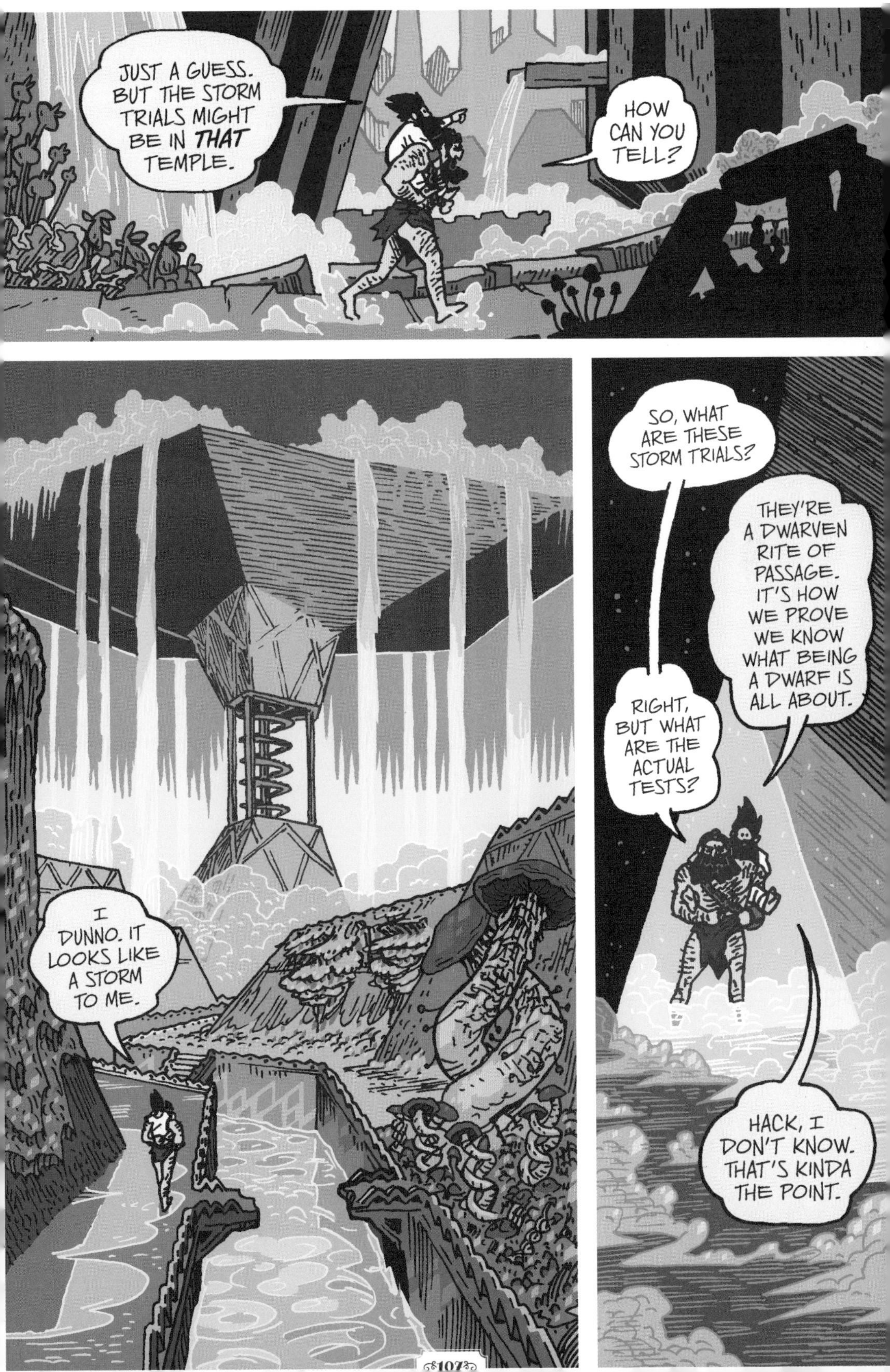
JUST A GUESS. BUT THE STORM TRIALS MIGHT BE IN **THAT** TEMPLE.
HOW CAN YOU TELL?
I DUNNO. IT LOOKS LIKE A STORM TO ME.
SO, WHAT ARE THESE STORM TRIALS?
THEY'RE A DWARVEN RITE OF PASSAGE. IT'S HOW WE PROVE WE KNOW WHAT BEING A DWARF IS ALL ABOUT.
RIGHT, BUT WHAT ARE THE ACTUAL TESTS?
HACK, I DON'T KNOW. THAT'S KINDA THE POINT.

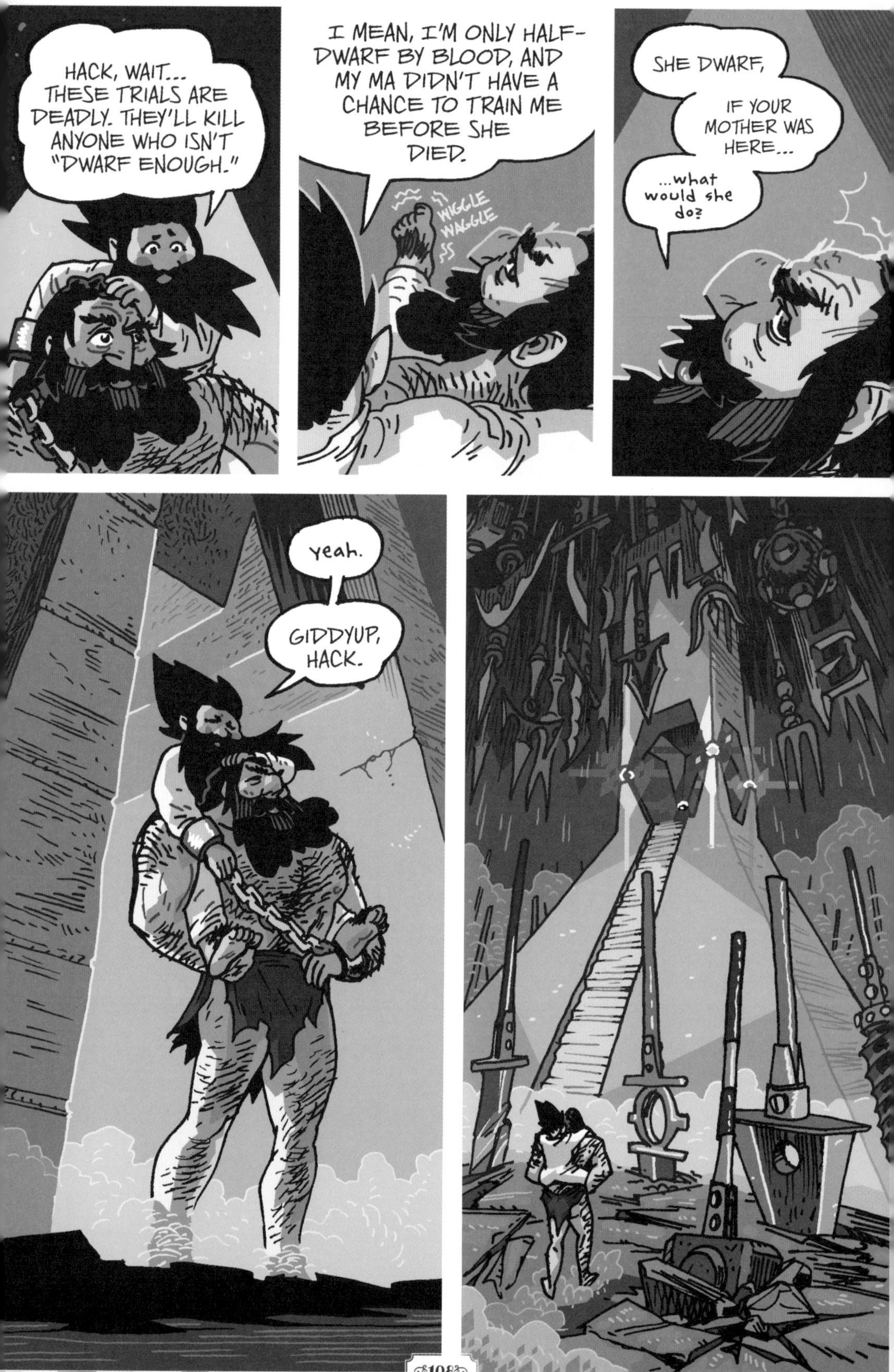
HACK, WAIT... THESE TRIALS ARE DEADLY. THEY'LL KILL ANYONE WHO ISN'T "DWARF ENOUGH."
I MEAN, I'M ONLY HALF-DWARF BY BLOOD, AND MY MA DIDN'T HAVE A CHANCE TO TRAIN ME BEFORE SHE DIED.
WIGGLE WAGGLE
SHE DWARF,
IF YOUR MOTHER WAS HERE...
...what would she do?
yeah.
GIDDYUP, HACK.

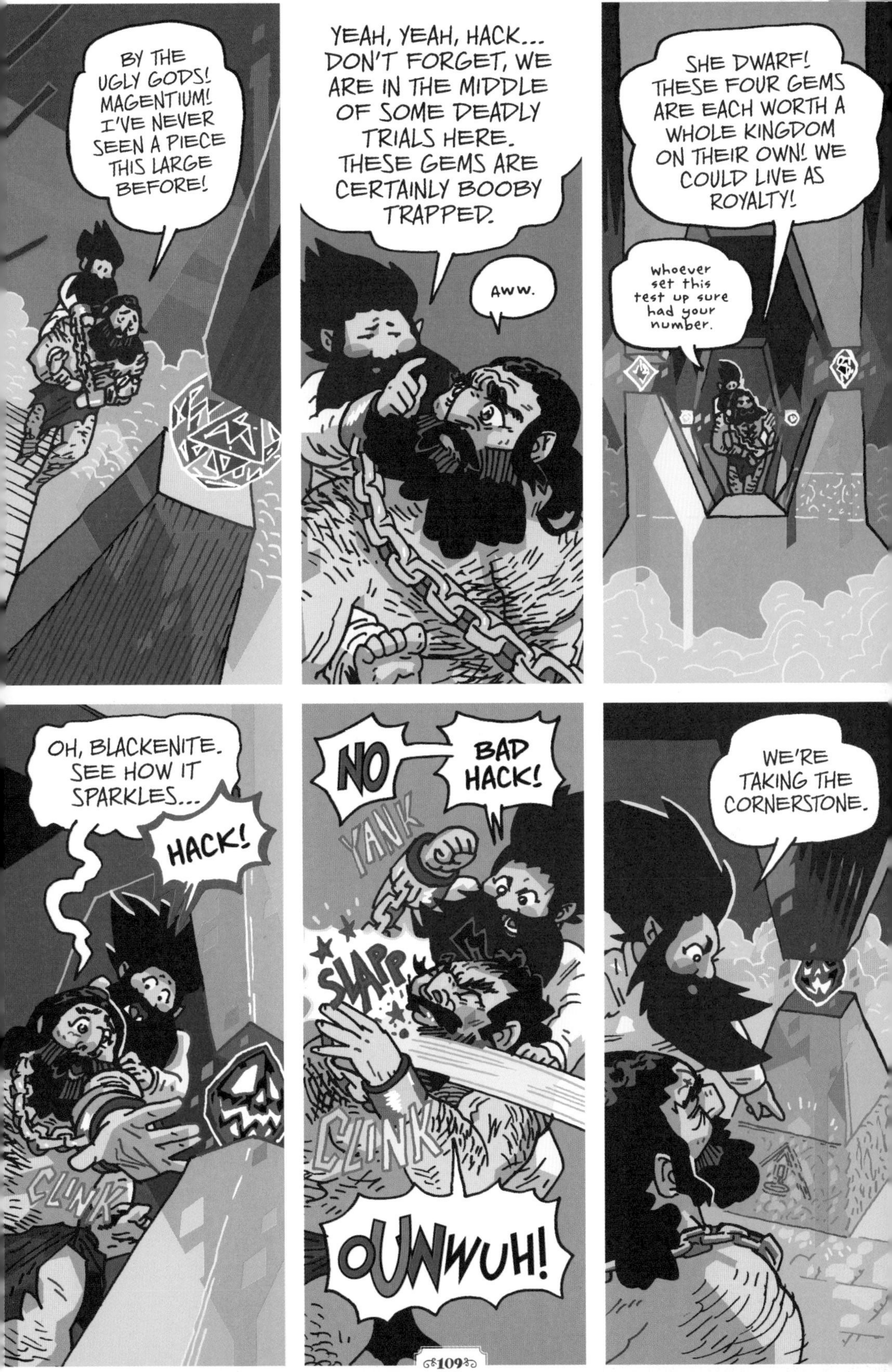
BY THE UGLY GODS! MAGENTIUM! I'VE NEVER SEEN A PIECE THIS LARGE BEFORE!
YEAH, YEAH, HACK... DON'T FORGET, WE ARE IN THE MIDDLE OF SOME DEADLY TRIALS HERE. THESE GEMS ARE CERTAINLY BOOBY TRAPPED.
AWW.
SHE DWARF! THESE FOUR GEMS ARE EACH WORTH A WHOLE KINGDOM ON THEIR OWN! WE COULD LIVE AS ROYALTY!
Whoever set this test up sure had your number.
OH, BLACKENITE. SEE HOW IT SPARKLES...
HACK!
CLINK
NO
BAD HACK!
YANK
SLAPP
CLINK
OUNWUH!
WE'RE TAKING THE CORNERSTONE.

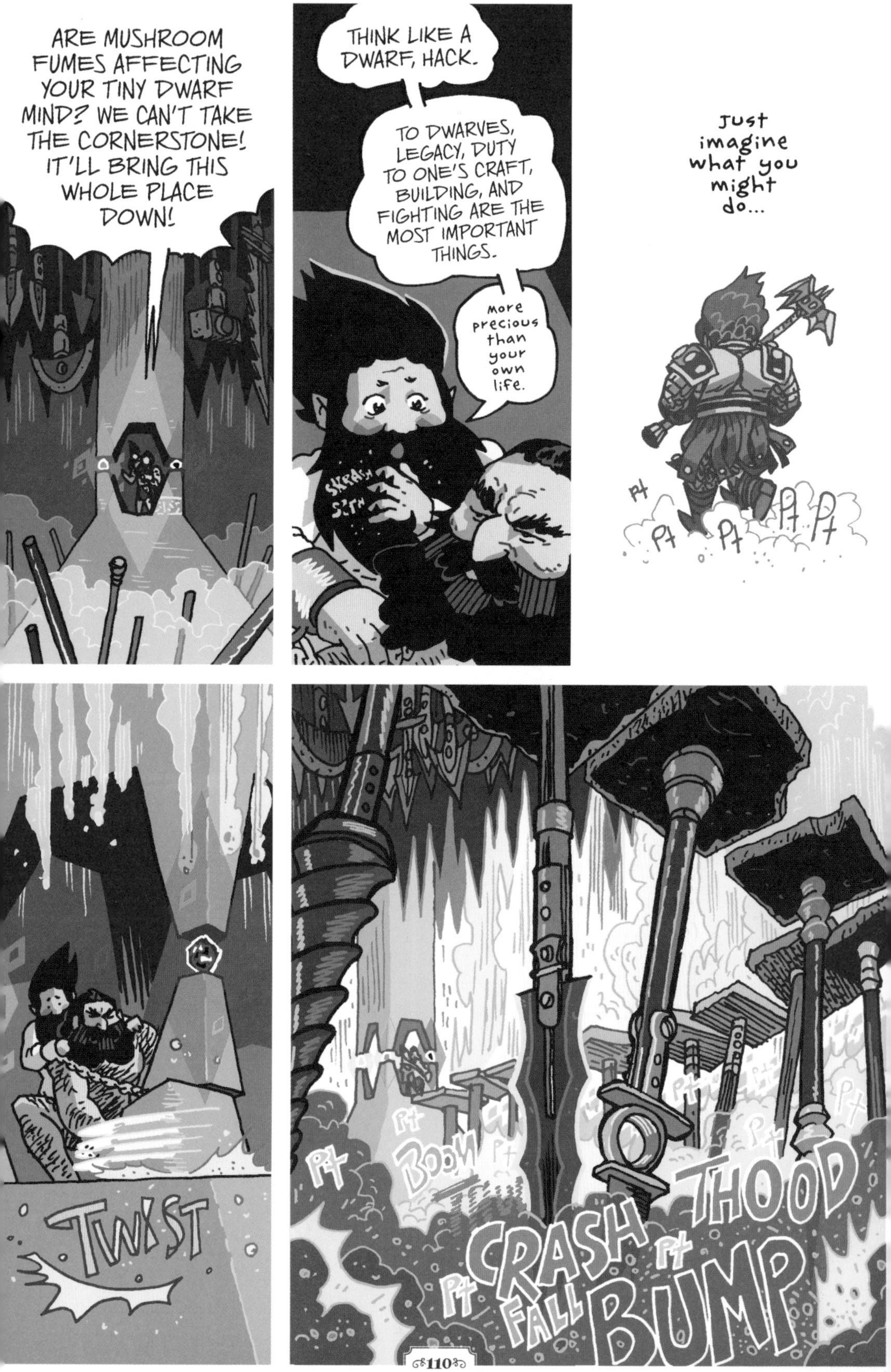
ARE MUSHROOM FUMES AFFECTING YOUR TINY DWARF MIND? WE CAN'T TAKE THE CORNERSTONE! IT'LL BRING THIS WHOLE PLACE DOWN!
THINK LIKE A DWARF, HACK.
TO DWARVES, LEGACY, DUTY TO ONE'S CRAFT, BUILDING, AND FIGHTING ARE THE MOST IMPORTANT THINGS.
more precious than your own life.
SKRASH
SCTH
Just imagine what you might do...
Pt
Pt
Pt
Pt
Pt
TWIST
Pt
BOOM
CRASH
Pt
FALL
THOOD
BUMP

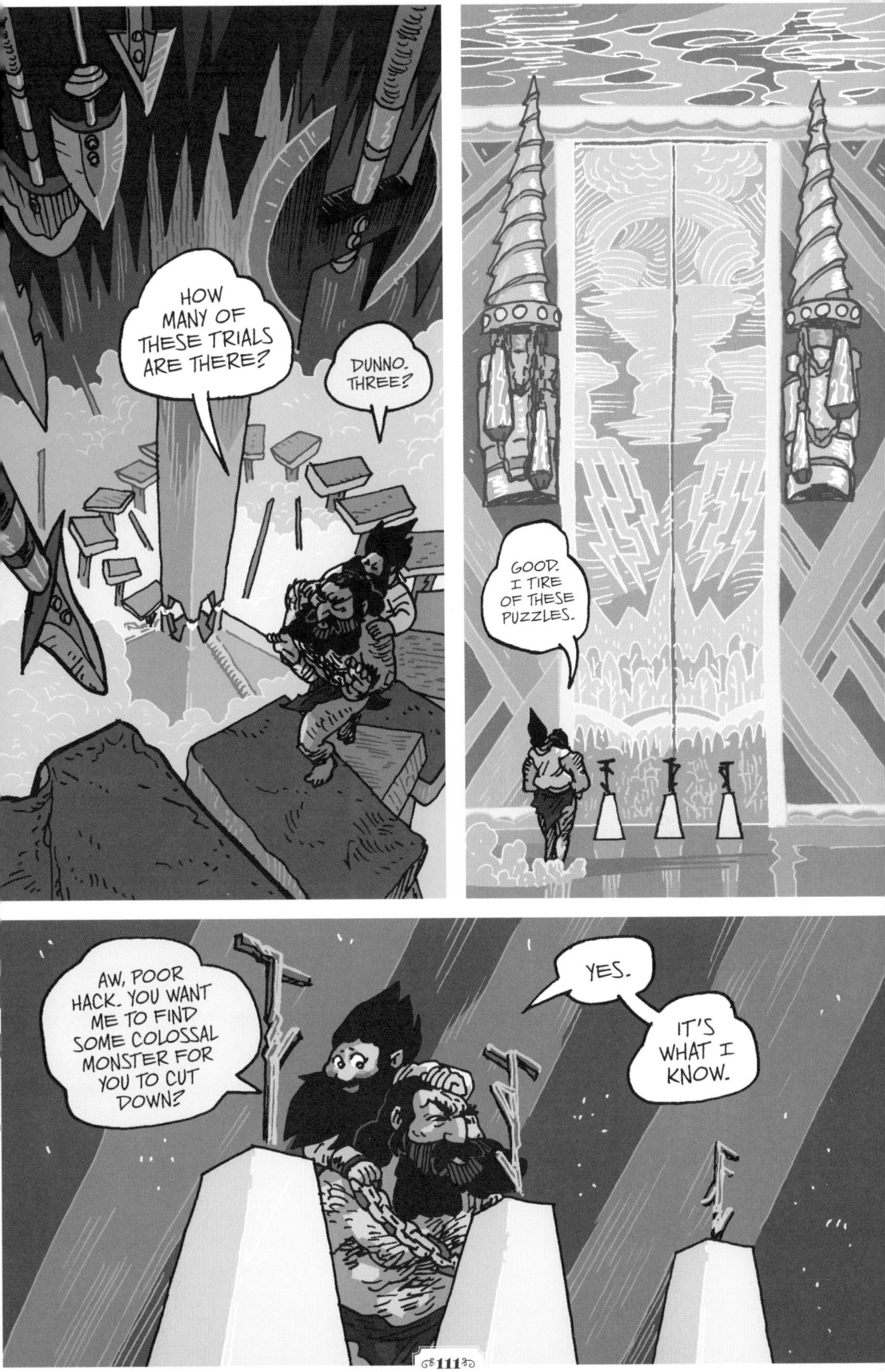
HOW MANY OF THESE TRIALS ARE THERE?
DUNNO. THREE?
GOOD. I TIRE OF THESE PUZZLES.
AW, POOR HACK. YOU WANT ME TO FIND SOME COLOSSAL MONSTER FOR YOU TO CUT DOWN?
YES.
IT'S WHAT I KNOW.

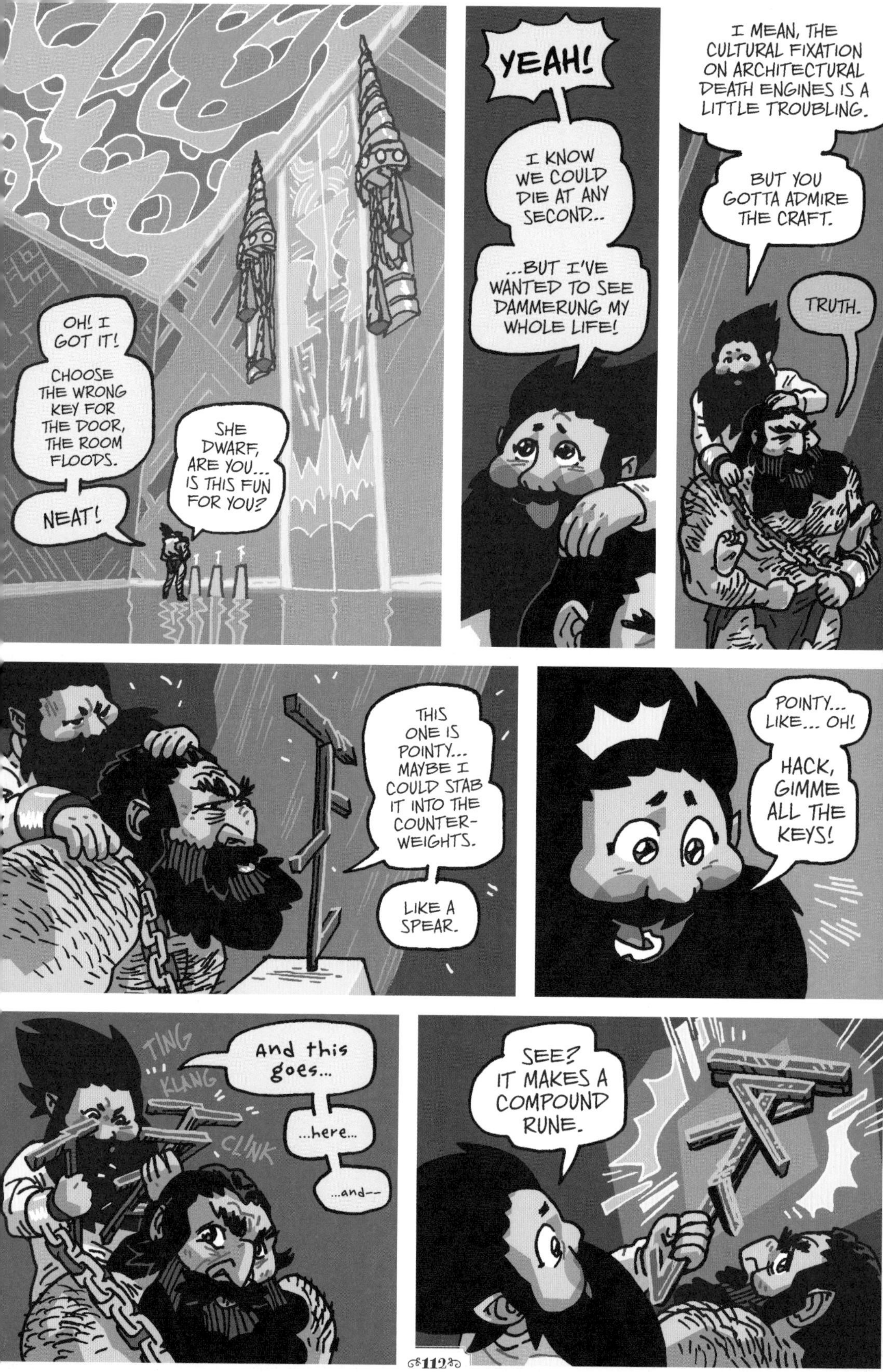
OH! I GOT IT!
CHOOSE THE WRONG KEY FOR THE DOOR, THE ROOM FLOODS.
NEAT!
SHE DWARF, ARE YOU... IS THIS FUN FOR YOU?
YEAH!
I KNOW WE COULD DIE AT ANY SECOND...
...BUT I'VE WANTED TO SEE DAMMERUNG MY WHOLE LIFE!
I MEAN, THE CULTURAL FIXATION ON ARCHITECTURAL DEATH ENGINES IS A LITTLE TROUBLING.
BUT YOU GOTTA ADMIRE THE CRAFT.
TRUTH.
THIS ONE IS POINTY... MAYBE I COULD STAB IT INTO THE COUNTER-WEIGHTS.
LIKE A SPEAR.
POINTY... LIKE... OH!
HACK, GIMME ALL THE KEYS!
TING
KLANG
CLINK
And this goes...
...here...
...and--
SEE? IT MAKES A COMPOUND RUNE.

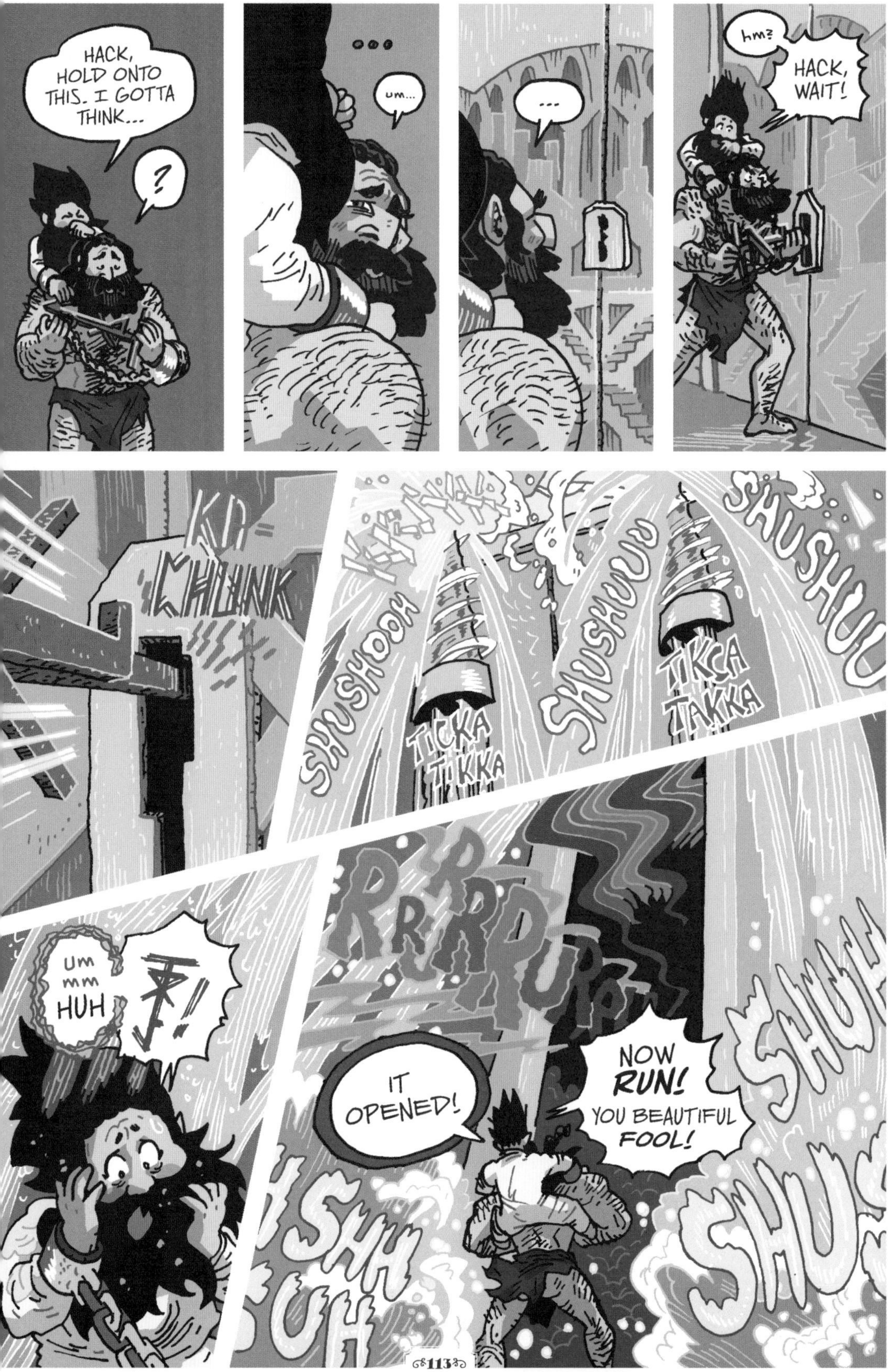
HACK, HOLD ONTO THIS. I GOTTA THINK...
?
...
um...
...
hm?
HACK, WAIT!
KA CHUNK
SHUSHOOOH
TICKA TIKKA
SHUSHUUU
TIKCA TAKKA
SHUSHUU
RRRRRRURR
Um mm HUH
IT OPENED!
NOW RUN! YOU BEAUTIFUL FOOL!
SHUSH
SHUSH

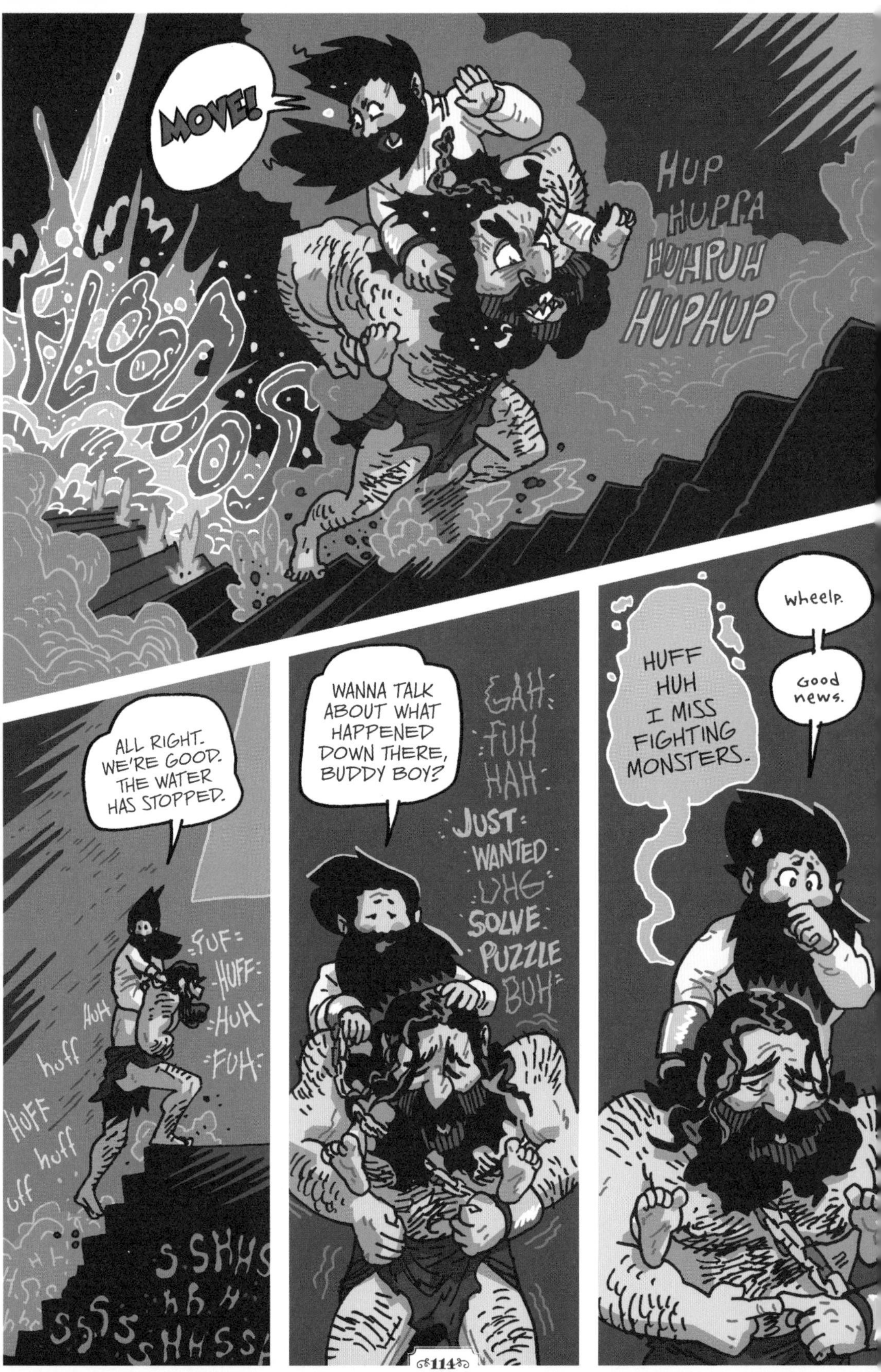
MOVE!
FLOOOOSH
HUP
HUPPA
HUHPUH
HUPHUP
ALL RIGHT. WE'RE GOOD. THE WATER HAS STOPPED.
FUF
HUFF
HUH
FUH
HUH
huff
HUFF
huff
uff
SSHHS
hh h
SSSSHHSSA
WANNA TALK ABOUT WHAT HAPPENED DOWN THERE, BUDDY BOY?
GAH
FUH
HAH
JUST
WANTED
UHG
SOLVE
PUZZLE
BUH
HUFF HUH I MISS FIGHTING MONSTERS.
wheelp.
Good news.

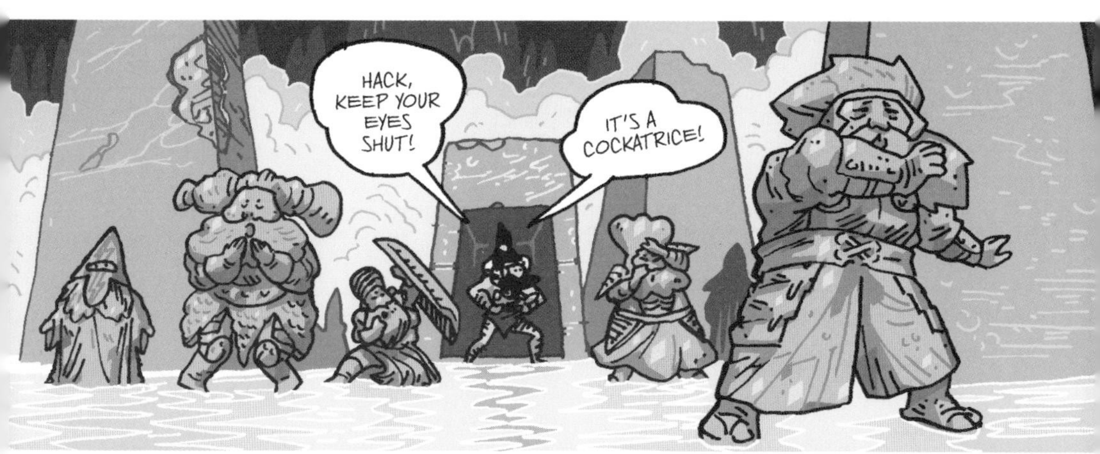
HACK, KEEP YOUR EYES SHUT!
IT'S A COCKATRICE!

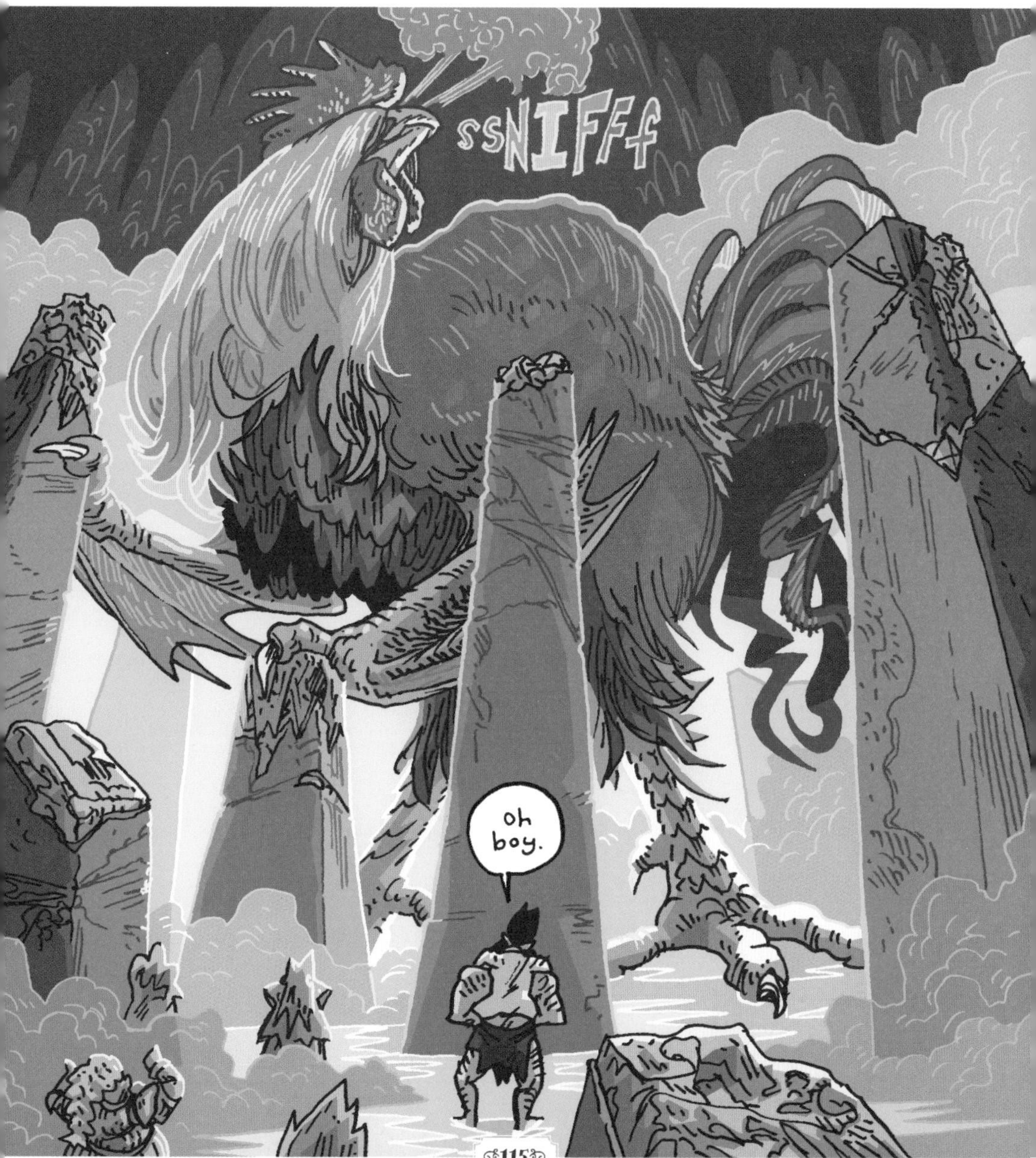
ssNIFFf
oh boy.

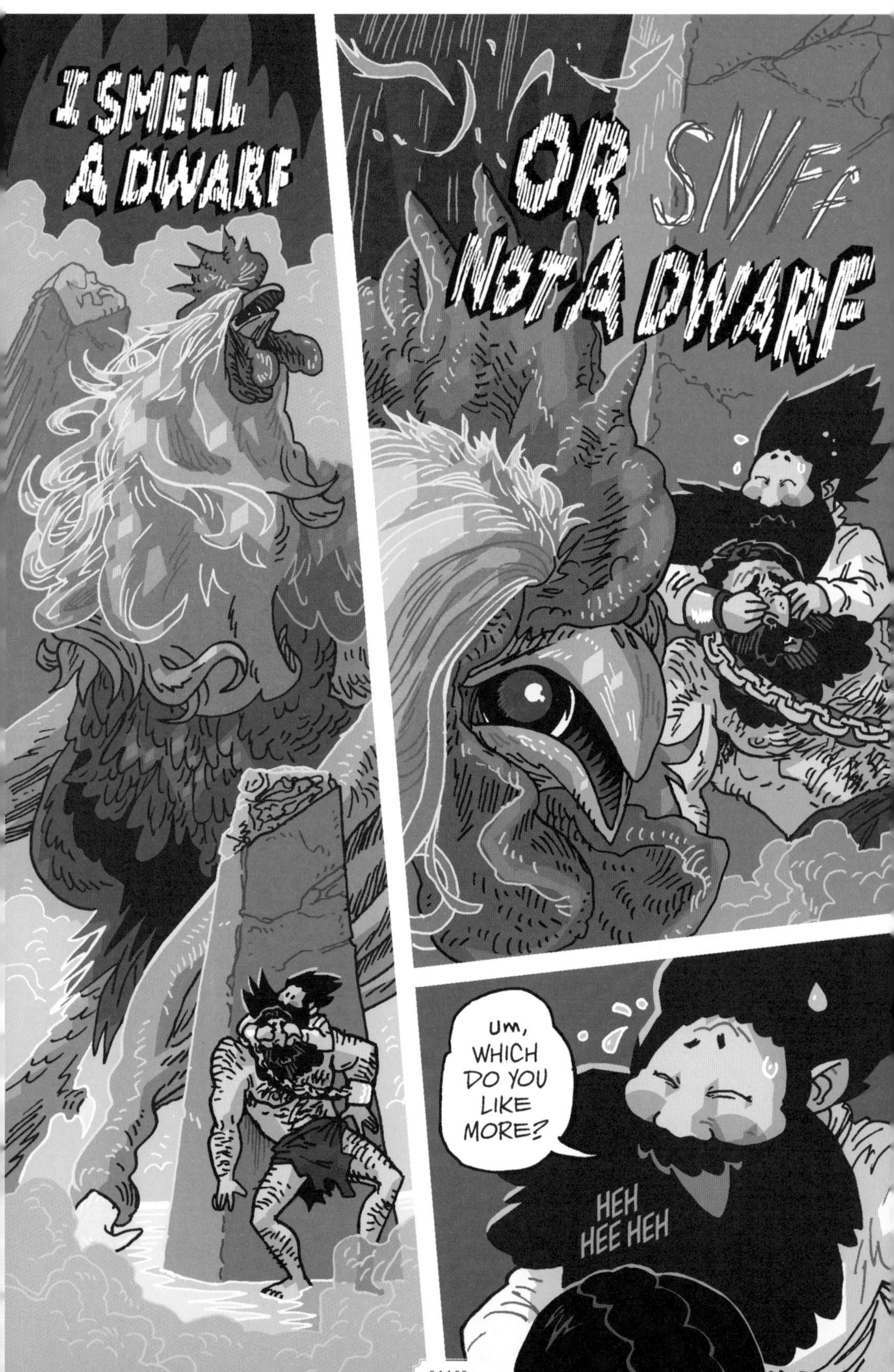
I SMELL A DWARF
OR SNFF
NOT A DWARF
UM, WHICH DO YOU LIKE MORE?
HEH HEE HEH

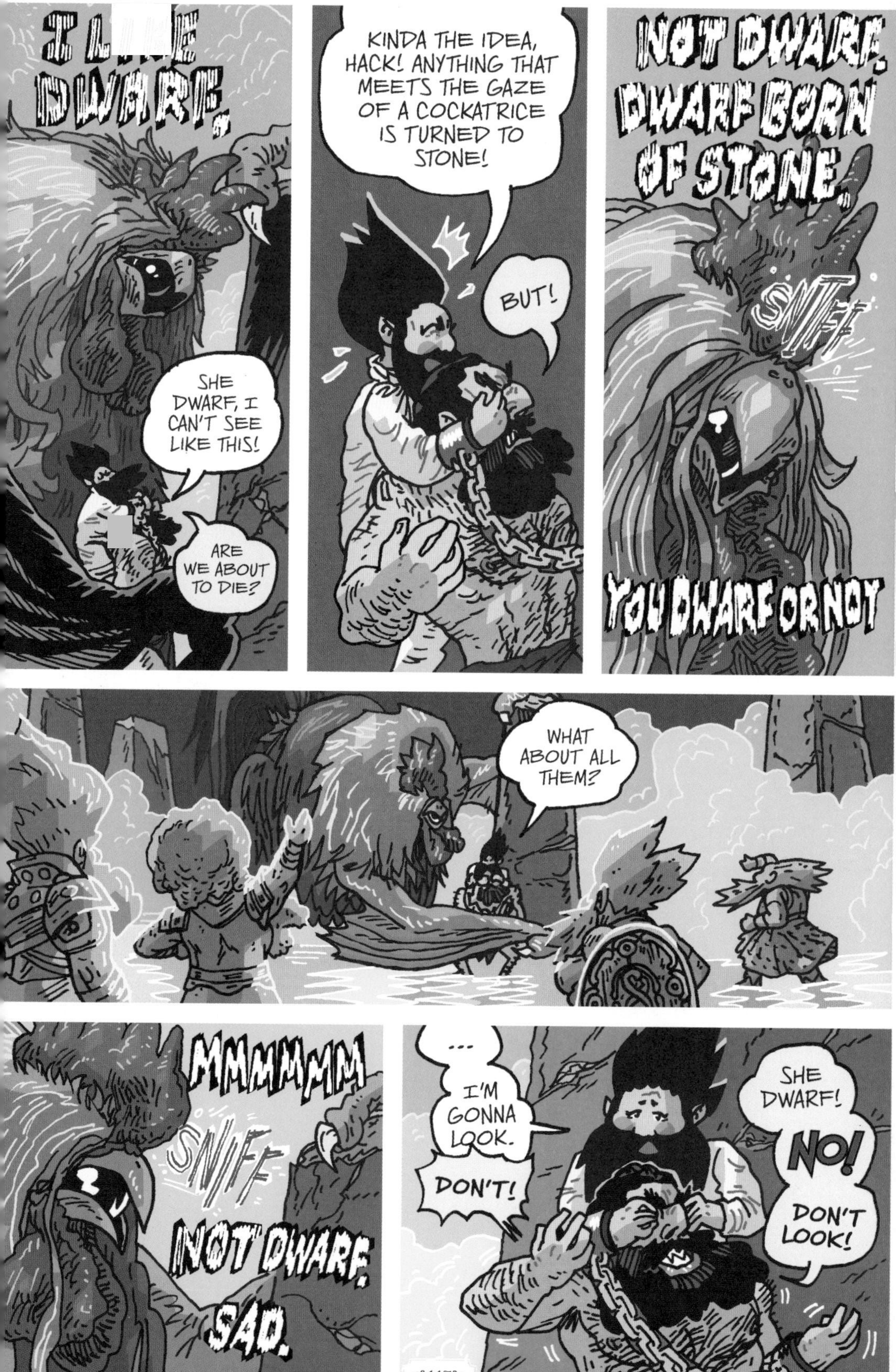
I LI E DWARF.
SHE DWARF, I CAN'T SEE LIKE THIS!
ARE WE ABOUT TO DIE?
KINDA THE IDEA, HACK! ANYTHING THAT MEETS THE GAZE OF A COCKATRICE IS TURNED TO STONE!
BUT!
NOT DWARF. DWARF BORN OF STONE.
SNIFF
YOU DWARF OR NOT
WHAT ABOUT ALL THEM?
MMMMMM
SNIFF
NOT DWARF. SAD.
...
I'M GONNA LOOK.
DON'T!
SHE DWARF!
NO!
DON'T LOOK!

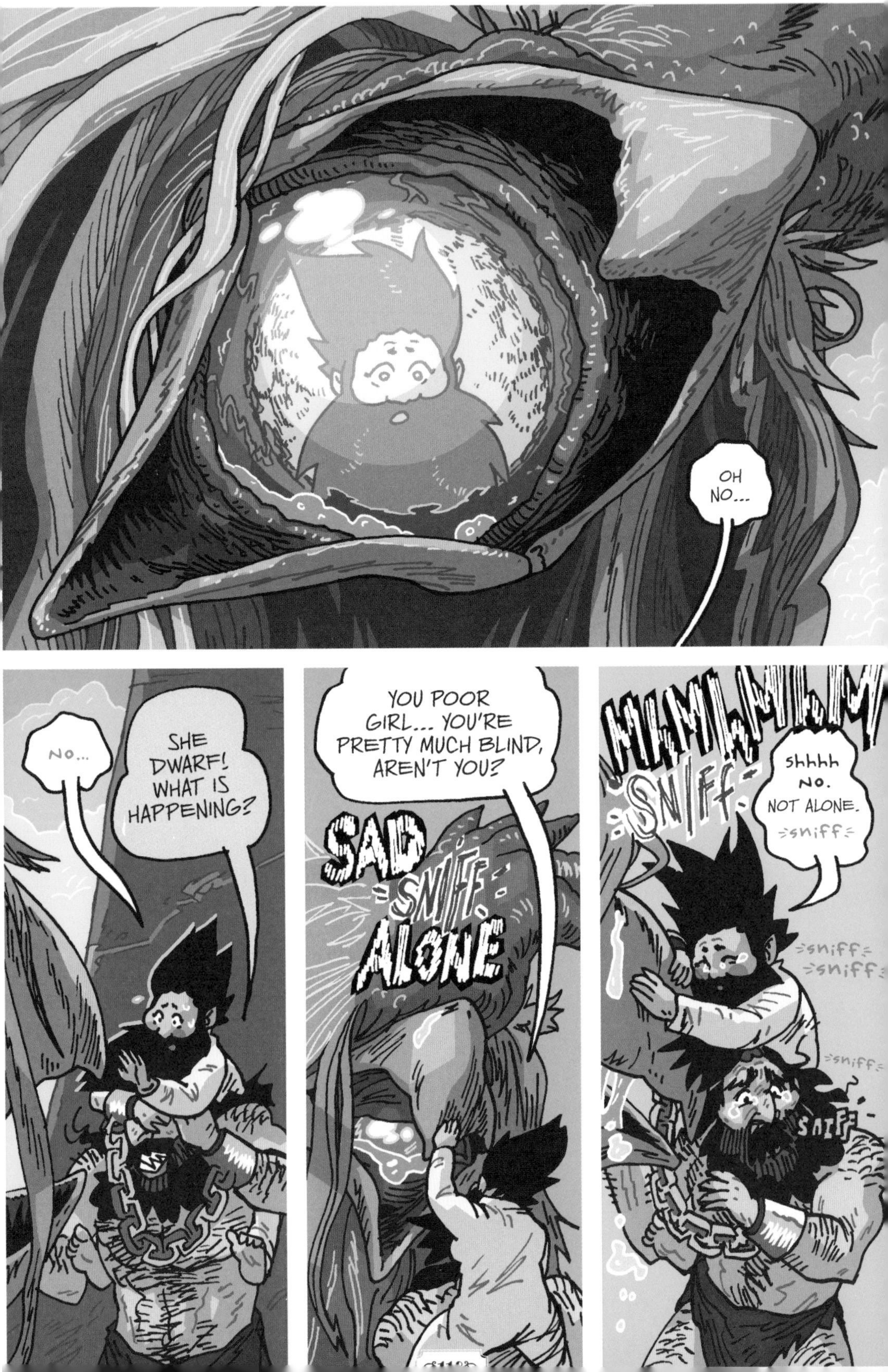
OH NO...
NO...
SHE DWARF! WHAT IS HAPPENING?
YOU POOR GIRL... YOU'RE PRETTY MUCH BLIND, AREN'T YOU?
SAD
SNIFF
ALONE
SNIFF
shhhh NO. NOT ALONE.
sniff
sniff
sniff
sniff
SNIFF

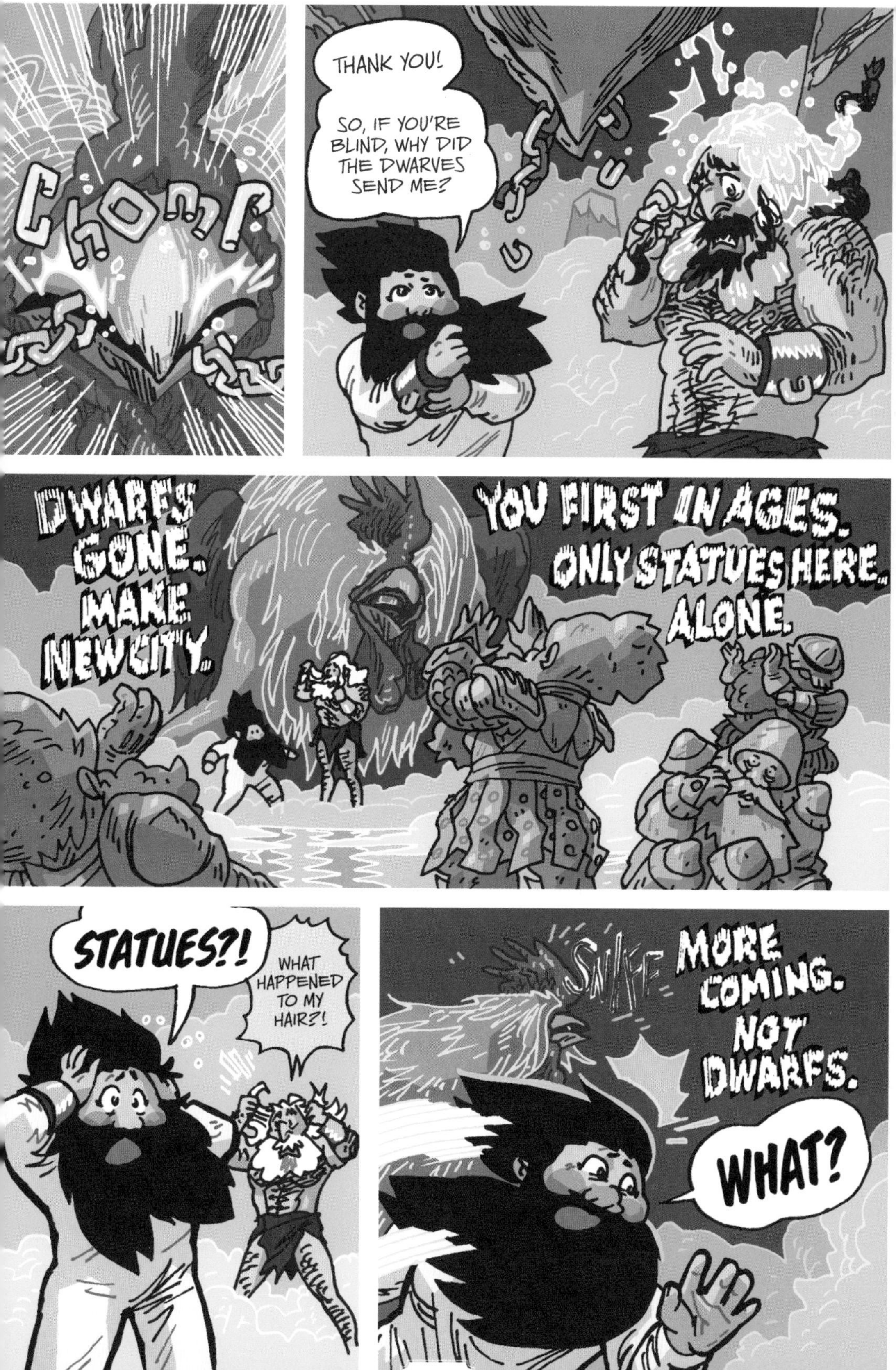
CHOMP
THANK YOU!
SO, IF YOU'RE BLIND, WHY DID THE DWARVES SEND ME?
DWARFS GONE. MAKE NEW CITY.
YOU FIRST IN AGES. ONLY STATUES HERE. ALONE.
STATUES?!
WHAT HAPPENED TO MY HAIR?!
SNIFF
MORE COMING. NOT DWARFS.
WHAT?

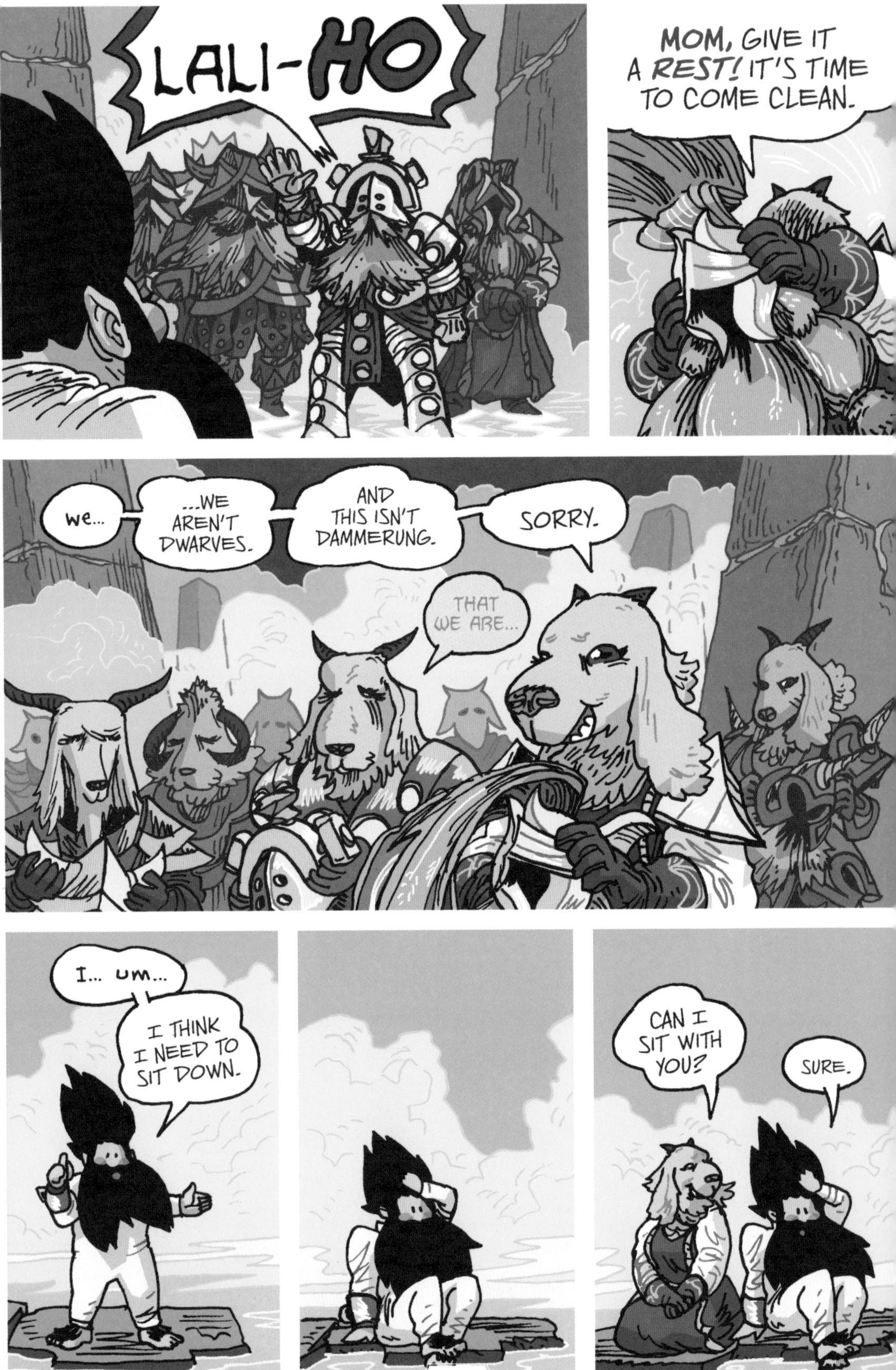
LALI-HO
MOM, GIVE IT A REST! IT'S TIME TO COME CLEAN.
WE...
...WE AREN'T DWARVES.
AND THIS ISN'T DAMMERUNG.
SORRY.
THAT WE ARE...
I... UM...
I THINK I NEED TO SIT DOWN.
CAN I SIT WITH YOU?
SURE.

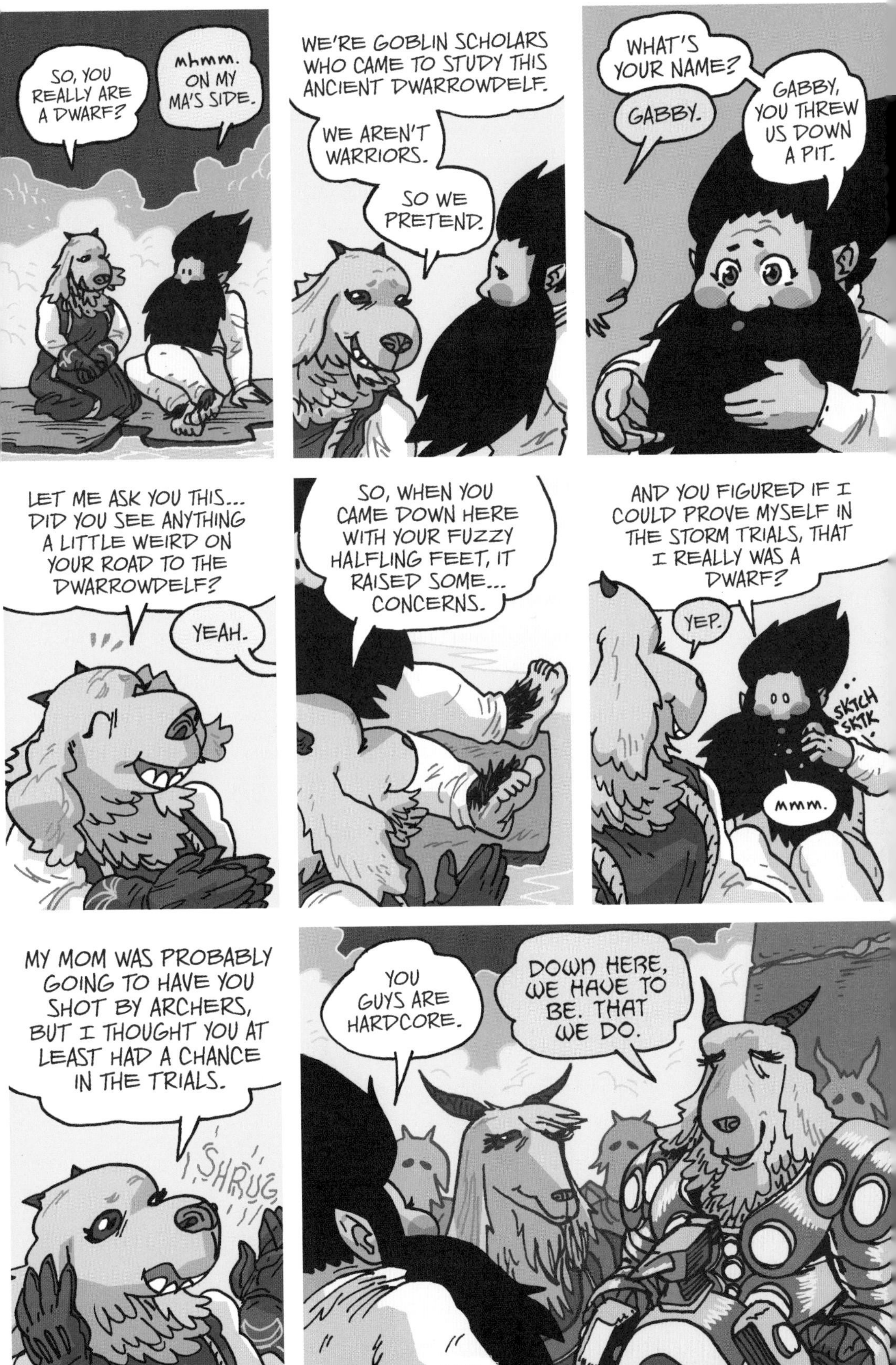
SO, YOU REALLY ARE A DWARF?
mhmm. ON MY MA'S SIDE.
WE'RE GOBLIN SCHOLARS WHO CAME TO STUDY THIS ANCIENT DWARROWDELF.
WE AREN'T WARRIORS.
SO WE PRETEND.
WHAT'S YOUR NAME?
GABBY.
GABBY, YOU THREW US DOWN A PIT.
LET ME ASK YOU THIS... DID YOU SEE ANYTHING A LITTLE WEIRD ON YOUR ROAD TO THE DWARROWDELF?
YEAH.
SO, WHEN YOU CAME DOWN HERE WITH YOUR FUZZY HALFLING FEET, IT RAISED SOME... CONCERNS.
AND YOU FIGURED IF I COULD PROVE MYSELF IN THE STORM TRIALS, THAT I REALLY WAS A DWARF?
YEP.
SKTCH SKTK
mmm.
MY MOM WAS PROBABLY GOING TO HAVE YOU SHOT BY ARCHERS, BUT I THOUGHT YOU AT LEAST HAD A CHANCE IN THE TRIALS.
SHRUG
YOU GUYS ARE HARDCORE.
DOWN HERE, WE HAVE TO BE. THAT WE DO.

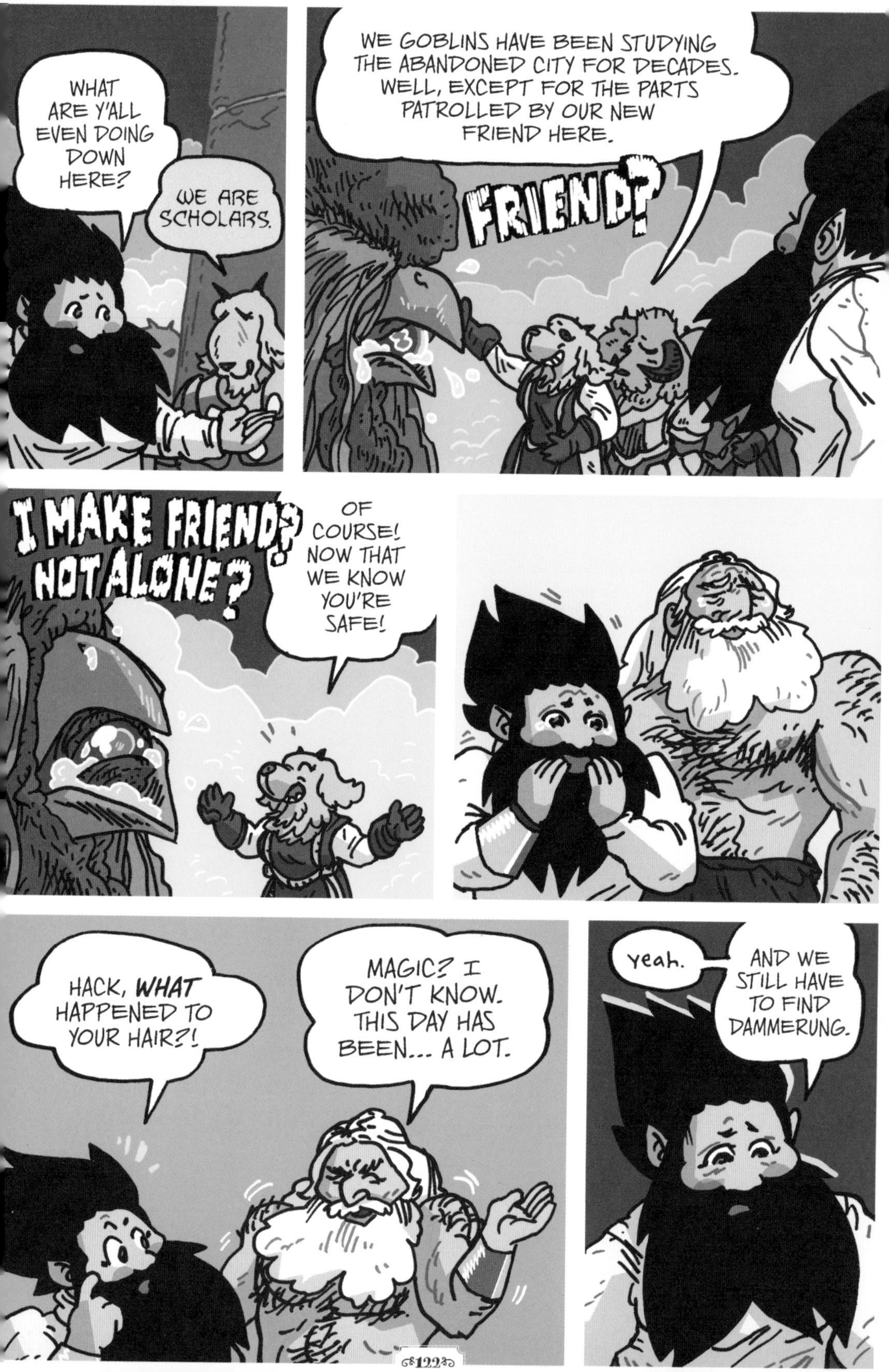

WHAT ARE Y'ALL EVEN DOING DOWN HERE?
WE ARE SCHOLARS.
WE GOBLINS HAVE BEEN STUDYING THE ABANDONED CITY FOR DECADES. WELL, EXCEPT FOR THE PARTS PATROLLED BY OUR NEW FRIEND HERE.
FRIEND?
I MAKE FRIEND? NOT ALONE?
OF COURSE! NOW THAT WE KNOW YOU'RE SAFE!
HACK, WHAT HAPPENED TO YOUR HAIR?!
MAGIC? I DON'T KNOW. THIS DAY HAS BEEN... A LOT.
Yeah.
AND WE STILL HAVE TO FIND DAMMERUNG.

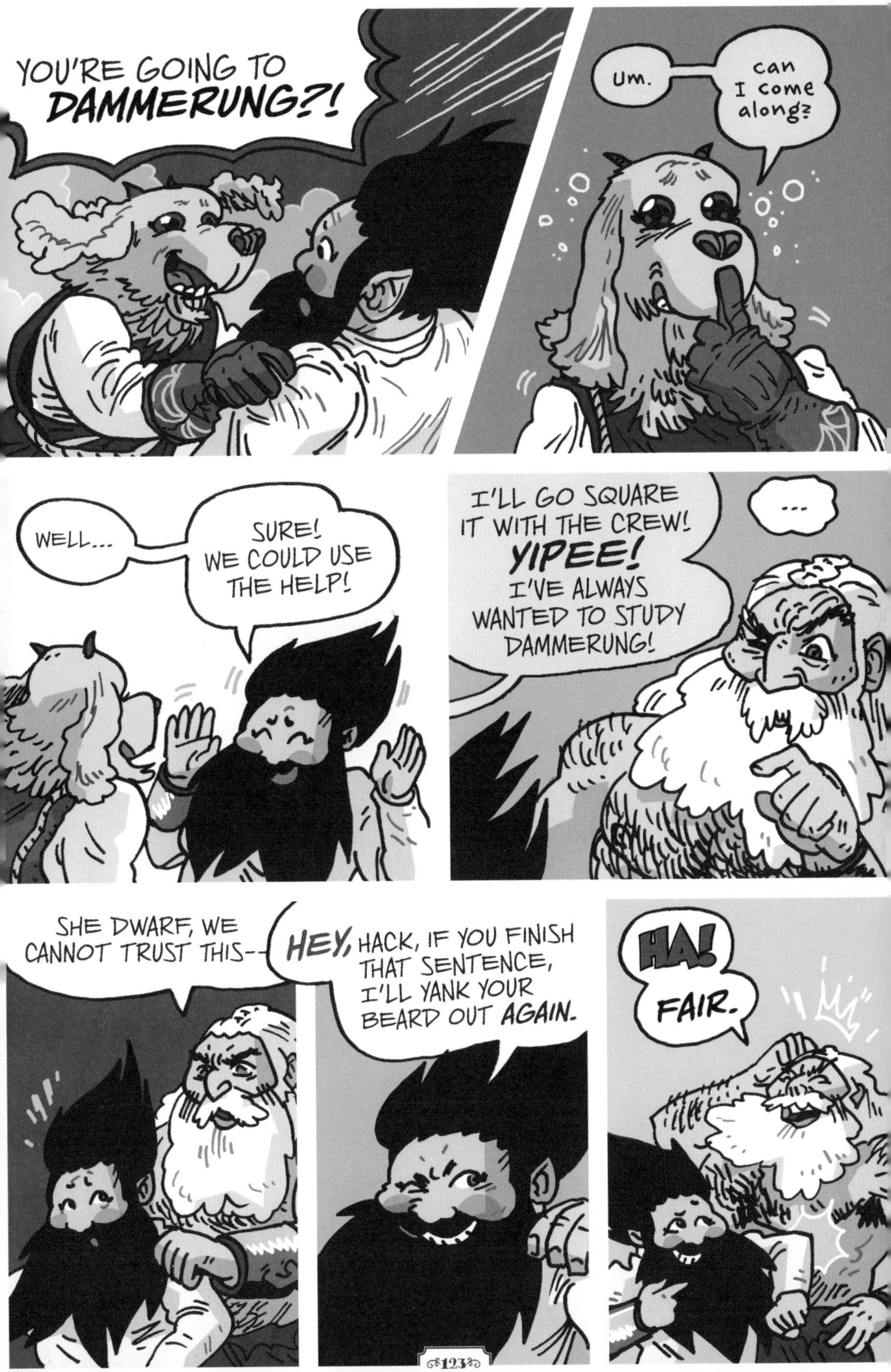
YOU'RE GOING TO DAMMERUNG?!
Um.
can I come along?
WELL...
SURE! WE COULD USE THE HELP!
I'LL GO SQUARE IT WITH THE CREW! YIPEE! I'VE ALWAYS WANTED TO STUDY DAMMERUNG!
...
SHE DWARF, WE CANNOT TRUST THIS--
HEY, HACK, IF YOU FINISH THAT SENTENCE, I'LL YANK YOUR BEARD OUT AGAIN.
HA!
FAIR.

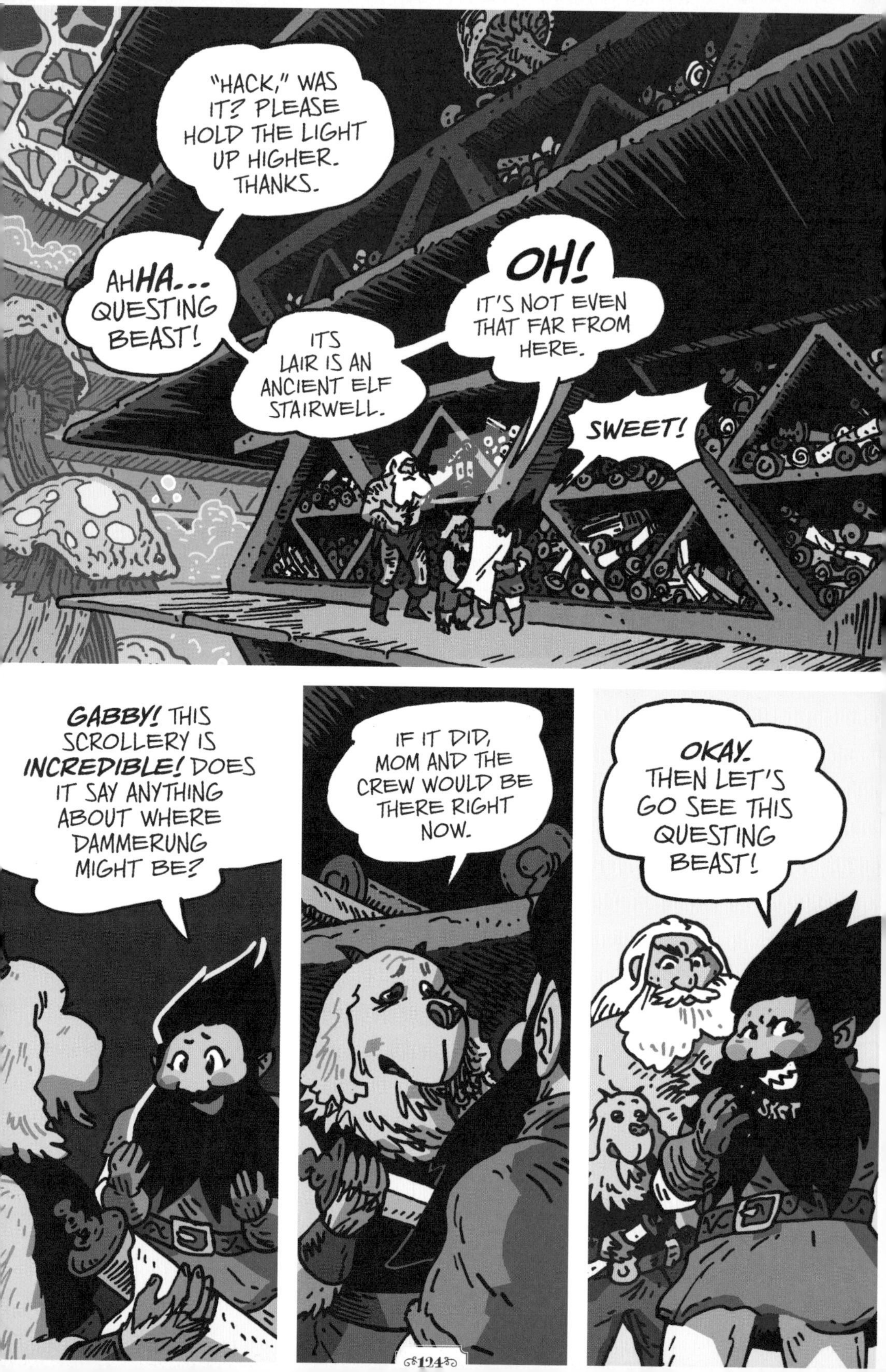
"HACK," WAS IT? PLEASE HOLD THE LIGHT UP HIGHER. THANKS.
AHHA... QUESTING BEAST!
ITS LAIR IS AN ANCIENT ELF STAIRWELL.
OH! IT'S NOT EVEN THAT FAR FROM HERE.
SWEET!
GABBY! THIS SCROLLERY IS INCREDIBLE! DOES IT SAY ANYTHING ABOUT WHERE DAMMERUNG MIGHT BE?
IF IT DID, MOM AND THE CREW WOULD BE THERE RIGHT NOW.
OKAY. THEN LET'S GO SEE THIS QUESTING BEAST!

CHAPTER
⟊VII⟐

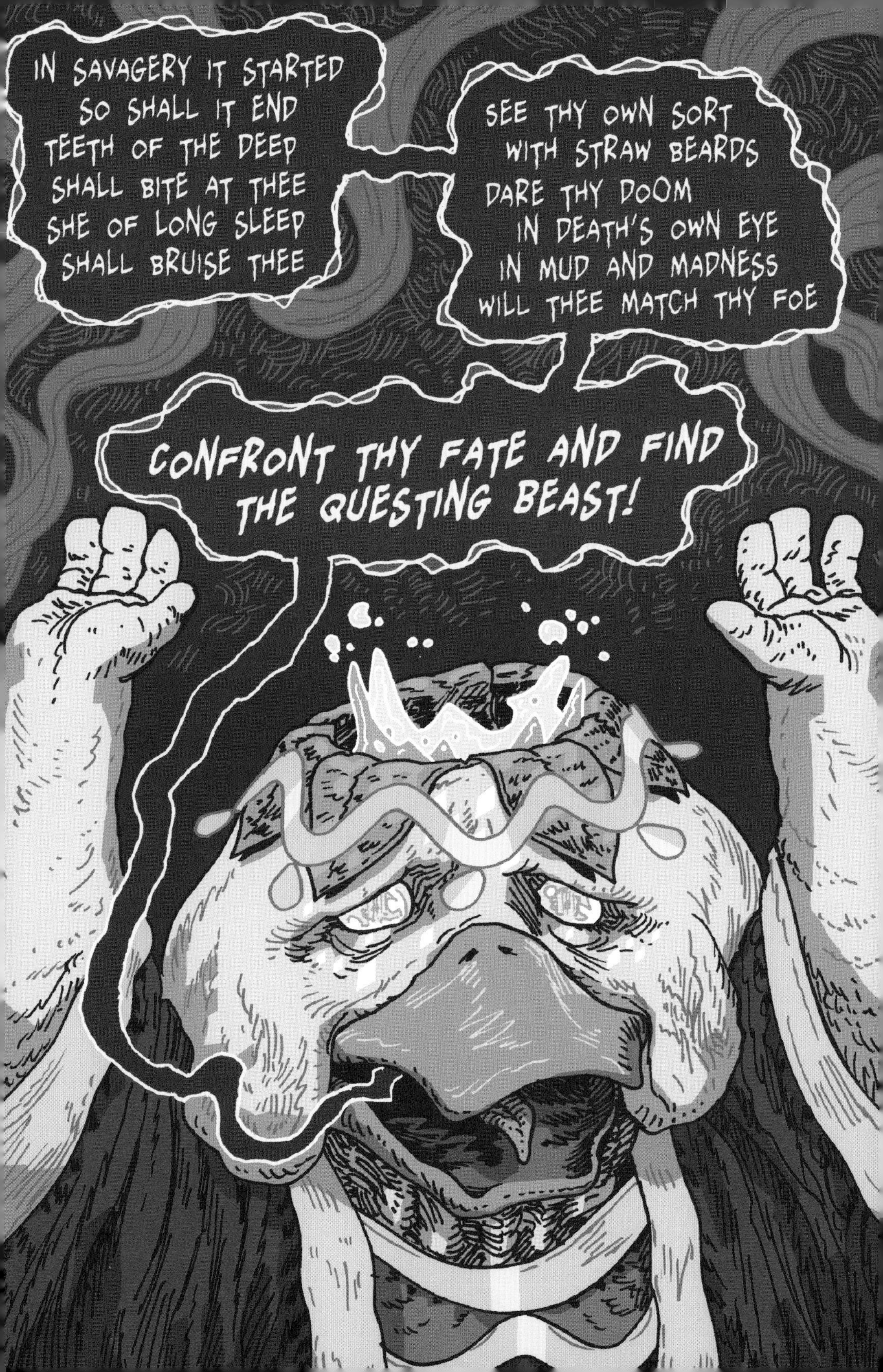
IN SAVAGERY IT STARTED SO SHALL IT END TEETH OF THE DEEP SHALL BITE AT THEE SHE OF LONG SLEEP SHALL BRUISE THEE
SEE THY OWN SORT WITH STRAW BEARDS DARE THY DOOM IN DEATH'S OWN EYE IN MUD AND MADNESS WILL THEE MATCH THY FOE
CONFRONT THY FATE AND FIND THE QUESTING BEAST!

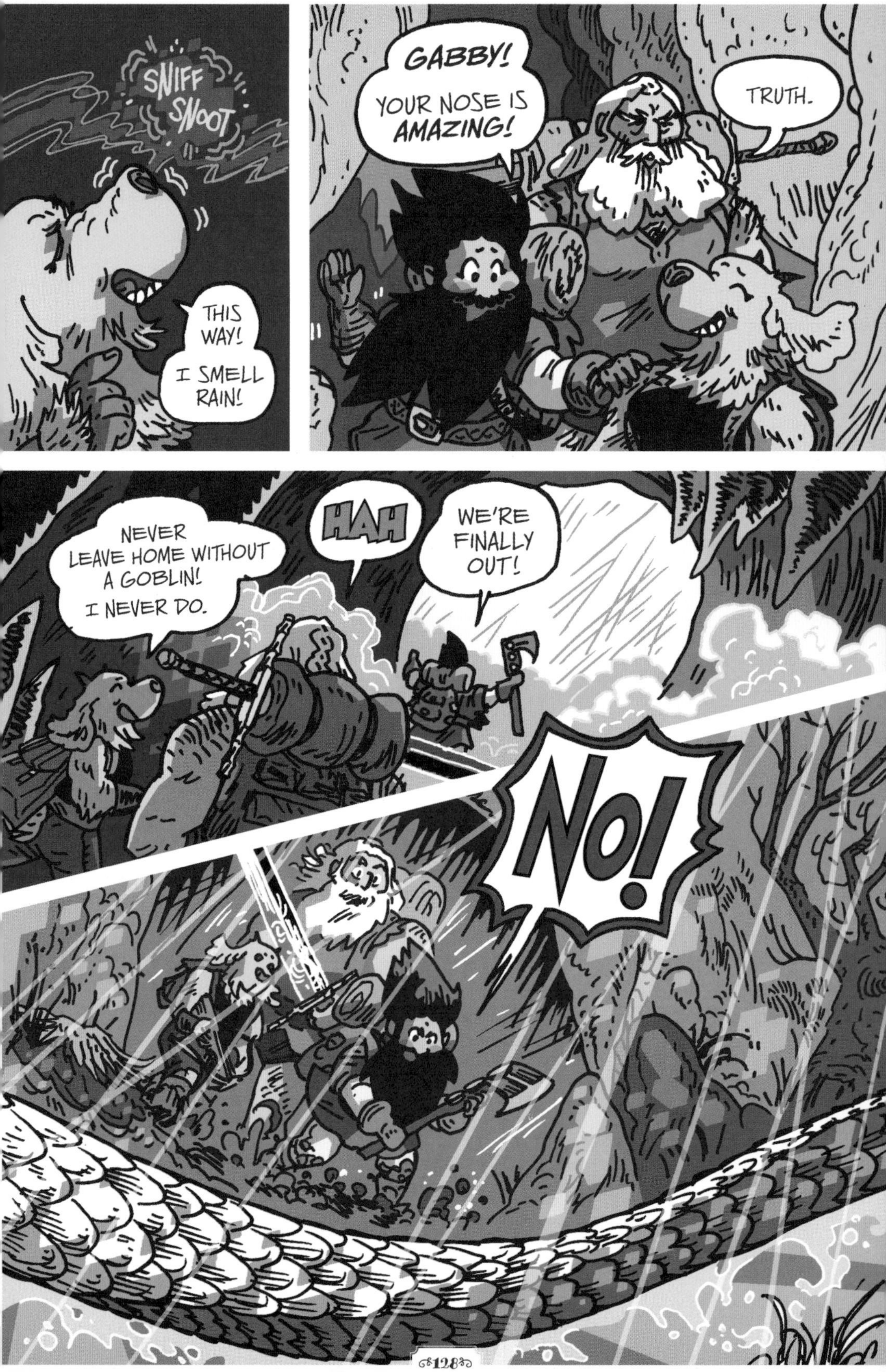
SNIFF
SNOOT
THIS WAY!
I SMELL RAIN!
GABBY!
YOUR NOSE IS AMAZING!
TRUTH.
NEVER LEAVE HOME WITHOUT A GOBLIN!
I NEVER DO.
HAH
WE'RE FINALLY OUT!
NO!

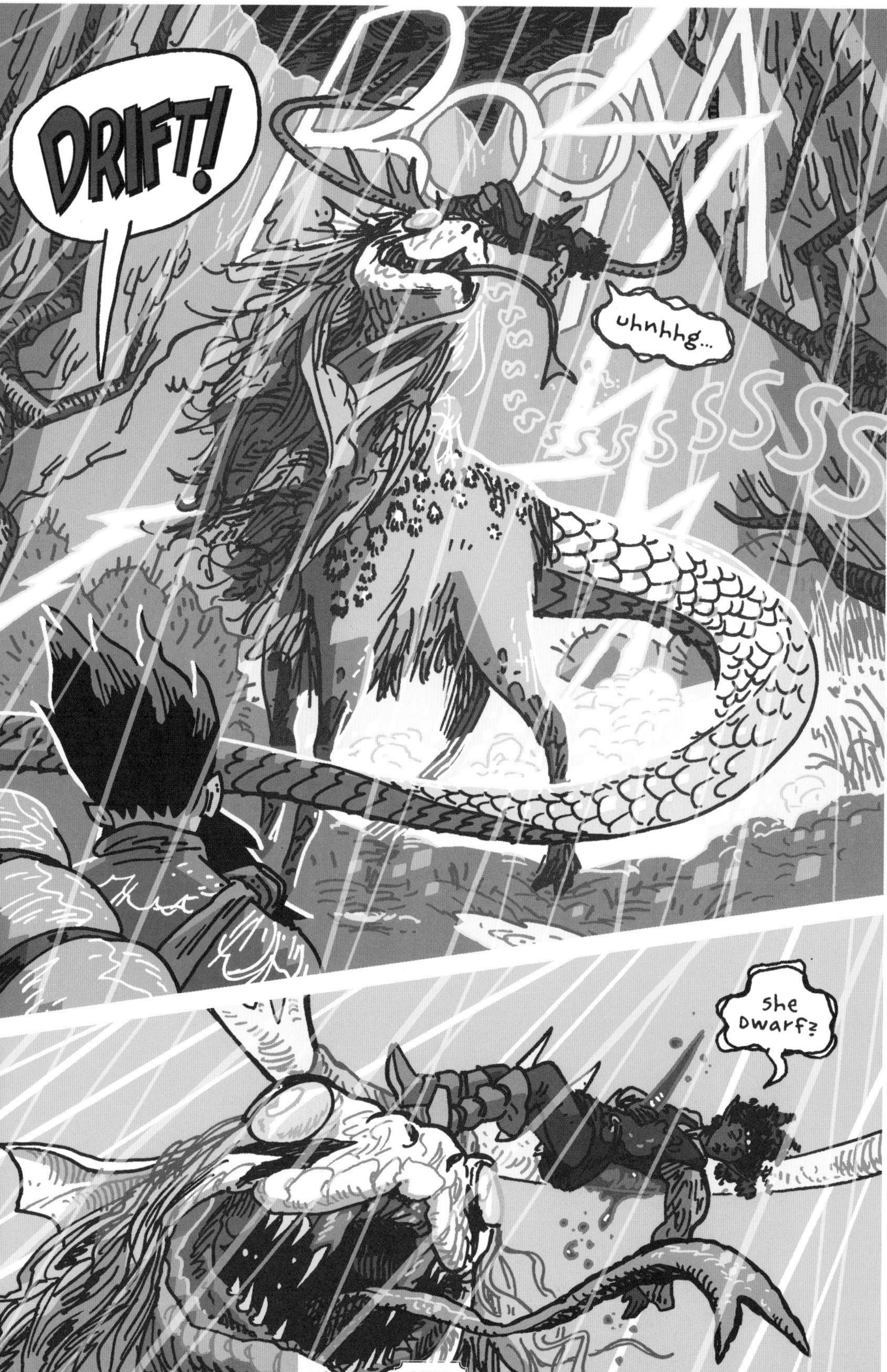
DRIFT!
uhnhhg...
she
Dwarf?

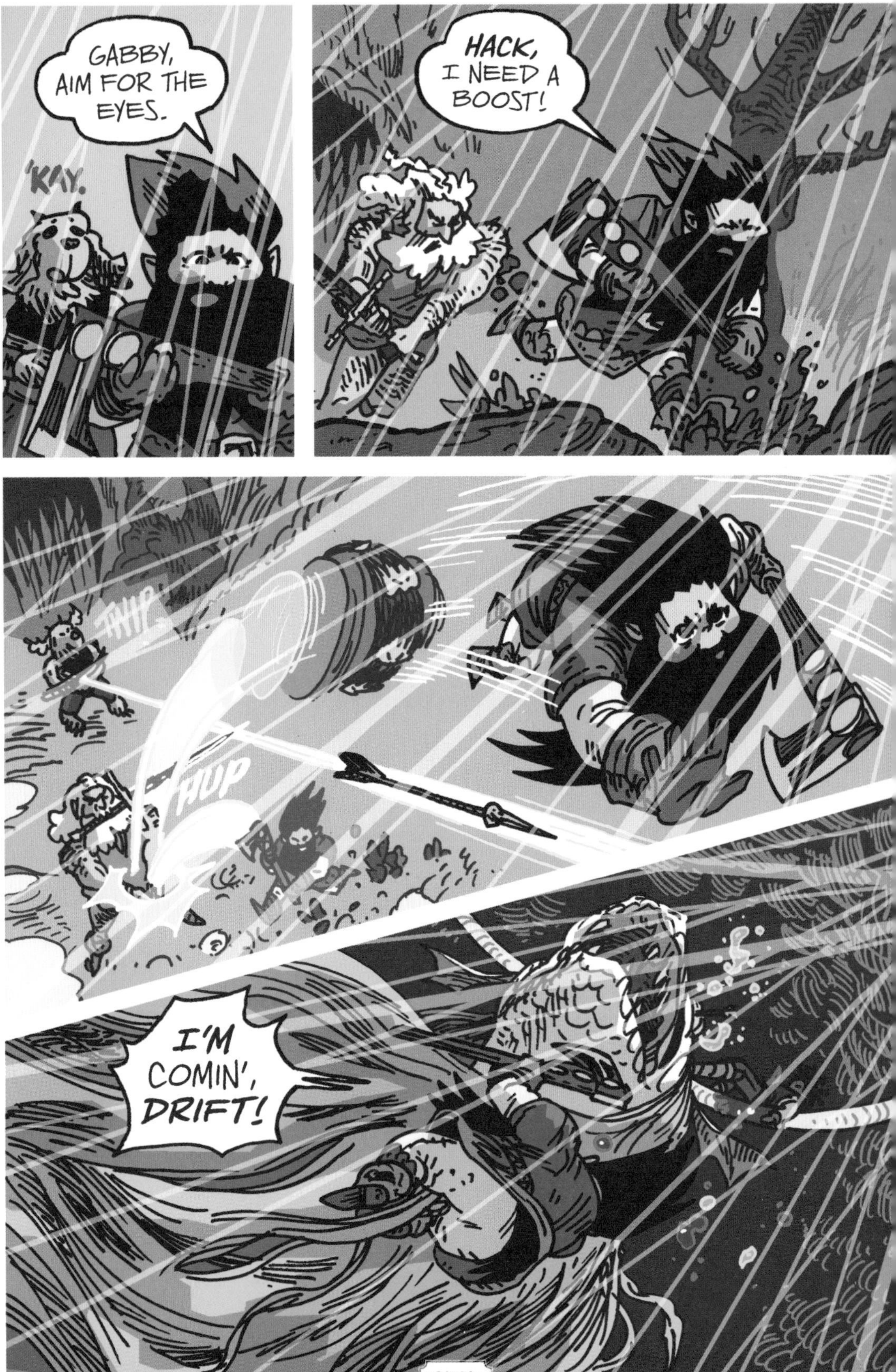
GABBY, AIM FOR THE EYES.
'KAY.
HACK, I NEED A BOOST!
THIP
THUP
I'M COMIN', DRIFT!

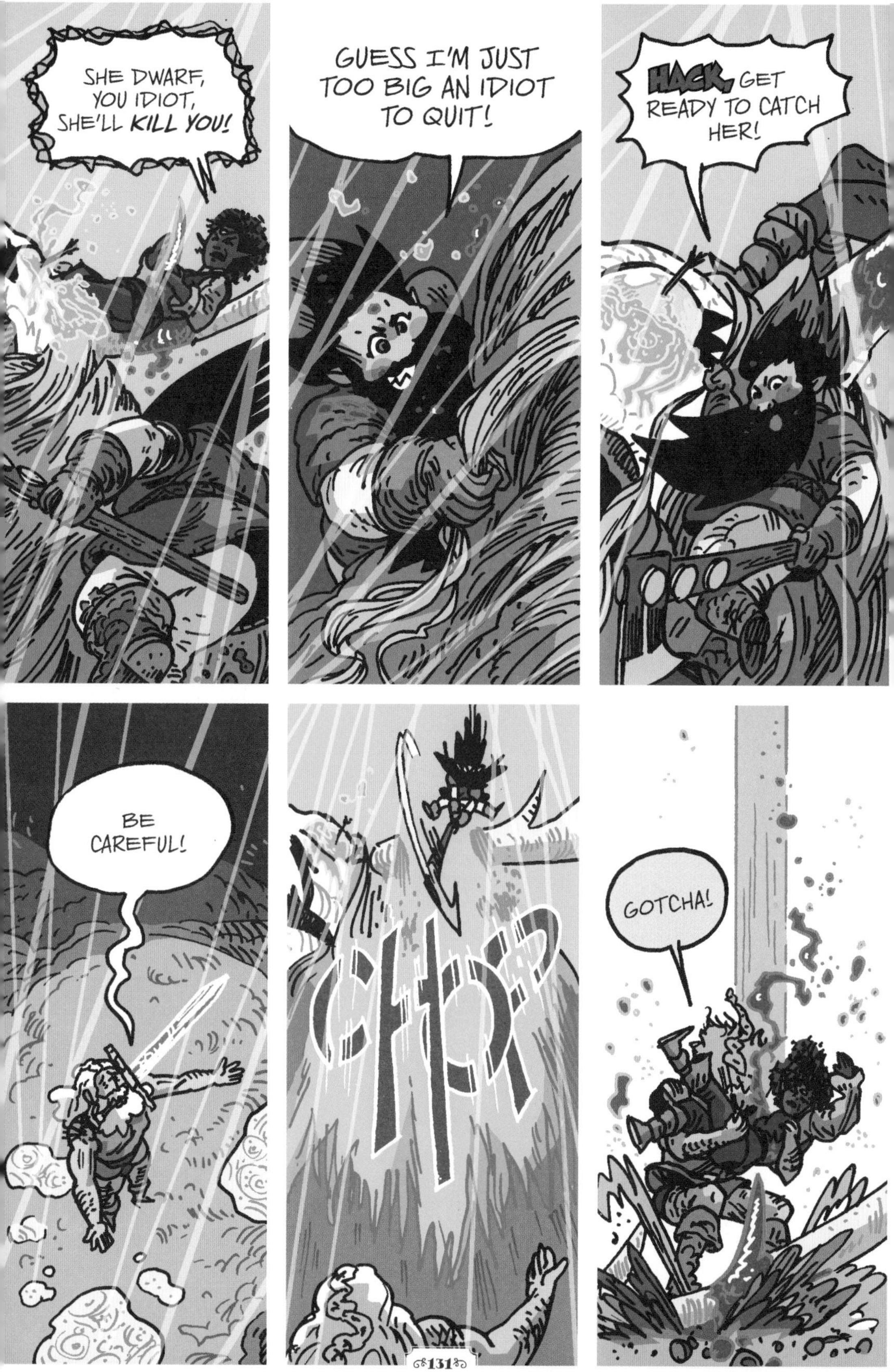
SHE DWARF, YOU IDIOT, SHE'LL **KILL YOU!**
GUESS I'M JUST TOO BIG AN IDIOT TO QUIT!
HACK, GET READY TO CATCH HER!
BE CAREFUL!
CHOP
GOTCHA!

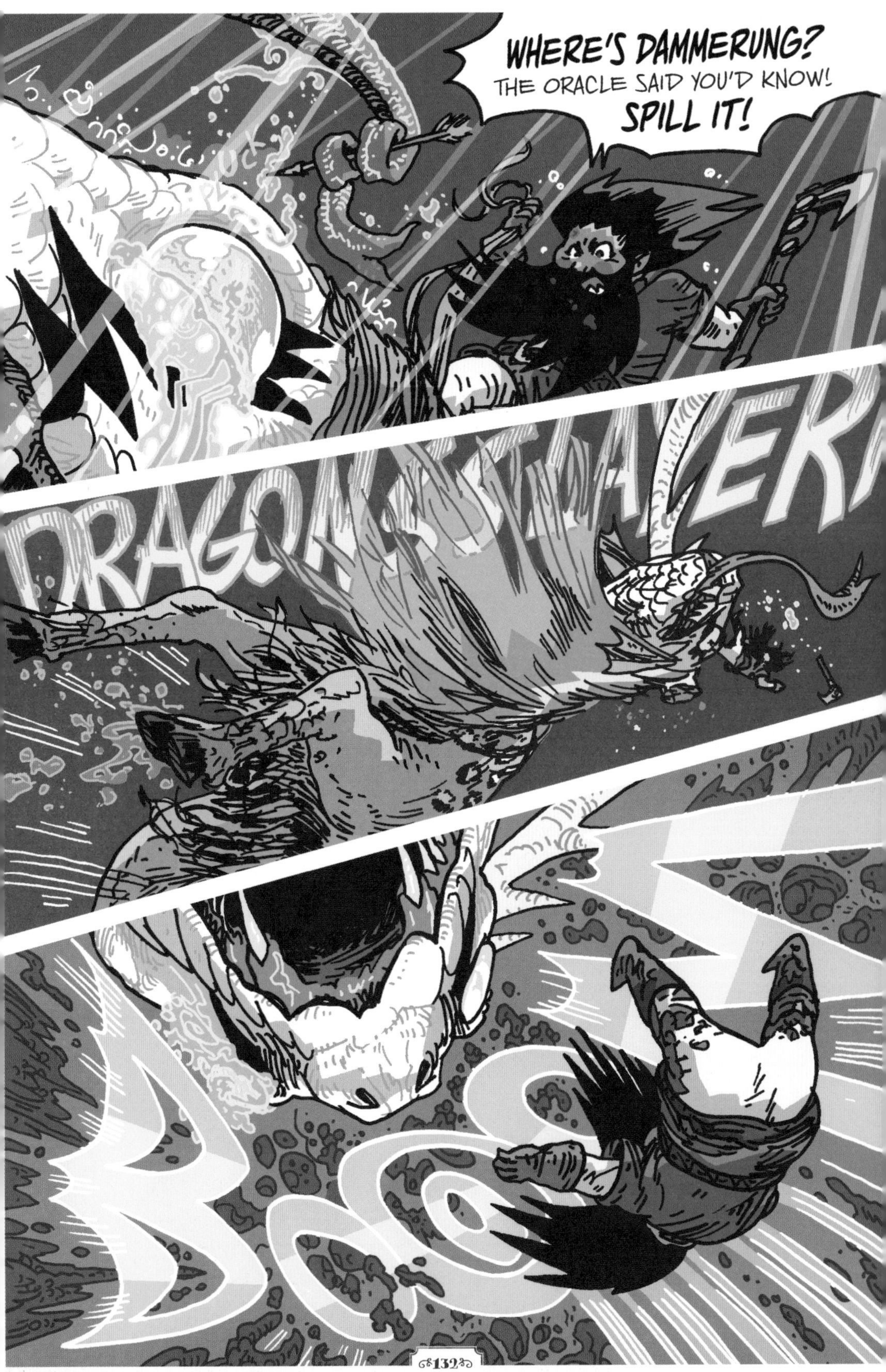
WHERE'S DAMMERUNG?
THE ORACLE SAID YOU'D KNOW!
SPILL IT!
PLUCK
DRAGONSLAYER!

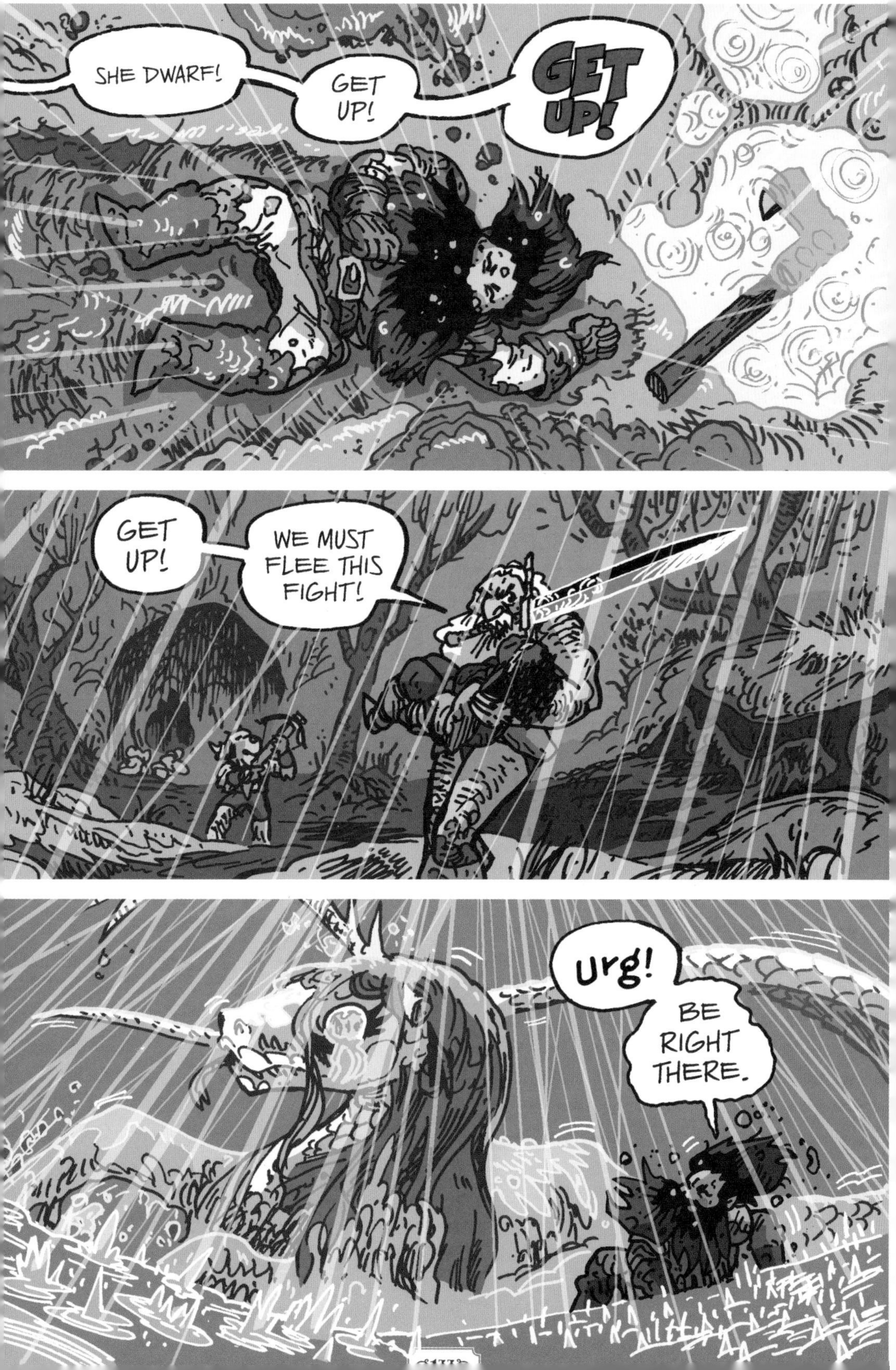
SHE DWARF!
GET UP!
GET UP!
GET UP!
WE MUST FLEE THIS FIGHT!
Urg!
BE RIGHT THERE.

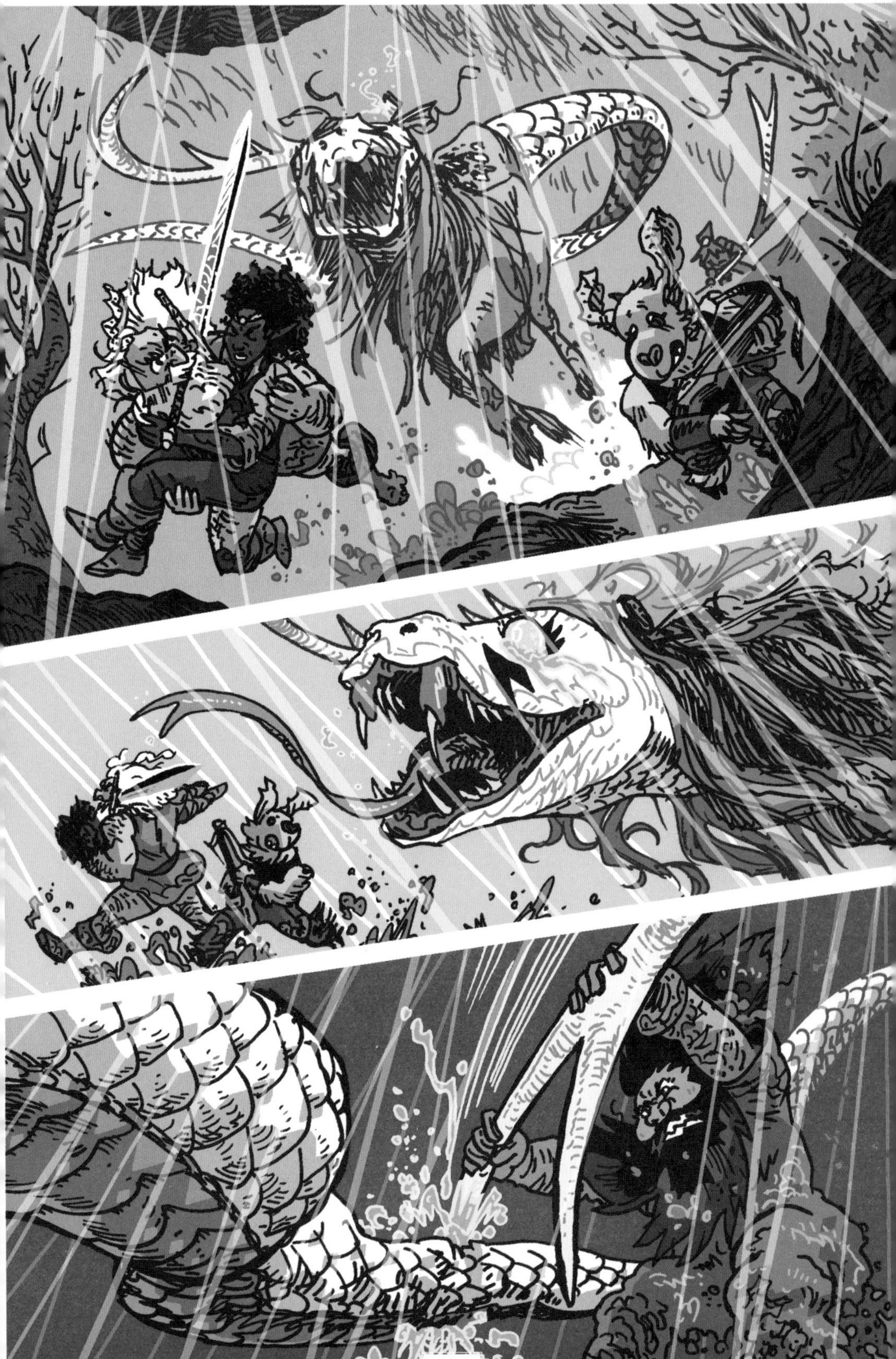

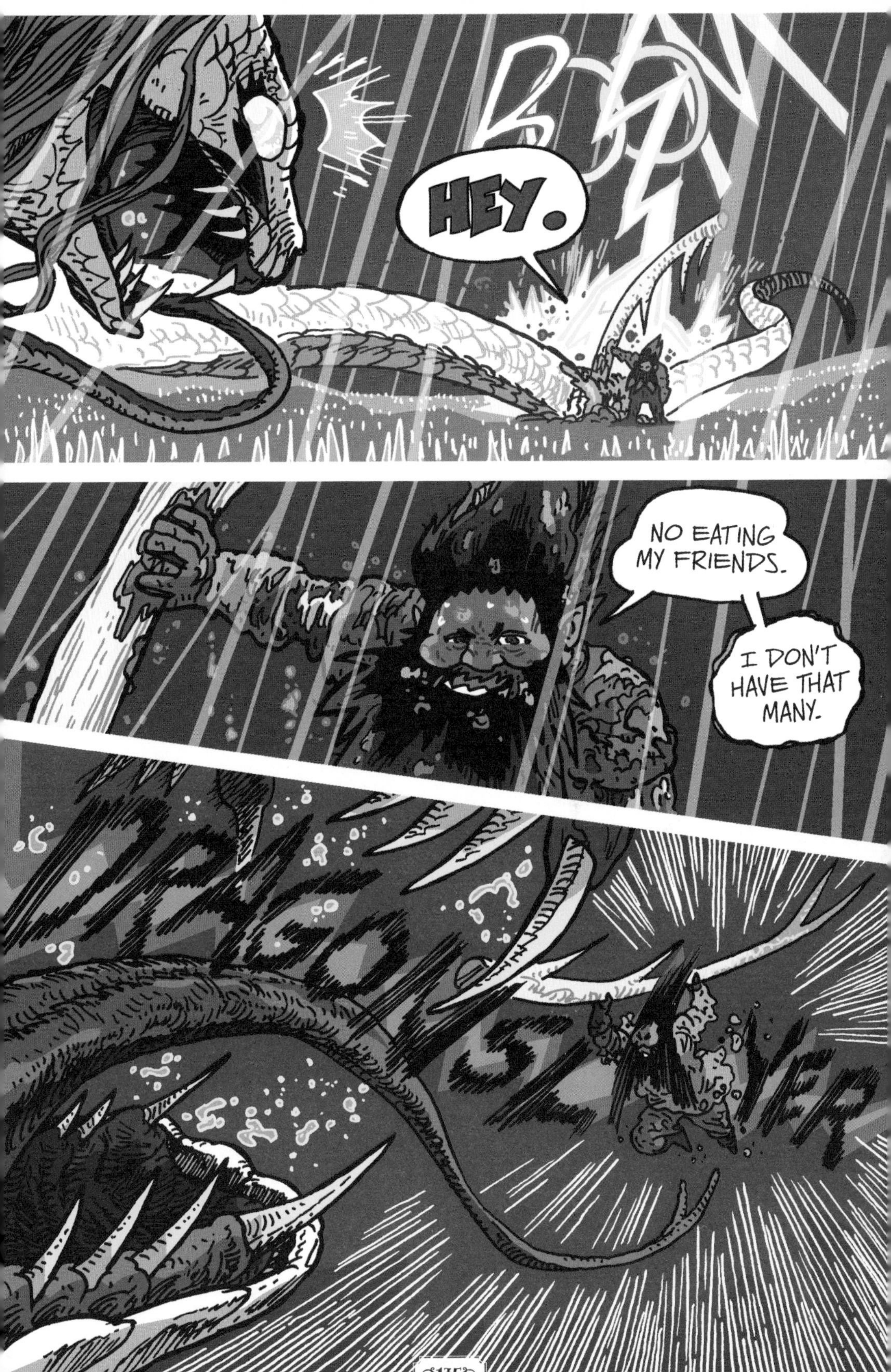
HEY.
NO EATING MY FRIENDS.
I DON'T HAVE THAT MANY.
DRAGON SLAYER

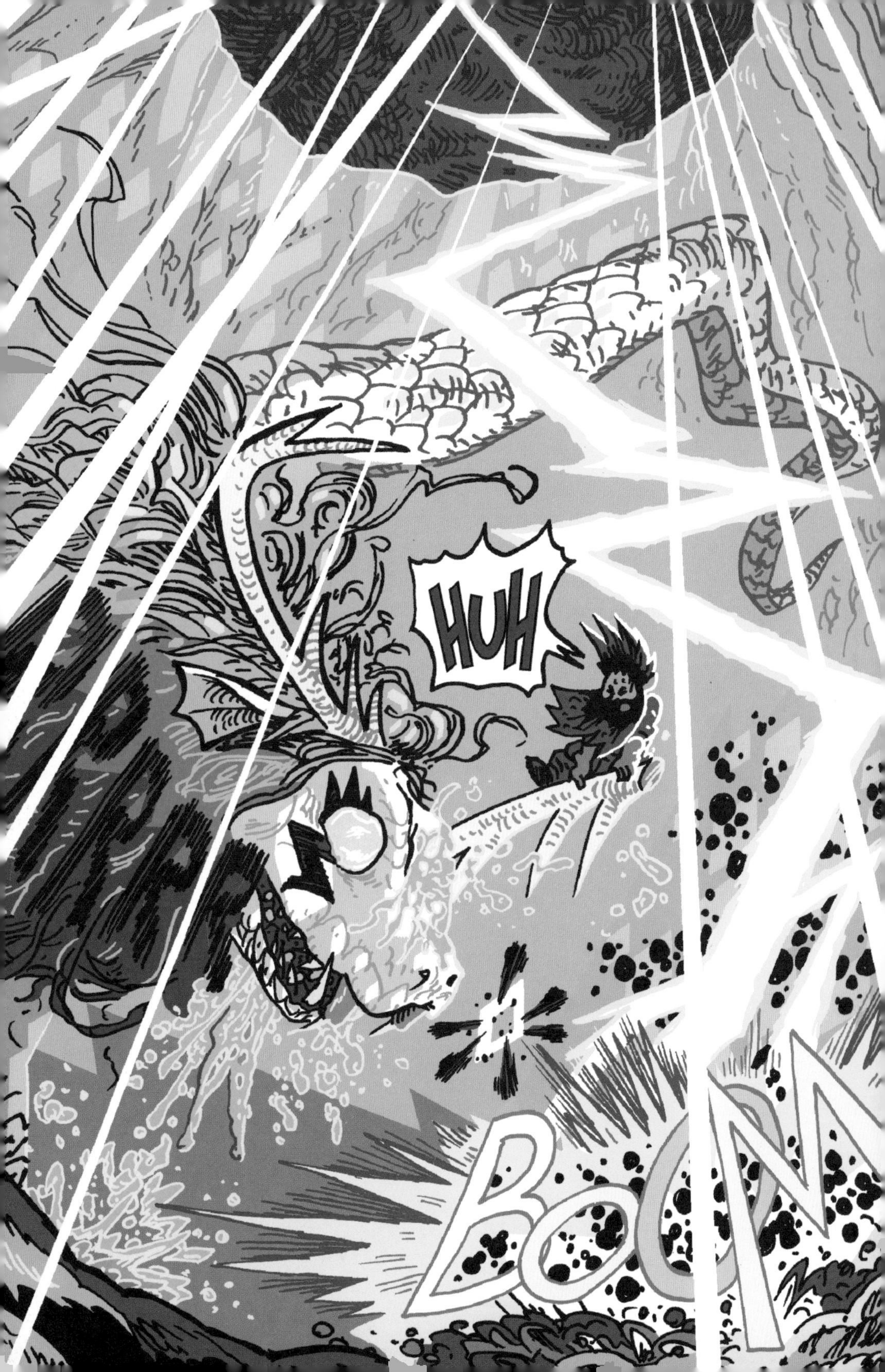
HUH
BOOM

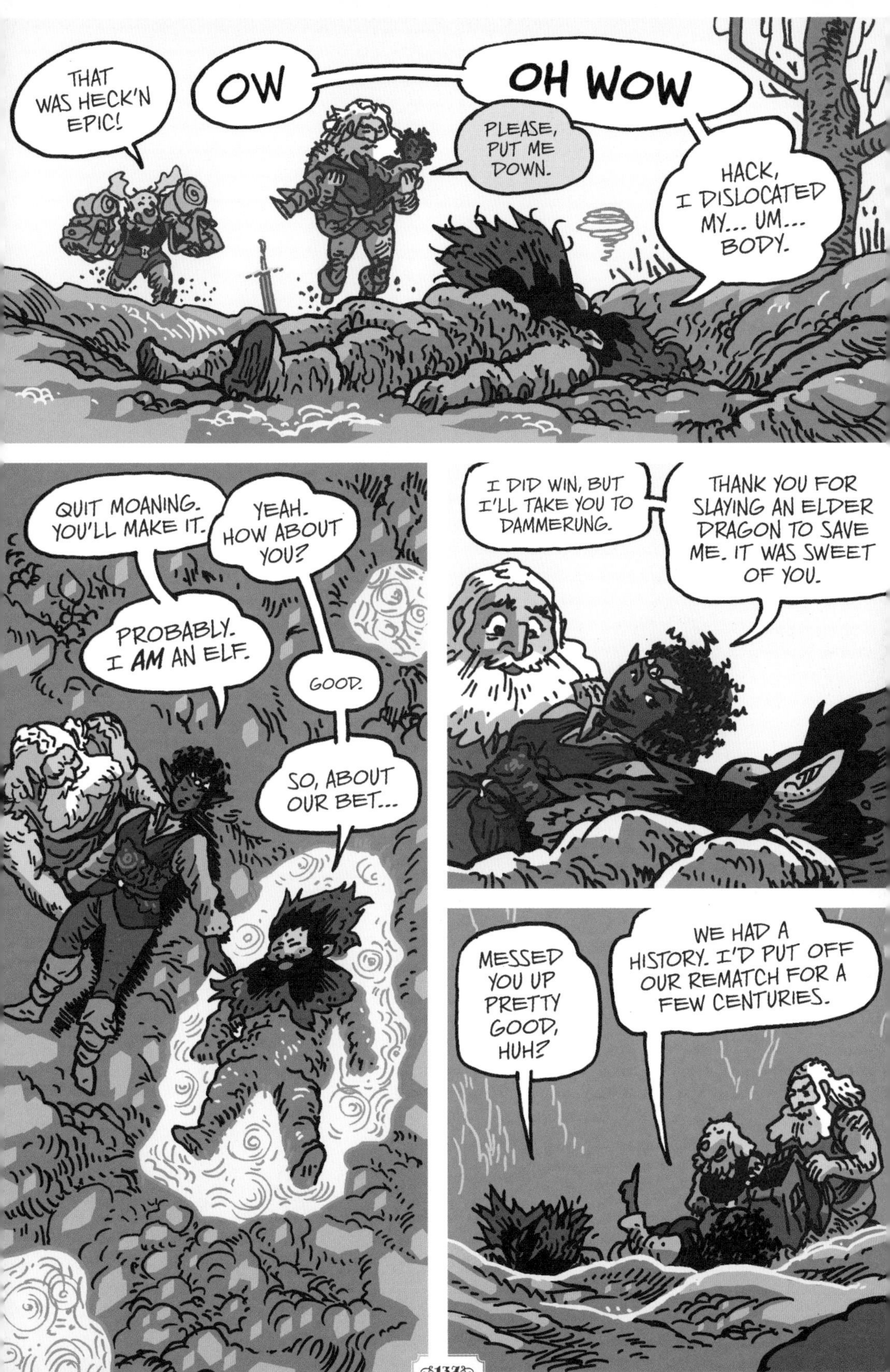
THAT WAS HECK'N EPIC!
OW
OH WOW
PLEASE, PUT ME DOWN.
HACK, I DISLOCATED MY... UM... BODY.
QUIT MOANING. YOU'LL MAKE IT.
YEAH. HOW ABOUT YOU?
PROBABLY. I **AM** AN ELF.
GOOD.
SO, ABOUT OUR BET...
THANK YOU FOR SLAYING AN ELDER DRAGON TO SAVE ME. IT WAS SWEET OF YOU.
I DID WIN, BUT I'LL TAKE YOU TO DAMMERUNG.
MESSED YOU UP PRETTY GOOD, HUH?
WE HAD A HISTORY. I'D PUT OFF OUR REMATCH FOR A FEW CENTURIES.

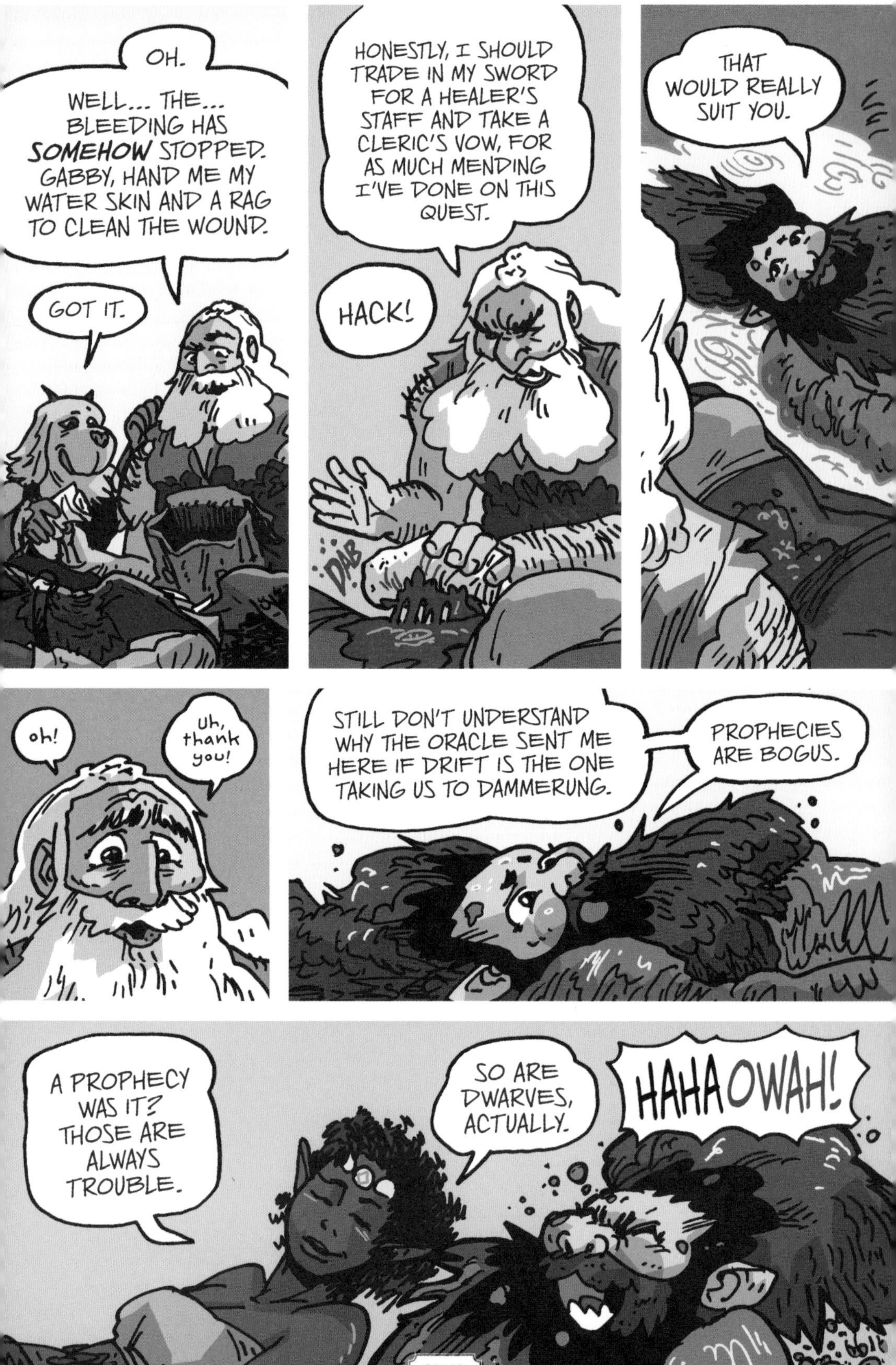
OH.
WELL... THE... BLEEDING HAS SOMEHOW STOPPED. GABBY, HAND ME MY WATER SKIN AND A RAG TO CLEAN THE WOUND.
GOT IT.
HONESTLY, I SHOULD TRADE IN MY SWORD FOR A HEALER'S STAFF AND TAKE A CLERIC'S VOW, FOR AS MUCH MENDING I'VE DONE ON THIS QUEST.
HACK!
DAB
THAT WOULD REALLY SUIT YOU.
oh!
uh, thank you!
STILL DON'T UNDERSTAND WHY THE ORACLE SENT ME HERE IF DRIFT IS THE ONE TAKING US TO DAMMERUNG.
PROPHECIES ARE BOGUS.
A PROPHECY WAS IT? THOSE ARE ALWAYS TROUBLE.
SO ARE DWARVES, ACTUALLY.
HAHA OWAH!

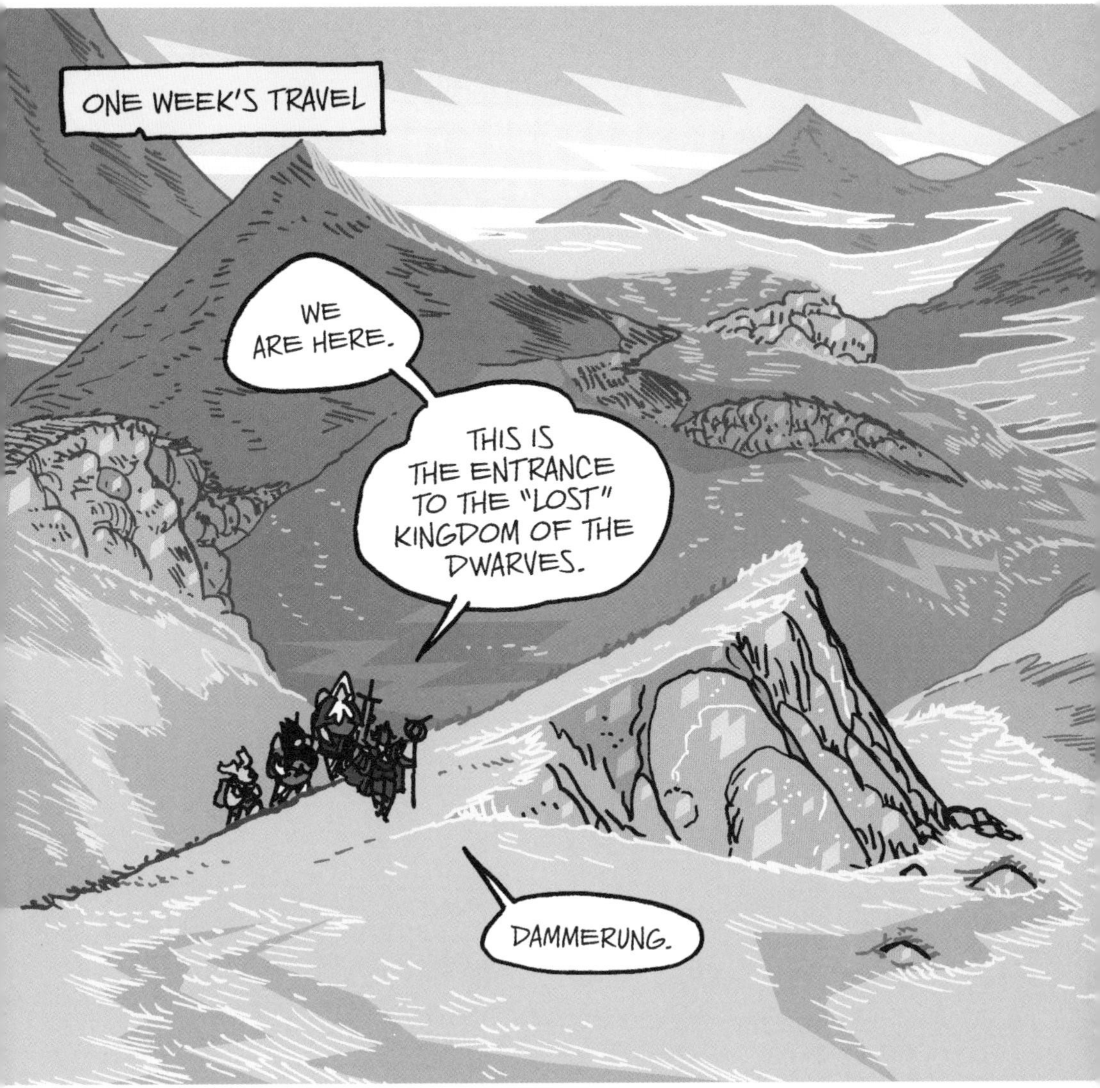
ONE WEEK'S TRAVEL
WE ARE HERE.
THIS IS THE ENTRANCE TO THE "LOST" KINGDOM OF THE DWARVES.
DAMMERUNG.

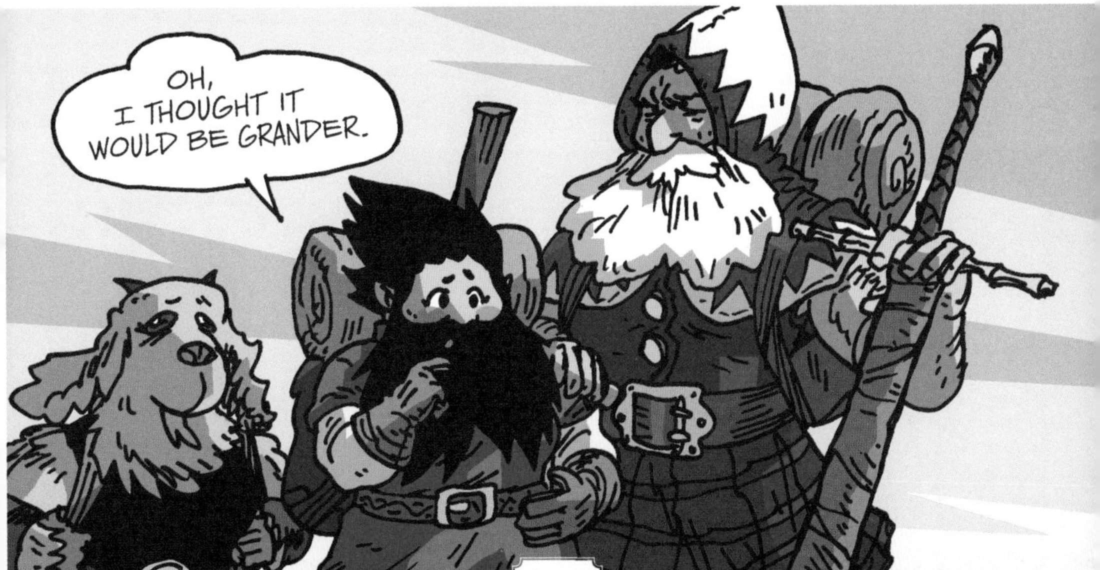
OH, I THOUGHT IT WOULD BE GRANDER.

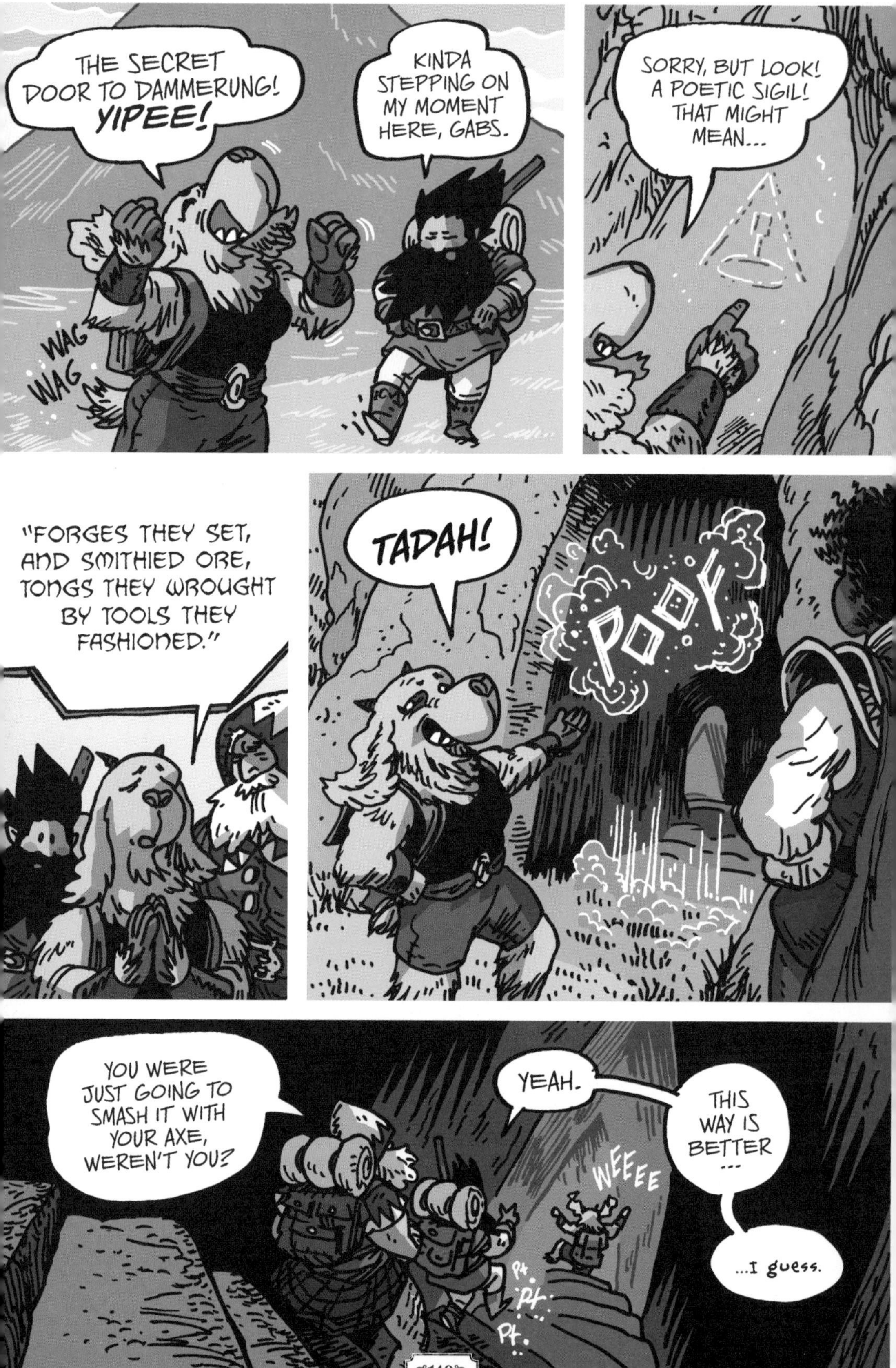
THE SECRET DOOR TO DAMMERUNG! YIPEE!
KINDA STEPPING ON MY MOMENT HERE, GABS.
WAG WAG
SORRY, BUT LOOK! A POETIC SIGIL! THAT MIGHT MEAN...
"FORGES THEY SET, AND SMITHIED ORE, TONGS THEY WROUGHT BY TOOLS THEY FASHIONED."
TADAH!
POOF
YOU WERE JUST GOING TO SMASH IT WITH YOUR AXE, WEREN'T YOU?
YEAH.
THIS WAY IS BETTER ...
...I guess.
WEEEE
PT PT PT

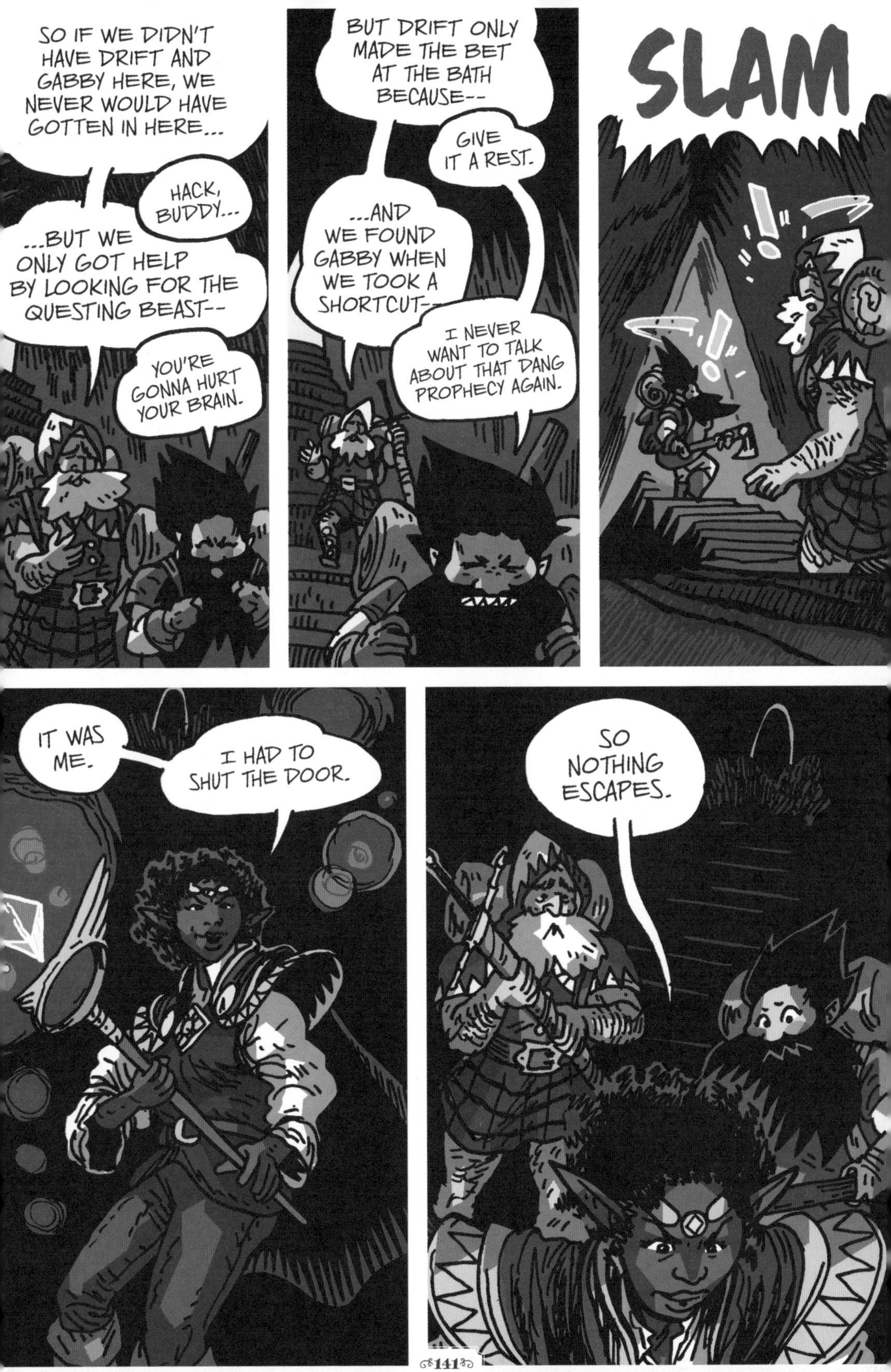
SO IF WE DIDN'T HAVE DRIFT AND GABBY HERE, WE NEVER WOULD HAVE GOTTEN IN HERE...
...BUT WE ONLY GOT HELP BY LOOKING FOR THE QUESTING BEAST--
HACK, BUDDY...
YOU'RE GONNA HURT YOUR BRAIN.
BUT DRIFT ONLY MADE THE BET AT THE BATH BECAUSE--
GIVE IT A REST.
...AND WE FOUND GABBY WHEN WE TOOK A SHORTCUT--
I NEVER WANT TO TALK ABOUT THAT DANG PROPHECY AGAIN.
SLAM
!
!
IT WAS ME.
I HAD TO SHUT THE DOOR.
SO NOTHING ESCAPES.

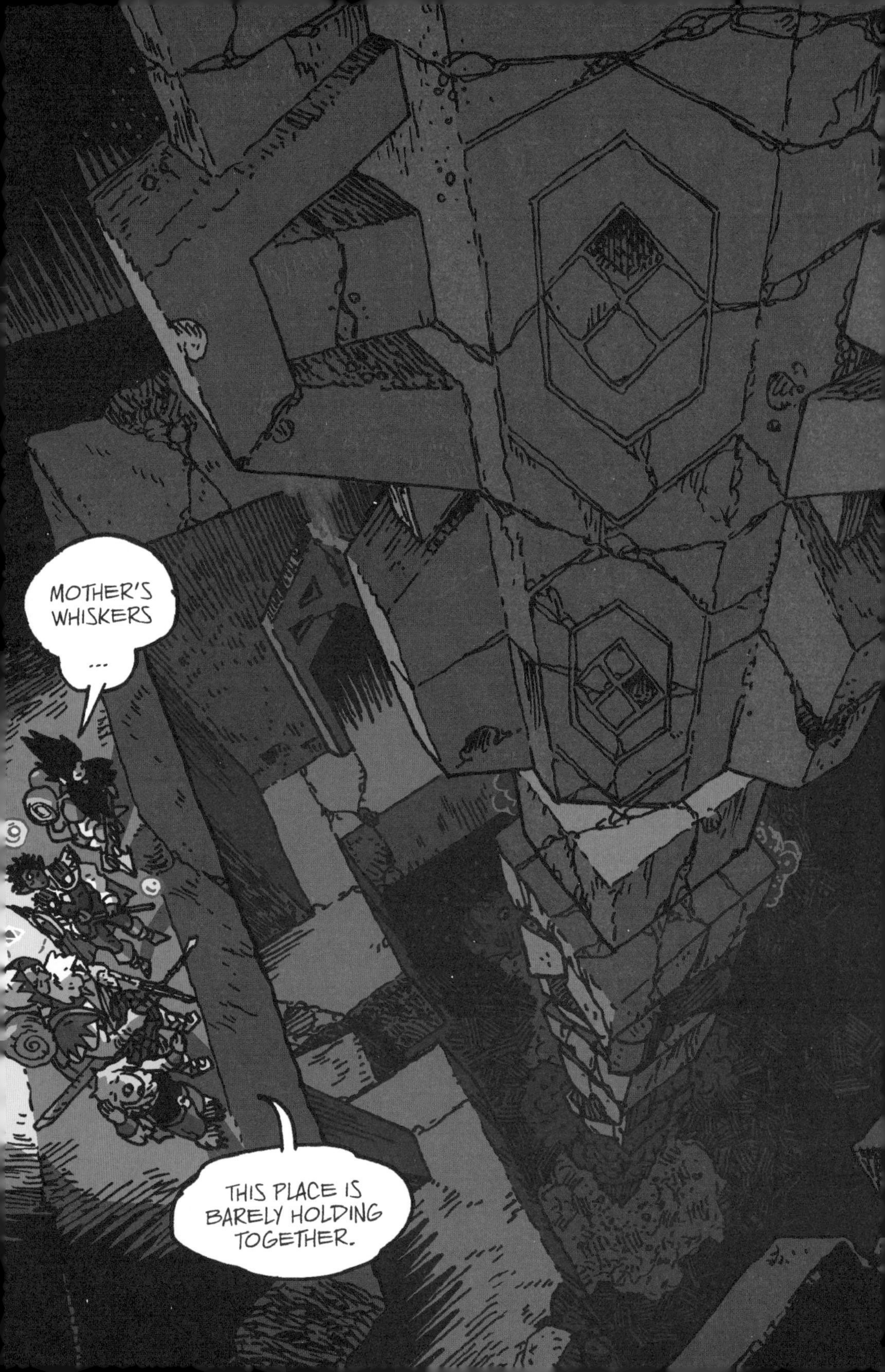
MOTHER'S WHISKERS ...
THIS PLACE IS BARELY HOLDING TOGETHER.

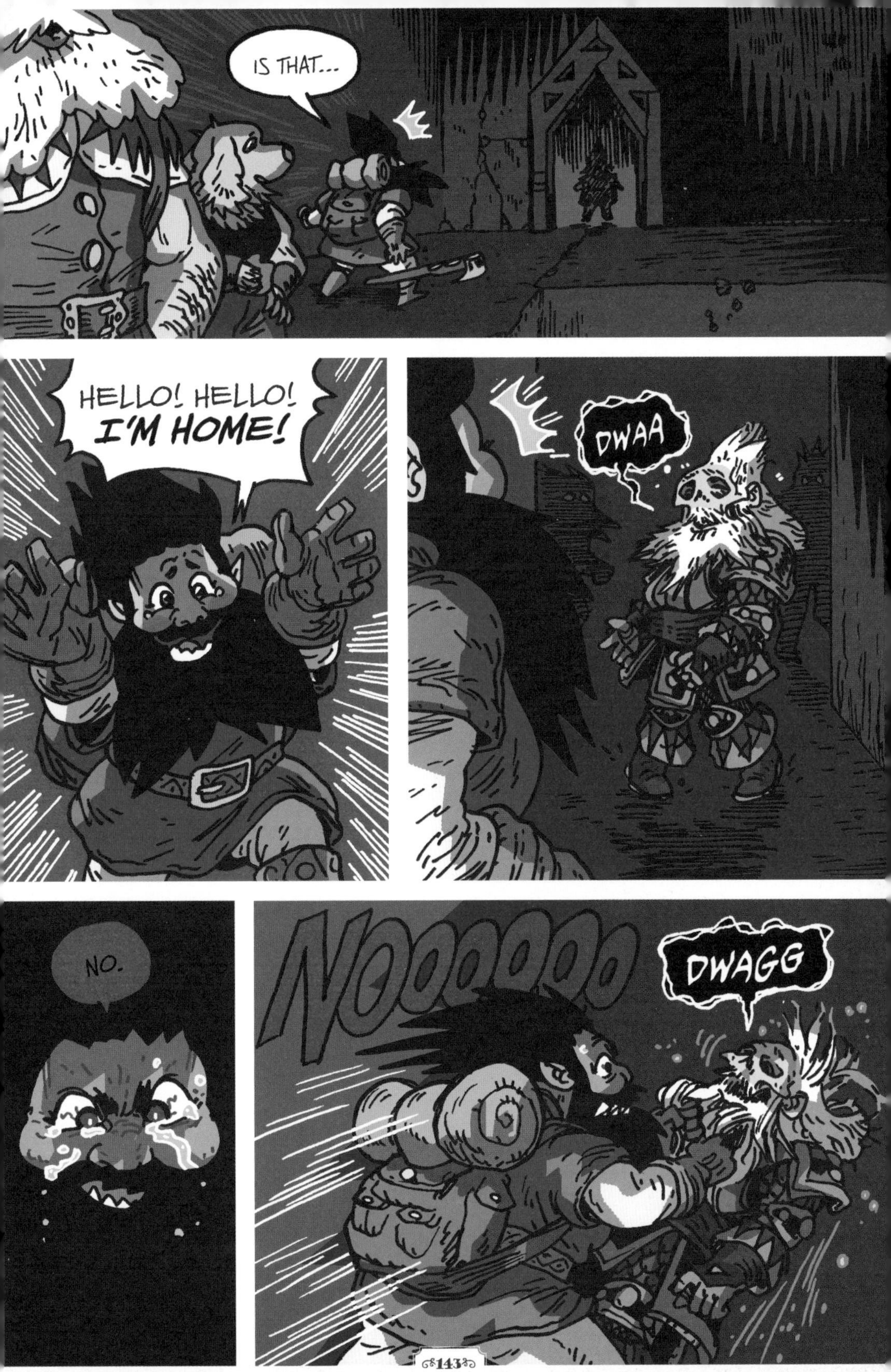
IS THAT...
HELLO! HELLO! I'M HOME!
DWAA
NO.
NOOOOOO
DWAGG

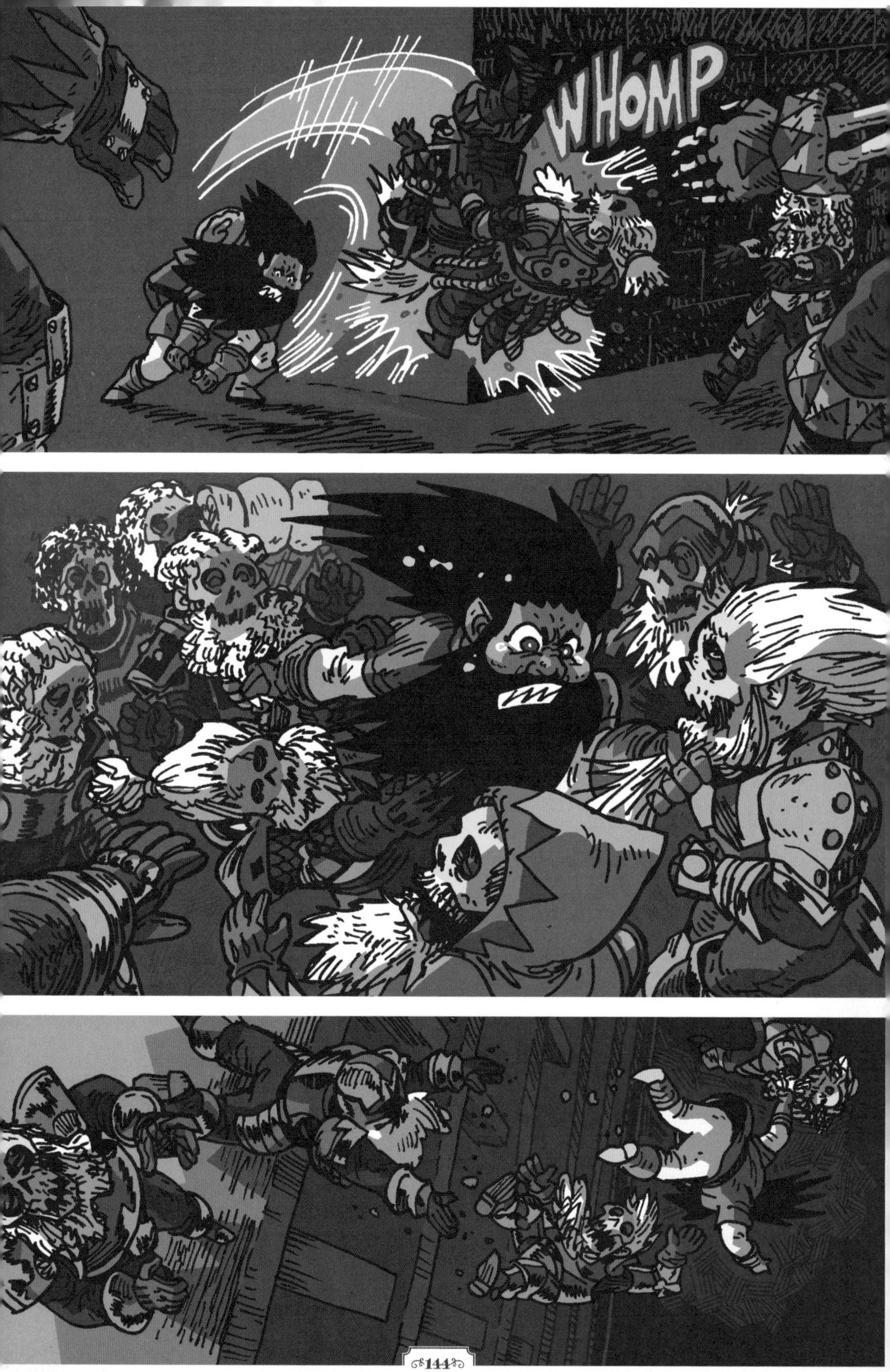
WHOMP

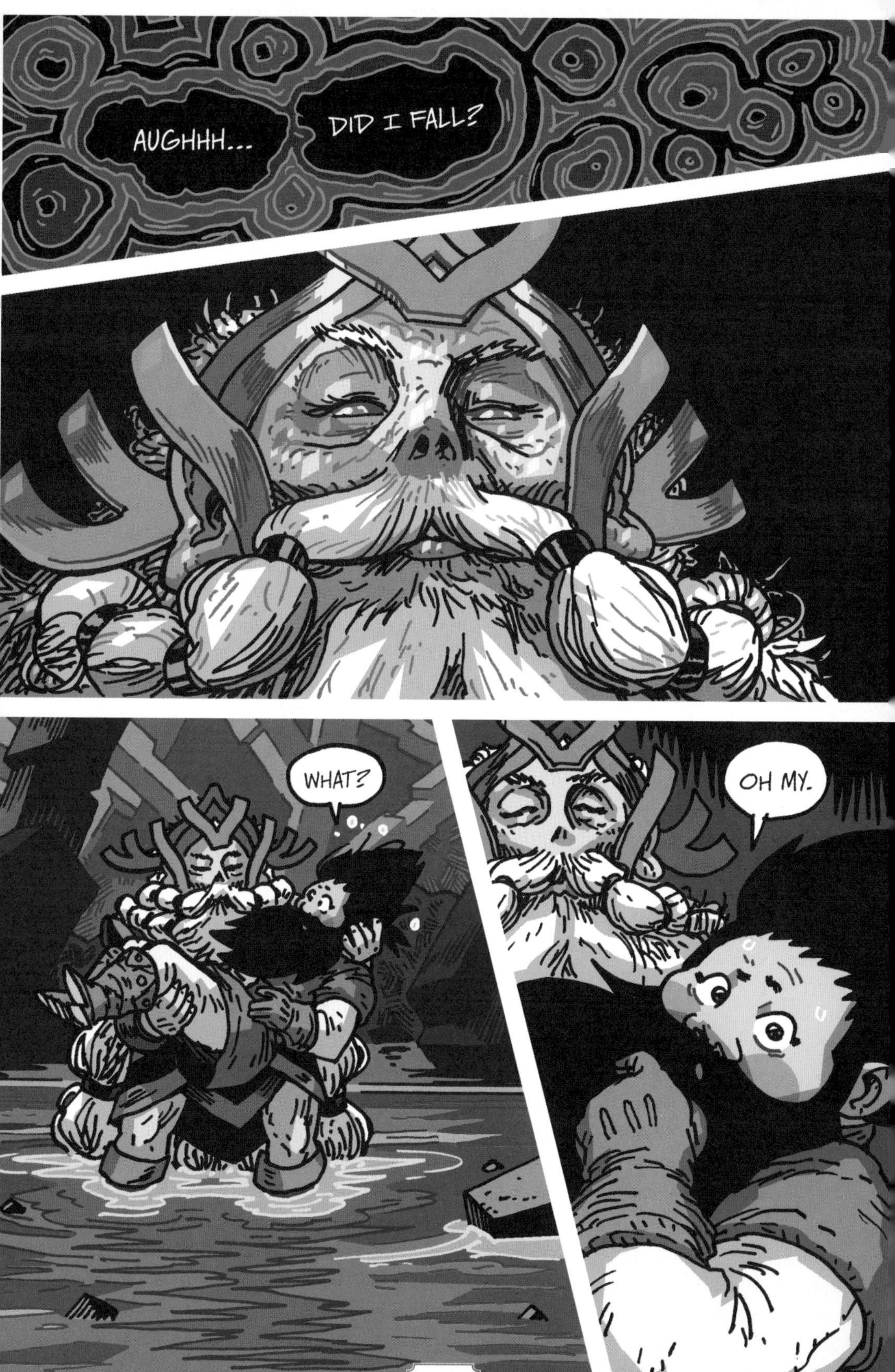
AUGHHH...
DID I FALL?
WHAT?
OH MY.

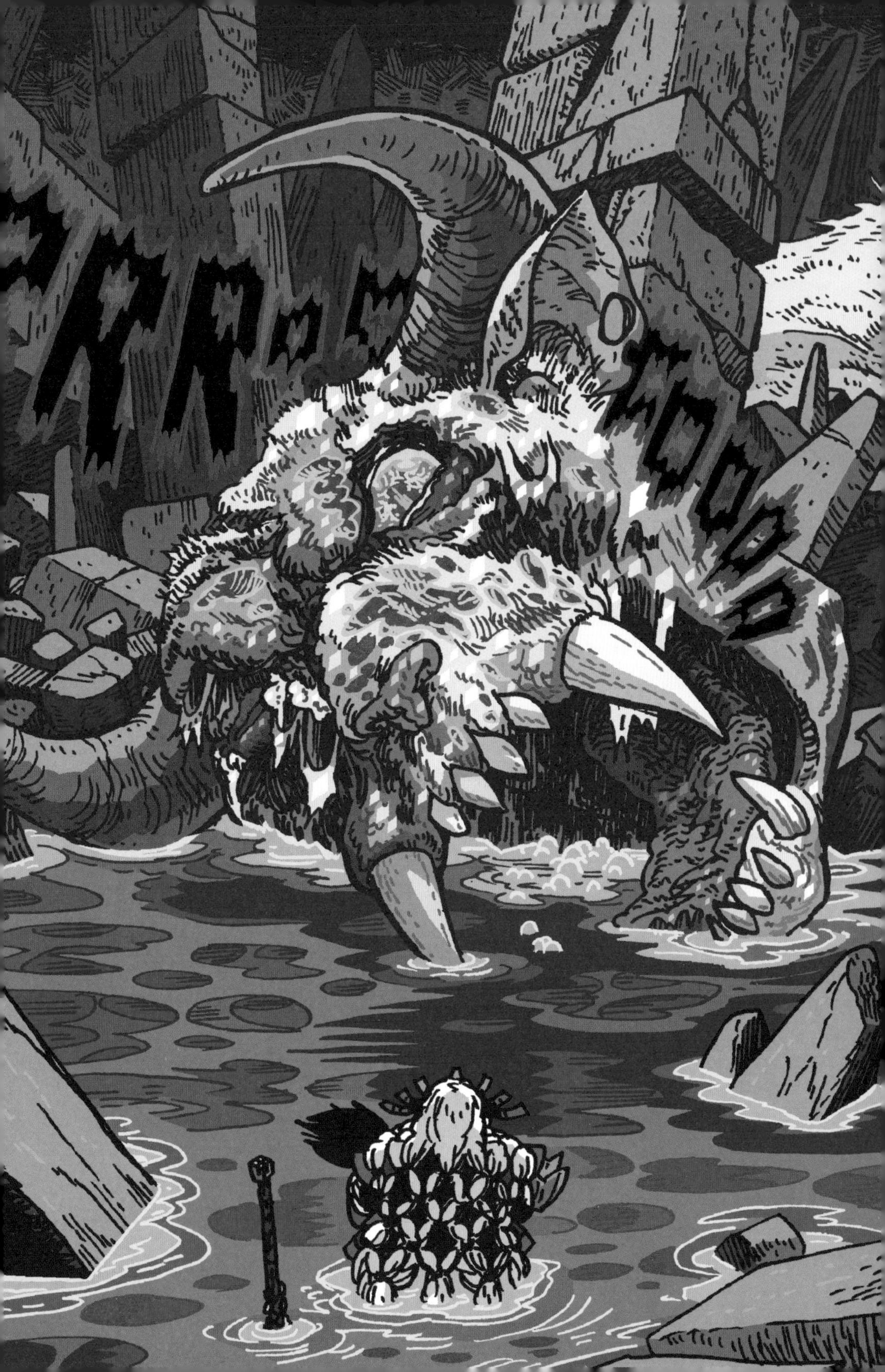

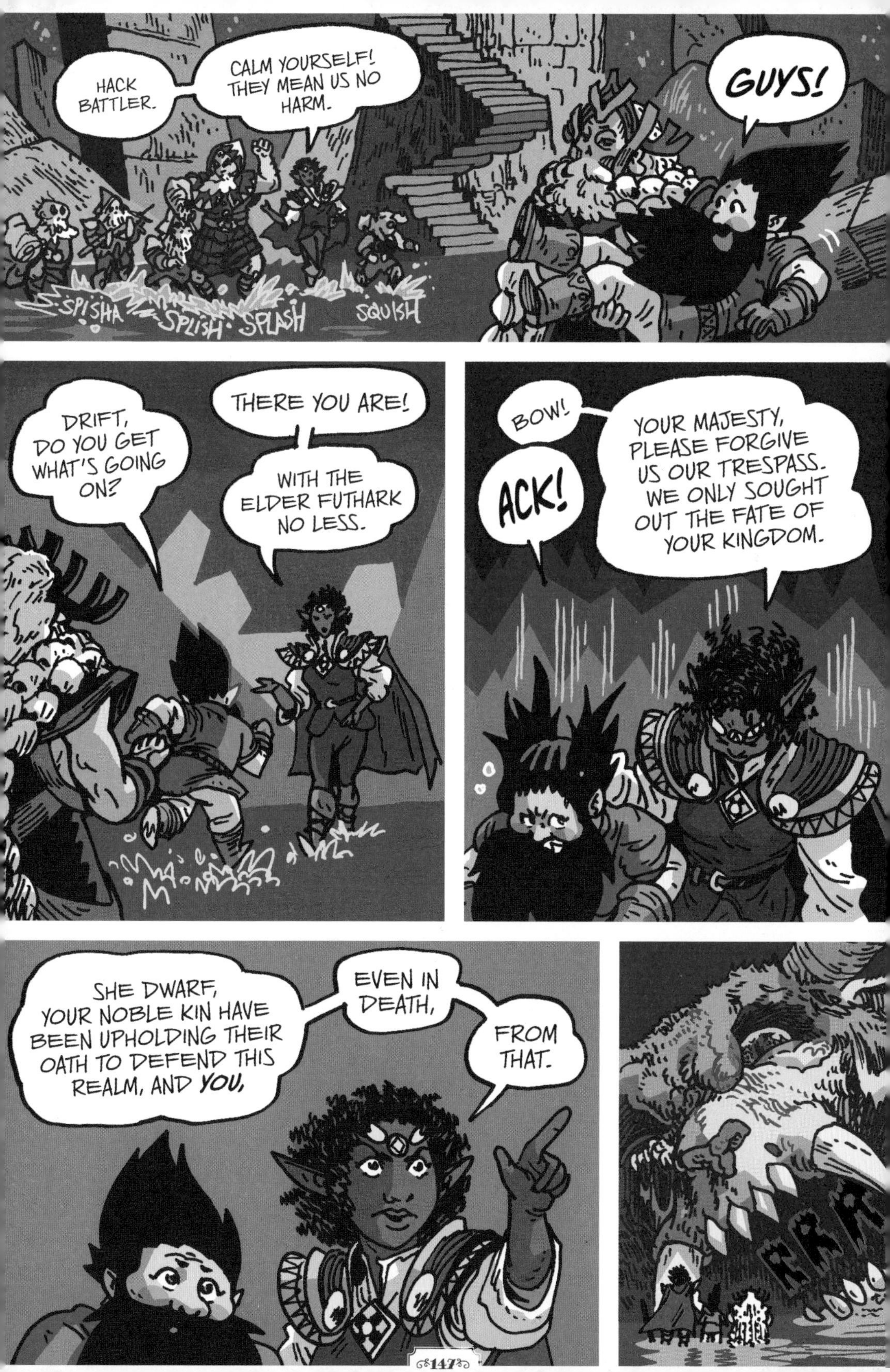
HACK BATTLER.
CALM YOURSELF! THEY MEAN US NO HARM.
SPISHA SPLISH SPLASH SQUISH
GUYS!
DRIFT, DO YOU GET WHAT'S GOING ON?
THERE YOU ARE!
WITH THE ELDER FUTHARK NO LESS.
BOW!
ACK!
YOUR MAJESTY, PLEASE FORGIVE US OUR TRESPASS. WE ONLY SOUGHT OUT THE FATE OF YOUR KINGDOM.
SHE DWARF, YOUR NOBLE KIN HAVE BEEN UPHOLDING THEIR OATH TO DEFEND THIS REALM, AND *YOU*,
EVEN IN DEATH,
FROM THAT.

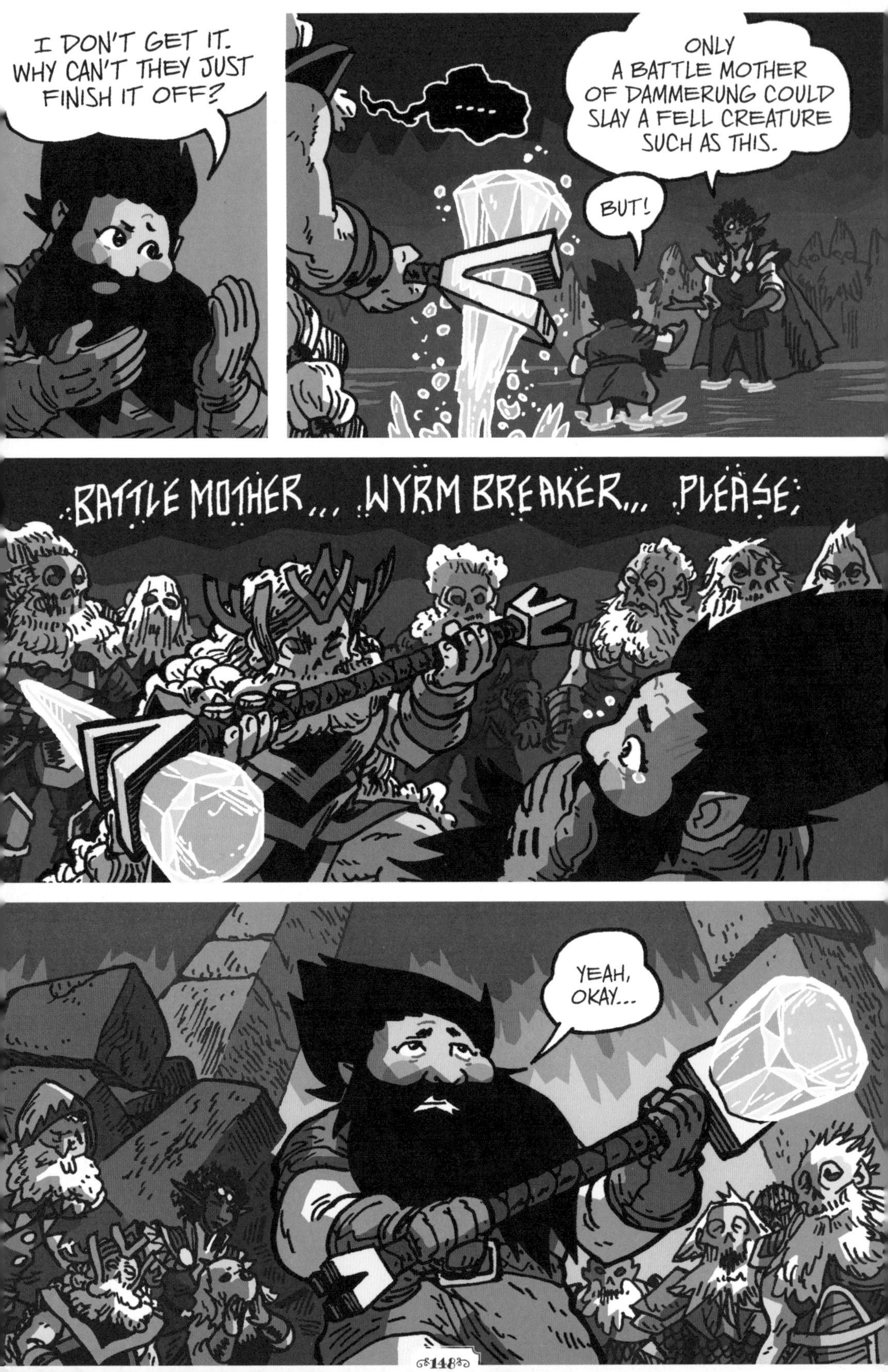

I DON'T GET IT. WHY CAN'T THEY JUST FINISH IT OFF?
....
ONLY A BATTLE MOTHER OF DAMMERUNG COULD SLAY A FELL CREATURE SUCH AS THIS.
BUT!
BATTLE MOTHER... WYRM BREAKER... PLEASE;
YEAH, OKAY...

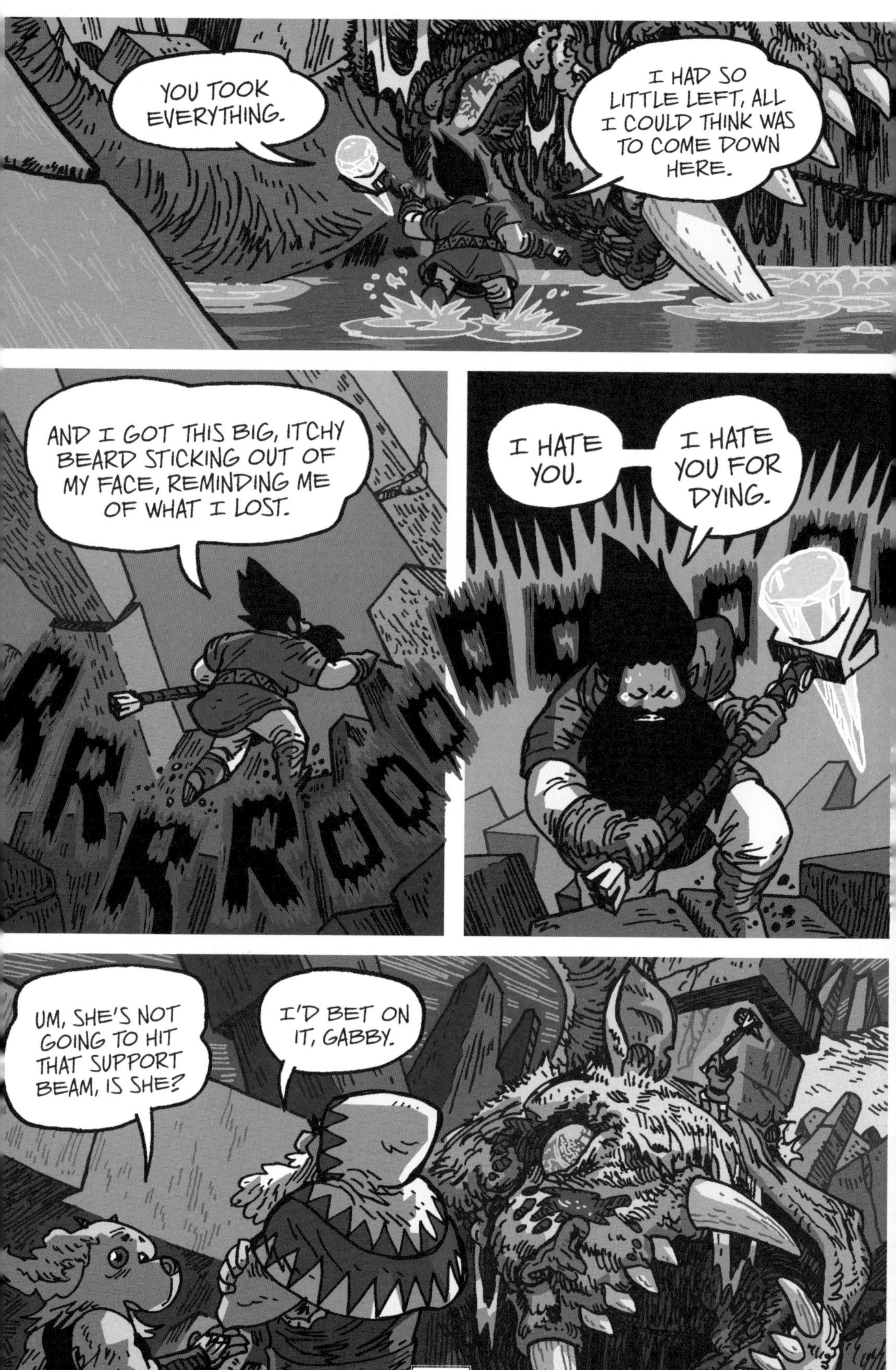
YOU TOOK EVERYTHING.
I HAD SO LITTLE LEFT, ALL I COULD THINK WAS TO COME DOWN HERE.
AND I GOT THIS BIG, ITCHY BEARD STICKING OUT OF MY FACE, REMINDING ME OF WHAT I LOST.
I HATE YOU.
I HATE YOU FOR DYING.
UM, SHE'S NOT GOING TO HIT THAT SUPPORT BEAM, IS SHE?
I'D BET ON IT, GABBY.

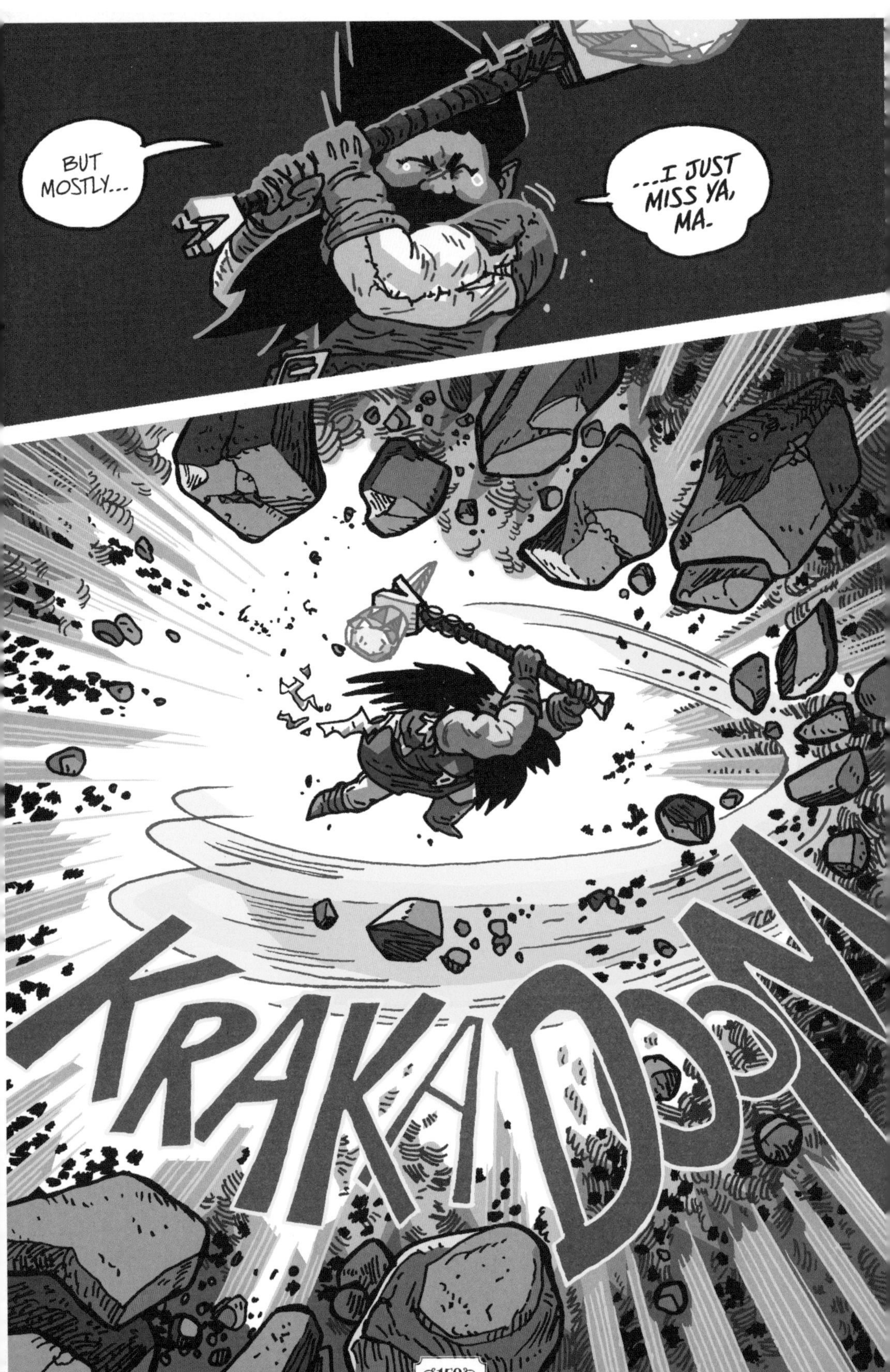
BUT MOSTLY...
...I JUST MISS YA, MA.
KRAKADOOM

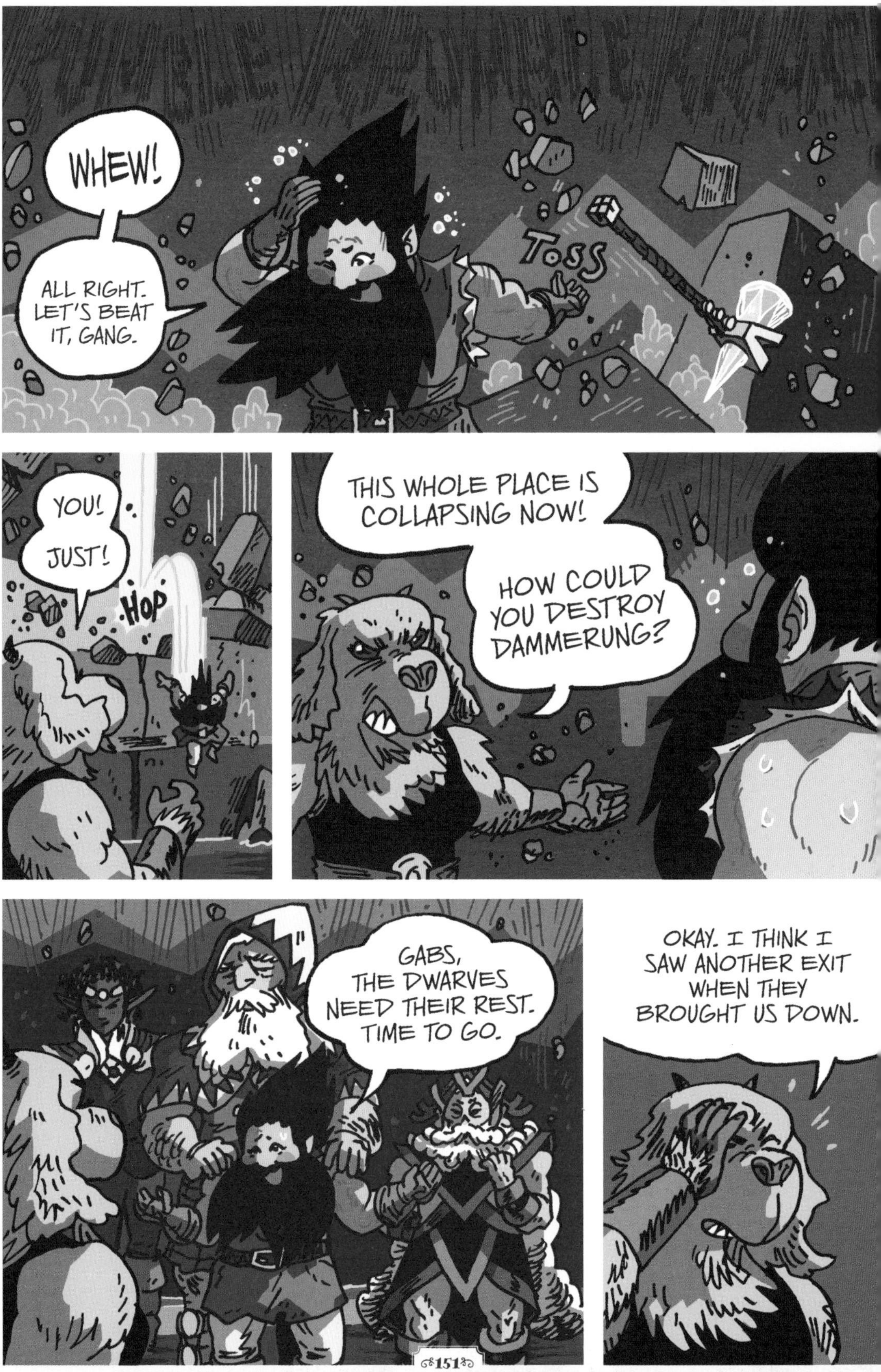
WHEW!
ALL RIGHT. LET'S BEAT IT, GANG.
TOSS
YOU! JUST!
HOP
THIS WHOLE PLACE IS COLLAPSING NOW!
HOW COULD YOU DESTROY DAMMERUNG?
GABS, THE DWARVES NEED THEIR REST. TIME TO GO.
OKAY. I THINK I SAW ANOTHER EXIT WHEN THEY BROUGHT US DOWN.

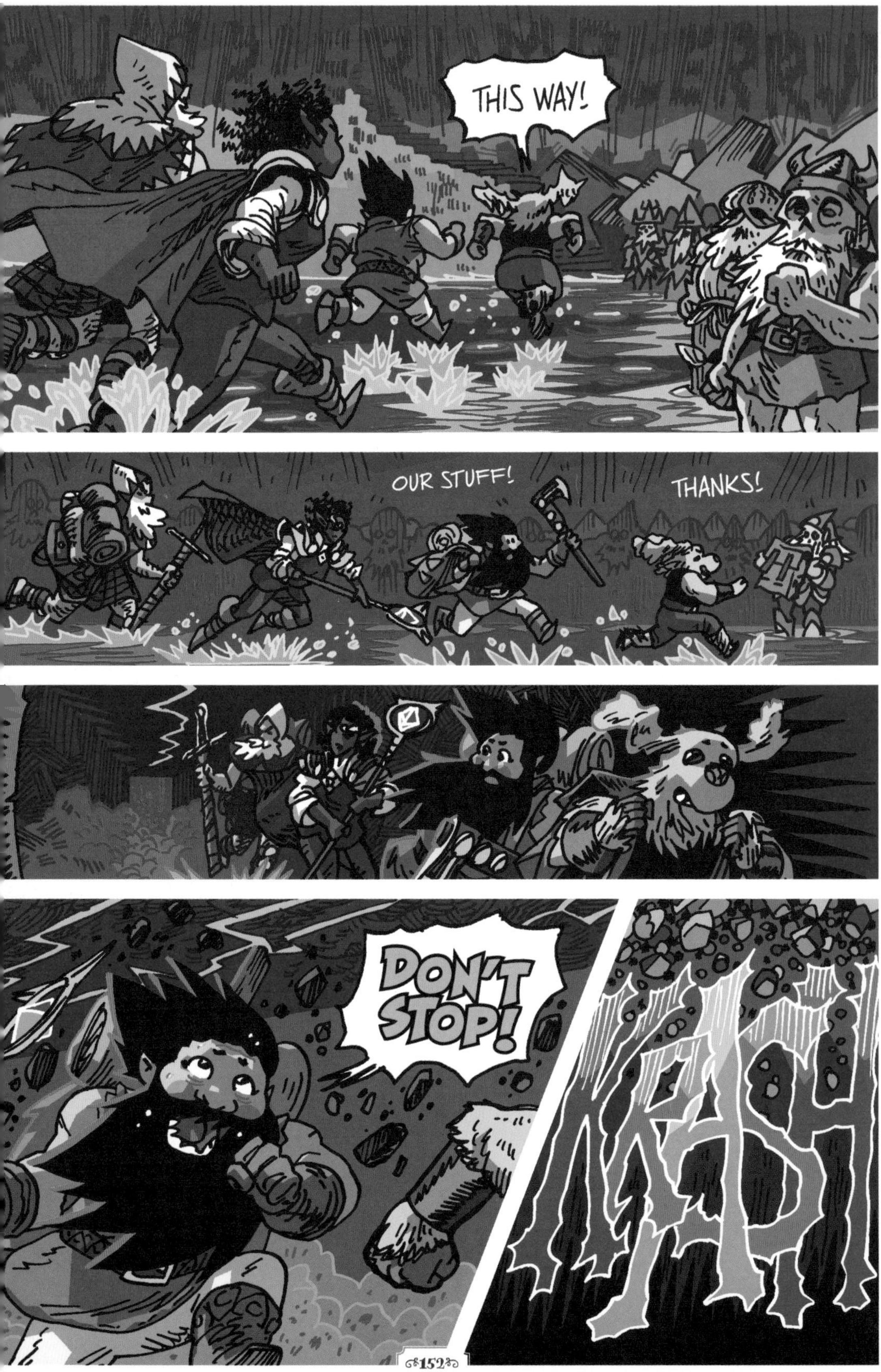
THIS WAY!
OUR STUFF!
THANKS!
DON'T STOP!
KRASH

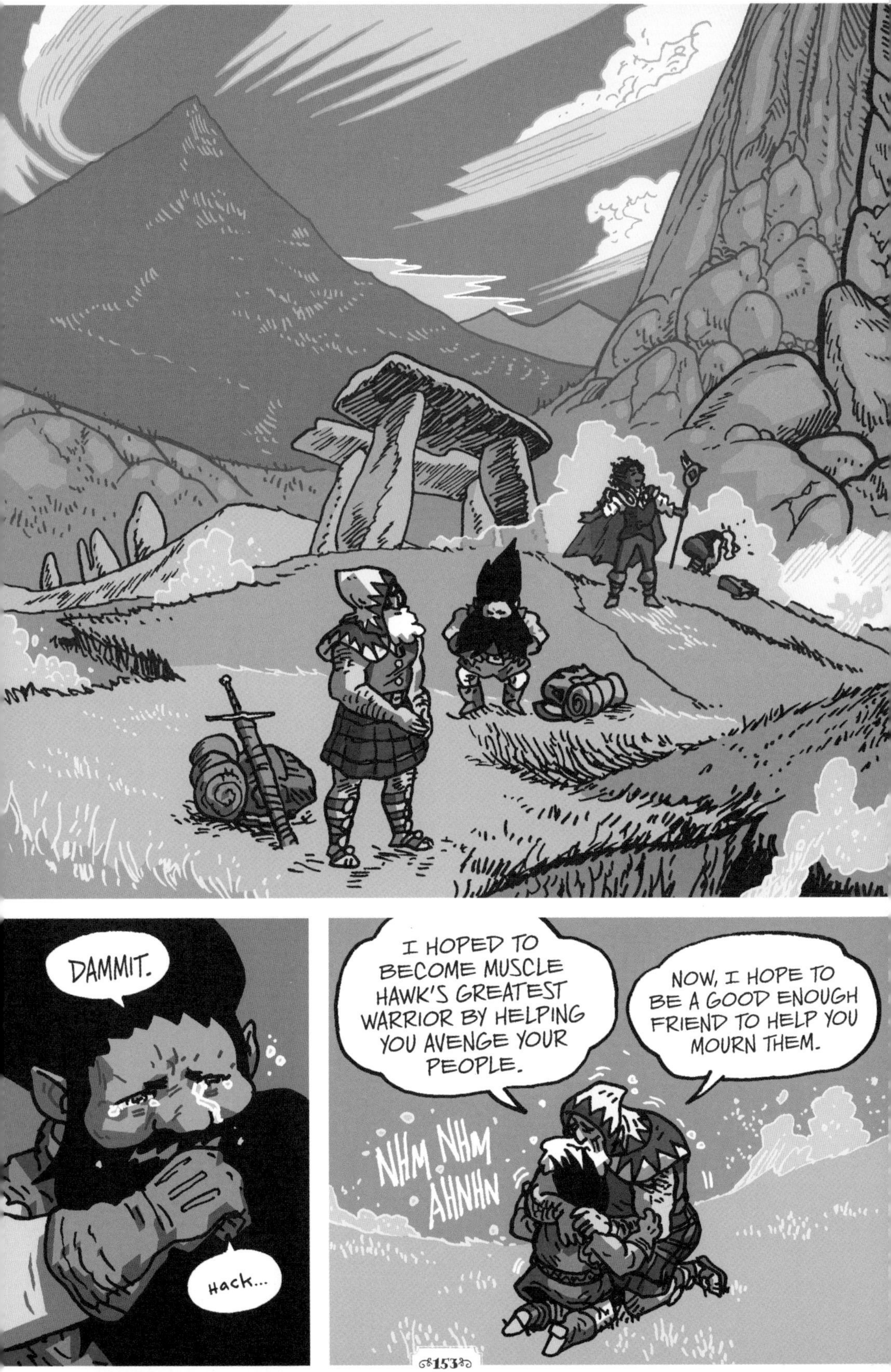
DAMMIT.
Hack...
I HOPED TO BECOME MUSCLE HAWK'S GREATEST WARRIOR BY HELPING YOU AVENGE YOUR PEOPLE.
NOW, I HOPE TO BE A GOOD ENOUGH FRIEND TO HELP YOU MOURN THEM.
NHM NHM AHNHN

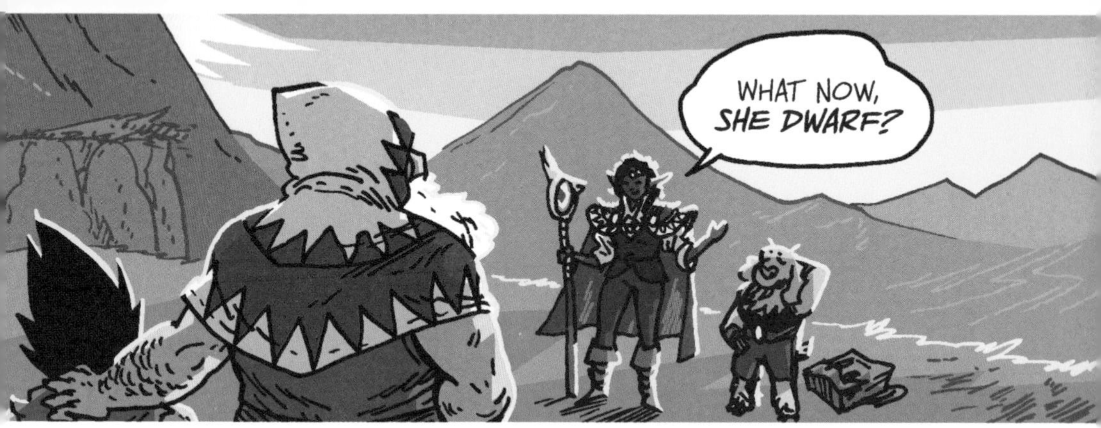
WHAT NOW,
SHE DWARF?

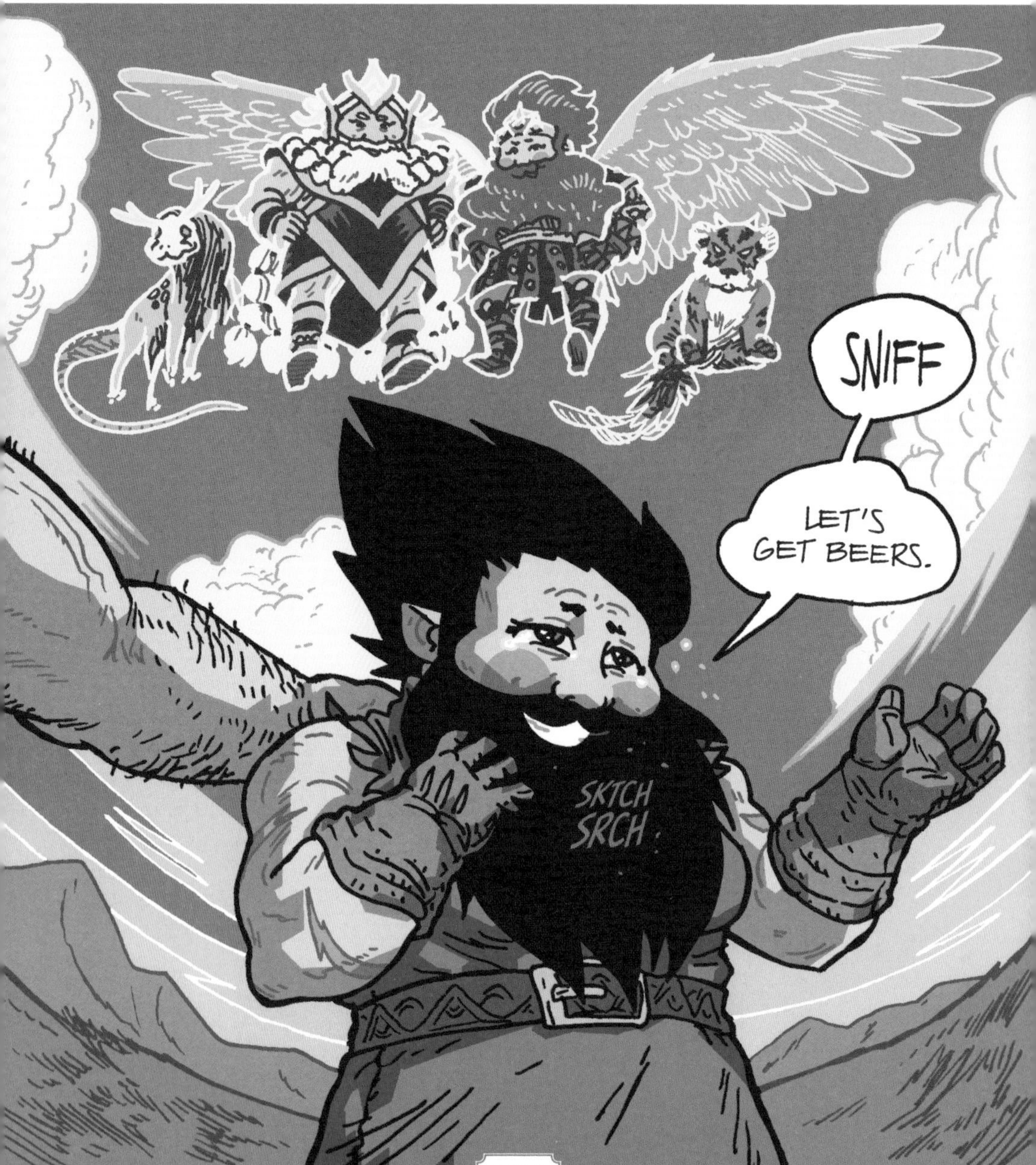
SNIFF
LET'S GET BEERS.
SKTCH SRCH

MONSTER BONUS SECTION!

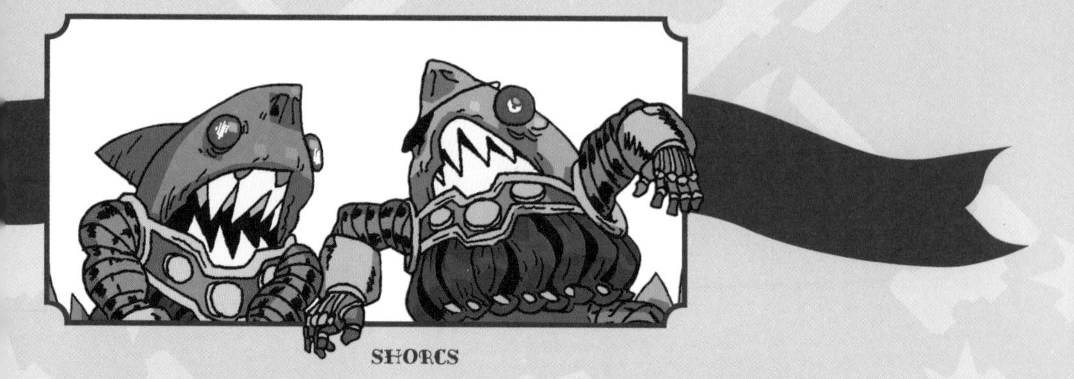

SHORCS

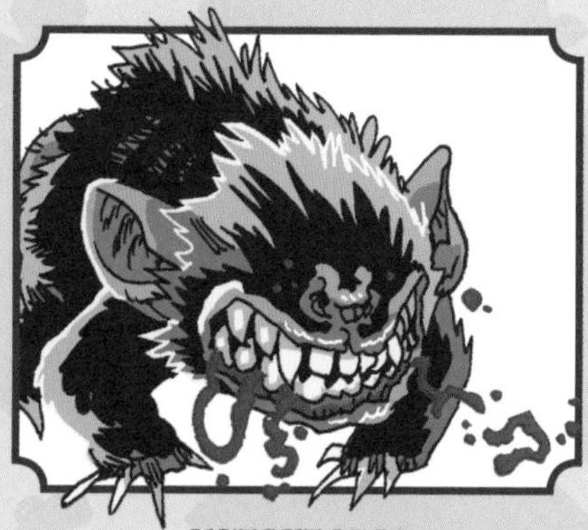

MUTANT BEAR

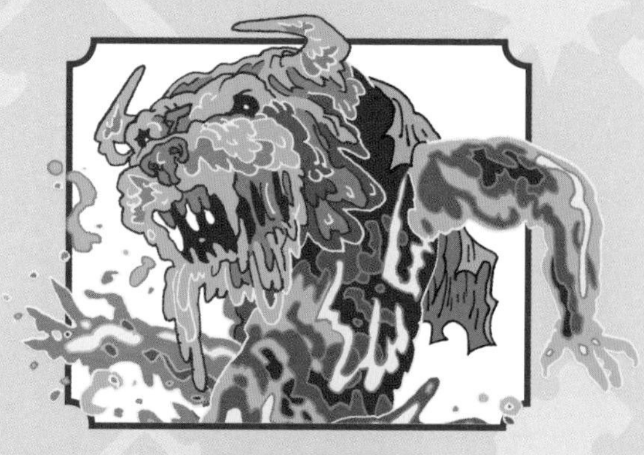

SLUDGE DEMON

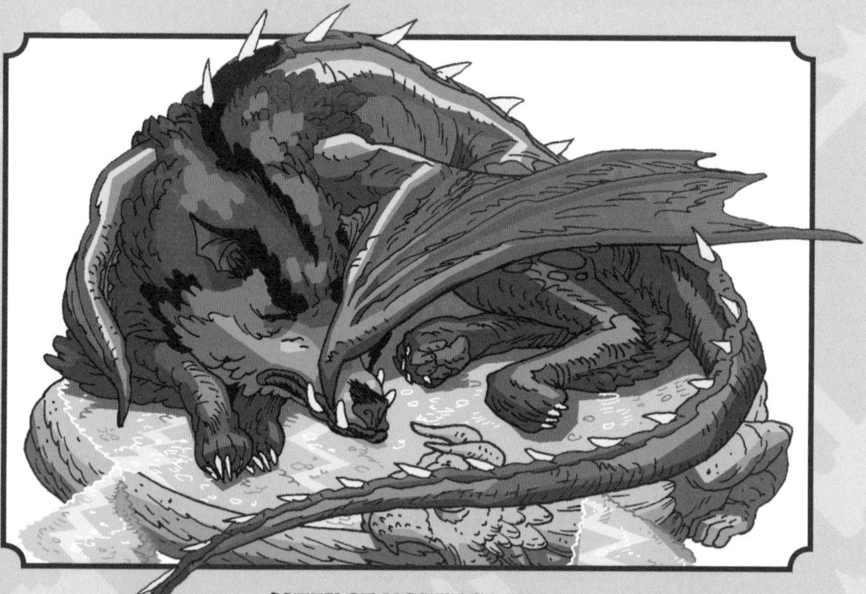

QUEEN OF MOUNT GRAVE

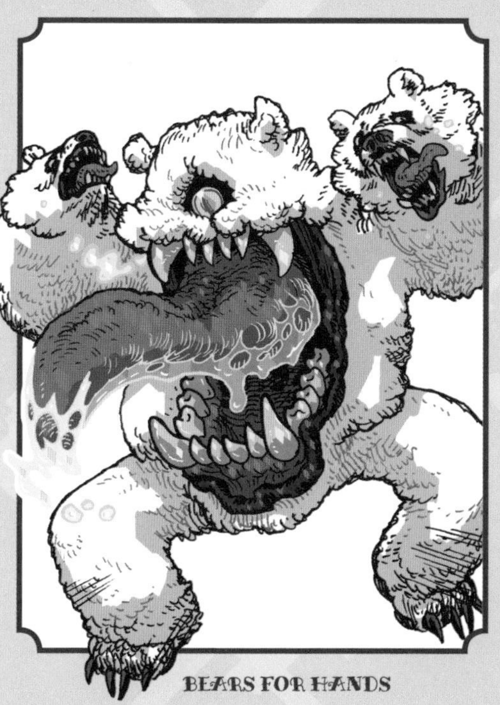

BEARS FOR HANDS

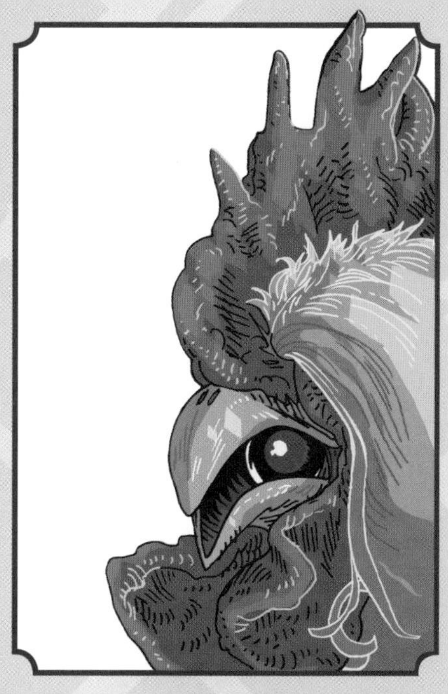

COCKATRICE

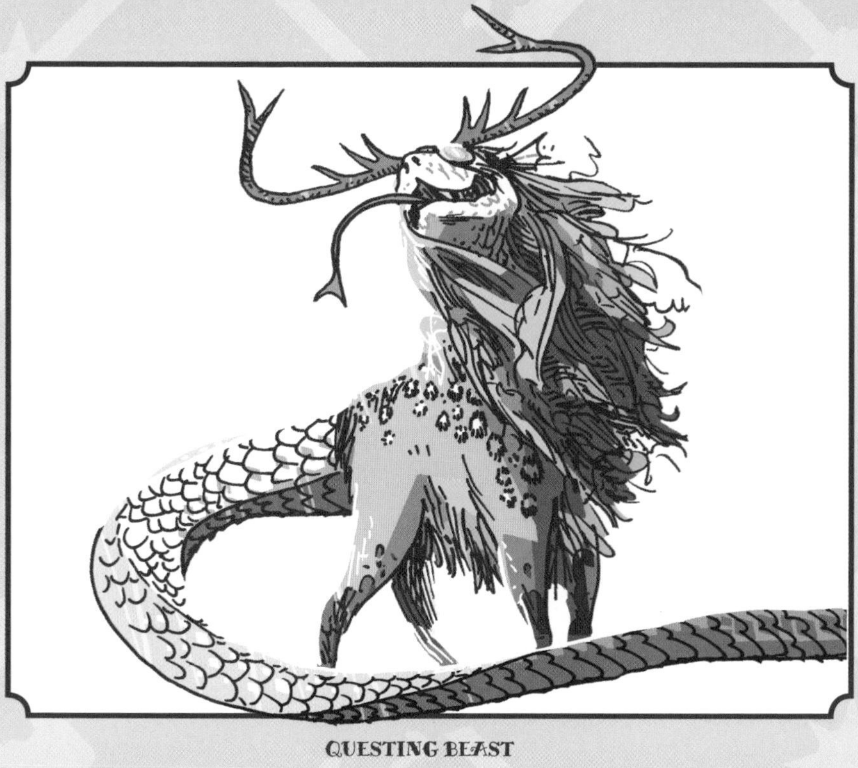

QUESTING BEAST

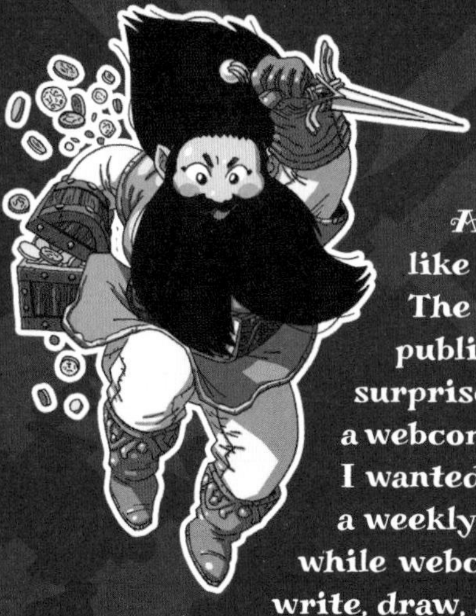

HOWDY, FOLKS!

American cartoonist Kyle Latino here. I would like to talk about this book you're reading for a bit. The fact that *The Savage Beard of She Dwarf* is a published book at all would have been an absolute surprise to me in 2015. I originally launched the story as a webcomic with no intention of publishing in print at all. I wanted to play with the spralling and endless space of a weekly webcomic. What I eventually discovered is that while webcomics can be endless and spralling, my time to write, draw, and color them was anything but. Moreover, the more that I wrote and drew of our plucky hero, She Dwarf, the more that I came to understand what she needed as a character. I initially contrived her to be a fortune-hunting, tomb-plundering, barbarian type, like Conan or Xena. But shortly after chapter two had wrapped up, I came to understand that she was actually just looking for a home that didn't exist anymore. My engenius and articulate ex-wife, to whom this book is dedicated, was enormously helpful in rediscovering and renegotiating the character of She Dwarf. Also, if it wasn't for her, Hack Battler would likely have never re-entered the story.

For that matter, Jen Van Meter pitched the idea of She Dwarf being the last dwarf in the world on a quest to discover the fate of her people before the webcomic even launched. You should really also know that if it wasn't for my editor, Grace Bornhoft, I probably would have quit drawing this dang old comic. I would have been stuck in mud without Bri, Gin, and Chris. And, of course, without the incomparable literary agent, Charlie Olsen, contacting me in the first place, *She Dwarf* would have only been a charming, yet brief, webcomic experiment.

I started *She Dwarf* largely out of spite for the default assumption that comics are a collaborative process. But I produced and finished *She Dwarf* entirely because of collaboration with wonderful people. In so many ways, my journey as an artist mirrors She Dwarf's journey from being an overly confident wanderer to a humbled and weeping mess surrounded by a glorious support system. I stand before you now as a lapsed auteur theorist. My message to any frustrated artist reading is this: the best thing you can do for your practice is to seek out capable people who want to help you and, for land sake, listen to them! For everyone else reading this, let me lay this on you: find the people you love and eat many meals with them.

Anyway, enough blubbering. In every chapter, *She Dwarf* surprised me and refused to behave. Would that all cartoonists were so lucky to be so thoroughly bamboozled by their own characters as I was. –Kyle Latino.

KYLE LATINO is a cartoonist and illustrator from Indianapolis. His work has appeared in the pages of comics such as *Fresh Romance, Rolled & Told, Outlaw Territories,* and many self-published projects. Kyle received a BFA in Biblical Literature from Taylor University (2007) and an MFA in Visual Fine Arts from the University of Cincinnati (2020). When he is not at the drawing desk, Kyle is often wishing he was playing Dungeons & Dragons.

MORE FROM ONI PRESS!

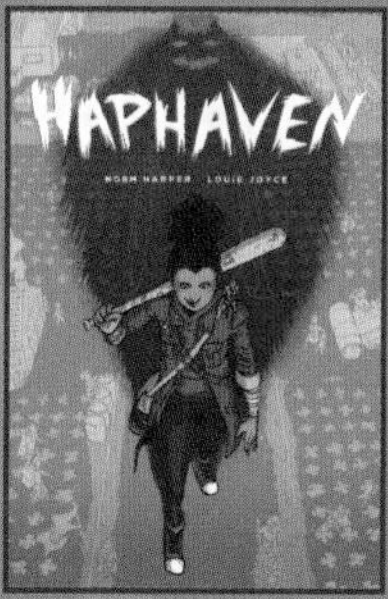
HAPHAVEN
NORM HARPER LOUIE JOYCE

Haphaven
By Norm Harper and Louie Joyce

When ever-superstitious Alex Mills steps on a crack and it actually breaks her mother's back, she must journey through a rainbow to the land where all superstitions draw their power in order to save her mom.

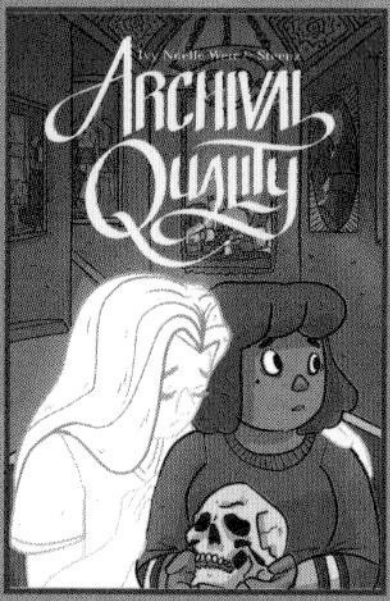
ARCHIVAL QUALITY

Archival Quality
By Ivy Noelle Weir and Steenz

After losing her job at the library, Cel Walden starts working at the haunting Logan Museum as an archivist. But the job may not be the second chance she was hoping for.

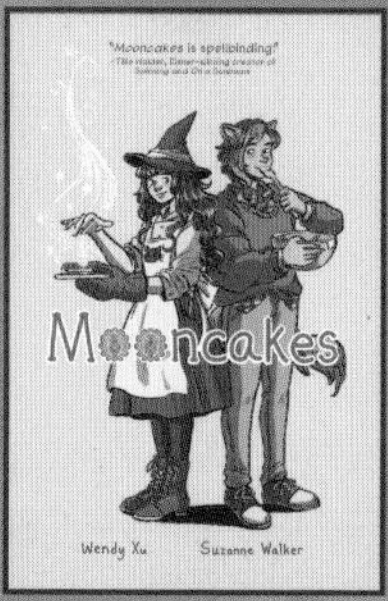
"Mooncakes is spellbinding!"
Mooncakes
Wendy Xu
Suzanne Walker

Mooncakes
By Suzanne Walker and Wendy Xu

Teen witch Nova Huang and werewolf Tam Lang must join forces to fight the supernatural powers eager to claim wolf magic for evil, all amidst a rekindling of an old romance.

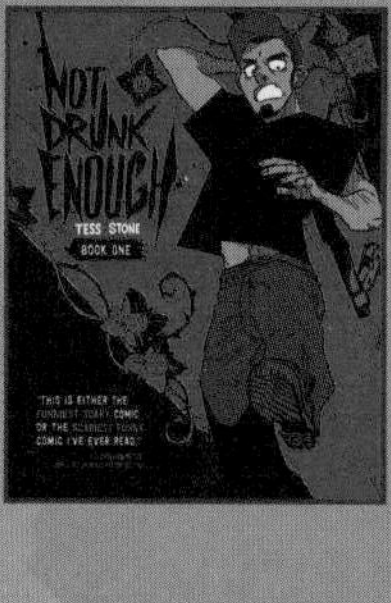
NOT DRUNK ENOUGH
TESS STONE
BOOK ONE

Not Drunk Enough: Book 1
By Tess Stone

Logan is a repairman in the wrong place at the wrong time—which is a creepy corporate lab in the middle of the night. After fighting off a freaky creature, he joins forces with three other poor souls trapped inside the building.